Novels by Rick Stiller

Fiction

Dealer

The Redemption Series

Nellis Gray – Volume I
SunnyBreeze – Volume II
Elect Mac Murphy - Volume III

Young Adult

The Morgan's Knot Serial Fantasy

Morgan's Knot
Island of the Children
Ice Island
Islands of Concrete and Steel
Islands of the Mind
Islands in the Sky
Islands of Dark Miracles
Islands of Wisdom

Visit: www.rickstiller.com for more of his books,
photographs, and music and www.morgansknot.com for
the latest on the Morgan's Knot series.

The Redemption Series
Volume IV
By
Rick Stiller

Text Copyright © 2022 by Rick Stiller
Cover Illustrations © 2022 by Mark Leavitt
All Rights Reserved
House of the Four Seasons Publishing

ISBN - 978-1-7326505-7-2

Visit www.rickstiller.com

For
Steve Strong
Loren Basch
Karin Whang

THE FORGE

By

Rick Stiller

Democratic Presidential nominee, Stanton Spratlin scowled into the television camera set up in the grand entry of stately Spratlin House, perched on a ridge overlooking the town of Cameron, Oklahoma which was erected in a crook of the meandering Arkansas River. His speech was being broadcast by every news network in the country and his voice echoed off the walnut paneling and tiled floor. "My fellow Americans, I want to speak to you tonight about the assassination of our Presidential candidate, Tyrone Turner, at the debate in Madison, Wisconsin, ten days ago by a paid assassin, who shattered history with a single shot.

I want to talk about the suicidal plane crash that killed or maimed hundreds of innocent people at the All People Matter rally in Chicago, the disgusting firebombing massacre of desperate demonstrators in Denver, the brutal white-nationalist riots in Atlanta, the deadly bombing in Houston, and so many other attacks by the foot soldiers of a very exclusive group of people, who have every intention of deconstructing our government and dismantling our democracy."

His eyes softened, "As all of you know, I am the most unlikely candidate in the history of presidential elections. I've been a loyal Republican for my entire life but…in hindsight, I've come to realize that through all those years, I was too comfortable in my belief system to pay attention to the lies, the clever catch phrases excusing and promoting hate, bigotry, and racism at the very core of the party platform. I contributed to the truckloads of dark money behind the elections of subservient lackies and completely unqualified candidates, who were tasked with passing legislation in every State House and both Houses of Congress to promote and protect the financial welfare of a small cadre of the wealthiest citizens in our land.

I was absolutely astounded, when Mayor Turner insisted that I be his running-mate. I hesitated for about two seconds because, first, I believe in everything the man stood for and, second, you don't say 'no' to Tyrone Turner, a six-six All-Star linebacker for the Atlanta Falcons and a Rhodes Scholar, with a doctorate in economics from Yale. He was bigger than life and he had a vision to unite all the citizens of this country to create a future for everyone together. I will do everything in my power to make his dream our reality."

He paused, "I'm sure that most of you are familiar with the brutal attacks on the All People Matter movement and our campaign, so I want to assure you that, no matter what the Republican propaganda machine splatters across the media, there is absolutely no doubt about who is responsible for the deaths of hundreds and injuries to thousands. We will be presenting proof in Congress, over the next few weeks, and we'll see whether the Justice Department is truly invested in justice.

In addition to all the murders, it appears they've entered a new phase of their offensive, which involves the kidnapping and disappearance of a number of people who have been at the forefront of the All People Matter movement. So far, we know of thirty-eight people in six different cities, who were visited and taken into custody by a clandestine governmental force known as the Alien Relocation Command and there are literally hundreds that we haven't been able to contact. None of the people who were arrested has been seen or heard from since they were detained without warrants or judicial oversight.

There is no record of charges being filed or any of them appearing in any court."

His spine straightened, his chin rose in defiance, "My staff has learned that this secret agency is funded through Homeland Security, as a black operation for counter-terrorism, but it appears to have been used to round up Latino immigrants who lacked proper documentation on their person, dispatching them across the border without a hearing before a judge or an opportunity to say goodbye to their loved ones. Like our patriotic associates, they just disappeared.

As you should know, the Republican Senate refused to confirm three different candidates, nominated by our hamstrung Democratic President Gonzalez, for the Secretarial seat for Homeland Security and the second and third in command quit in protest of blatant racism. So, the Department is being run by Ozzie James, a radically conservative former Republican Representative from South Carolina, who resigned when four-thousand forged ballots turned up after his election. His office did not respond to our inquiries but I can assure you that he will be brought before the Oversight Committee to respond to these accusations."

He paused again, "I honestly don't know whether my opponent is involved with this plot to hand the Federal Government over to the sponsors behind this enormous conspiracy but I do know that he is compromised by their financial support for his campaign.

Considering all that's happened over the past few months, combined with this paramilitary operation to silence and eliminate the opposition, I believe the coming elections should be postponed, until Congress and a special prosecutor can guarantee truly free and fair balloting in every district in the country. We must have some assurance that this isn't just a sham produced by people who believe they deserve vast power and riches at your expense. At the very least, you should be able to trust that your votes will actually count.

Ladies and gentlemen, we've been working on our democracy for nearly two-hundred and fifty years. Hundreds of thousands of patriots have fought and died, defending the very concepts that make our nation the envy of the entire world but, in spite of how far we've come, we still have a long way to go before we finally become that shining city on a hillside.

I don't know about you but I'm not ready to hand all of this over to the richest few to raid and pillage, until our Constitution and the Bill of Rights have no meaning, no value, and no purpose. I don't believe we should return to the barbarity of feudalism or bow to the cruelty of fascism and neither do you.

We have to restore the hope and confidence of our people and the only way to save our country is for every one of you to demand a full and honest investigation before one vote is cast. I call on my opponent to join me, if he's truly not in the pocket of the conspirators.

Every citizen needs to contact your senators and representatives, your governor and state legislators, your mayor and town council. I hope to see massive peaceful crowds shut down every city in the country until we learn the truth!

Let's stand together to defend the future of the nation and the promise of our democracy against this most vicious and virulent conspiracy festering inside our borders. Thank you and God bless the America we all believe in."

Derek Rangle, proprietor of the Tropical Paradise Art Gallery on St. Michael's Circle, drove his vintage British Racing Green Jaguar XKE across the causeway, skirting traffic in the little town of Dolphin Bay, down the Tamiami Trail, turning off on Poinsettia Avenue. His feature tropical landscape artist and dear friend, Jessie Cotton, and his girlfriend, editorial writer Kate Crockett, both Founding leaders of the All People Matter movement, were not answering their phone and people were concerned.

The last time this happened, they'd been kidnapped by a squad of fake police officers and incarcerated in an abandoned derelict jail a hundred miles south down Florida's scenic highway Forty-One in Naples. The powers that be in the community could not tolerate massive protests over wages and benefits at the height of tourist season but the kidnapping failed when they were rescued.

Massive crowds jammed into the town square as the first storms from hurricane Dot unleashed a deluge, while planted provocateurs detonated explosives to create live television images of chaos, but the pluck and determination of the protestors in that demonstration grew into a national movement representing the plight of millions of unemployed working people. Their success transformed the leaders into enemies of the syndicate of fascist families at the center of the clandestine network known as The Forge.

Jessie's VW bus and Kate's old BMW were parked in the driveway of the transformed carriage house and the front door was standing open. He knocked on the screen and a dog yelped but no one responded, so he stepped inside to find young Johnny Warmington sitting in the middle of the studio floor hugging Jessie's limp and barely responsive Shepherd-mix Gracie. "What's wrong?"

"The bad cops took Jessie and Kate again."

"What cops?"

"Four big guys dressed in black armor, with shiny face shields like in the movies, and four more outside."

Rangle knelt down to pet Gracie, "How do you know?"

"Jessie and I were going fishing and he was late getting ready. The scary guys knocked on the door, came inside, one of them showed a gold badge with a shiny shooting star on it. Gracie growled at them and one of them shot her with that dart," said the boy, pointing to a slender silver tube on the floor. "He told Jessie they needed to answer some questions about the assassination."

"And they went with the bad men?"

"Yeah, they had these big guns and one of them aimed it at me."

"Did Jessie or Kate say anything?"

"Jessie hugged me and told me I could use his tackle box and they'd be back in a little while."

Rangle walked over to the kitchen counter and opened the kit, where, underneath spools of line, leaders, bobbers, a stout fisherman's stiletto, and a plastic box of hooks and lures, he found a hefty envelope wrapped in plastic. "Perhaps this is what he wanted us to find."

"What is it?" asked Johnny.

Rangle tore off the wrapper, then the seal, and unfolded a thick sheaf of papers, with a note in journalist Kate's elegant script clipped to the packet.

Should you find us missing and you're clever enough to discover this letter, please take this file to my publisher Tabitha Hall. She'll understand the contents and know what to do with it.

He licked his thumb to turn the page, "Let's just see what the first page has to say…"

Gracie groaned and rolled over on her stomach, squinting her brown eyes and ducking her head to blunt a stunning headache. The boy hugged her gently and looked up, as Rangle's eyes scanned the pages. "What's it say?"

"It says that Miss Kate was investigating a secret government agency called the 'Alien Relocation Command', who are responsible for rounding up and deporting people who are in our country illegally." He looked over his reading glasses, "Just about our whole population descended from immigrants who came from other countries to escape oppression or violence or starvation and everyone who comes here dreams of freedom and opportunity in a land where everyone is equal.

The 'Relocation Command' seems primarily interested in finding brown people, who came from Mexico or Central America, but they're also arresting people opposed to the right-wing plan to take over our government."

"That's what Jessie and Kate have been fighting for."

"Exactly." He flipped through a few more pages, "Turns out they can't just ship these people back across the border. By law, they have a right to a trial in front of a judge to decide who stays and who goes and…because there are so many people being arrested, they've…built giant prison camps out west to hold them until judges can get to their cases."

Johnny hugged Gracie and started to cry, "Is that where they've taken Jessie and Kate?"

Rangle folded the papers and knelt down again, "First, we should call your mother and tell her what's happened. I'd be surprised if she didn't want you home until we know what's really going on and, maybe, you should take Gracie with you. I assume you came in your boat?"

"Yeah."

"I'll walk you down to the dock and then I'll take Kate's investigation to Mrs. Hall's house and see what she can find out. Okay?"

"Okay," replied Johnny, helping the unsteady dog to her feet.

"I need to use their phone for a moment to let your mom and Mrs. Thompson know what's going on." He picked up the receiver from the wall phone and dialed the number he had scratched on the back of one of his engraved business cards. "Alva, it's Derek Rangle." He paused, listening, "Yes, it's as bad as we thought. I'm here with Jessie's young friend, Johnny Warmington, and he witnessed them being detained by the Alien Relocation commandos. Kate left an extensive article about the Command, which I'll take to Tabitha Hall as soon as I leave here."

He glanced at Johnny, "So, they've taken Jessie, Kate, Eddie Glover, and Benny…oh, and Sammy Ball too? Alright, I'll see what else I can find out and I'll call you back. Thank you."

Gracie groaned, as the man patted Johnny on the shoulder, "You helped save Jessie and Kate and Sammy Ball, when they got kidnapped before, because you told your mom and she told me and eventually we got them back. At least this time, we know what to do."

Nellis Gray and his new bride, Katherine escaped apprehension by a squad of sanctioned thugs in black uniforms and mirrored helmets, when neighbor girls Sammy and Sissy, daughters of Representative Stanton Spratlin, galloped up to the house on horseback to rescue them before the goons could rush the gate at Nellis's farm in the hills above Cameron. Twelve hours later, they were concealed with jet-set land developer Tate Sloan in a cocoon of immaculate clothing hanging on racks in the back of Ned Perkins' newly painted 'Acme Uniform' step-van, as he eased up to the security gate for the private hangars at the Cameron Municipal Airport. Ned glanced around the airfield and said without turning, "I don't see any sign of your troopers or their black Humvees hiding in the bushes."

Nellis whispered, "There ain't no bushes at an airport."

Their getaway driver grinned and pulled back on the sliding window, "Yup, that explains it."

A flabby guard leaned out of his little shed, "Aren't you supposed to deliver in the mornings?"

Ned held up a clipboard, "Yeah, usually, but it says here that I'm supposed to deliver ten dress uniforms to the Mid-American hangar before midnight. Guess they've got folks flying out early, huh?"

The guard scratched his scruffy beard and yawned, "Yeah, I guess. You don't have any extra bodies in the back of that rig, do you, brother?"

"Well, if I was hauling a rolling party around, I'd only carry beautiful women and I'd sure invite you!" Ned laughed, "Why do you ask?"

"We've got some intimidating government troopers from some secret outfit called the Alien Relocation Command roaming around asking lots of questions about some mysterious missing couple. Evidently, they're wanted by the Feds for questioning but they didn't say about what. Hell, other than them, you're the only vehicle to pass through here tonight, so I'm guessin' their dogs are barking up the wrong tree, when the coons hightailed it hours ago." The old man chuckled and waved his hand, "Be quick about it, I'm too tired to wait around to check your sorry ass out."

"Yes, Sir! Lickidy split!"

The step-van motored along the service road and around the front of the huge hanger, to roll under a partially opened door emblazoned with the Simonson Air logo into a palatial shrine to aerial speed and comfort.

The enormous door rattled into a groove in the floor with a modest 'clunk', before Ned turned to say, "All clear."

Tate led the newlyweds through the cab, down the steps, three paces across a shiny gray floor, into a twelve-seat Gulfstream, with barely a glance at the half-dozen gleaming silver darts parked in pools of amber cascading down from the darkness of the lofty ceiling. The cabin lights were dimmed and all the window shades closed, as he leaned into the cockpit, "We're ready to roll, when you are."

"Roger that, we'll be wheels up in five minutes," replied the pilot.

Ned bounced up the stairs, "This is where we part company for a little while. I'll catch up with you at your destination."

Nellis hugged him and patted him on the back, "I'm thankful for your foresight in putting the clues together and saving our asses."

"I hate to admit that I couldn't restrain myself from reading the file you gave me the last time I was through here, because I knew something bad was about to go down. All I had to do was think like you and I knew exactly where to find you."

"Great minds," said Katherine with a kiss to each cheek. "We owe you."

"No, you don't," he replied with a hug, pointing, "but that guy you just married is on the hook for some serious smoked pork ribs as soon as I land wherever you are. If I can find charcoal, he's cooking."

"Do me a favor and make my seasonal gifts to Sister Gwen at the orphanage, Hank Garrett at the soup kitchen, and Constance Calhoon over at the homeless shelter, they'll be needing our contributions ahead of the holidays. And give Sissy and Sammy some money to cover their expenses feeding all our critters. I sure do appreciate their help," said Nellis.

Ned laughed, "They shared the story of saving your sorry ass, on horseback no less! I'm thinking you owe them big but they've got the animals under control. No worries. Oh, and Brad's getting in touch with his old military buddies to see what they know. The Gestapo seems to understand that nabbing the opposition candidate's son might not make for good press, while the leader of a national movement and her enforcer don't seem to be much of a publicity problem."

"Knowing how they're moving hundreds or thousands of people around the country without anybody noticing would be a good place to start!"

Tate gripped Ned's hand, "You got everything under control?"

"Yeah, man. Just deliver these two to the theater and I'll meet up with you in a couple of days."

"Thanks. Be safe," replied Tate with a hug.

The air inside the fuselage compressed for a moment as the copilot closed and sealed the hatch and turned into the cabin, "Please buckle your seatbelts, we've been cleared to taxi to the runway for immediate take-off. I'll be back to take drink orders, once we reach altitude." He started towards the cockpit but stopped to say, "Oh, and please don't open the blinds. Our manifest says the aircraft is flying empty."

The engines whined, as the huge door rolled up, and the sleek silver sprint slipped out of the air-barn onto tarmac and along the taxiway to line up at the end of the runway. The twin Rolls Royce engines revved up to speed and the jet streaked down the strip, lifting into dark clouds streaking in from the northwest.

Katherine exhaled a long breath and squeezed Nellis' hand, then looked into Tate's famous blue eyes, "We need to thank you for saving the day but...I have to wonder how all of this came about and where have you been since you supposedly died?"

Tate's publicity smile was captivating, in spite of several day's stubble, "First, it's my honor to transport you to a sanctuary where you can lead your movement to save the nation from certain damnation. With all you've accomplished for the desperate middle-class of this country and your work in Tyrone Turner's historic run for the presidency, you and your friends are venerated gurus of the new revolution to reclaim our democracy."

"Do we have any news about the rest of our campaign?" asked Katherine.

"At this point, I'm not privileged to that information. My job is to deliver you to safety."

"There are a lot of good people missing, including Jessie and Kate," said Nellis.

"I know and I wish I knew something I could share with you but you probably know more than I do. To answer the first part of your question," he glanced at Nellis, "I met your friend Ned through some mutual friends and he's been instrumental in keeping me incognito. It didn't take long to connect me to Mavis to you. Oh, and he knew about your rather unusual charity work, so he led me right to you."

"I'm not sure whether to hug him or punch him, next time we meet?" said Nellis.

"Personally, I think he's a magician but we'll get to that," replied Sloan. "I've had a lot of time to think about my life, before hurricane Dot destroyed everything I worked so hard to build and promote, and I realized that the publicity and fame, the wealth and the status, the whole image that Mavis and I learned to project was…completely fake. It was all gilt and glitter that became more important than the relationship we had when we were ambitious kids with big dreams fresh out of college. We became high profile actors playing the roles that were expected of us. Success and accomplishment became the only glue that held us together, when the lights went out and the cameras stopped rolling."

He paused, his eyes wandering around the plush interior of the jet, as he remembered, "When Hurricane Dot was clawing through the last structures in SunnyBreeze and I was stranded on the battered remnants of Jessie's demolished boat bridge, I honestly prepared myself for death. In the fury of the storm, clinging to floating debris, bounced around by huge waves, relentless winds, mind-numbing thunder, and vicious lightning, my whole life whizzed through my mind.

I realized that nothing that I had ever done had any positive or lasting meaning. It was all self-serving narcissistic gluttony, my life was overflowing with riches but there was nothing inside my soul, nothing to leave to the children we never had, nothing to claim that I had ever done for anyone else, besides sharing my ill-gotten wealth with my impoverished family.

Mavis followed her conscience to become the business brains behind your All People Matter movement, as well as constructing dozens of self-contained communities that have provided thousands of destitute people with jobs and pride and dignity. I lost my soul on a sure bet that promised glory and riches, until Mother Nature swept the entire project into the bay and I knew there was nothing to go back to."

"So, how did you survive the hurricane?" asked Nellis.

"I honestly don't know. Huge winds whipped the string of boat carcasses around the little bay and I got tossed around like a guppy in a tidal storm. I remember barely reaching consciousness, lying on a crumbling slab of asphalt, looking up at the battered front fender of a yellow school bus with its caution lights flashing through buckets of rain falling from swirling clouds illuminated by crackling lightning. All these faces were leaning over me, their voices like murmurs drowned out by deep rumbling thunder and the machine-gun patter of raindrops splattering on the pavement. Lots of hands picked me up and carried me inside. The next thing I knew, I woke up in a bed in a dark room, attended by several very kind women and a flock of children. You'll meet them soon enough."

"So, Mavis didn't know you were alive?" asked Nellis.

"Not until Turner was shot. We've talked on the phone but we haven't seen each other since before the storm."

"She's one powerful woman, as you well know, so, I'm guessin' you might be in a heap of trouble."

Tate nodded, "That goes without saying."

"I don't know whether it's impolite to ask, but where are we going?" inquired Katherine.

"We'll be landing at Teterboro Airport, just north of New York City, in a couple of hours."

"Isn't it dangerous for us to be out and about in a huge metropolitan area with cops on every corner?" asked Nellis.

"I've been invisible for nearly two years and I travel all over the world," replied Tate. "For the time being, you'll never be exposed to the public. We'll travel by helicopter to land on a spit of concrete in the East River, where a car will deliver us to a tunnel beneath the city streets, that leads to the home of a rather inspiring community."

~

Ultraconservative radio talk-show host and renegade Republican nominee for the office of President of the United States, Mac Murphy, was famous for arriving late and thoroughly inebriated for his nightly shows in the tiny, overcrowded studio in WBFK, 'World Broadcasting from the Konfederacy', ten-forty on the dial, just outside Cincinnati.

Tonight was no different, except his battered gold Cadillac convertible was replaced with an armored limousine in a convoy of black Secret Service Suburban's and official vehicles from at least twelve local municipalities. Hundreds of flashing red and blue lights transformed dusk into dawn on the gravel lot outside the shabby cinderblock building, the birthplace of his fledgling and entirely fraudulent campaign.

Dr. Theodore Billings, quack physician who signed on to the campaign to manage Murphy's many addictions at the behest of the stymied power brokers behind The Forge, handed the candidate a small white paper cup. "Time for your vitamins."

Murphy peered into the cup, containing two black amphetamine capsules to jag his primal rage and a blue football to spike his libido, "Considering I popped a couple before you showed up, these should put me in prime form."

"That's my job, keeping you ready and on the edge for the next appearance."

Dowdy former station receptionist and Personal Assistant to the Candidate, Milly Clark, offered a tumbler of Jack Daniels.

"Are we set on how you're going to handle your response to Spratlin's blather?" asked campaign director Casper Wein.

He chugged the bourbon and handed the glass back to Milly, as the thick door opened from the outside, "I'm going to make him look like the impotent wimp he is!"

Two Secret Service agents reached to grab his arms, as he stumbled out of the car and shuffled up the steps, through armed security, into a tiny reception area crammed with staff and volunteers clapping and cheering, "Murphy! Murphy!"

The candidate smiled and bowed, touching his flabby chest above his heart, in the pose of a distinguished thespian entering a theater to present an inspired dramatic performance to a house packed with fans enthralled with his every syllable or gesture.

He assumed his role as defender for a whole class of invisible evangelical far-right nationalists almost five-years earlier, while filling in for an ailing political radio host, at this barely subsisting rural radio station with an audience of approximately twelve active listeners. His predecessor's death provided the only employment opportunity at this end of the tragically self-inflicted demise of a once promising acting career, soiled by scandal and addiction. "Thank you! Thank you! With your help, we can win this election!"

Shepherd Stone, assistant campaign manager and political operative, grabbed his elbow to guide him back to the studio, where Haden Crawley and his video crew were setting up lights to tape the broadcast.

Penny Baker, voluptuous make-up artist and occasional lover, pushed him into his worn leather chair and covered him with a towel. She wiped the oil from his cheeks and forehead and dusted his face with a translucent powder to cut the glare and reflections. "You should be wearing shades! Your eyes look even worse than usual, what's wrong with you?"

He placed her hand on his crotch, "I just need a little inspiration to get primed for my performance!"

"You sleaze-ball," replied Baker, reaching under the towel with her left hand to fondle his limp member, while brushing a glaze on his lips with her right. "If your fans knew the truth about what an impotent asshole you are…"

"Even more of 'em would vote for me! I represent the flawed hero they wish they could be, the insolent personality who'll stand up for their weird conflicted convictions. Even if it is all a bunch of hooey, I make the perverted crap they scream at their televisions sound sane and normal and that's all that counts with them."

"Sane and normal?"

He sat up, as she whipped the towel from his chest and walked behind his chair to brush and spray his thinning salt and pepper hair to mask the bald spot, "You know what I mean, it's all a show and, if the voters want to sign up for additional episodes for the next four years, they can check my name on their ballots."

"You don't really believe that you have any chance of winning this thing, do you?" inquired the stylist.

"Before Turner's assassination, I treated the whole campaign as a joke, a chance to bank my retirement, jump some pretty girls, have some fun embarrassing the straight-laced morons, and ride off into the sunset. But now, I'm not so sure. The polls show me running neck and neck with Spratlin and he doesn't have any more political qualifications than I do."

"Somehow, I don't think that's what elections should be about…which guy is less qualified?"

"I think the fact that I was nominated as the Republican nominee says everything you need to know about the hypocrisy and lies, bigotry and hate at the heart of the party. Either way, we're going to expose them for exactly what they are."

She poked him in the chest, "You've been an absolute creep to me since the first day I met you but now, I know your truth and you'd best change your ways or I'll share your secrets with the guys who own you."

He pushed her against the desk and started grinding between her legs, "Don't threaten me, girly. You're on the most fantastic trip of your life and you better hang on tight, if you want to be there when we reach the Holy Grail."

Studio manager Jack Hannah's baritone rumbled over the speakers, as he peered down from the window in the engineer's booth, "One minute and counting."

Penny gathered her things and hustled across the studio, disappearing into the glare of the studio lights, while Murphy donned his headphones, lit a cigar, took a swig of bourbon from the WBFK coffee cup on the cluttered desk, and leaned back in the large chair under a battered Old Glory and the Confederate battle flag.

The studio crew settled into silence as Hannah counted down, "Five, four, three, two, and we're on the air!"

The candidate morphed into character, "Good evening! This is your next president, Mac Murphy, bringing you the unvarnished truth about your world from WBFK, 'World Broadcasting from the Konfederacy', ten-forty on the dial, just outside Cincinnati.

Tonight, I'd like to welcome all of you for a chat about my opponent, Representative Stanton Spratlin, traitor turncoat Republican, who's running for the White House as a Democrat, and the ridiculous speech he gave last night. He sure looked like a wet mangy dog trying to find shelter from a storm, don't ya' think?

He's ranting and raving about some hairbrained conspiracy by the wealthiest of our citizens, who might be scumbags screwing the working people of this country, but they sure as hell aren't in the business of hiring bands of thugs to carry out terrorism and assassination. Credible reports suggest that the deaths of hundreds or maybe thousands of protestors at the All People Matter rallies were paid for by members of their own executive committee, in a sad twisted effort to gain sympathy and support from moderate Republicans.

We have yet to see any evidence that Tyrone Turner's assassination was anything more than the act of a very sick human being, who thought he was doing mankind a favor. I won't speak ill of the dead, of a man who should be respected, even if I didn't agree with a single thing he stood for, but I don't think any of us could imagine him being elected as our president."

Murphy paused, toked on his cigar and retrieved his bourbon-filled coffee cup from the mounds of clippings of outrageous and completely untrue stories from the far-right fringes of the media piled on the desk. He blew a long slow stream of gray smoke towards the camera and jumped out of his chair, screaming, "My opponent wants to postpone the election until his PR people can figure out how to sell the fantasy that all the tragedies surrounding the All People Matter movement were ordered up by a few wealthy Republicans! Really, the party of justice, patriotism, and evangelical ethics? Even with today's phony journalism, that's a little hard to swallow.

You know what I think? I think he's a chicken-shit, who's in way over his head and lacks the gonads or the intelligence to win a fair fight. Let the best man win and we all know he doesn't have the backbone! If he's afraid to take me on, can you imagine what a mess he'd make of our relations with leaders of all the other countries in the world, friend and foe alike. They'd clean his clock and empty the treasury in the first hour of his administration!

Spratlin knows the truth is going to come out about the front office at Stanton Oil pillaging the employee's pension fund to keep the company afloat after years of criminal corruption and mismanagement. He knows he can't hide from the truth about his sleazy dysfunctional family and his long-term affair with his former secretary, Katherine Kennedy, spokeswoman for the All People Matter movement. Hell, the only way he got seated in the House of Representatives was Oklahoma's corrupt governor needed to cover-up his own participation in the scandal to elect more incompetent nincompoops to Congress.

Spratlin has no business being in government, let alone leading our nation right down the tubes to economic and moral bankruptcy. He's a joke, a conman, an imposter trying to steal your votes, so the real conspirators can take over our government, our democracy, and our lives. We can't let that happen!

We have to triumph in this election, because defeat would mark the first step in dismantling our society, our beliefs, our dignity, and our country! We can't hand it over to the infestation of dirty immigrants pouring across our borders, to the violent vermin packed into the disgusting ghettos in our cities, to the arrogant liberal elites who have dominated and abused our democratic institutions for long enough! And we sure don't want those greedy bastards on Wall Street running the economy!

They've destroyed our America, sullied the purity of our Founding Fathers' sacred covenant, and desecrated the graves of all the patriots who fought and died to protect our ideals over the centuries, since our revolution finally defeated the British oppressors at Yorktown.

It's time to take back control of our nation! It's time to stand together in demanding that my opponent stop hiding behind the tragedy surrounding Tyrone Turner's death and come out and fight like a man! This isn't an election for the school board! All of you are about to elect the next President of the United States and the candidate you choose is going to determine the future direction of this nation. You have the power to decide whether you want to rebuild our national glory or bow down to the demands of international pirates, who can't wait to pillage and plunder the corpse of our once glorious nation."

He sat down, sipped from his cup, puffed on his cigar, and blew a long slow funnel of gray smoke at his audience. He leaned back, laughing, "Can you imagine Stanton Spratlin facing down our most dangerous enemies in a crisis? Really? He'd be shaking in his boots if Russia or China or, hell, even little Belgium called his bluff.

America needs a leader who isn't afraid to thumb his nose at second-rate nations or poke our enemies in the eye or kick our allies in the ass when we need their assistance. You know what America needs, that's why I'm asking you to get on board and help us take this election for our people and the future of our country. Get all your friends, your family, your family's family, and everyone you know to the polls on the first Tuesday in November to vote for the only candidate who represents you! A vote for Mac Murphy is a vote for freedom, liberty, and the American Way! God bless our flag, our country, and all of you! Good night!"

The studio crew broke into cheers and applause, as Jack Hannah's baritone rumbled through the speakers, "This has been The Mac Murphy Show on WBKF, World News from the Konfederacy, ten-forty on the dial. We appreciate your support but we still need you to send those contributions to the Mac Murphy Presidential Campaign at WBFK, P.O. Box 1040, Cincinnati, Ohio. Let's take our country back, elect Mac Murphy President!"

~

Steel magnate, Conrad Blaho's aging tennis knees ached, as he settled into a plush leather chair inside a luxurious lounge, buried in the bowels of Dynamic Devices' sprawling complex near Willow Run Airport, just west of Detroit. Over a half-century, Stanley French parlayed an insignificant materials contract with the Air Force to become the single largest contractor for advanced weapons systems in the country, supplying many foreign governments as well.

The bunker offered all the amenities of a modern office suite, with advanced communications and direct links to the Pentagon and the White House. It was shielded from any form of external monitoring and swept for bugs before and after every meeting.

Blaho accepted a tumbler of amber Scotch and toasted a decidedly stout Stanley French, who was sporting a trim goatee, "I'm impressed with your SCIF (Sensitive Compartmentalized Information Facility) - confidential, tasteful, and comfortable."

"The development of high-tech weaponry requires secure facilities for discussions and communications. Our competitors and our enemies are all too eager to gain information about our systems and our plans."

"We have the same problem but, I must say, your designers provided more luxury and style than our rather sterile chambers." There was a pause and, knowing that Stanley had recently lost his second wife, Conrad asked, "How are your boys?"

"It's kind of you to inquire. I'm not sure how, but they're both grown men. It doesn't seem that long ago that they were just little kids, when we first met with Tomlinson and Reverend Godwin at the ranch in Sixty-eight to begin planning this campaign. John's MBA from Yale made him the perfect choice to coordinate our suppliers' implementation of just-in-time scheduling that's enhanced our quality control and saved a bundle on warehousing. MIT transformed Michael into a mechanical engineering phenomenon, who earned the leading role in our concept and design department. They've worked their way up through management, just like we did, and they're firmly committed to the cause."

Blaho grinned, "With just a little nudge from the old man?"

"They're the future leaders of our campaign and they're well-prepared."

"We might actually live to see the ultimate fruition of this transformation we set into play so many years ago."

The stiff white shirt collar disappeared beneath French's heavy jowls, as he leaned in to growl, "It's obvious the Republican's trickle-down miracle gave us a nice little tax break, before it fizzled into a recession that dumped millions of working people out on the street and kept our wetback Democrat in the White House for two terms. Those workers pay taxes for roads and schools and government services, so we don't have to. How's all that affecting your heavy-metals industries?"

As COO and heir to the vast holdings of Lebanon Steel, Blaho was tasked with expanding a legacy of power and profitability for several more generations of his great-great grandfather's heritage. That tradition demanded absolute commitment to the family ethic of maintaining undisputed dominance in every facet of their industries and a diligent intolerance of competition or government interference.

"Sales to manufacturers, inside the United States, are down by twenty-percent over the past two years. The Koreans and the Chinese are dumping crap product on the world market at prices well below cost and we can't compete." He sipped, "Time for another convenient conflict in the Gulf to push us all into the black again."

"Hell, we'd have more to gain if we invaded Venezuela, so we could open up our leases and start drilling again."

"If all this works out, our people will make that happen."

"With the real costs of the wars added in, the government's in the red and our lame-duck Commander-in-Chief is trying to raise taxes on big business and old money, before he leaves office next January."

"That's why we're here, isn't it?"

"Yes, but the more important question is whether we can handle Murphy, once he's in office?" inquired French.

"After his performance, holding Turner's bloody corpse in his lap after the assassination at the debate before tens of millions of viewers, I'm sure we'll take the White House and majorities in both Houses of Congress too. Red or blue, the general population is totally freaked out by everything that's happened. Disappearing hundreds of opposition organizers can't hurt either.

Besides, we have several operatives inside the campaign, including Dr. Teddy Billings, who has our candidate on a schedule of medications that keeps him in prime fighting form, when he's needed, and in something close to a coma when he's not. As you know, we've been supplying an endless parade of professional women to service his ego and I've been assured that we have hours of compromising video, if we need it."

"Is that the good news?"

Blaho smiled, "The good news is that we're seeing a rather remarkable trend in our polling numbers across the Midwest and the South. Reverend Godwin's association of ministers are delivering the Gospel according to Saint Ethan Tomlinson, to growing congregations of our unemployed or barely surviving nationalist core.

ImageSculptor, Tomlinson's public relations firm, created a clandestine publishing wing that bought hundreds of small town newspapers that run stories about immigrant drug gangs invading white suburbia, black hooligans raping defenseless white women, Haitian prostitutes spreading HIV to white teenage boys, bogus news about the IRS threatening evangelical ministries with investigations into tax evasion, the ATF moving to require background checks and licensing of every firearm in the country, even Asian students being given preference on college entrance exams over white scholars. Some of these reports ricochet through the community, like political pinballs with flashing lights and clanging bells, until they become accepted as truth."

"And everything is blamed on the liberals?"

"Of course, our constituency has to be convinced that the Democrats are plotting to destroy their basic rights and freedoms, murder unborn babies, promote fuzzy scientific theories that threaten their extreme religious delusions, and, of course, equal rights for niggers, faggots, women, and foreigners. Hate is the galvanizing elixir and we provide the boogieman everyone can blame for their misery."

"What about our slate of candidates?"

The balding man put down his glass, "We've selected three-hundred and forty-six extreme white-nationalists, as the next class of candidates. Our sponsor families have groomed their political pedigrees, dressed them in fancy suits, run them through our academies for psychological evaluation of their fidelity and commitment to our priorities, coupled with rigorous training in debate and public speaking before the cameras and large crowds. We've provided substantial funding and teams to run their campaigns, Tomlinson's supplying scripted talking points, and his pal, Will Terry, has created a really aggressive political advertising genre designed to leave the ignorant masses terrified and frothing for revenge to finish off the campaign."

"All they need are beat-up flags and well-worn Bibles."

"Already supplied." He paused and looked up, "We knew this was going to be a long slog over the last six decades but, with everything we've been promoting, the country has become more and more tribal. People are taking up violent opposition over very specific personal issues that supersede other disputes and the major parties are becoming more polarized, which has forced them to shift to the extremes, leaving a huge percentage of the population abandoned in the political wilderness.

Our projections indicate that Spratlin can't carry the Democrats to victory, even with a massive sympathy vote, he doesn't have that personal charisma that sparkles in the glowing gloom of reality. After suffering through the administration's incompetence and the violence that commands the headlines every day, the country is ready for dramatic change. If everything falls into place, almost every legislature in the country will be populated with our people. Pouring money into gerrymandering over the years and contesting every close election across the country pays dividends."

"And so many districts turned red! Do think we're grooming enough committed candidates to follow through?"

"Oh, there are platoons of qualified people being trained. Our foundations and think-tanks are narrowing the choices to fill Cabinet positions and the support staff, the well of prospects is bottomless, and the to-do list doesn't end until we turn out the lights in D.C." Blaho paused, his eyes intent, "When our boy, Creighton Steil, assumes control from Murphy, the system will be primed to begin dismantling the government in earnest."

"What about the project states?" inquired French, pouring two fingers of Scotch from an antique crystal decanter.

"We've got committees working in every state and the looming possibility of another recession is making converts out of desperate Democrats, who have no problem blaming the unions that were supposed to protect them and their own bumbling president." Conrad raised his glass, "Our polling continues to expose the dark underbelly of American society as racist, nationalistic, completely self-absorbed, and pretending to be Christian."

"Pretending?"

"Of course, contemporary evangelical ministry is pure hypocrisy - you can beat your wife, cheat your neighbor, and screw his daughter, knowing that you'll be forgiven by a raving minister, who had to be born again, because he's a complete moral failure as a human being and has no more connection with God than the loon on a soapbox screaming for salvation. It's big-money entertainment that plays to the fears and flaws of their flocks to make a whole bunch of charlatan-ministers rich."

He paused to sip, "Monday morning, the sinners are free to go out and sow their anger and hate all over again. They're too ignorant to read real newspapers or follow factual news, have no understanding or respect for science or facts for that matter, and honestly believe that there's a secret society behind the government that's out to get them personally. A good dose of evangelical fundamentalism, doused with a steady stream of racist propaganda and carefully constructed lies, drives those losers right into our ranks."

"Well, they're right about a conspiracy to take control of the government, because they're going to help make it happen," chuckled French.

"Our campaign against unions has taken flight across the rust belt. Our folks in Wisconsin built a grassroots campaign to hijack the school boards and cripple the teachers' union, which lost its grip on public education before the evangelical community took control.

As you know, we've promoted legislation in Indiana, Michigan, Ohio, and Pennsylvania to force large manufacturing to stop requiring mandatory union membership and force current employees to pay union dues directly, instead of as an automatic deduction. They'll be less inclined to pay up, if they have to take the cash out of their pockets."

"That's fairly brilliant, just keep your troublemakers away from my front door!" replied French.

"The ministries in Oklahoma expanded their attack on public education, forcing the legislature to cut funding by another three and a half-percent for the coming year, which makes the entire budget less than half of what it was when we started. Test scores have dropped every year, leaving Okie kids second from the bottom, just ahead of Mississippi.

The state Board of Education in Texas has the final say on the approval of a majority of the textbooks used in most school districts across the country. Our board members have forced changes in a number of texts - questioning the validity of scientific theories, including evolution and the big-bang, the accuracy of historical facts, particularly the Civil War being fought over State's rights instead of slavery and casting doubt on the holocaust. They're also working diligently to remove any references to mistakes and tragedies that sully the glorification of flag and country, so the little guys will grow up to be rabid supporters of white-nationalist heroes."

"An ignorant populous is far easier to manipulate than well-educated liberals!"

Blaho nodded, "We convinced the residents of Kansas that the entire tax system was rigged and state government corrupt and wasteful. We expect to add another dozen dedicated representatives to the legislature this fall to push through a final package of patriotic tax breaks for our patrons.

Will Terry teamed up with Bill Mendelson to form a broadcasting company that bought up hundreds of rural radio and television stations across the country to deliver our message to feed and reinforce society's fear, anger, and frustration. Our goal is to get all the red states to mimic Alabama, Mississippi, and Louisiana, where we could get the devil himself elected, if he was against integration, immigration, and abortion, and for expanding Second Amendment rights and our brand of Evangelical Christianity."

"Amen."

"And let's not forget the outstanding work of the Alien Relocation Command, who have picked up twenty-seven thousand illegals and thousands of opposition operatives in the past month," added Blaho. "I still find it astonishing that the whole operation is sanctioned by the Congress in the budget."

"What do you mean?"

"Buried in the fine print is a directive granting 'extraordinary powers' to indefinitely detain people and suspend habeas corpus during times of natural disaster, civil disobedience, or other emergency situations, applicable to any statutes or rules of procedure otherwise affecting pre-arrest, post-arrest, pre-trial, trial, and post-trial measures in criminal and juvenile proceedings and all civil processes and proceedings."

"I can't believe the Democrats didn't find that."

"We didn't give them time to read the preamble, let alone the thousands of pages of allocations."

"They just gave the Command free rein to conduct mercenary operations inside our borders against our own citizens!"

"And they're doing a bang-up job too!" Blaho smiled, "How are we doing with the law schools?"

French laughed, "It's absolutely astonishing how the most intelligent and gifted people on the planet can be so gullible. We dangle new buildings and patronage to the most liberal institutions in the country and they're perfectly willing to disregard their arrogant privileged principles and accept our conservative lawyers and judges to run their faculty. Over the years, they've redirected the curriculum to reflect a more libertarian tenor.

Money talks and, while we're dismantling the government, Congress is going to offer broad support for the elimination of taxes for the families who invested billions to fund this revolution and we'll have our own judiciary to back it up. The members of The Forge will be pleased."

"There is one more thing," said Blaho.

"What's that?"

"The Nucleus is up and running. Our world-wide web of massive computers, controlled by advanced artificial intelligence, has been programmed to manage everything from the global economy to organizing the population to serve the foundation of the new order. We've been using it to guide the Relocation Commandos to find and capture enemies of the state and, in short order, we'll be able to pull up full backgrounds and trace any individual in the country."

"How are we gaining access, if it's a government operation?"

"The central core controlling the programs is called The Kernel and it's housed as a black operation under Homeland Security. Our people have been administering the project since conception and our Forge brother, Harry Wilson's computer company, Primary Tech, is the sole contractor."

"I know we've talked about all of this a number of times over the years but I find myself rather awed by the idea that we can manipulate the past, present, and future of any individual we choose simply by pressing a button. That's certainly the ultimate tool for sculpting and reordering the population of this country."

"That's why we started this campaign in the first place, to replace our failed experiment in democracy with an economy that benefits those who possess the knowledge and power to run things with extreme efficiency for maximum profits."

~

The wheels of the Gulfstream touched Teterboro Airport's tarmac at four-fifty-eight on a damp cloudy morning and taxied into a white hangar emblazoned with a giant Simonson Air logo. The plane rolled to a stop in the enormous cavern, the overhead door closed, and the pilot appeared in the cabin. "We are secure. There's a van waiting to take you to the helicopter."

Tate unbuckled and stood to shake his hand, "Thanks for getting us here."

"I'm honored to help." He turned to Nellis and Katherine, "The All People Matter movement is the only hope for millions of desperate people who are struggling to survive. I thank you for all you've done in uniting and inspiring us all to save this country."

Nellis stood "It might be easier to pull off out here in the real world, as opposed to sitting in a dank dungeon someplace far from civilization."

The copilot released the hatch and cold air rushed into the plane, as Tate led the newlyweds down three steps, five strides across the glistening floor to hop in the back of a black Ford utility van.

The Hispanic driver slid the door closed and trotted around to climb in the front. His tiny strip of a moustache arched into a grin, "We'll be taking the scenic route past a stunning collection of dumpsters behind this line of hangars, with no stops for burgers or restrooms. Travel time should be less than four minutes and I'm told the coast is clear."

"I'm not used to sneaking around, especially in this luxury," said Katherine.

Tate patted her hand, "A private jet that whisks you from the grip of the Gestapo to freedom is not a luxury, it's a tool that provides invisibility and liberty."

"I know her old man owns the charter company but, if you talk to Mavis before we do, I hope you'll thank her for all of this."

"That's going to be an…interesting conversation."

Nellis squeezed Katherine's hand, "I don't envy you that one, brother."

"I could claim amnesia from a bash to the head but I was a Big Twelve college quarterback when we met, so that's never going to fly."

"You might need to claim that after she gets finished with you," laughed Katherine. "I know she's honestly missed you."

Tate glanced out the windshield, as the van braked and stopped next to a red Bell helicopter with its engine running. "I think this is our flight. When we exit the van, walk directly to the open door of the helicopter, keep your head down, and do not look to either side. Make yourselves unrecognizable."

Nellis wrapped an arm around Katherine, "Did you bring our disguises?"

"Sorry, all I could find was the front and back ends of a Jersey cow but I didn't think you'd go for it," laughed Sloan.

The driver slid the door open, "You have a safe journey."

"Thanks for helping us," said Nellis, turning up his collar and donning an orange and blue Mets ball cap, the cupped bill pulled low on his forehead, while Katherine tied a floral scarf under her chin to hide her thick auburn hair and donned oversized sunglasses. He kissed her cheek, "Now you look like a movie star."

"It's been my honor, sir," said their chauffer, his Latin accent tinged with a hint of Bronx brogue.

Katherine touched the man's shoulder, as she climbed out, huddled close to Nellis and trotted over to climb into the helicopter under the draft of the rotating blade. The driver latched the door behind Tate, who offered headphones before he buckled up.

The pilot's voice sounded sharp and crackly against the roar of the engine, "If everyone is secure, we'll lift off. Travel time is approximately twelve minutes. We hope you enjoy the flight."

The helicopter rose into the air, tilted forward, and flew southeast across the meandering Hackensack River to turn south over the Hudson, as the sky brightened briefly, the light reflecting between a forest of glass skyscrapers, then around the southern tip of Manhattan to land on a broad stretch of concrete jutting into the inky water.

The copilot pulled the door open and Tate hustled Nellis and Katherine into the back seat of a waiting Yellow Cab, which pulled away before the rear door closed. The cabbie turned, "Where to?"

"The underground," replied Tate.

"I thought we were going to a theater or something?" inquired Katherine.

"Oh, we'll get there, but there's something we need to see first," replied Tate.

The taxi turned west, then north around the toe of Manhattan, before dropping down a curved ramp into an open tunnel near South Cove Park, pulling to the curb in front of an unfinished subway station beneath Battery Park. Tate stepped out of the car, "C'mon."

Nellis and Katherine followed, "Why are we stopping at a construction site?"

"I haven't seen it yet but I'm told that there are three stations along this line that were never completed, so they've been put to other uses," replied Tate, walking to a row of doors, as the taxi pulled down the lane and parked.

He pulled on one, then another, and finally walked along the line until he spied a square of red tape in the middle of the glass panel on the second last door. He tapped twice with the gold wedding ring on his left hand, waited, and tapped twice again. The door swung open and the escapees strolled inside, as it closed and locked itself.

A rapid patter of footsteps preceded a slender man, in a gray suit, crimson bowtie, and little round wire-rimmed glasses, who appeared out of the darkness. "I'm Dr. David Cohen and you must be Tate Sloan, I'd recognize that famous face anywhere, with Nellis Gray and Katherine Kennedy. I'm thrilled that you're safe."

They shook hands all around and Tate said, "I've had a brief overview of your operation but I'm afraid I don't really know any details."

Cohen shook his head, "The Alien Relocation Command, who have evidently been chasing our most esteemed guests, have been at this for quite some time, pursuing and capturing thousands of innocent civilians, mostly immigrants and people of color. They seem to be the direct beneficiaries of the secret intelligence databases containing extensive files on every person in the country or, perhaps, the industrialized world. The government has been denying that they've collected those illegal records for decades, but we know they actually exist, because our team has hacked the Command's link into the system to retrieve the identities of those at risk.

Once the underground understood the challenge, they started a campaign to infiltrate the communications of the Command and interrupt, interfere, and rescue as many potential prisoners as possible."

"But how is all of that possible?" asked Katherine.

"First, because there is a secret authority, within every level of the bureaucracy of our government, that answers to and is directed by the nationalist confederacy that attacked your rallies and murdered Tyrone Turner. They're tasked with removing the opposition before the election by any means necessary. Second, because technical experts, who have spoken out against the right-wing coup, are at the top of the 'enemies' list. Many of them are staying with us."

"Staying with you?" inquired Nellis.

"Yes, as you'll see in just a moment, we've filled these three stations with a growing colony of fugitives, who have transformed their exile into a functioning society." He took Katherine's arm, "Come along and I'll show you."

They walked back into the structure through broad darkened hallways that opened into a blazing lobby lined with silver escalators and a dozen elevators with doors in rainbow colors. Nellis leaned to the murmurs of many voices and a continuous circulation of bodies moving around the lower level.

Dr. Cohen tapped his arm, "If you'll follow me, I think I can introduce you to the big picture."

He walked over to a red elevator and pressed a glowing button. A tiny 'ding' announced the retraction of the cherry slabs, before they stepped inside and rose two floors. The doctor led them along a hallway to a balcony overlooking concourses on each side of two lines of track disappearing into dark tunnels under a soaring white ceiling arching over the massive space.

Tate whistled under his breath, watching thousands of people moving around the enormous cavern in a very organized manner, in spite of the early hour. Everyone marched with purpose and conviction and no one seemed to be wandering aimlessly. Little human eddies peeled off to visit well-stocked shops lining the stations - offering clothing, office supplies, newspapers and magazines, a lending library with an impressive collection, and lots of stalls with personal items.

"These people, working at the clusters of desks and tables below us, administer the functions of the facility - from who's here, to their assigned living space and job, to their medical records and their preferences in the cafeteria." Cohen pointed, "That dimly lit cave, behind the heavy glass doors on the opposite balcony, houses our technical wizards, who are the only ones allowed access to the outside world. Obviously, security is a primary concern. We call them wizards and that's Oz.

The tunnels have morphed into the biggest dormitories in the city, the station to the south has been transformed into a hospital and a school. We even have a basketball court set up and teams compete every night." Dr. Cohen hooked a thumb over his shoulder, "The facility to the north is our canteen."

"How many do you feed," asked Katherine.

"Last official count had us at just over forty-five hundred."

"That's a lot of folks to feed every meal every day," said Nellis. "How do you import your supplies? And why haven't the cops figured out you're here?"

"None of this could possibly work without help from very high places in the city. We have a lot of powerful allies trying to sabotage the conspirators and their Storm Troopers and protecting these people is part of the battle.

Food and supplies arrive on special trains in the wee hours of every morning. A massive crew spends four hours unloading and transporting the supplies throughout the complex and you could be standing on the next platform and never hear a sound. Everyone who lives down here has a job."

"How do these people find their way to you?" asked Katherine.

"Well, they don't. We have specially trained teams, who go out to collect them, when we receive information about impending arrests from the Command's lists. It's a race, from the moment we learn a new identity, to facilitate a rescue before the Black Shirts have a chance to nab them. We have a fairly stellar record but we all regret every one we miss."

"How'd all this get started?" asked Sloan.

The doctor laughed, "Actually, it started with a bunch of high school musicians holding underground concerts for their friends and fans. They'd haul their gear down here and party for days because no one could hear the racket outside. One of their grandmothers figured out what was going on and conned the kids into putting on concerts for thousands instead of a few hundred. They still play on the weekends."

"Smart woman."

He gazed around at the hive of activity, "There are a lot of brilliant people in our midst, patriots who are chomping at the bit to take our country back."

"I know how they feel," said Katherine.

"Would you be willing to address them? Just knowing that you're here, that the movement is alive, would give them hope."

"I'd be happy to talk with them," replied the brunette, "because they, and the millions of workers who've been screwed by the oligarchs, are the movement."

Nellis quipped, "Be careful what you ask for, get her cranked up and you might have a riot on your hands."

Katherine raised her chin defiantly, "If memory serves, you have a well-deserved reputation for being…disruptive, to use a polite term. Clips of your brutally honest cameo, after the massacre in Denver, are still playing on the news networks almost every day!"

"Good! We want everyone to remember what those butchers did to our people." He turned to Cohen, "We've only been married for like eight or ten hours and she's already starting to yank my chain."

The doctor laughed, "I've been married for thirty-seven years and my wife leaves no doubt that I have yet to master the very basics of house-training."

"Nellis has a long way to go, if we ever get back home."

"Freedom will require the cumulative strength and bravery of every one of us," said the doctor. "Have you heard about the protests?"

"No, where?"

Cohen smiled, "Everywhere, starting today. There's been an enormous response to Representative Spratlin's speech. They're expecting a hundred-thousand at noon in Central Park and similar gatherings are going to be held in every major city in the country."

"I'll bet Tabitha Hall has a hand in this," said Nellis.

"I can hear her saying, 'Let the people speak!'," added Katherine. "I wish we could be there."

"Neither you nor any of these other fugitives can be seen in public or allowed to communicate with the outside world for the safety of everyone else. I think of the Alien Relocation Command as a modern reincarnation of the Gestapo, except these devils are armed with weapons and technology that the Germans could only dream about in their campaign of cruel tyranny and ruthless slaughter."

"Let's go have a chat with our people," said Katherine.

The red elevator dropped three stories before the doors slid open to the bustle of the west concourse. People stopped to stare as soon as Nellis and Katherine emerged from the lift and several started to clap, which enticed crowds to gather and join in cheers and applause. More refugees poured out of the tunnels to fill the station with hope.

Dr. Cohen handed Katherine a microphone and she stepped to the edge of the platform. The crowd clapped and waved, cheered and cried out to her for several minutes, before they finally settled into moderate pandemonium. "Ladies and gentlemen, I think we all treasure and have a new appreciation of the privilege of freedom. I know I do, as I stand before you today, because we barely escaped the clutches of the Alien Relocation Commandos at our farm in Cameron, Oklahoma, yesterday, only because a couple of very brave young ladies road in on horseback to rescue us, just like in the old black-and-white westerns."

The crowd cheered and a bearded man down front yelled, "You're a long way from home, lady, but you're more than welcome here!"

"Thank you, thank all of you for resisting!"

Applause.

"I'm told that massive protests are planned for later today in all the major cities in the country and I wish we could join them but I understand that, if we value our freedom and we care about each other, we can't. Instead, we're going to join forces to work from the underground to reveal the real puppeteers who have been buying elections for decades. They think they can take it all in this shady election…the House, the Senate, and the White House…and we have to prove them wrong!"

The merchandise on the shelves in the little shops rattled with the raucous roar.

"We've just escaped, so, to be honest, I don't know how many of our associates have been seized but we have to assume that a great number of our leaders are missing. Until we have better intel, we'll begin by encouraging what's left of the All People Matter movement to do everything possible to promote the candidacy of Stanton Spratlin. Let's reveal the unvarnished truth about Mac Murphy and the Republican White-Nationalist Party to the American people before they vote on election day. And, while we're about it, let's expose the chain of command behind the American Gestapo!"

Chapter Two

The Yellow Cab slipped into a flock of identical taxis in congested traffic heading up Church Street through Soho and, after several turns, eased into an alley and stopped next to a large slatted overhead door inset in a windowless brick wall that rose five stories, with a black steel entry off to one side. A small sign read, 'The Playhouse – Deliveries. Please ring bell'.

Tate pressed the button and a red light on a small camera mounted above the door glowed for a moment before the lock clicked. He turned the handle and stepped into a gigantic warehouse overflowing with costumes, props, and scenery.

Katherine picked up a pink boa and flicked it at Nellis, "This place is every little girl's fantasy! Everything you could need to put on any play you could imagine!"

"Mavis would love it, too," said Tate, pointing to a rainbow of gowns hanging on a rack.

A small stout elf of a man, with bushy brows and twinkly eyes peering over little glasses perched low on a broad nose beneath a weathered train engineer's cap, stepped from a dusty yellow streetcar parked in the corner of the cavern beneath the snout and wings of a DC3 diving out of the wall. "It wouldn't surprise me, if we hadn't produced just about every play worth performing over the past fifty years, as well as vaudeville nights, poetry readings, community gatherings, and musical concerts, too."

Katherine reached her hand to shake, "I'm Katherine Kennedy."

"I'm Burt Sutton and I'm fairly certain that everybody, who knows anything about what's going on in the world, knows who you are. Likewise, Mr. Gray of course, and, risen from the dead, Tate Sloan - stellar quarterback, entrepreneur, and international sex symbol. Welcome to The Playhouse…which is our family home as well."

"We appreciate your sanctuary," said Nellis, shaking his hand.

"You'll be safe here." Sutton turned to Tate, "Did you take them by the underground?"

"Yes, Miss Kennedy gave a rousing speech."

"Actually, I'm Katherine Gray, now."

Nellis squeezed her hand, "Kind of spur of the moment decision that should have happened a long time ago."

"Congratulations," said Sutton with a grin and a slight bow. "If you'll follow me, I'll introduce you to the rest of the clan. Oh, I hope you don't mind children, we have more than our share."

"I have two grown children and whole tribe of youngsters who descend on our farm far too often."

Katherine gripped his arm, "He says that but he wouldn't trade a moment with any of them and, in a way, they're kind of responsible for us getting to know each other."

"There's a long story," laughed Nellis, following Sutton through endless rows of shelving rising from planked floors to a very high ceiling, stuffed with props and furniture, an armory of weapons, a menagerie of lifelike animals, trees, plants, rocks and boulders, rolling racks of costumes from every historical period, hundreds of faceless heads covered with wigs of every color and style, and nooks and crannies dedicated to glittering jewelry, shoes, hats, and a vibrant collection of ties.

"Is there anything you don't have in here?" mused Tate.

Burt stopped, "A weapon to end fascism."

"I think the most powerful weapon we could conjure is the energy I felt from all those patriots in the underground waiting impatiently for their chance at retribution," said Katherine.

"If the folks marching in these rallies around the country are half as passionate as the refugees in those tunnels, this could be the start of a revolution," added Nellis.

"One that's been a long time coming," said Burt, climbing the stairs to a landing overlooking the entire warehouse, which was neatly crammed with scenery, props, and clothes to fashion any performance.

He pulled open one of a pair of steel doors at the end of a long dark hallway and pointed to rooms and alcoves along each side, "These are rehearsal and dressing rooms for the stars. We're right under the stage but our living quarters are through here."

He turned right and climbed another steep staircase that opened into a large kitchen, with twin commercial ranges, enormous ovens, double refrigerators, four sinks and dishwashers, and a commercial milk machine.

Three women turned from browning meat for a massive stew at the stoves with welcoming smiles and Burt said, "I'd like to introduce my wife Matty, field general of this operation, and our daughters, Sally and Alison."

Matty wiped her hands on a towel draped over her shoulder and hugged Katherine, "We're so glad you're safe."

The adult daughters curtsied and shook hands with Tate and Nellis and fit and lithe Alison asked, "Can we offer you something to drink?"

Katherine lifted her nose to inhale the rich, earthy aromas rising from the stove, "It smells like a warm loving home in here. A cup of hot coffee would be wonderful."

Alison was a natural for a role of the athlete or peppy young housewife, while Sally might be the smoldering vamp in a soap opera with thick auburn hair, sultry eyes and a deep melodic voice, "We've always got a pot going in this kitchen, just to keep our energy up to feed this clan. We clean up from breakfast just in-time to start dinner."

"Burt said you have a bunch of children," said Nellis, accepting a steaming cup.

"Last count was fifteen, if I'm not mistaken," said Matty, sly blue eyes sparkled as she stirred small mountains of vegetables and potatoes in two large pans, "plus assorted strays who show up for meals."

"This is the calm before the storm," added Alison, laying out loaves of bread, extra-large jars of peanut butter and jams, baskets of fruits, and a platter of fresh baked oatmeal cookies on an endless table stretching through an adjoining dining room. "They'll start arriving home from school soon and they'll all be starving."

"Are they all yours?" inquired Katherine.

"We were blessed with three wonderful independent children, who went off into the world, collected spouses, had a bunch of kids and, without so much as an 'Oh, by the way,' they all moved back home! Plus, we've sort of adopted another half-dozen or so who happened into our lives." Burt grinned, "If you add Nell, Matty's mother, we've got four generations living under one roof."

"You qualify as a clan," said Nellis.

"Clan with a 'C', if you don't mind," said Matty. "We don't have much truck with the other kind but, after all you suffered at your rallies, you already know about them."

"Intimately," replied Katherine, glancing at Nellis. "After Houston, Atlanta, Chicago, Denver, and the assassination, their cruelty is etched into my soul."

"If you called a rally tonight, half the city would show up," said Sally. "You and your campaign have lots of support up here in the urban north."

"Dr. Cohen said there were going to be protest marches today?"

Alison punched a button on a remote and a large screen above the refrigerators displayed enormous crowds carrying signs, 'Shut it Down!', 'Free our leaders', 'End American Fascism', and, most poignant, 'VOTE!'. She turned up the volume and caught the reporter in mid-sentence, yelling over the protestors' chants, "The city has never seen a march of this magnitude. Our police force is used to dealing with major events but nothing like this."

The camera panned across the river of humanity flowing down Fifth Avenue, as Tatum Freese, the studio anchor, replied, "I'm seeing a true sampling of American diversity and everything seems to be peaceful so far."

"I think trouble-makers would be hard pressed to find any supporters in this crowd. The atmosphere is kind of jovial, people are enjoying each other's support but, at the same time, they seem resolute and determined. Several leaders, that I've spoken with, said they plan to shut the city down until legitimate investigations are underway. These people are demanding truth.

Our march might be the biggest but it certainly isn't unique. Virtually every major city and most college campuses across the county are hosting similar protests with record participation. Representative Spratlin's speech struck a note and the country's reacting in a very powerful way. There are rumors that he'll appear at one of these demonstrations tonight."

Freese's blond co-anchor, Madeline Post, smiled into the camera, "There has been no reaction to these gatherings from Murphy Campaign Headquarters but House and Senate Republicans are calling this a 'Communist putsch', a revolution to overthrow the next 'rightfully elected' government…and, adding an ironic twist, they're actually defending their sworn enemy, Democratic President Gonzalez…at least until they can drive him out of office."

"Congressional leaders have said they view these demonstrations as an attempt by desperate Democrats to postpone the election and the Republican caucus is threatening to demand a vote on a bill to force the voters to decide on election day by abolishing early or after hours balloting and mail-in ballots."

The sound dimmed and Burt pointed to the marchers, "This is the real voice of America but the opposition is so tone-deaf, they can't hear it."

"They're being paid to deny that it even exists," said Tate. "The Republicans aren't a political party anymore, they're an entertainment business, contrived to keep the masses distracted and riled up, while their lackies destroy the government and cover their crimes. I should know, there was a time when I was a major contributor."

Nellis grinned, "You're forgiven."

"Absolution from you is quite a compliment."

"We're all just pilgrims on this journey through life, seeking redemption for the parts we got wrong by trying to set things right before it's too late. Best we can do."

"Amen," replied Tate, turning as a mob of children bounded into the kitchen like a herd of hungry scavengers.

Each stopped to hug Burt, Alison, and Sally, before Matty quieted the hubbub, "Children, we have guests! Let me introduce…"

A long, lanky girl with dirty blond hair and puppy dog brown eyes interrupted, "Katherine Kennedy! You're my hero!"

Katherine smiled, "Thank you! And who might you be?"

Matty wrapped an arm around her granddaughter's waist, "This is Adel and, like all her siblings, she is very special…and you'll find that she won't hesitate to tell you so."

The girl blushed, "If you're Katherine Kennedy, then you must be Nellis Gray. Your interview after the bombings in Denver was one of the most powerfully honest moments I've ever seen on television."

He winked at Katherine.

Adel turned to Sloan, "And you're Tate Sloan. My mom used to have lots of magazines with your picture on the cover and I thought you were the most handsome man in the world…but didn't you die last year?"

Tate held his index finger to his lips, "Technically, I'm still dead, just don't tell anyone, okay? Let's pretend we're all on a secret mission."

A boy with wavy blond hair grinned, "If this is a secret mission, what's the password?"

"Freedom! We demand freedom and we're going to earn it by keeping the family secrets to protect our guests." Burt waved his hand towards a tall boy with a tri-color Mohawk and dangly peace symbol earring, "Let me introduce the rest of this mob. This is our budding rock-n-roll star, Little Mac, his gorgeous sister and amazing songstress, Nikki, twins Bailey and Thomas, wee Melody, Patrick - our resident Irishman, and Rusty our techno-genius. When we get you settled, you'll have to see the train yard he's got set up in the basement. It's all computerized."

The children bowed, cheered, and pushed into the dining room for a rowdy snack.

"That's quite a pack you've got there," said Tate.

"That's just the first wave, another eight or ten will wander in shortly looking dangerously ravenous," said Alison.

"How do you maintain all of them and this theater too?" asked Katherine.

Matty laughed, "We don't, they do. Every one of them has a job in the theater, even the youngest can move scenery, help with makeup and costumes, run the lights and sound during a performance. Most know every line of every part and could step in on a moment's notice and all of them are disappointed when they don't get time on stage in front of an audience."

"That's amazing."

"Yes, it is," replied Sally, "and each of them has at least one formidable talent."

Burt turned to Nellis, "I've been asked to pass along a message."

"From who?"

"Bruce Spratlin."

"One of my heroes," said Nellis.

"He said his brother has contacted some of his associates across the country in an effort to determine where the Alien Relocation Command is holding your friends and how they're transporting them to wherever the captives are being confined. I'm told that more information will follow as he receives it."

"Thanks, that's a start. Question is whether they can be rescued before they reach their final destination? It's already been a couple of days since they were kidnapped."

"Local scuttlebutt has it that there's a detainee processing center up near Indian Point and we're getting reports of sleek white windowless mystery trains rolling south through Hoboken and Jersey City in the wee hours of the morning."

"This isn't just some renegade government agency, this is a fully-functional para-military branch of Homeland Security seizing thousands of 'enemies of the state' all over the county just like us!"

"And they must have huge facilities set up somewhere to hold all the detainees and kangaroo courts to sentence them. Plus, they'd need an army of people to deposit anyone of color on the other side of the border," added Burt.

Nellis shook his head, "My journey to this reality started with exposing our Congressman as a nightrider for the Ku Klux Klan, then taking down his hand-picked totally unfit replacement, and it keeps expanding out in every direction, from the poorest in our society to the wealthiest and most powerful."

"Their civilian militia killed hundreds and injured thousands at our rallies," added Katherine. "It reminds me of Hitler's Brown-Shirt thugs attacking the opposition in the streets and the government-sanctioned Gestapo disposing of the 'undesirables' in the dark of night."

"Only it isn't the Fuhrer calling the shots, it's a gang of tycoons."

"Yeah, but Hitler couldn't have pulled off his march to power without the support of the German industrialists and these guys are just a modern reincarnation of their greed and lust for power."

Doc Billings leaned close to Murphy's face, pointing a penlight into the pinpoint pupils of his jaundiced eyes. He grasped the candidate's wrist between his fingers, counting the sluggish thump-thump of his pulse. Finally, he pulled away, "You're a mess."

"Yeah, I know and I've got to be in character on that stage in an hour. Think there's any hope?"

"That's why I'm here, isn't it? But first, I want to know how you're holding up inside that brain of yours?"

Mac grinned, "Hell, I'm less than two weeks away from winning the election, how do you think I feel?"

"I think you're probably scared to death and completely depressed that your ruse didn't work. You expected to skate through this campaign and exit gracefully into a million-dollar book deal with a bevy of bimbos in tow. We both know you never expected to win."

"True that," said Murphy, "but I'll play it through the final performance."

"You don't have a clue what comes after that do you?"

"None."

The doctor held up a little white paper cup and his patient counted the pills, "Seven?"

"Our usual cocktail with some vitamins for your state of mind. I'm absolutely sure that you'll be ready to rock in an hour."

Mac tossed down the pills with a chug of bourbon. "I put my faith in you, Doc."

"Enthusiastic fans have been lining up since noon and you'll have a friendly crowd of more than seventeen-thousand cheering you on, so go out there and lock down North Carolina. Charlotte's Murphy-country and you're on the brink of victory!"

Stylist Penny Baker marched across the dressing room and set her kit on the table next to the candidate. She pulled out a rag to wipe the sweat and shine off his cheeks and forehead and pushed him back into the chair to cover his chest with a towel. "You look worse than usual. Good thing the fans are too far away to see that you're actually a cadaver that someone dug up from a shallow grave in their back yard."

She reached to close his eyes with two fingers and dusted his face, "I can't believe you've only got a couple more rallies before the vote."

"How'd we get here?"

"I don't have any idea but I'm glad you talked me into sticking it out. I can't wait to be there when you declare victory."

His hands twitched, his pupils snapped open, and the corners of his lips curled into a sadistic grin. He grabbed her hand and shoved it under the towel, "You know how to get me ready, make him salute old glory."

Penny squeezed the soft lump in his pants but excused herself as Jack Hannah, Casper Wein, Shepherd Stone, and financial titan, Turner Graves, pulled up chairs. Murphy asked, "How are the numbers tonight?"

Campaign manager Wein scanned a sheaf of papers, "Nationally, you're hovering around forty-eight point three and Spratlin's at forty-six nine. I think the electoral college is leaning our way, especially if we can take a couple of rust-belt states."

"We've got the base sewed up tight but we need to pull in those middle-of-the-road, undecided voters to push this thing over the top," added Hannah.

"If you can pull this off, you're going to drag a lot of down-ballot candidates along with you and the party will bow to your mandates."

Turner Graves grinned and nodded to a shapely blond and a dramatic redhead across the room, "Inspiration."

"We've been through this a hundred times, you old 'pro's' keep trying to screw with my head, when the message is in the magic I gin up with the audience. This is grand theater, an organic ritual that always enthralls the crowd, because it's a funhouse-mirror reflection of their glorified ignorance and bigotry. I give them permission to hate…and they love me for it."

Milly Clark walked up and handed him a tall glass of Kentucky's finest, "This is your audience but you should know that several friendly networks are broadcasting live across the country."

"I wish this was a debate instead of a rally, I'd kick his ass!" replied Mac, chugging the bourbon.

Wein laughed, "Just don't kick Jefferson Hick's ass after he introduces you. We want these folks to re-elect him!"

"I'll convince 'em he's just a regular old guy dedicated to God, guns, and apple pie, instead of a con artist and a sadistic pedophile."

"He's been approved by the committee," cautioned publicist Stone.

"Committee my ass, they're a bunch of arrogant fools and that guy's a piece of shit and you know it!" screamed the candidate. "Now get out of my face, I have to prepare for my performance."

Dowdy Milly Clark patted him on the shoulder and kissed his forehead, whispering, "We're almost done, Sweetheart. A flurry of virtuoso performances to close out the show to a standing ovation. You can do this."

A stage manager stuck his head in the door, "The band's about to finish up, the mayor will introduce the Congressman, who will speak for five minutes before welcoming you to the stage. Are you ready."

Murphy stood up, buttoned his suit jacket, and checked the mirror, "I think the question is whether they're ready for me?"

Packs of dignitaries milled about backstage and turned to applaud, shake his hand, and pat him on the back as the candidate marched along the hallway to the bottom of the ramp leading up to the stage at the end of the Charlotte Spectrum Center arena.

Jefferson Hicks, a tall slender charmer with pale skin, ruby lips, and jet-black hair, stood in a spotlight, trying to deliver his blather but every time he stopped to take a breath, chants of "Murphy! Murphy!" rolled over his speech. He smiled and waved, "Your candidate will be here in just a moment but I want to remind you that, to fulfill the promise of his movement, he needs his own candidates in Congress to turn his ideals into laws to protect our democracy. I hope I can count on your votes next Tuesday!"

The churning crowd roared.

"It's a great honor to introduce the spokesman for our righteous cause and the next President of these United States, Mac Murphy!"

Mac inhaled deeply and exhaled slowly, hesitating as he shifted into character before marching up the ramp, waving to ecstatic fans screaming adoration as they were crushed against a security fence ten or twelve feet from the edge of the stage by a surge of rowdy bodies. He walked over to shake with Hicks, raised their arms in a grasp of unity, then trotted to the far side of the stage into a shower of lacy lingerie.

Several dozen women were leaning over the barrier with their breasts exposed, reaching out to offer room keys or slips of paper with their phone numbers. He blew a kiss to them, then turned back to the podium and waited for the crowd to calm. The chants and the roiling movement slowly settled into a rumbling murmur.

He smiled and shouted. "Good Evening! And welcome to our future!"

Fervent cheers shook the massive structure with the force of a minor earthquake.

"I'm glad to see we're on the same page! This campaign's going to Washington, D.C. because you're going to show up at the polls and vote!"

"Murphy! Murphy!"

"I need to thank your representative, Jefferson Hicks, for his kind introduction. I'm told that I'm supposed to toss in a lick for him because he's one of 'our people' but I think I should ask the people who elected him in the first place, what do you think?"

Polite but muted cheers rippled through the crowd, overwhelmed by boo's and catcalls.

"You like him that much, huh? Well, let's at least give the man a round of applause for the good work he's already done."

Spotty clapping.

"You know, I've always thought that our system has got this election thing all backwards. We're supposed to pick the best of the worst from a bunch of shady fools who have no brains and are completely controlled by a clique of greedy tyrants. I think the "Founding Fathers" wanted local residents to nominate citizens from their own communities, folks who actually possess intelligence and qualifications to serve our people. After a couple of terms, they automatically retire and go back to being normal citizens again. Screw the political parties who keep the same lame candidates in office for decades, let the people decide!"

He could sense the reaction of the party elite in the wings, as the enthusiastic crowd responded. "With your help, we're going to win this election but that doesn't mean diddly-squat if you don't give me a Congress that's ready to rock from the first day of my term.

This country is facing the most dire challenges of our lifetime and we need to find common sense solutions to protect the very foundations of our democracy. Unfortunately, my opponent seems to think this is little league softball, where you can call 'time' whenever the other team's running up the score against you. He wants to postpone the election, until the Justice Department makes a thorough investigation into the self-inflicted violence that plagued the All People Matter rallies and the assassination of Tyrone Turner by a sad twisted psychopath. And that would leave powerless President Gonzalez in office way past his expiration date!"

The crowd erupted.

"We don't have time for that, it could take years to document what we already know. They did it to themselves, so the public would sympathize with their cause and make the executive council rich. We have the most powerful nation on the planet to run and the world isn't going to wait around for us to get our shit together!

Let the people decide whether they want a wimp in the White House or a leader who won't hesitate to spit in the eye of anyone who gets in our way or tries to alter the course to our destiny. I want our foes to cower and our friends to obey, simple as that. I don't think that's an unreasonable expectation, when we all know that the United States of America is the economic engine that produces more output than most other developed countries combined and there is no other military in the world that could stand for even a few days against our might.

This country needs a leader who's got the guts to tell the world that they can cooperate or they can suffer the consequences and there's only one guy in this race who can and will do that!"

"Murphy! Murphy!"

"You're God's chosen people and you have the power to change the course of history, to return us back to a time when our brothers and sisters, who gave their blood, sweat, and tears to build this country and defend our shores, were honored and respected. A time before our society was infected with swarthy immigrants swarming through our porous borders, before Congress created outrageous benefits for millions of vagrants too lazy to hold a job, or the liberal courts destroyed God's social equilibrium by granting 'equality' to groups who mock his sacred commandments through their beliefs and behaviors.

Our forefathers founded this great nation on the democratic concept of reaching consensus by granting one vote to every free man and we'll rebuild our laws and institutions to honor their vision. They never expected that every individual would be qualified for the responsibility of governing of this fledgling nation without regard to their background, heritage, or allegiances. We all know that you can't just let any fool march into the polling booth to cast their ballots without some way to verify that they actually have a clue about who they're voting for and what their candidate stands for! That's not democracy, that's communism!

That's political anarchy which guarantees that we'll continue to elect these pre-packaged, incompetent marionettes, who vote as they're instructed by the real powers behind our fraudulent government. You have the power to end this circus and restore order to the madness. You have the power to evict the traitors and criminals and replace them with true patriots, who will pass laws to protect your rights first, last, and always!

I need your votes and your spouse's vote, and your mom's and your dad's, brother, sister, kids, aunts, uncles, best friends, worst enemies…drag them all to the polls! I need every vote we can muster! Are you with me?"

"Murphy! Murphy!"

The crowd heaved forward, squashing the people hanging over the chain-link barriers, which toppled over and a stampede trampled the fallen in a rush for the stage. A posse of Secret Service agents stormed out of the shadows to surround the candidate and lead him down the ramp and out of danger.

The live broadcast captured a tsunami of enthusiastic supporters attempting to scale the stage in pursuit of their hero but the campaign's private security forces waded into the fracas swinging batons and tossing bloodied bodies back into the melee on the floor of the arena.

The stage lights dimmed and blazing spots followed members of The Kentucky HiJinx band, who opened the show, scampering onto the risers at the back of the stage to crank up a rousing country rendition of 'Happy days are here again…', an ironic soundtrack for the raucous brawl swirling through the darkness.

Four agents maneuvered Murphy down the ramp, through a tangle of party officials to snag a wake of staff and inner circle supporters trailing along a fluorescent hallway to a waiting armored Suburban.

The candidate screamed, "What the fuck are you doing? I was just getting them cranked up!"

There was no acknowledgement from his security team, who ignored his protests until he was sealed inside the vehicle. They permitted Hannah, Wein, Stone, Doc Billings, and Milly Clark to join him before the motorcade roared through the tunnel and out into the night, heading for the airport.

"Why'd you let them ruin the show?" yelled Murphy. "The next five minutes would have sealed the deal!"

Milly handed him a mug of bourbon, "Because it was getting dangerous and the campaign needs you alive."

Billings offered a paper cup full of pills but Murphy brushed them away. "If you want me to put this election away, let me do my thing. The voters don't want some sissy-ass imposter being dragged away every time the crowd gets rowdy. They want to see this fearless character we've created stand up to the threat of danger, like the generals of old! They want their fictional hero to act like a hero and I can't do that with these mugs jumping in way before they're needed!"

Hannah looked him straight in the eye, "I've been with you since long before this carnival got launched and we both know that you can't impersonate a stoic Tyrone Turner standing up to an airplane streaking straight for him. That is not your character and your audience doesn't expect that from you. We're almost at the end of this roller coaster, stay in character, do your bit, and we'll win this thing."

Murphy grimaced, his hands curled into tight fists in frustration, a massive amphetamine rush tensed every muscle in his flabby old body. He was cocked and ready to spring at the slightest provocation, until Milly Clark patted his knee, "You can do this, I know you can."

~

Sissy's leather heels clacked on the oak flooring in the vestibule, as she walked up to the two agents standing outside the door of the study and curtsied, "May I see my father?"

The taller man leaned over, "I'm sure he'd make time for someone as cute as you."

"Can I knock?"

"Go ahead, there's no one with him at the moment," said the other guard.

The little blond sprite marched up to the heavy door and knocked three times. After a moment, her father's voice bellowed, "Come in."

"Do I have to make an appointment to see you?"

Stanton rose and walked around the carved mahogany desk to hug her, "I've been so absorbed in this campaign that I've neglected the people who make it worth the effort. How are you?"

"I'm fine but your guardians keep following us over to Nellis' farm, when we go to feed the animals and clean out the stalls. They finally quit asking questions, then I told them I was trying to earn extra money because you donated my allowance to your campaign."

"You didn't?"

"I did," giggled his daughter.

"How's that going? Taking care of the animals, I mean."

"You can tell they miss Nellis, especially Gracie. She lies in the driveway, gazing down the lane, waiting for him to come back. It's so sad."

"I've been looking into the 'Alien Relocation Command' and they're basically a secret army being run from inside the government by people who have no authority to run anything." Spratlin leaned against the desk, "I'm sorry, honey. I'm frustrated because I'm running for the highest office in the land and there's nothing I can do to protect hundreds or thousands of people who have disappeared over the past few weeks, including Katherine and Nellis, and many of the people associated with the All People Matter movement."

He reached to wipe a tear from her cheek, "I don't know how or when Nellis and Katherine will be back but a little bird told me that they're safe for the moment."

Sissy grinned, "I already knew."

"How'd...?"

"Brad told me they got away and that he's got a bunch of friends trying to find out where all the prisoners are being held, so they can try to get them back."

"He's kept me abreast of his investigation and his guys are mostly retired military intelligence officers."

"Intelligence officers?"

"The people who run the spies and tap into the secret communications of our adversaries...our enemies. They know how to find out classified...secret things."

The lithe girl stared at the floor, "Sammy told me that he used to get crazy, like he couldn't figure out whether he was in the war or he was here, and he told her that he did some bad things."

Stanton hugged her, "Sometimes, like in wars, people do terrible things to each other and lots of people die...but those who survive carry those nightmare memories around for the rest of their lives, even if they didn't cause it. Your brother didn't know how to deal with his pain and confusion, until you and the rest of the kids inspired him to talk to some professional therapists, who have been through similar experiences. He takes special medicines that let him focus on the good part of life. Does that make any sense?"

"Yeah, I didn't understand when he used to get weird and angry but I'm glad he's back to being part of the family again. I like it when we all look after each other."

"Me too."

"What's happening with the election?"

"Well, I'm going to be gone, giving speeches in towns from coast to coast until a final rally in Detroit next Monday night, because all the citizens across the country are going to the polls next Tuesday. I'll fly home, so we can all watch the returns together."

"Do you think you're going to win?"

"Honestly, no…no, I don't. In spite of all the protests going on around the country, a sizable portion of the population is too afraid to stand up to demand a real fairly-elected government. They want someone who will protect them from the chaos and violence that fills the headlines every day."

"I don't think Mr. Murphy could protect anyone from anything. He's too old and too fat."

"Well, you do have a point," laughed Stanton. "I'll tell you what I really think. I think that I'm going to work as hard as I can, every minute, until the voting begins, to convince the people of our nation that they hold the power to take back our democracy, to restore common sense and common decency in government, and reclaim a confidence that we can all share in the future. That's what we need and that's what I believe in."

"If they're smart, they'll vote for you," said Sissy, with a hug.

Chapter Three
Election Day

Mindy Hoffman led thirteen of her friends and neighbors, minus Bob Gorman who was laid up in the hospital with pneumonia, through a crowd of shivering reporters and news crews, stranded in a minor blizzard until they would be invited inside for the voting and the official announcement a few minutes past midnight. The only eligible voters in the tiny town of Dixville Notch, New Hampshire, stamped their feet and brushed the snow off their coats, as they marched up the steps into the grand ballroom in The Balsams Hotel on beautiful Lake Gloriette nestled in the White Mountains.

Bobby Thompson, mayor of neighboring Colebrook, wearing a red, white, and blue bow tie beneath a distinguished smile, greeted them at the entry to the infamous Ballot Room, where the first votes in the country had been cast in every national election since 1960. He hugged Mindy, and shook hands with each eager voter. "I see that Warren and Fred, our selectmen are here, as well as Sally, our town clerk, and Chief Shannon and Betty Barnes are qualified as supervisors. So, I think we have all the officials we need to start this historic election."

The voters applauded and filed into the wood paneled room, where a simple wooden box sat on a long table draped with the original flag of the Continental Congress, bearing thirteen red and white stripes with a circle of thirteen stars on a blue field. Our contemporary flag was draped from a tall brass pole on the left and the New Hampshire flag on the right. Black and white framed photographs of famous people and every group who had voted in presidential elections over decades covered the walls. Seven white vertical boards were lined up along each side as temporary voting booths, connected by a narrow shelf for marking the ballots.

Thompson glanced at the clock, "We've a few minutes yet, before we begin, and I'm sure that after all these years you're familiar with the rules regarding your vote. So, I'll ask you to sign in, collect your ballot, and keep your choice secret until all the votes are counted. I know

I've said this before but I believe that this might be the most historic election any of us have ever participated in and your votes might well offer a clue to the nation about the outcome and the future of the country."

Barry Hinkle laughed, as he signed the form on the table, "If memory serves, we've been right more often than not."

"The nation awaits your decision, I would hope that you cast it wisely," said the mayor, holding up his hand as he watched the second hand on the old clock tick down to midnight. The chime sounded with a regal gong, "You may begin."

Reporters and film crews crowded, respectfully, in the doorway to record the momentary celebrities stepping into the temporary booths to cast their votes, then returning the folded ballots to the slot in the top of the fine birch box with a small plaque that read, 'The Town of Dixville', beneath the city crest.

When the last voter dropped her paper into the chest, Mayor Thompson said, "If all the eligible voters have finished, I hereby declare these polls closed."

He inserted a key into the brass lock on the ballot box, retrieved the contents, and handed them to Sally Yoder, the town clerk. "If you would be kind enough to report the tally?"

A barrage of flashes fired in rapid succession, as she sat down at the table to scan each new page and tabulate the results. "In the local elections, all of our current office holders have retained their positions. In the State results, Governor Pete Morrison and Lieutenant Governor Bruce Banner have been re-elected and Robert Mayweather has been elected as our Representative to the House. In the presidential race – Republican Mac Murphy has six votes and Democrat Stanton Spratlin has seven.

Cameras turned to correspondents from all the major news networks, to report the first results to the world, while their producers ushered the voters through the small crowd for an interview. Pamela Paulsen, of International News, smiled at Mindy Hoffman, "Tell us, what's your reaction to casting the first votes in the nation?"

"It's always exciting," replied the housewife, "but humbling. I think we all take this very seriously, because we know that our decisions might affect how the voting goes across the country. We hope that every voter will take the time to understand the issues before they cast their ballots."

"Any chance you'd reveal your choice for president?"

"I think the Founding Fathers had it right, when they prescribed 'secret' ballots. So, I think I'd like to keep that to myself, until a winner is declared."

Paulsen turned to the camera with a confident smile, "There you have it, ladies and gentlemen. The first votes have been cast and, in about twenty hours, the final polls will close. If these results are any indication, this should be a very close contest. I'm Pamela Paulson in Dixville Notch, New Hampshire, for International News."

Stanton Spratlin settled back in his plush leather seat on the Boeing 737, nicknamed 'The Spratlin Satellite', that had transported the campaign staff and members of the press to nineteen cities in the past seven days. He opened the previous morning's Detroit Free Press, ignoring the political headlines, turning directly to the comic strips. Donny Seamans, his press secretary, sat down on the opposite side of the aisle, "I can give you more accurate numbers than you're going to find in yesterday's news."

The candidate grinned and shifted the page to display the cartoons, "I've seen all the numbers, I just want to make sure that the real world of kids and everyday problems is still out there. I feel like I've been charging around the country in a political bubble since the convention and I can't wait to be at home with all the kids."

"You gave a great speech tonight, Ford Field was jam-packed and the crowd was enthusiastic. With all the local coverage, I think we might just take Michigan. Great way to finish up."

Spratlin shook his head slowly, "I was overwhelmed by their energy but we both know that, no matter how we juggle the numbers, it's going to take a miracle to turn the tide."

"It's been a long haul and I know you're exhausted, but don't give up yet. We've got several hours before the polls open on the east coast and rumor has it that our supporters are going to be out en-masse in every city in the country."

"Good, we might lose but at least their voice, their desperate plea has been heard."

Captain Martin's voice interrupted, "Our congratulations to Representative Spratlin for his strong dignified campaign. We're proud to have had the opportunity to transport you from place to place and hope that our next trip will be to your inauguration!"

The staff and press clapped and cheered.

The pilot continued, "Please take your seats and buckle up, we've been cleared to taxi out to the runway for takeoff. Travel time to Cameron will be approximately two hours and forty minutes. Settle back and enjoy the flight."

The engines whined as the plane rolled out onto the tarmac and Seamans leaned across the aisle, "I know you've been worried about Katherine and the rest of the people who are missing. Have you learned anything new?"

"The minority on the Intelligence Committee have subpoenaed the documentation of the creation and funding of the Alien Relocation Command and we've requested testimony concerning their ongoing operations from Director Jonathon Hughes but the Republicans are claiming that it's a black anti-terrorism operation and they're refusing cooperation."

"Any idea of where they're taking these people and how they're getting them there?"

"Actually, my son Brad, the former commando, informed me that they have processing centers in strategic locations that are accessible to what seems to be a clandestine railroad that's ferrying the prisoners from point to point but we don't have any details yet."

Donny nodded, "That's totally astonishing. The U.S. government has its own Gestapo rounding up 'enemies of the state' and rolling them around the country in cattle cars! Congress doesn't have any right to know what's going on?"

"The Republicans are doing their best to stymie the Democrats' best efforts but none of this could have been instituted without senior members of the Republican caucus writing it into a budget that nobody got to read before it was put up for a vote. I think I heard that it was fourteen-thousand pages and the details of the Alien Relocation Command are buried in a secret appendix someplace out of sight."

"Maybe being president would give you more sway."

"I doubt it, I've talked with Phillipe about this and his Secretary of Homeland Security claims his staff can find no record of it. But I'll guarantee you that win, lose, or draw, I'll pursue this until I find the answer and a way to bring our people home."

"I'm right there with you."

~

Mac Murphy stumbled down the ramp to a waiting limousine, steadied by a tall curvy platinum blond on his right and a striking brunette with ruby red lips and dark dangerous eyes that flashed as she leaned close to casually fondle his erection and whisper, "I can't wait to be the first to play with the next President of the United States while he's still a virgin."

He squeezed her soft rump, "I might be looking for a first lady, if you're not busy?"

She licked his ear, "I could make time, if you need me."

"Honey, I need you now," moaned the candidate, as they loaded him into the broad backseat and cuddled close.

Doc Billings held up a paper cup and a tumbler of bourbon, "Time for your vitamins."

Murphy sneered, "I've done everything everyone's asked me to do, so, if those aren't more of whatever you gave me before the gig, I don't want to come down. Keep me going, Doc, these ladies are counting on you."

Billings handed him the bourbon and opened his black bag to dump the cup and refill it with Mac's favorite combination of stimulants. He handed the cup to his patient and the blond leaned to look inside. "Oh, I hope you've put enough in there to make sure he's fit to service both of us."

"I can promise he'll be randy for hours," smiled the physician.

Wein started laughing, as he ruffled through a sheaf of papers, "I'll be damned."

Milly Clark turned from watching Murphy paw the prostitutes, "What are you laughing about?"

"The latest polls have us down by three points nationally but when the states are broken down by votes in the Electoral College, we're up by nine."

Murphy met Milly's gaze, as she turned back to him with an astonished grin. He released the women and leaned forward, scanning the faces of his gang of mavericks, "While I was out there hawking the baloney, all of you were doing the real work of transforming this preposterous prank into a winning campaign. I have each and every one of you to thank for making this happen and I hope that at least one of you has some clue about how to organize whatever comes next."

Shepherd Stone replied, "Don't worry about it, the wheels are turning and we'll have all the help we need."

"We already have a fairly expansive list of qualified candidates to fill the roster and we'll transform your campaign promises into a coordinated agenda of legislative proposals in a few days," added Casper Wein. "The national committee is already laying the groundwork."

"I hope those assholes have their resumes up to date, because most of 'em are going to be looking for new employment opportunities as soon as I sit down in the Oval Office and take control of the Party. We're going to clean house!" yelled Murphy. "I promised our supporters we'd get rid of the privileged bastards who made this mess and that's exactly what I intend to do."

Jack Hannah said, "You don't need to sell us, we're on your side."

He settled back between his escorts, "Good, because we're about the change to world!"

Stone leaned over to Wein, "He might actually believe his own bullshit."

"Don't worry, I'm sure we have the situation well in hand," replied the campaign manager, glancing at Dr. Billings. "Once the initial rush of victory wears off, he'll be more manageable."

"After the pace he's kept during the campaign, I can guarantee that the exhaustion will catch up with him and the recovery could drag on for a while."

"Creighton Steil will be in town for the celebration and I've scheduled a strategy meeting before their appearance at the Energy Center tomorrow night to smooth the transition. By the time Murphy's finished his acceptance speech, Steil will be in charge."

Bruce Spratlin bounded down the stairs from his painting studio above the garage with his hands clamped over his ears to dampen the thunder of Brad's Harley-Davisson. His hulking brother pulled him close and leaned to whisper in his ear, "We have to assume everything is bugged and I need to get a message to Nellis."

"I can do that."

"You have to make sure you don't use any of our phones or make the call when any of the Feds are hanging around."

"I know just the place."

"If you're wrong, you'll expose more of our people."

"I know how to do this."

"Okay."

An hour later, Bruce's baby-blue VW Beetle pulled out of the garage and putted out through the portico, down the meandering drive beneath barren sycamores, oaks, and maples - skeletons standing tall against a dull gray sky, to exit under the arch with the stately 'S' embossed on a burgundy crest suspended between regal golden lions to the security gate on Maple Ridge Boulevard. The fat county cop lifted the gate and walked over to the car, "Where you think you're headed without an escort?"

Spratlin slipped into his rich-bitch gay persona, "They just don't seem to have any respect for patrons who value erotic art and, as you already know, I can't deliver pornographic images to horny clients if I have a Secret Service entourage following me around. That would be scandalous!"

The cop ducked his head to catch a glimpse of the muscular nude male with an enormous erection on the canvas, "I don't know, my boss was pissed the last time you took off."

"You should get down on your knees and kiss his ass more often but he'll still treat you like the dirty slut you are. In the meantime, my old man might be rich and famous but this is how I earn my keep, so get the fuck out of my way!" Without waiting for a response, he gunned the engine and wheeled the little car through a gauntlet of official vehicles lining both sides of the narrow road.

The blue bug whipped down the winding lane to spit out on Fourth Street and circled one block after the next until he was sure no one was following. Finally, he parked in the alley behind the Quiky-Mart and marched into a residential neighborhood to make sure. After several blocks, where he found dogs barking and children playing kickball in the empty streets, he walked up to the playground gate behind Saint Francis Orphanage, where Sister Gwen waited with a warm smile in the midmorning chill. "Did your passengers arrive at their destination safely?"

"Yes, word has it that they're safe and working on the movement. Which is why I'm here. Could I use your phone to pass a message to Nellis?" She took his arm and guided him, through wafting whiffs of frying chicken, to the kitchen door.

"I take it security is of primary importance?"

"Yes, extremely."

"Fine, if you'll tell me where the destination is, I can have our private service make your call connect through a church or monastery nearby, so the final leg will show up as a local call."

"The Church has its own private communication system? That's incredible."

Her gentle smile felt like the blessing of angels, "Let's call it separation of church and state."

Bruce followed her into an expansive kitchen, where three nuns were preparing the dinner meal, and through a hallway to a narrow staircase. "How many kids do you have living here?"

"It varies as children arrive and then move on but, at the moment, we have a little over three-dozen. If you'll follow me to my office, I'll set up your call."

Her robes barely fluttered as she climbed the stairs silently. Bruce shook his head, "I'll bet the kids call you a ghost because you move so quietly."

On the second landing she looked back at him, "I'd rather they be surprised, given the choice."

"If they're anything like my sisters, I'll bet they're a handful."

"The cure for their misery is the same for each, finding someone to love them unconditionally. God will connect a few of them with the right people but, certainly, not enough."

She unlocked a slender door at the top of the steps, which opened into a small cramped office with a large desk piled with paperwork between two dormer windows looking over the rooftops to the steeple of the abandoned Praise the Lord Temple sprouting high above every other building in the town square.

Bruce stood awkwardly, as she picked up the receiver of a very old black rotary telephone and asked, "Where would you like this call to go?"

"I'll be calling a number on Lake Travis, outside of Austin, Texas." He handed her a small slip of paper.

The nun dialed several numbers, "Hello, Sister Margaret, this is Sister Gwen in Cameron, Oklahoma, and I was wondering whether you would be kind enough to route a call through Saint Mary's in Austin?"

"Oh, bless you, I do so appreciate it. Here's the number…512-555-0555."

The nun looked up, handed him the receiver, and left the room.

He sat down hesitantly in Sister Gwen's chair, as the ancient black phone clicked and buzzed. The desk was covered with tall neat piles of folders, bills, and unsorted mail stacked around a black and white framed portrait of a young soldier in front of palm trees, his handsome face crinkled into a genuine smile. File cabinets lined one wall with an overflowing bookcase from floor to ceiling opposite and a small sleeping nook tucked under the eve at the back of the room. Other than a small television wedged into a shelf and a crucifix on the wall next to the door, there were no hints about the character or nature of the woman inside the habit.

He was startled when a man answered the call, "Simonson residence."

"Hi, I was wondering whether I might speak with Mavis Sloan?"

"Who, may I say, is calling?"

"I'm sorry, I'm Bruce Spratlin, Stanton Spratlin's son."

"If you'll hold for a moment, I'll try to track her down."

"Thank you."

The line went dead for several minutes before Mavis's sensuous voice said, "Bruce Spratlin, Mavis Sloan. How's your old man holding up?"

"His team is watching the projected returns but he's been hanging out in the kitchen with all the kids since lunch."

"I know exactly how he feels, I'm just in from riding my horse, just to burn off some steam and I'm heading down to watch the returns with Tabitha in a little while."

"My brother, Brad, was wondering whether you could get a message to Nellis?"

"That's possible, what's up?"

"Well…he and his marine buddies think they've figured out how the Alien Relocation Command is stashing their captives and then moving them around the country," said Bruce.

"Why don't we stop fooling ourselves and just call those bastards The Gestapo?"

"I'll agree with that, it seemed like their black SUV's were all over the city when I snuck Nellis and Katherine to a safe sanctuary, where they could hide out until someone you know pretty well swooped through town and made them disappear."

"I hear they're safe and sound…and busy," said the Texan beauty.

"That's good. Nellis strikes me as the kind of guy who can't sit still for more than a couple of minutes at a time."

"I don't think anyone will argue with that assessment," laughed Mavis. "So, what do you want me to pass along?"

"Brad says they've got centralized processing centers in key spots around the country and they're moving the prisoners on secret trains at night. His guys still haven't figured out the final destination where they're being delivered."

"Is there more?"

"They think the system was designed to move illegal immigrants across the southern border but it got more complicated when they started picking up American citizens who have to be processed somehow. So, there's a bottleneck someplace and maybe some of those people could be liberated by guys who know how to do those sorts of things."

"I'll pass that along but they're going to want to know if and when anything is going to happen."

"That's all I've got at the moment but I'll call you back when I know more."

"I trust that you're using a secure line?"

Bruce grinned, "I think it's actually the safest means of communication in the country."

"Okay, give my sincerest best wishes to your father." She paused, "If you're sure about your security, I'll give you a number and you can tell him yourself."

"Can do, and thank you."

"Hey, we're all in this together, just make sure you're safe."

Nellis found an old Martin guitar in a dressing room, during a pensive wander through the bowels of the old theater, and stood on the stage, strumming chords and humming a tune that had been rattling around in his head for weeks. His eyes scanned hundreds of red velvet seats perfectly aligned in curved rows climbing the incline into darkness beneath baroque balconies, until a blazing blue spot skittered across the curtains, a radiant wraith racing to envelope him, followed by a youngster's giggly voice erupting from the speakers, "Grampa says there's a phone call for you."

"I thank you for taking the time to track me down but who am I speaking to?"

The blue spot withered and, after a few moments, the gawky young boy with tousled blond hair and a goofy smile strode down the aisle, "I'm Rusty."

"Oh, I'm afraid I'm still trying to get everyone's name straight, there are quite of few of you youngsters running around here. You're Sybil's son, right?"

"Yeah."

"I've only had a chance to talk with her for a few minutes but she sure seems like a very smart lady."

"She runs the theater, books the acts, does all the advertising, and takes care of the money."

"Everyone in this family seems to have some special talent, you included. Your grandfather seemed mighty proud of your abilities with computers. He said that you have a model train set up someplace in the building?"

"Yeah, it's down in the basement."

"Well, I'd love to see it but how about I find a phone to answer the call and then you can show me your operation?"

"Only if you finish playing that song."

"Deal. Now, where's the phone?" He set the guitar on the edge of the stage and hopped down to follow Rusty up the aisle, out through the small ornate lobby, and into the business office behind the ticket window. The boy picked up a phone on a desk and dialed. After a pause, he handed the phone to Nellis and disappeared through another door.

"Hello."

"Nellis, this is Bruce."

"Lordy, it's nice to hear your voice but I sure hope you covered your tracks, if you know what I mean."

"Sister Gwen says this call is sanctioned by the highest authority, higher than the president."

"I'll take your word for it and give her our thanks. How're my critters?"

"The girls are spoiling them. Sissy said they took the horses for a run yesterday and most of the dogs tagged along."

"Good, keeps 'em all too tuckered out to cause any trouble. Hope you'll pass along my appreciation and a big hug for each of them."

"Can do. Listen, Brad wanted me to tell you that his guys have identified several processing centers in different parts of the country and they think the prisoners are being moved around on special trains."

"Yeah, I've heard rumors up here about white trains with no windows that only move at night."

"They're trying to figure out the destinations but they haven't got that yet."

"There's no way of knowing but I'd sure be interested to know how fast folks move along that system. We've got a lot of friends who are probably staggering through different phases of the process."

"I'll call you back as soon as we know more. How are you and Katherine holding up?"

"Actually, even though we've just got here, we're finding ways to be actively involved from behind the scenes, so, considering the alternatives, we won't complain…for the moment."

"Gotcha'!"

"We've been watching the news about the election but nobody seems ready to even hint at a winner, the exit polls are too close. How's your old man doing?"

"He's exhausted from spending the last couple of weeks on the road, doing multiple appearances every day, but I think he's resigned to wait it out. He was hanging with all the kids in the kitchen when I left the house."

"I don't blame him, I can smell Mama Louise's fried chicken from here and those kids are way more fun than campaign managers and pollsters!"

Bruce was quiet for a moment, staring around the cramped but sparse office, "He's come a long way since this whole thing started."

"Be proud of your old man, he's one of the good guys. Call me when you know more."

"Thanks, be safe."

The line went dead and Nellis stared at the receiver, wondering how those electronic signals, blessed by the Lord himself, could skirt the electronic surveillance that monitored every call or communication everywhere. He could only have faith that young Spratlin and his beloved nun knew what they were doing.

Rusty opened the door to the inner office, releasing the chatter of a television reporter's voice, "We've never seen anything like this. The crowds flooding through Time's Square are bigger and rowdier than anything we've experienced before and it's happening all across the country. One thing we can say for sure, these people are riled up and I've been told that they won't stop these protests, no matter who wins the election."

Sybil appeared in the doorway, a tall radiant brunette with big almond eyes, past her prime but stunningly beautiful, "It looks like your organization is still effective in turning out the true believers, in spite of the Alien Relocation Command."

"Win, lose, or draw, this won't be over until everyone involved in the conspiracy to destroy this country has been brought to justice."

"I wish we could put you on stage to tell the folks what's really happening," said Rusty.

Nellis blushed, "I've been banned from speaking publicly, since I got a little bit carried away after the massacre at the rally in Denver."

"Considering what they did, I thought your reaction was honest and genuine. You said what everyone was feeling," added Sybil. "I'm glad we can help."

"We appreciate your hospitality."

Rusty grinned, "C'mon, I want to show you the railroad."

"I'm with you," replied Nellis, following him down two flights of stairs and along a darkened hallway to a white steel door.

The boy pulled a key from his pocket, toggled the lock, and flipped a switch to turn on spotlights, scattered across the ceiling. Pools of amber illuminated twelve separate tracks roaming through a landscaped countryside with bridges over flowing rivers and tunnels feeding into a rail yard with a turntable at the terminal in the center of a small city. Animals grazed around barns and farmhouses with tree-lined fields full of crops on the outskirts of a thriving metropolis with large buildings, cars and pedestrians traveling on paved streets with sidewalks and streetlights. Each scene was complete in exquisite detail.

Rusty walked into an alcove in the panorama to ignite the blue glow of a computer monitor and pecked at several keys before train whistles sounded and tiny engines pulling cars filled with cattle and piled with goods rolled down the tracks heading in and out of the town.

Nellis marveled, "This is incredible. Did you and your granddad build all of this?"

"I guess parts of it have always been here, we just enlarged it and computerized it."

"I noticed you were directing traffic from your station, how's that work?"

"Actually, it's the same software that real railroads use to keep track of the trains, change signals and switching stations, and stuff."

"How'd you get your hands on that and how do you know how to use it?"

Rusty looked up with a sly grin, "There's nothing complicated about the code, I figured that out in nothing flat."

"So, how'd you get a copy of their software?"

"Well, I kind of borrowed it, to figure out how it worked…and then I rewrote most of it to work better." He paused and looked down at his shoes, "They don't know it yet."

"You mean, you're hooked into the real system?"

"Sure…"

Nellis stared at the boy, "Can you tell which trains are going where?"

"Yeah, they're all identified with badges of their routes and destinations."

"Could you…make them go where you want them to go?"

"I just watch them coming and going, so I've never tried, but…sure, it's possible."

~

Mavis settled back into the sofa, surrounded by a testament to the luxury and style of a previous century where crystal chandeliers glinted above black and white tiled floors, Persian carpets, and priceless antique furnishings. Most of Tabitha's artwork and sculptures were period pieces by ancient masters, with the exception of two of Jessie Cotton's large canvases in the drawing room. Over the fireplace, a brilliant sunset peeked beneath a violent storm charging the beach with towering surf and howling winds assaulting battered palm trees. On the opposite wall, low lazy light filtered through a jungle to reveal a roost of coastal birds in vibrant plumage.

She was elated by the massive marches in every city in the country, organized by the sheer will of her aging hostess and the coordination of the movement by secretary Bobby Warmington, but anxious for the muted talking heads to release the first returns from the Midwest. Spratlin held his own in the northeast but Murphy swept the South. She sipped her Chardonnet, "I think Ohio, Michigan, Illinois, and Wisconsin will determine the winner."

The old publisher smiled, "You might as well throw in Indiana, while you're at it, but I think you are correct, M'dear. The Republicans own most of the west, except Colorado and maybe Arizona, but the liberals will carry the West Coast. From our polling, I'll bet it comes down to the very last vote."

"Actually, it will come down to who has the votes to win the Electoral College, not who gets the most popular votes," replied Mavis. "Assuming the polls are right and the rest of the country balances out, two or maybe three of those could decide it."

Tabitha sipped, "I do miss talking with Katherine and Kate, they'd be proud of the incredible turnout across the country because of the All People Matter movement."

"Me too. I keep wondering whether they're safe and where they are…and how we're going to free them," said Mavis. "Oh, I forgot to tell you, I transferred a call from Bruce Spratlin to Nellis this morning. Brad thinks he's figured out how the Gestapo is moving prisoners around the country."

"How?"

"By a twenty-first century version of the cattle car."

"Haven't we seen this nightmare before? I talked with Stanton several days ago, while he was being whisked from one city to the next, and he has had no satisfaction in his inquiries into how this operation is being run from Homeland Security."

Mavis sat up, "The only way anyone's going to break through that bureaucracy is when we take back the Congress and I don't see that happening with this election."

"The local balloting for governors and the state houses is going to elect more liberals and women than ever before, perhaps enough in some places to tip the balance from red to purple, which would give more of our people a voice in local issues."

"But that's not going to slow down the deconstruction of our democracy, unless something totally dramatic happens."

The elderly woman smiled, "Like what?"

"Oh, a revolution would be a good start!"

"This from the woman who built the most exclusive condominium project on the west coast of Florida, catering to a well-heeled clientele!" scoffed Tabitha, before her eyes softened and her matronly voice whispered, "Tell me, you've been avoiding the subject of the resurrection of your dead husband, how do you feel about that?"

Mavis stared at the golden liquor inside her crystal goblet, "We've talked on the phone and I'm so very relieved that he's alive but…"

"But you want to throttle him for deserting you and putting you through all this pain?"

"Something like that. Someday soon, we'll sit down and talk this through, after I punch him right in the mouth." She looked down at her drink, "I don't see us getting back together. But…I don't know, I'm so confused by everything…Tyrone getting killed, our friends disappearing down a bureaucratic dark hole, the success of the movement in rallying the people who need the most help to fight back, but we both know that we're probably going to lose this election and I can't imagine how bad things might get with Murphy in the White House and the oligarchs calling the shots."

"That's a fairly dark perspective but one that I will probably site in my editorial in tomorrow's Dolphin Times. Do you think another glass of wine would buoy your spirits or drag you into complete depression?"

Mavis smiled her magazine cover smile, "You are insufferable, you know that."

"Of course, dear, how do you think a cub reporter managed to take over a publishing empire?"

Chapter Four

Ultraconservative Public Relations consultant, Ethan Tomlinson, stood on a small stage in an opulent lounge behind the banquet hall and lifted a glass of rare Krug Champagne to toast members of The Forge, as they called themselves, "The imminent election of Mac Murphy proves that the secret, to galvanizing the ignorant and enraged core of the population into a dominant majority, is to give them something to hate together, some group to blame for everything that's been denied from their naïve expectations. Hitler and Goebbels' second commandment was to craft the big lie that denigrates your enemy's integrity and repeat it often enough that it becomes truth!"

The crowd cheered, exchanging congratulations all around.

"And we succeeded!" He raised his glass again, "I think it only appropriate to salute our host for this marvelous event, Harvey Summers!"

Summers, an international real estate developer, founded The Golden Key Golf Resort and constructed the hotel, a challenging course, and ninety-six palatial homes nestled onto a very private spit of sand in Biscayne Bay. In early November, warmth and sunshine made it the ideal site for a fiftieth anniversary reunion of several dozen like-minded patriots, who also happened to be moguls within their own international empires and charter contributors to the campaign to deconstruct representative government, dismantle socialist welfare, eliminate federal regulations that restrained their industries and restricted their profits, and shut down the IRS.

The guest list included an inner circle of media and political consultants, who transformed the national dialogue into a barrage of blatantly false charges and dumbfounded denials that dominated the headlines, created a ratings bonanza for the news networks, and dispensed with any discussion of issues of consequence.

More than five decades ago, these old guard conservative tycoons became incensed with the impending election of a liberal Democrat to the nation's highest office with modest majorities in both

Houses of Congress. They formed The Forge Foundation to reconfigure the boundaries of every Congressional district in the nation, while they developed and supported carefully vetted candidates to wreak havoc on the democratic process and repulse any effort at compromise by the opposition.

Conrad Blaho, COO of multinational Lebanon Steel, and Stanley French, CEO of Dynamic Devices, the single largest contractor for advanced weapons systems in the country, hired Tomlinson, Will Terry, and their cronies to create and execute a well-financed nationalistic action plan to retake the government and reshape the allegiances of a vast and invisible populace hiding in plain sight.

The dirt-farmers were being forced off their land by club member Augie Phillips' gigantic corporate farms that drove the price of land up and the price for grain down, through high-tech mechanization, scientific research, and employing seasonal armies of illegal aliens to plant and harvest tender crops.

Unemployed rustbelt workers followed generations of their forefathers into the factories only to be left destitute in decaying cities fouled by industrial pollution, devastating poverty, and senseless carnage. All the result of several members of this group and their international conglomerates deciding that manufacture and assembly was cheaper and more profitable in Shanghai than Youngstown.

Similar stories defined the slow tragic stagnation of the Appalachian coal country that threatened to starve and eradicate a unique culture, with roots stretching back to a forced relocation of the most incorrigible prisoners, delivered from England on wooden slave ships before the revolution. Inexpensive natural gas made coal too dirty, dangerous, and costly to compete. They trotted Murphy out to pledge the return of 'clean' coal jobs to rile up desperate voters but everyone except the miners accepted the death of the industry as inevitable.

The list of the slighted was virtually endless but, as Tomlinson pointed out, "If you add the evangelical fanatics and the fringe groups of the radical-right, the common denominator is hate and resentment of just about anyone who is not an ignorant white Christian bigot."

The men in this room precipitated and profited from the expanding epidemic of poverty and unemployment, which was devastating the middle-class and provided motivation to keep the herd angry and desperate enough to vote for their loutish puppets who actually believed their own rubbish.

Hand the candidates a flag, selected passages from a well-worn Bible, and a script that pounded on primal patriotic themes of gun rights, abortion as murder, threats to 'religious freedom', liberal support of gays and blacks and immigrants, international corporations shipping middle-class jobs overseas, government overreach, and a rigged economy that left this massive block of uninformed and uneducated citizens behind. Blinded by hopes and dreams, overwhelmed by a churning media, and battered by an endless barrage of rumors and half-truths, ardent supporters failed to grasp their role in the clandestine quest for dictatorial power and absolute economic control.

Tomlinson and his associates crafted an exquisitely brutal campaign that stoked those subliminal embers into a wildfire that scorched the political map and rendered the voices of political dissent mute.

"As we discussed in our executive session earlier, we expect to add another dozen seats to our majority in the House and perhaps another pair of seats in the Senate. We'll add another conservative justice to the Supreme Court in January and, in spite of having Gonzalez in office, the program to dismantle inconvenient Federal regulations is moving along much more rapidly than we anticipated."

"Why is that?" asked Casey Buck, owner of the largest private oil company in the world.

Ethan smiled, "The opposition has absolutely no chance of success in delaying or denying a flurry of coordinated efforts in every agency in the Federal government, because we own the votes and the courts."

Laughter and whistles.

"The Democrats will protest but after tonight, they can't do anything but whine!" laughed Sam Snider, who owned ritzy resorts and luxury cruise ships.

Harvey Summers raised a hand for quiet, "We'll be moving on to cocktails with our guests, then a sumptuous dinner and entertainment in the banquet hall. I would request that you save a little room and just a smidgeon of sobriety for a glass of rare Moyet Cognac in the library, when the celebrations wind down. We still have much to discuss and a full day of golf tomorrow."

"The compensation for our efforts and investments begins in the morning!" shouted Jack Simpson – national and international heavy construction.

~

Two muscular Secret Service agents coaxed a stumbling Murphy through the back door, down the long narrow hallway to the WBFK studio. He insisted on doing his election-day show early in the evening, to comment on the returns and thank his supporters.

Jack Hannah liked the idea of the tiny radio station winning its largest share ever but Stone and Turner argued against it.

Casper Wein objected, "If you blow off steam on the show, any hope of a rousing patriotic speech inviting everyone to participate in a new beginning of a bipartisan national dialogue will be down the tubes. You'll look like a hypocrite."

Austin Crouch added, "If you get this wrong, we'll have rioting in the streets instead of peaceful protests and you'll be fighting for credibility and respect through the rest of your term."

Murphy was having none of it, "Fuck all y'all, I'm the guy who's going to be elected president, that makes me the boss and I make the final decisions. All these folks out in radioland helped win this thing and I think a nice big 'Thank you' is in order. I can crow about winning the Southeast, react to the returns from the Midwest, then pull the plug until my victory speech at the Netherland Plaza later."

Milly Clark stood in the doorway to the studio and looked up into his bloodshot eyes, "Are you sure this is the right choice?"

"My character's got one more show and an acceptance speech and then he's going to retire to rest, while we begin the job we've been elected to do."

She cocked her head, "I truly hope the real you means that, because the other Murphy will make a mess of it, if you let him."

"That's why he's got to finish this tonight."

She grabbed his jacket and pulled him down to kiss his cheek as he whispered, "Thanks for being there through all of this, I couldn't have survived without you."

"I'm glad we both agree that you're still full of shit, now get going."

The studio crew applauded as he lurched across the room to flop into his big chair behind the desk. He took a slug from the bottle in the bottom drawer, lit a cigar, and shuffled through piles of clippings, a repository of racist hate and preposterous conspiracies that fueled nonsensical tirades, which garnered an audience of millions of fake Christian bigots faithfully tuning in five nights a week, expecting him to quench their thirst for venomous comradery and meaningless significance.

Doc Billings leaned on the desk, "How are you holding up?"

"The finish line's in sight and I want to cross it in style!"

"This is going to be a long night, so I'm going to try to ease you through it without pushing too far too fast. How are you feeling?"

"Fairly drunk but zipping right along."

The doctor frowned, "How many Black Molly's did you take?"

"Since when?"

"Since you got out of bed."

"Oooo, she was nice too…ah, probably six, two of the blue ones to keep my pecker vertical, and one of those yellow ones a couple of hours ago to smooth things out, along with several fingers of Jack."

"Sounds like you've taken over-prescribing your own meds to a new level," replied Billings, dropping pills into a tiny paper cup. "Here, these ought to keep you going until the speech later. We'll talk before you go on."

Milly handed him a WBFK coffee cup brimming with golden bourbon and patted him on the shoulder, just as Penny Baker sashayed across the room with her kit to attempt to make him look half-human for the video.

"You're in fine form, I could tell watching you stagger across the studio."

Murphy blew a perfect smoke ring, "Just getting in the spirit of the moment, darlin'."

She pushed him back in his chair and draped the towel across his chest, "Yeah, your skin's all flaky and yellow and your eyes look like you tangled with an angry chicken! Now, hold still and let me scrape this grime off your face."

He grinned, "Do you believe we're at this end of this thing?"

"Stone says you've got a good chance of winning."

"Do you want to be in charge of makeup for me at the White House?"

"No, I want to be Secretary of State."

He grabbed her left hand and shoved it under the towel, "How 'bout First Lady?"

"How many of those pills did you take?"

"Enough to make him salute all night long, so keep him frisky until showtime."

She poured drops into his eyes, dusted his face with powder, with a little rouge to his cheeks, touched up his lashes with mascara, and smoothed gloss on his lips. Without a squeeze goodbye, she snatched the sheet and patted his cheek, as a jovial Shepherd Stone, the cool calm messaging chief, walked over.

"You ready for all of this?"

"Well, the show's always the same old schtick with some improvisations but the victory speech needs to be strong and patriotic. Do you have the final draft yet?"

"We'll have it by the time you've finished the show but there will be time to read through it and make any final changes you think necessary. When you approve, we'll load up the teleprompters at the hotel."

"This wasn't supposed to happen, so I'm having trouble believing it'll be a victory speech."

"All our polls say you're going to take the electoral college by six or seven. That's enough."

Murphy shook his head, "You've just pulled off the biggest scam in the history of American elections."

Stone's dark eyes shifted from the warm friendly voice that guided the campaign to the intense focus of a political pro, who has completed the assignment of delivering his candidate to the Oval Office and is no longer bound to playing his part, "No, this victory is the culmination of decades of massive investments by a dedicated group of patriots, who bought every election they could grab from the school boards to the presidency. You didn't win it, they did."

Murphy sputtered, "But...?"

"Don't act surprised, underneath all the bluster and bullshit, you're an intelligent grifter who knows that no one gets this office without a lot of help from the people who actually run the show. You might become the President-elect but you're just another employee and, after tonight, you'll be taking orders like the rest of us."

Jack Hannah's voice rumbled through the speakers, "Two minutes to air."

Stone started to walk away but turned, "Don't let this show get out of hand. We need you to be the dignified Commander-in-Chief when you give your speech tonight. Don't screw it up."

The candidate's hands were shaking as he lifted the coffee cup to his lips, a splash of whiskey dribbled down his shirt. Murphy coughed up a cloud of smoke and mopped the stain with his red tie, as Hannah's voice rumbled through the studio, "This is the Mac Murphy Show coming to you on this momentous election night from WBFK, 'World Broadcasting from the Konfederacy', ten-forty on the dial. I'm honored to present the next President of the United States, Mac Murphy!"

The video crew settled in, waiting impatiently, while Murphy took another long slow drag on the cigar and stared at the microphone, dithering between the loudmouth racist bore who was birthed and nurtured in this studio and some vague phantom from a soul that once dwelt in the empty hollow of a promising actor's tarnished dignity.

"Ladies and gentlemen, I'm honored to have the privilege of talking with you tonight and I want to say thanks to each and every one of you, because this may well prove to be a historic milestone for working-class Americans! I also want to thank the talented people who transformed an impossible, ridiculous prank into a winning campaign.

This studio is full of the folks who make up my inner circle. They're magicians, every one of them – campaign directors Casper Wein and Shepherd Stone, impresario Austin Crouch, video-wizard Haden Crawley, my personal assistant, Milly Clark, our producer Jack Hannah, and so many others who have dedicated their lives to our success during the past year.

We swept the South and now we're marching through the center of the country from Texas to Minnesota, the part that's populated with real Americans who don't mind working hard and getting their hands dirty, who drive Dodges, Fords and Chevys, whose clean pair of jeans is their Sunday best, and who aren't embarrassed to salute the flag or say a prayer or sign up to serve our country.

I'm proud to stand up for a whole segment of our society who have been ignored and denigrated for generations. You have a right to be heard and respected for everything you contribute to this country and our society."

He lifted his eyes to stare directly into the lens of the video camera peering through the glare of blazing light panels, for a long moment, before scanning enthusiastic smiles and thumbs up.

"Used to be, back when I was a kid, every child went to school and was expected to work hard at their lessons, which were based, for the most part, on proven facts…two plus two is four, it's not three and a half, it's four. George Washington was our first president and they named the Capital in his honor. The moon orbits the Earth and the Earth orbits the sun. These were all facts that we accepted as truth and, when we took tests in class, the answers to the questions were either right or wrong and we didn't argue about it.

Today, I find too many people willing to believe absolute poppycock without proof or hesitation and they're far too quick to spread unfounded rumors as absolute truth, to divide the population into us and them, to demonize anyone who looks or talks or believes differently than they do. Folks, I have to tell you, if we don't put an end to this, it will be the death of our democracy and the working poor will suffer most."

He paused, sipped and puffed, absorbing the tension, the anticipation, the confusion ebbing through the campaign staff. "Have I ever told you how I came to have the privilege of talking with you every night? No, probably not. Well, about five years ago, former racist host and a real charmer of a guy, Bernard Schott, had a heart attack, so I filled the chair while he was in the hospital, which was all well and good, until he died.

I once had a promising acting career and I spent years doing everything possible to destroy my talent and my reputation through drinking, drugs, and debauchery, until the only option was to spout racist bullshit five nights a week to an audience of illiterate morons, who are too stupid or too lazy or too scared of anyone who isn't a white-supremacist Evangelical to join the rest of humanity.

You'd rather worship the twisted Biblical nonsense that your drunken preacher spews every Sunday, citing little bits and pieces of verse that always add up to why you sinners are going to be saved, along with a side of ecclesiastical permission to hate anyone different and screw anyone who gets in your way. Do you actually believe those brown savages are the reason that white people can't get a good job or a decent education?

The only reason that poor white people can't get ahead is because they don't want to put in the effort to make themselves into something better. Oh, and by the way, your preacher, who's all pious and holier-than-thou while he's molesting your wife or your children, yeah, he's receiving a hefty salary from the very same folks who own the radio and television stations and newspapers that reinforce your sad illusions of superiority over everyone else under God's grace.

It's all nonsense and you know it! I'm sitting here at my studio desk that's covered a foot deep with publications that you find at the checkout counter in the grocery, featuring half-naked blond white women on the covers and hate filled articles built on outrageous lies that are designed to convince you that those 'other' people are coming to take your job, your home, your woman, and your future. They're just over the horizon and they'll come pounding on our door in the middle of the night. You better fortify your house and buy more guns and ammo, survival gear and dehydrated food, the invasion's about to happen!

The news media is designed to get you to turn on the channel that starts every show with a murder or a violent wreck with bloody casualties or some immigrant of color being charged with raping a child or a white woman. They keep repeating those same themes over and over, until you're convinced the world has gone to shit and you're living on a tiny little island surrounded by shark-infested waters. Unless you're smart enough, brave enough to change the channel to get a different perspective…that's your reality and I don't blame you for being terrified.

Problem is…none of it is true. The crap that I've been screaming about for the past five years is all rotten baloney. The crazier I get, the higher my ratings go and the more money I make. You, my dear listeners, tune in to hear me rant because no one with half a brain will listen when you expose your ignorance, you're just repeating rumors that reinforce your own prejudices…and you wonder why the rest of the population mocks you?

I've been demonizing the power brokers who've done their damnedest to deconstruct the middle class, destroy public fact-based education, and eliminate your rights and your benefits. It's not the immigrants with brown skin who've taken your jobs, it's the white honkies in expensive suits that run the corporations that have shipped your future to Korea or Singapore or Venezuela.

All the folks who show up at my rallies and scream and yell, when I talk about the 'Deep State' or the 'Liberal Elite' taking over the power structure of our country, are missing the obvious. Rich Republicans have been picking away at everything that used to make America the greatest country on the planet for decades and you can rest assured that they don't give a damn about you…but they sure know how to use their billions to convince stupid people to vote for the completely unqualified fascist candidates they've paid for. I should know because I'm one of them."

Murphy hesitated, as a collective gasp broke the escalating intensity and absorbed all the oxygen in the studio.

"This will be my last show on WBFK and chances are good that either I'll be assassinated by my sponsors before dawn breaks or I'll be sworn-in as the next President of the United States. Unfortunately, I've already been informed that, if elected, I'll be a mere figurehead, a powerless front-man to distract your attention while the oligarchs finish the job of tearing the government apart piece by piece under the direction of their vice-presidential candidate, Creighton Steil.

I thank you all for your support through the years we've been doing this radio show together and your enthusiasm driving this campaign. It's all been a cheap, sleazy carnival sideshow to keep you folks angry and riled up enough to vote for the kind of shady people you wouldn't allow into your living rooms."

He was distracted by Shepherd Stone pounding on the window into the control booth. Jack Hannah laughed hysterically and offered a thumbs-up as the Communications Director slashed his finger across his throat, demanding the producer cut off the mic.

Murphy paused, glancing from one confused and astonished face to the next, "So, I'll leave you with this…there is redemption for each of us. Our brothers and sisters in the All People Matter movement are marching in the streets of every town and city. Unless you approve of a small group of arrogant rich guys selling you out, I suggest you ditch your racist ignorance, swallow your pride, and start acting like the Christians you claim to be. Go march with the true patriots who are standing up for your rights before it's too late. You need and want the same things – respect, dignity, a job, and a future, so shut this country down until we weed out the traitors who paid for this mess.

Thank you for allowing me to play this insane and ridiculous character in our tragic farce…but I want to apologize for allowing it to molt into this disgusting monster that took on a life of its own. I never had any intention or expectation of winning the nomination, let alone the election, and we all know that I never had any credentials that might qualify me for this great office in the first place.

So, along with my apology, I will promise you this…if I am installed as President of the United States in January, my first act will be to make sure that everyone involved in this charade is brought to justice, so this can never happen again. God bless you, God bless our great nation, and protect us from our own stupidity. Thank you and good night."

Nobody moved or spoke for a long moment, before the red lights on the cameras blinked off and the video crew shut down the floodlights and started packing their gear. Turner Graves stared at him coldly, for a moment, and followed Casper Wein through the padded doors without a word. Shepherd Stone stood with his arms folded across his chest, scowling like a high school coach whose best player just threw the championship game and his future fortune, spat on the floor, and avoided confrontation with the rest of the inner circle.

Murphy puffed and sipped, watching the slow procession empty the room, until finally, only Milly Clark remained with tears running down her cheeks and a smile curling her lips. She walked over to the desk, grabbed armfuls of racist propaganda rags and dumped them on the floor, scratching and pawing until only the telephone, microphone, and an overflowing ashtray remained. "You sure know how to throw a monkey wrench into any hope for your future."

The candidate started laughing, "I'm surprised one of them didn't pull out a gun and shoot me before I got half-finished."

"You were too busy running your mouth off to notice how the communal tension in the studio slowly increased as you built to a narrative peak. The further it went, the more everyone suspected that the old Murphy had been replaced by an imposter but no one was quite sure how far you'd go."

"Hell, if you're going skinny dipping, you might as well go all in."

"Do you have any idea of what comes next?

"Nope," said Mac, exhaling a huge cloud of smoke, "but I do know one thing for certain."

"What's that?"

"Those bastards plan to drug me into a stupor and lock me in a closet someplace, while that faggot Creighton Steil takes over as 'acting' president during my incapacity, to put the deconstruction of the government into high gear."

"So, you decided to quit acting?"

"Yeah, I'm sick of listening to myself and I suck at it anyway."

"No, you're actually quite convincing, but while you're back in real Mac Murphy mode, I've got somebody you need to meet before the bad guys shoot you."

"Who's that?"

"My college roommate."

"How?"

"Well, I'd suggest that we sneak out of here before your Secret Service detail figures out you're gone."

"And how are we going to do that?" replied Murphy leaning back in his chair with an amused inebriated grin.

Milly walked behind his desk and eased a sliding door into the wall. "This provides access to the electronics of the station in the basement."

"So?"

"So, there's a utility tunnel that opens on the other side of the parking lot. Don't ask me because I don't have any idea of why it's full of pipes and heavy cables, maybe it serviced a factory or something that was here before they built the station. As far as I know, Jack and I are the only ones who know about this."

"You expect me to just waltz out of here, without so much as a 'See ya', bye'?"

"I think you've got about two minutes before your minders with the sunglasses and earplugs come marching through those doors to take you to the celebration, so make up your mind. It's now or never," said Milly.

"Fake president or fugitive, that's a tough choice and either one will probably get me killed."

~

"Does that bastard have any idea of what he's done?" screamed Wein. "Spratlin's not going to give a concession speech after that performance. He'll call for new elections!"

"Murphy's opened it up for a Congressional investigation," added Stone, "and we've got no cover."

"Someone go get that son of a bitch, I want to know why...what's his motivation?"

"I'm ready to punch the guy out! Hell, being convicted of assassinating a future president almost sounds justifiable at the moment!" said Stone. "Send Penny, so I don't do something stupid."

Wein stuck his head out the door of the office, "Penny, go get Murphy. I want him here now!"

Penny Baker's heels clacked on the stairs down to the back hallway, where two agents stood in front of the studio doors. She added an extra wiggle to her walk, "I need to see Mac."

"He said he didn't want to be disturbed for a few minutes," said the guard on the left.

"I'm pretty sure he'll see me. Can I knock?"

The agent scanned her curves, "Sure."

She stepped up to the padded door and hammered it with her fist, "Murphy, I need to talk with you!"

There was no answer. She banged again without response and, finally, pulled the door open and stepped inside. The studio was dark, save the fluorescent glow from the window of the control room, illuminating piles of magazines and cuttings scattered all over the floor around the desk, but there was no one in Murphy's chair. "Murphy! Where are you?"

The two agents entered the room with the guns drawn, each moving silently along the walls to meet behind the desk. "He can't have disappeared into thin air, we've got this place locked down."

"Maybe he went to the men's," said Penny.

"Where?" asked the shorter man, who spoke into a microphone on his lapel, "The package is missing! I repeat, Blunderbuss is missing."

Her stiletto heels tapped out a seductive rhythm as she strode across the room to open a door on the far side but it was dark and empty. "Nope."

"Is there another way out of here?"

"I don't know, I only come here to do makeup for his show."

"Turn on the lights."

She reached for a panel on the wall and flipped switches. Ceiling lights blinked on and the taller agent started knocking on the paneling behind Murphy's chair until he hit a hollow sound. Panicked voices screamed in his earpiece but the panel moved as he pushed, so he slid it back into the gap in the wall, "Here it is."

"Where's it lead?" asked his partner, before they scrambled along the narrow passage, clattering down a of flight a metal stairs to sprint along the damp tunnel beneath aging pipes and heavy cables. A heavy steel door blocked the end of the channel and it was unmoving.

"Shoot the lock," shouted the agent, stepping back as his partner fired three shots into the lockset. He grabbed one handle but it fell free before he tugged on the other and the door swung open, revealing a muddy staircase with two sets of footprints climbing up into darkness in a grove of trees next to a lane that fed into an alley, behind the security fence, and spit out on the next street over. There was no sign or sound of a car moving and a moderate breeze erased any trace of engine exhaust.

~

Nellis and Katherine were sitting on the edge of the stage in The Playhouse Theater, deep in quiet conversation as Nellis strummed the Martin, when Rusty appeared from behind the curtain, "Here you are."

"Were we lost?" replied Nellis with a grin.

"No, I guess not, but Grandpa asked me to come find you. There's something you might want to see on the television."

Nellis helped Katherine up and set the guitar on the padded seat of a gilded throne backstage, as they trotted after the slender boy up the stairs and into the apartment. A gaggle of children surrounded Burt, Matty, Marty, Sybil, Alison, and Sally standing in the kitchen staring at the screen.

Marty's daughter, Adel, turned, "Oh, you won't believe this."

Katherine clutched her husband's arm as blond anchor Paige Phillips droned, "As we reported, the network has called the presidential election for Mac Murphy but hours before the final count was announced, Murphy did one last radio show and claimed that his candidacy was a complete fraud financed by a small clique of Republicans who are on a mission to destroy the American government from inside the administration."

The camera panned out to include her co-anchor Trevor Hobbs, "We haven't corroborated his claims but he called his millions of followers ignorant evangelical white-nationalists who are too lazy or too dumb to understand what's really going on in this county and suggested that they should reject their bigotry and join the All People Matter protestors in shutting down the country until Congress carries out an investigation."

Paige Phillips stared into the camera for a moment, listening to her producer through an earpiece, before she said, "Trevor, I hate to interrupt but Stanton Spratlin is about to speak to his supporters from the Great Plains Hotel in Cameron, Oklahoma."

"We go now to Democratic candidate, Stanton Spratlin."

The audience in the darkened room clapped and cheered, as Spratlin appeared in a spotlight at the podium with Marjorie, Brad, Bruce, Samantha, Sissy, and Maybelle Brown's four children.

After a minute of smiles and appreciation, he held up his hands and the crowd settled. "I must say that this has been an interesting day, a day that may change how our democracy works in every future election."

Applause accompanied whistles and cat calls.

"As all of you know, my opponent, Mac Murphy, seems to have lost the popular vote by several million ballots but it appears that he won a majority of the electoral college, which technically makes him the next President of the United States."

Boos and hisses.

"You may also know that he made an astonishing announcement on his radio show tonight. He said that his candidacy was a monumental prank paid for and orchestrated by that same group of wealthy Republicans the All People Matter movement has been trying to expose for more than a year.

These are not imaginary conspiracy phantoms that some nutcase dreamed up, we all see these very prominent citizens appear on magazine covers or on news programs with glossy stories recognizing their patronage just often enough to maintain their public image as a distraction from their darker associations."

He paused, gazing around at the crowd, "I prepared a concession speech, with warm congratulations for the winner and an offer to support his administration, but I'm afraid no one really knows the status of today's election. The numbers say one thing but my opponent seems reluctant to accept victory and I have absolutely no idea how this muddle might be reconciled. It may take days or weeks to establish an outcome."

He smiled, "If Murphy thinks it's rigged, why should we doubt him? I know we don't have to ask you, who you think won!"

The crowd exploded with cheers and applause. "Spratlin, Spratlin, Spratlin!"

"We started fighting political corruption during the last Congressional elections but, when we exposed the Brantleys and so many other illegitimate candidates, we had no idea of how far or how deep the cancer had spread. We couldn't fathom how insidious and successful their campaign had been over decades of buying elections to install thousands of their lackeys, whose primary allegiance was to the protection and fulfillment of their sponsor's financial goals.

The outcome of this presidential election leaves little doubt that, if Murphy hadn't exposed the ruse, they would have achieved their ultimate goal of dominating our government with the sole intent of dismantling our democracy."

Boo's and jeers.

"They might still, if we allow them to get away with it."

"No!"

"Then I'll start by saying that I will not concede this election until a legitimate inquiry is conducted to investigate all of the allegations of who and what might have influenced the outcome. I know that some of you have been outside marching around the square, protesting our crooked political system, and I would hope that our brothers and sisters across the country will continue their massive demonstrations to put an end to 'business as usual' until there can honestly be 'business as usual'!

I welcome folks who voted for Mac Murphy to join us, we're all fighting the same enemy for the same goal and there's strength in numbers.

I call on Congress to convene tomorrow to begin organizing our investigating committees to decide how we can reach equitable agreement on procedures to collect evidence and call witnesses to determine who is responsible.

Therefore, I will not concede this election nor recognize my opponent's apparent victory until we're all satisfied that we can believe in our leaders and our system of government. Thank you all for your support and I look forward to joining you in the streets!"

Glittering confetti and patriotic balloons showered down on the crowd, who clapped and danced to music from Jazz Taggart and his Merry Men, as Spratlin and his family greeted friends and supporters from the stage.

Bruce squatted to shake hands with Sister Gwen, who was accompanied by Hank Garrett, who ran the soup kitchen. "I never thought of you as political."

"It's just an extension of my service to God, standing up for what's right and true."

"You're a shining example of what the rest of us might hope to be but I couldn't have said it better."

"You come by and visit whenever you need a little ecclesiastical motivation from a mob of love-starved kids."

"I'll take you up on that," replied Bruce with a wink.

The Secret Service agents appeared on each side of the stage, which was their way of suggesting that the cavalcade was ready to roll. Brad and Bruce followed their parents into the first limousine and settled in at the back of the bench seats, near their father.

The agents closed the door and tapped on the roof before the huge car rolled into the square, preceded and followed by a parade of black Suburban's. Sheriff's deputies and Cameron City Police on motorcycles blocked each intersection until the procession rumbled through.

The Service decided that Representative Spratlin might somehow become the next president and they were not going to relax their vigil until the results of the election were cleared up. One president-elect disappearing before the vote was tallied was viewed as one too many.

Brad leaned close to his father, "My guys think they're starting to understand the system and some of the destinations. I want to keep you in the loop."

"I appreciate that, how 'bout we chat over the kitchen table when we get home?"

"Deal."

~

Brad and Bruce turned from the rebroadcast of snippets of Murphy's radio show interspersed with parts of their father's speech on a television above the kitchen table, when Stanton appeared wearing corduroys and a heavy sweater and rubbing his hands together, "It's starting to feel like winter again."

"Do you realize that last Thanksgiving we had Nellis and Katherine over for dinner and you suggested that everyone should get involved with Mavis's campaign to organize the resistance against the boogedy-boogedy guys who were throwing elections everywhere?"

"I have to admit that I was reflecting on that same thought on the flight home last night. How did we go from trying to prevent a fraudulent election in our little burg to winning the election as the next almost-president?"

Brad's lips curled into a sarcastic smile, "Personally, I'd blame it on Nellis, myself, if he was here."

Spratlin shook his head, "I've had everyone from President Gonzalez on down trying to dig up information on how the Alien Relocation Command was established, funded, and who's running it now. The Republicans have constructed a cocoon around the whole program and they refuse to reveal anything. Which makes me angry on a personal level, because I'm desperate to track down Kate and Jessie and all the other dedicated people who have disappeared into a black hole."

"We might have some threads to follow," said Brad.

"Like what?"

"Well, we already knew that they're using massive warehouses as local processing facilities, sorting their prisoners according to their crimes or status. My intel suggests that illegal aliens are being tossed across the Mexican border without an inquiry or trial but the political detainees are shipped to regional centers on white windowless trains that only travel at night. We've identified two sorting houses, one just outside Macon, Georgia, and another in Fort Worth. Obviously, they have at least one in every region. We just haven't found them yet."

"Where's the ultimate destination?"

"We think they're using remote abandoned military bases out west in the boonies for long-term storage or disposal."

Stanton hesitated, "And one might presume that conditions are somewhat less than optimal."

"From my experience in Iraq and Afghanistan, the mortality rate for political prisoners is usually a staggering percentage…on purpose."

Bruce stared at his brother, "I'm sorry I couldn't be more help in bringing you back to this reality."

"Hey, little brother, we're here now and we've got work to do. Don't fret it."

"You've both come a long way in the past year and I'm very proud to have my boys back with the family. We need each other."

"Yeah, we do," said Bruce. "And we need to find out how to spring our friends from the ghouls who kidnapped them."

"I have buddies in sixteen states working on this, we'll find some answers soon."

"Let's hope we haven't missed the opportunity to make a difference."

"Well, we did find an interesting bit of information. They've introduced a new identification program, called ATIS or Automatic Train Identification System, to identify which trains are where and they've identified the Alien Relocation trains with ARC and an identification number."

"So, you could pick out which trains are carrying prisoners?" asked Stanton.

"Yes."

"That's interesting," said Bruce, "but what could you do, if you knew where and when those trains were running?"

"I could put together experienced teams to hijack them, if we need to," said Brad.

"I'm not supposed to be hearing this, considering I'm almost a president, but my reaction is that we need to move as soon as we've identified the whole circuit or at least how it functions."

"We're working on it," said Brad.

"I think Nellis needs to know about this," added Bruce.

"Yes, he does." Stanton pursed his lips, pondering, "There's something else that I'd like to understand."

"What's that," asked Brad.

"Where the powerbrokers recruited their army of thugs and how they're being paid?"

"They're everywhere and they justify themselves as patriots because the "Founding Fathers" built in safeguards to protect minority rule by white men.

My first instinct is the Pacific Northwest. There's a huge well-organized white-supremacist movement up there. I'm sure the FBI has files on those guys."

"I'll sniff around and see what I can find out. Meanwhile, I'm sure your guys will have some thoughts on that too."

"Absolutely."

The only possessions Murphy grabbed, before stumbling after Milly through the equipment closet, lurching down the steel stairs, and tottering through the dark grimy tunnel, were his stout little satchel of stashed pills and his nearly-full bottle of Jack Daniels. He popped two yellow ones with a splash of Jack to mellow him out and settled back into the passenger seat of Milly's car. His fingers fumbled to remove the American flag pin, that the Secret Service had supplied, and tossed it out the window.

"I just got rid of the bug they planted on me but you know they're going to come looking for us and everyone knows that you just bought this car…and how long have you been planning this?"

Milly turned to him with a grin, "It's been in the back of my mind since you started this whole charade. You're a very smart man but you can't see any further than the tip of your rather prominent nose and I knew you wouldn't build yourself an escape hatch."

"So, you're my shining knight and this is your steed!"

"I'm not your savior, you're going to have to deal with that yourself, but I am providing you with transportation and support from some very special people, if you're willing to accept it."

Murphy took another swig, "I don't think I have much choice, they're probably going to shoot me on sight, when they catch up with us!"

"With good reason too!"

"Hey, whose side are you on?"

"The real Mac Murphy's. Now start acting like him."

"But...?"

"But nothing, put that damned bottle away. I need you to act sober, while we switch cars."

"You had this planned."

"You're right about that." She pulled the car into a parking lot behind a Kroger grocery and parked next to an old ratty minivan with weathered blue paint scraped off the driver's side. "Get out."

He struggled to open the door and staggered as he started around her car. She took his arm to deposit him in the worn passenger seat of the van. "I like your new car better."

"Me too. Buckle up."

Twenty minutes later, she wheeled into the Clark Heating and Air parking lot in Milford and pulled the blue van next to a black Mercedes. "What's this?"

"My uncle's company. We're borrowing his car for a few days. He won't mind."

"He won't mind if you rip off his classic ride in trade for this piece of crap?" asked the almost president, teetering between open doors.

"As you suggested, I've been thinking about this for a while."

"While I was off being an asshole and chasing beautiful women? You must be a masochist."

"You really are dumb, aren't you?"

"What do you mean?"

"I've been in love with you since the first time we talked at my reception desk all those years ago. You were too wrapped up in yourself to notice. Now get your butt in the car and let's get out of here before someone tracks us down."

The black car was thirty miles down the back roads of central Ohio before Murphy spoke, "I really do owe you an apology."

"There are probably forty or fifty million people who are pretty sure you fucked them over too, so you might want to include them in your regrets."

He was quiet for another few miles, "Where are we going?"

"Well, there seem to be several choices - first, if you're an asshole, I'll just drop you at the White House and you can invent some bullshit to cover your tracks. Or, a better alternative is my friend in New York. She'll take us in, until we figure out what comes next. We can be there by morning."

"Let's check out the second choice first," pulling the cork from his bottle for a little nip before he leaned back and started snoring.

Chapter Five
Election +1

A bewildered Matty replaced the receiver in the cradle and bowed her head in contemplation, her lips pursed, her pale eyes darting around the worn tiles on the kitchen floor.

Sally asked, "Who was that?"

"Milly Clark."

"Wasn't she your roommate in college?"

"Yes, freshman year in the dorms. She went home to Ohio for the summer and couldn't afford to come back."

"You haven't heard from her for quite a while."

"That's true." The soul of the theater and matriarch of the Sutton clan glanced at the grandfather clock next to the stairway.

"What is it? You're chewing on something."

"That was the weirdest phone call I've ever received, especially from her."

Katherine walked into the kitchen as Sally asked, "So?"

"So, she's coming for a visit and…"

"And?"

Matty walked over to pour herself a hot cup of black coffee, avoiding her daughter's inquisitive gaze, "And she's bringing someone with her."

Sally leaned against the counter and put an arm around her mother's shoulders. "Who?"

She glanced up at Katherine, "It seems she ended up being second in command at radio station KBFK out in Ohio."

"Isn't that the station that broadcasts Mac Murphy's rants?" asked Katherine.

"Yeah, she said that he did the final show last night and admitted to his millions of listeners that his candidacy was just a lark, financed by the same rich guys who paid the assassins who attacked your rallies, and he's walked away from accepting victory. Actually, they snuck out, when the Secret Service wasn't looking, and they're coming here."

"That's dangerous," said Nellis from the hallway. "We've already got the Alien Relocation Command hunting for us, now you're going to have the Secret Service looking for him."

Matty's dour expression melted into laughter as she walked over to pat Nellis on the chest, "We do entertain the most interesting people!"

"You'll forgive me, if I want to punch his lights out."

"I understand how you feel but let's find out the whole story before we resort to violence, shall we?"

Sally hugged Katherine, "Who knows, maybe Spratlin will end up the winner."

"Wishful thinking," replied the voice of the All People Matter movement. "If Murphy won't take it, the Republicans will install that sleazebag, Steil."

"He's scarier than Murphy!"

"When are they arriving," inquired Nellis.

"Late morning," said Matty. "Milly said she was staying on back roads as long as she can."

Burt emerged from the hallway shaking his head, "I could hear your chatter all the way at the bottom of the stairs."

"Did you get things set up for the rehearsals," asked Matty.

"Yeah, the kids did a great job cleaning up the dressing rooms and the set designers are coming in tomorrow to lay out the stage."

"What's the production," asked Nellis.

"A kind of jazz interpretation of King Lear...more music and dance, with less poetic dialogue."

"That could be interesting," said Katherine.

"This could turn into Shakespearean cops and robbers," said Nellis. "And the cops are looking for us."

"We've got enough hidey-holes in this old building that we could make you disappear without a trace or we could stash you at the underground," said Burt.

"Naw, I need to be in the middle of what's really going down. Everything and everyone involved might be affected by what this nitwit's trying to do."

Two hours later, the buzzer from the back door jingled and the camera captured Milly propping the newly elected drunk against the wall.

Burt hit the switch to unlock the door and lumbered down the stairs to fetch the new arrivals in the warehouse.

He found them just inside the steel door, gaping at the endless props, costumes, and backgrounds, "Glad you found us!"

Murphy seemed barely able to stand, his eyes were droopy, and before he could speak, Milly said, "I'm afraid we haven't met, I'm Milly Clark."

"I'm Matty's husband, Burt Sutton. She talks of you in humorous wistful moments of remembering your time together." He turned to Murphy, "And, if I'm not mistaken, this must be our future president."

"Yes, he's in fine form this morning and I'm hoping you have someplace where he can sleep it off. It's been a…turbulent twenty-four hours."

"I can only imagine," replied Burt, as an athletic man trotted down the stairs. "This is my son, Marty. If you'll give him your keys, he'll stash your car."

He scanned a barely conscious Murphy and shook Milly's hand, taking the keys. "My mom used to talk about how much fun you two had sharing a dorm room."

"We used to call each other 'big trouble' but I'm afraid that's what I've brought with me this time. I know this is a weird imposition but I couldn't think of anyone I could trust as much as Matty."

"We seem to be collecting America's most wanted lately," laughed Marty. "Do you need some help with him?"

"How far do we have to take him?"

"It's up a couple of flights of stairs but we could take him part way in the freight elevator," said Marty. "I'll help keep him upright."

Murphy groaned, turning to stare at Burt's son, "Are you Secret Service? You're out of uniform."

"I'm undercover but don't tell anyone. We're trying to get you to safety and you have to help."

"Okay."

Burt and Marty shuffled him along the aisles between fascinating islands of fantasies and decades of entertainment. The lift took them to stage level and they scaled the metal staircase to the apartment, then up to the bedroom wing, where they deposited him on a spare bed.

"He's going to be out for a while," said Burt. "Does he have a stash of booze or drugs?"

"He left an empty bottle of bourbon in the car and I know he's got a bag of pills that he pilfered from the huge doses his doctor provided to keep him going."

Marty ruffled through his pockets, finding twelve dollars secured in a money clip bearing a Shakespeare medallion, a greasy comb, a tiny tin of breath lozenges, and a cloth bag full of pills. He dumped out a handful, "I think we'll put these in a safe place until our doctor can determine whether they're medicinal or recreational, but I'm pretty sure these little black caps are amphetamines and the yellow ones are downers. Was he being treated for any medical conditions?"

"I know he's overweight, out of shape, has high cholesterol, and is stoned out of his mind during most of his waking hours."

"That bad, huh?" asked Burt.

"He's not the person the public sees and hears, he's been playing this outrageous character for the past five years and he has a hard time transitioning back and forth. I know he doesn't believe most of the nonsense he spouts and he never had any intention of winning the nomination or the election."

"He sure fooled a lot of people," said Marty, "and most of them are going to be pissed that he screwed them over."

Milly shook her head, "Some people were violently opposed to his personification of ignorance, bigotry and hate. Now, all the people who believed his rants are realizing that they might end up with Creighton Steil, who doesn't represent anyone but the guys with big money and you can be sure they're going to want to recoup some of the millions they invested in Mac's campaign one way or another."

"Yeah, that pretty well includes everyone in the country," said Marty, turning to his father. "How 'bout you take Milly downstairs and get mom to call Doc Schumer and I'll go disappear the car?"

"What about Murphy?" asked Milly.

"We'll lock him in for the moment and he'll have plenty of chaperones when the kids get home."

"How many children do you have?"

Burt and Marty broke up, "Well, last count was somewhere around fifteen, give or take."

"Really? Did you breed them or collect them?"

Burt laughed and took her arm, guiding her down the hall, while Marty locked the door. "Well, our three kids had more than their share, then we acquired a few and several others just sort of appeared, and I wouldn't be surprised if we took in a few more before it's all finished."

Matty met them in the hallway at the bottom of the stairs with a long tender hug for her former roommate, "I want to hear your story but I also want you to know how much it means that you called me in your hour of need. I'm glad we can still count on each other in times of real trouble, after all these years."

"I wish it was under better circumstances but I've never kidnapped a newly elected president before either, so naturally, I thought of you first."

"This is going to provide the makings for one crazy novel before we're finished," laughed Matty. "We'll be rich!"

"I'm sure the Secret Service is desperate to find him and I still can't believe we got away but the guys behind his campaign would just as soon kill him on sight and probably me too."

Sally turned up the volume on the television, "Ladies and gentlemen, the President of the United States, Phillipe Gonzalez."

The president appeared in the Oval Office, "Good morning, I come to you today because our entire election system was confounded by the President-elect's radio broadcast last night. During his program, he claimed that his entire campaign was a fraud financed by a small clique of extremely wealthy donors. It is my understanding that he declined to accept the office before he vanished, in spite of being under heavy security.

Every bureau of The Secret Service is involved in a nationwide search but no one knows whether he was kidnapped or just walked away from the pressure of his responsibilities. There has been no trace of him nor any requests for ransom.

In the meantime, I have authorized the Attorney General and the FBI to open an inquiry and I have requested that Congress convene to organize bipartisan committees to begin an investigation into the irregularities at every level of these elections. If we find illegal activities, I want everyone involved and those who sponsored the corruption of our free and fair electoral process to be brought to justice to answer for their crimes.

It's time to reign in the corrupt influence of big money buying elections. The very foundations of our democracy depend on an informed electorate having confidence that each and every vote will count. This election illustrates how we've ended up with a government that refuses to function, to serve the needs of all of the people in our country, and deal with its own amoral dysfunction. I propose banning all corporate political involvement, all political action committees, and putting a cap on spending in every election in the country. Each candidate should receive equal amounts to finance their campaigns and nothing more. It's time to get back to electing people for their character and their merits instead of suffering through an endless barrage of false and misleading propaganda to pick the one you hate the least.

Although I am humbled by my distinct and everlasting honor of serving as your president, I have no desire or ambition to continue in this office any longer than I am required by law or tradition. I know that our Republicans will scream and howl but I believe that I have the support of the vast majority of Americans when I declare that, until such time as we as a nation can have confidence that the people we elected have earned their positions fairly and honestly, no one will be inaugurated or sworn in to any office in the land.

I expect these investigations to be handled expeditiously but thoroughly by unbiased professionals, who will report to a bipartisan panel of our most respected leaders. I promise to keep the American people informed as to the progress and the results of this effort, so we might ensure that we are indeed a land governed of, by, and for our citizens. Together we must protect everything this wonderful country stands for. God bless you, God Bless America, thank you and good day."

The telephone rang and Matty answered, "Playhouse."

She paused, listening, and picked up a pen to write on a yellow legal pad. Finally, she nodded, "Thank you, I think I've got the list. We'll send the Market Bus to fetch them."

"Market bus?" inquired Katherine, turning away from the news.

Matty tore the page from the pad and handed it to Sally, who scanned the list, "The Alien Relocation Command is going after these people today and we're going to do what we can get to them first."

Marty added, "We've got an old school bus that circles through the neighborhoods to carry needy folk to the market or the doctor or whatever but, when we get a call, we pick up everyone who's threatened and deliver them to safety before the boogiemen show up."

"How many do you have today?" asked Nellis.

"Eighteen," said Sally, "and there are other teams covering different parts of the city. We better get going."

They hugged Matty and trotted down the hallway, just as Tate Sloan and Ned Perkins, carrying a large burlap bag under his arm, wandered into the kitchen as the president finished his speech and Nellis wrapped his slender friend in a bear hug, "It's about time you showed up."

"Well, rolling cross-country in a step van is not a comfortable way to travel."

"Especially, one painted with that distinctive pink bowtie on the front and big 'Acme Uniforms' sign down each side," said Katherine.

"Yeah, I did stop to get it painted in St. Louis."

"What did you paint her as...?" inquired Tate.

"Kept the bowtie, only painted it silver with the rest of the body a high-gloss ebony and had 'em put on a couple of custom chrome bumpers and really cool running lights," said Ned. "It looks like a pimp's hearse. It's so gaudy, everyone who sees it is too dazzled to think about what's inside her."

"That's brilliant," said Nellis, accepting the heavy lumpy sack from Perkins. "What's this?"

"Hickory. You're cooking."

Nellis grinned, "Damn, caught again, only I'm thinkin' we're going to need a lot more kindling and someplace to build us a temporary smoker."

"Without getting busted in the process," said Tate.

"Is there something we should know about?" asked Burt.

"Well, this guy's a master barbeque chef," said Ned, "and, as repayment for me saving his sorry butt from the Alien Commandos, he's cooking me a rib dinner. I'd suggest you and the rest of the crew might want to sign on for a special meal."

Burt grinned and scratched his chin, "Let' see, that'll be about thirty of us, so we're going to have to do some hunting and gathering. How long do your ribs cook, Mr. Chef?"

"I usually allow about six and a half hours from setting up the cooker to putting them on the table. So, if we get our stuff together, we can probably have an early evening meal."

"Okay, give me a list and I'll get your supplies and I think I've got enough bits and pieces of steel, down in what used to be the boiler room, to build a rudimentary oven in the back alley."

Tate grinned, "In this neighborhood, this could get out of control real quick."

"Your neighbors get a whiff of his smoke and they'll be lining up to sample the real thing," said Ned.

"Just so they don't call the fire department instead."

"Okay, I'll do some cookin' but I need to know a couple of things first."

"What's that?" asked Ned.

"How the hell you two mugs got hooked up and why you didn't let me in on your secret?"

"Well, I've got several other little side businesses working that you didn't need to know about but my mom and Uncle Burt are brother and sister, so that connection started before I was even born."

Tate interrupted, "And the whole family was performing at a resort down the coast in Venice, when hurricane Dot came rolling in and they discovered me on the beach road while they were trying to find a way across the bay to get out of the storm."

"One of my side businesses was helping wealthy people disappear when they got into trouble, so Uncle Burt called me in to help Tate," said Ned.

"And he's really good at his trade too," laughed Tate.

"I've got a mind to slug both of you for keeping me in the dark."

Ned wrapped an arm around his shoulders, "Brother, it was safer for everyone if nobody, including you, knew what was going down."

~

An hour later, Nellis, Tate, and Ned carried and arranged sheets of rusty steel and several curved vent pipes to feed smoke into a chamber with three large horizontal grates stacked to hold the meat.

"If this thing works, it could hold twenty or thirty racks at a time," said Katherine.

"If?" said Nellis indignantly. "As with all forms of art, it's not what you have, it's what you do with it."

"Amen," said his new wife. "Alison said that her friend with the landscape crew from Central Park, will be by with a load of hickory and oak in a little while."

"Then, let's take this puny bag of sticks that Ned brought and soak them in water until we need them."

He put an arm around her shoulder and kissed her cheek, "I've had this thing running around my skull since the president's speech, something about seizing the moment and…I think the moment to take action might be upon us…or approaching."

"What do you mean?"

"Well…politically, everything's about to stop…to cease functioning for a little while. I have no idea about whether we can use the drunk upstairs or whether he'd even consider participating but the power brokers have lost their grip and it's going to take time for them to reorganize. With the help of all the people who are already out in the streets, maybe we can make change happen."

"We need to set up a secure communications network with everyone who's left," said Katherine, "starting with the Spratlins."

~

Stanley French eased his considerable bulk into a chair at a small table draped with a white linen tablecloth covered with china, silver, and crystal goblets in the hushed lounge of the clubhouse of The Golden

Key Golf Resort and folded his hands together in front of his chin, "I've been talking with our associates, who all seem to have completely lost focus."

"This could be a golden opportunity," replied Conrad Blaho. "Murphy's never been part of the team, so he's doing us a favor because Steil is next in line."

"What about the chaos? The markets are going to tank!"

"They'll drop until we provide them with a lifeline, a calm in-charge vice-president elect."

"I take it that's being handled?"

Blaho broke crusty toast into his soft-boiled egg, "I was on the phone with Tomlinson when Murphy lit up the airwaves last night. The wheels started turning before he signed off and the propaganda machine is already rolling in high gear. We had our guys on every news channel in the country first thing this morning."

"What about Steil?"

"We'll hold him back until we've had a chance to lay the groundwork to prepare the voters to accept this succession. It has to appear logical, legal, and bipartisan when the white knight begins to restore order to the madness."

"Who's coordinating the Congressional investigations?"

"The loyal Republican chairmen of the various committees will do their duty for God and country, after they fulfil their obligations to our campaign," said Conrad, wiping a bit of grapefruit from his lip. "I'm telling you that we can make this work and, when we're done, everyone in the country will have given their approval."

A waiter appeared with a menu and a silver carafe, "Good morning, sir. Coffee?"

French waved the menu away, "Yes, please. Two eggs, sunny side up, with a side of bacon, crisp, and I assume, being about as far south as anyone can be, you have authentic Southern biscuits and gravy?"

"Yes, sir," replied the attendant, backing away.

He reached for a blueberry muffin beneath a napkin, embroidered with the Club seal in golden thread, in a silver basket,

"What about the opposition? There are millions of marchers in every city in the country and they're all pissed off."

"Will Terry's started a media campaign to tie Gonzalez and Spratlin to a coup to overturn the election. It's everywhere."

"What about the Relocation squads?"

"After a very successful nationwide sweep, transportation got backed up during the final weeks leading up to the election but the trains will begin moving prisoners from our processing centers to the camps out west in the next few days. With massive protests everywhere, we've pulled the last enforcers off the streets for the moment. They've rounded up most of the leadership of the movement and their most vocal supporters. Obviously, we've stayed away from Spratlin's family, Mavis Sloan, Tabitha Hall but we are informed of every move and every meeting. We've also got people searching for Katherine Kennedy and Nellis Gray, who got away."

"Even if they're underground, they'll find a way to cause trouble."

"We've got almost all forms of communication under surveillance and, sooner or later, they'll pop up."

"The sooner the better," replied French, peppering his eggs. "We have to convince the country that Creighton Steil is the only person in the universe who can save our democracy, between now and inauguration day."

"As long as Murphy doesn't show up, it's doable."

"Do our associates agree?"

"The morning's early but I've encountered panic and elation, three or four really moronic conspiracy theories, and too few who were invested in finding facts and reliable information to make informed decisions."

"The only thing the members of The Forge have in common is greed and a lust for power," said French, mopping rich bacon gravy with a bit of biscuit. "Each brings a unique perspective on how they dominate their little piece of the world economic system and a few of them might be conscious of the downstream ripples they produce. I doubt any of them realize that the utopian fantasy of a smoothly functioning integrated economy bounded by these alliances between our various industries will only last until the few begin to flourish and the feeding frenzy begins."

Conrad groaned, "We have to take the White House first."

~

Nellis started a fire in a stack of kindling under hickory logs and climbed the stairs to season the meats destined for a date with his smoking smoker. He almost crashed into Marty's eldest daughter, Dakota, bounding down the hall and dancing into the kitchen, "Does anyone know anything about a grownup in the guest room banging on the door and screaming for someone to call the Secret Service?"

Matty and Milly started to respond but Nellis held up his hand, "Why don't you let me handle this? Where's the key?"

Matty flipped a damp towel over her shoulder, "Can I trust you not to throttle the guy on general principles?"

"We've only just met and I've already made a bad first impression," pouted Nellis.

"No, you were preceded and accompanied by a…reputation for creative responses to people who don't accept your best intentions."

"Now, that's a nice a way of saying that I take pleasure in my revenge when someone dearly deserves it but they usually can't prove it was me…so I think we're safe here."

"Fine, just…"

Nellis started down the hallway, "I know, I know…"

The howling grew more frantic as he mounted the wooden staircase, worn smooth by the tread of thousands of children's shoes. By the time he found the key in the corner of the second drawer of a bureau full of linens in the hallway, Murphy was hammering on the door, "Let me out! Call the Secret Service! I'm gonna be the next president of these United States and I've been kidnapped!"

He twisted the lock and pushed the door open to find the room a shambles - bedding and pillows stripped from an overturned mattress, a flickering lamp impaling a crumpled shade lying on the floor, curtains torn from the rod above the window.

Murphy staggered back, "Where's my security? Where am I and who are you?"

Nellis filled the doorway, "We've never met but I'm Nellis Gray."

The president-elect stared for a moment, his face pallid, pinpoint pupils darting back and forth searching for a path past this human barrier to escape, "You're the guy who hangs around with Katherine Kennedy."

"One and the same."

His hands shook, drool dribbled down his chin, "I thought you were disappeared or something?"

"Seems we're being pursued by the same guys and these kind folks are providing a comfortable place to hide."

Murphy spiraled to the floor and leaned to rummage through the rumpled bedding.

"What are you looking for?"

"My medicines, I can't seem to find them."

"My friend Marty put them away for safe keeping. A doctor is coming by to check up on you, so he can provide you with whatever he thinks you need."

"Doc Billings kept me sane and stable."

"Well, I don't know Dr. Billings but I'm sure your new doctor will take good care of you."

Murphy crouched in a corner, clamping his hands over his ears as a parade of chattering children trooped up the stairs and along the hallway. "The protestors are coming to get me. They want to lynch me! Find my security detail!"

He looking up with a start, as Matty led Doc Schumer, a small round man in a black suit and a bowler hat, carrying an umbrella and a small black leather bag, into the room, "Gentlemen, this is Doctor Nathan Schumer. He's come to make sure that you're fit."

The doctor draped the umbrella handle over his left wrist and reached to shake the future president's hand. Murphy looked up at him defiantly but did not respond, "How do I know you're not some quack assassin sent to knock me off?"

"Well, first because, in my real life, I'm an obstetrician and my patients are usually small, noisy, and precious. I don't make a practice of treating flabby out of shape geriatrics but Matty asked me a favor and I wouldn't deny this lady any request, so let's get on with it. If you'll open your shirt, I'll make sure that your heart is still beating, then we'll see if your lungs are functioning, and move on to determine whether you need my services or not. Shall we begin?"

Mac's jaw dropped open and he started to protest but, muddled in frustration, he fumbled with the buttons on his shirt and struggled to slide his back up the wall to something approximating a standing position. Matty marched over, "Here, let me help. I've got three children and fifteen grandkids who can dress and undress themselves without assistance."

Nellis piled the mattress on top of the box springs and Murphy collapsed on the bed. The doctor listened to his heart, then his lungs, felt the glands in his neck, flashed blue light into his droopy eyes, nose, throat, and ears, and strapped a blood pressure cuff on his arm. "While I'm here, I'd like to take a blood sample, so I have a baseline on your state of health, which is, as far as I can tell from this brief exam, beyond borderline terminal."

Matty rolled up his sleeve and the patient flinched when the doctor inserted the needle but sat perfectly still while he filled three vials.

"What medications have you been taking?"

"Well, Doc Billings gave me Black Mollies to crank me up, then the little yellow ones to bring me back down, the blue ones to make my pecker salute, and a couple of other ones that didn't seem to do much."

"I see. I assume you drink alcohol?"

"Does the Lord have mercy?"

"In quantity?"

"Til there ain't no more."

"Hmm. Do you smoke?"

"Only Cuban stogies, lots of them."

"Tell me, how are you feeling right now?" inquired the doctor.

"My head's throbbing, my stomach feels like a big vat of lumpy red-hot lava, and I'm feeling kinda tired, you got any Molly's?"

"No, but I do have something that will relax you until I can get the results of these tests back, so I know how to help you."

Within moments of inserting a needle, Murphy's trembling body relaxed and melted onto the bed. Nellis lifted his legs, straighten his torso, and removed his shoes. "What'd you give him?"

"Just a mild sedative. He's in the first stages of withdrawal from whatever assortment of chemicals they were pumping through his veins. I'll rush these tests and let you know what I find as soon as I get the results. In the meantime, he's going to sleep for several hours. When he wakes up, he'll be disoriented, needing a stiff drink or a fix, and perhaps even be aggressive. Is there anyone that he can identify with?"

Milly was standing in the doorway, "I've known him for five years. I'll stay with him."

"Good. This is going to be difficult for him and everyone around him. He won't abandon his addictions easily but he can beat it, if he's willing to help himself."

"Fine, let us know what else we can do," said Matty, pulling a blanket over the snoring president. She turned to Milly, "I'll just bring you a cup of tea and a biscuit, if you like?"

"That would be lovely," replied her former roommate, pulling a soft chair next to the window overlooking the alleyway. "I don't think I've stopped moving in days."

"I'll be back in a few minutes and we can chat," said Matty, following the doctor, Nellis, and Katherine, into the hall.

Young Rusty and his long lanky sister Adel trooped up the stairs and the boy smiled at Nellis, "I think I found some of your trains."

"Where?"

"On my computer. Only a couple of them were moving last night but there are a bunch more parked on side tracks up near Providence, over in the Meadowlands Maintenance Complex in Jersey, and I found more in a rail yard in Macon, Georgia. That's as far as I got but I'm sure I can find more in other cities."

"That's good information," replied Nellis. "How'd you find them?"

"Well, I started with their identification tags but, once you see them on the satellite scans, they jump right off the screen because they're all white. They kind of glow in the dark."

"We need to hook you up with our friend, Brad. With your guidance, he might be able to help rescue some of the prisoners on those trains."

"I'm glad to help if I can," replied the bashful boy.

"I've got to put our dinner on the smoker but I have one question first."

"What's that?"

"Could you set up a secure call that no one could trace on either end?"

Rusty pursed his lips, "Grandpa Burt objects when I venture too far out into the internet."

"You're messing around with hijacking real trains and he's worried about masking a phone call?"

"Well, yeah," said Adel, "he's grandpa's favorite."

"Can you do it?" asked Nellis.

"Yeah, I've got to go back to school after lunch but I can set it up when I get back this afternoon."

"I'll be easy to find, just follow your nose," said Nellis, patting the boy on the shoulder. "I promise to do my best to keep you out of trouble."

"From what Grandmama Matty told me, I'm not putting much faith in your promise," said the boy, trotting down the hall.

Katherine laughed, "Seems the family has no illusions about exactly who you are."

"How come I'm feeling ganged up on?"

"Cause you didn't come from a big family," replied his new wife, with a hug. "I'm with Ned, the sooner you get the meat started, the sooner we get to eat."

~

Marty wheeled the gleefully rendered Market Bus around Washington Square, past the arch at the junction of Fifth Avenue, and around the corner into MacDougal Alley to stop in front of a red brick building, where a tall gentleman in a long gray coat was locking a slender black door.

Sally gasped, pointing down the narrow street, "That's him but…look."

Two black Humvees pulled into the far end of the lane, blocking their escape.

Marty snapped the doors open, "Grab him!"

"But?"

"Now!"

Sally leapt from the fanciful bus, a rolling riot of cartoonish clowns and animals cavorting through fields of jubilant flowers, and ran up to the man, "Excuse me, are you Stanley Sullivan?"

"Why do you ask?"

She pointed, "Because the Alien Relocation Commandoes are just down the block and they're coming for you. I'm here to save you."

The man glanced down the street, then at the bus, "In that?"

"It's the best we could do on short notice," said Sally, grabbing his arm to direct him across the sidewalk.

Marty slammed the door as they climbed the few stairs, "Hold on to something, we're going for a ride!"

He crunched the shifter into reverse and pushed the gas pedal to the floor, reaching a hand to steady Sullivan, who tumbled onto Sally's lap in the first seat. He spun the wheel, bounding over the curb, stabbed the brake, and punched the accelerator to swerve in front of a semitruck creeping south on MacDougal Street to barricade the entrance to the alley, as one of the Humvees and a squad of troopers in black uniforms and mirrored helmets raced down the lane.

Marty skipped first and ground the gearbox into second as he turned west on Waverly and merged into traffic heading north on Sixth Avenue. He checked the mirrors and turned right into Ninth Street. "We might have lost them but we won't know until we cross Fifth Avenue. Are you alright?"

The distinguished man extricating himself from Sally replied, "I think so but I really don't understand what those men would want with me."

Marty's sister patted his shoulder, "They want to make you disappear, just like so many other folks brave enough to stand up to the oligarchs, who can't tolerate insurgency or insurrection. What do you do for a living?"

"I'm a lawyer."

"And who are your clients?" asked Marty, glancing left and right, as they bounced across Fifth Avenue, spying two Humvees racing south a block down.

"Mostly people who stand up to the authorities, because it's always an innocent and intimidated David against a corrupt and brutish Goliath flaunting bogus unsubstantiated charges."

"There you go," said Sally. "You make it harder for them to clear the city of anyone who opposes their control or happens to be some other shade of human besides lily white."

"I never dreamed they'd go this far," replied the tall man.

"Oh, it's way bigger than anybody realizes," said Sally, "as you'll see in a little while. Meantime, we have one more stop to make before we deliver you to safety."

"Where to?"

"Up near the United Nations."

"Who we looking for?" asked Sally.

"Hey look, it's starting to snow." He handed the clipboard to her, as he turned west on Forty-Second, "Black female, 28, listed as Billy Holiday."

"Great name. Great singer."

"I know the neighborhood," said Sullivan. "There's a pub, McFadden's, on the next corner, that caters to United Nations staff who can't afford to drink in the establishments their bosses frequent. It's just up here on the right."

Sally whistled softly, staring through the windshield at a black Humvee, wedged onto the sidewalk between concrete planters that resembled heavy gray coffins scattered along the curb with mangy tufts of evergreens poking out the top. A single commando in full uniform screamed at a woman in an elegant coat curled on the pavement with her arms clutched around her head as his baton struck again and again. "I have no doubt that that's our girl."

The bus slid on the slushy street and smashed into the back of the Humvee with a mighty crunch, pinning it between planters. Marty jumped out to tackle the trooper, while Sally and Sullivan collected the woman.

The commando emitted an electronic groan as he threw a wild right cross but Marty reached under his chin and yanked the mirrored helmet off his head. The stunned black man lunged again before Marty launched him head-first into the steel door panel of the enforcers' black truck. Two of his comrades were trying to crawl out of the windows, while the driver was gunning the engine in reverse, attempting to push the crumpled community bus back into traffic.

Marty followed Sally and the lawyer to lift the wounded woman up the steps, jumped into the driver's seat and threw it into reverse, crunching a Rolls Royce into a diplomat's limousine with little yellow, blue, and red striped flags fluttering above the headlights, before screeching through the intersection dragging a sparking bumper to head south on Second Avenue, snaking through a tangle of trucks and taxis to turn east on Fortieth, then south again on Tunnel Approach Street. He checked the mirrors and opened the window to listen for sirens but no one seemed to be following as they cruised past the towering Corinthian complex, the top lost in streaming clouds and soft flaky snow.

He turned to Sally, "How's our escapee?"

"Not so good. She took a good thrashing and might have a concussion."

"I'm not a doctor but she needs medical attention immediately," added Sullivan.

The woman moaned, "Don't take me to a hospital. That's the first place they'll look."

"She's right," said Sally. "Let's take her to the theater and let mom check her out."

"Are you sure you want to take that chance?" asked Marty. "It's not like we're riding around in some inconspicuous gray minivan. Everyone in this part of the city knows this bus."

"All the more reason to head for home. We can hide it in the warehouse."

"Yeah, like it'll fit."

"Hell, we've already got the Memphis Belle in there, she needs company."

"Who's the Memphis Belle," asked Sullivan, cradling the young woman and pressing a handkerchief against the gash on her forehead.

Sally laughed, "She's a famous streetcar we rescued from certain destruction."

She leaned down to the woman, "I assume your name is Billy Holiday?"

The black girl looked up, stammering, "How could you possible know who I am?"

"Your name was on the list to be arrested today, so we were sent to rescue you before the troopers showed up. Unfortunately, we were a few minutes late!"

"But…"

"Don't fret about it. You're in good hands and we'll take you someplace safe," replied Sally. "By the way, I know the commandos are brutal but why was that jerk beating you instead of just arresting you?"

"That was Credo, he used to be my pimp, before he beat the crap out of me, got busted for crack, and volunteered himself into the ranks of the Alien Relocation Command to save his sorry ass from spending a couple of years in the pokey."

"And how did he know that you'd be here at this time on this day," asked the attorney.

Billy's beautiful black eyes dropped to the floor, "I work as a makeup artist for a studio downtown but I have a date with an Ecuadorian diplomat every Friday afternoon, who likes to make himself feel dominant and superior after spending the entire week being insulted and ignored by the other ambassadors."

"And he meets you at McFadden's?" asked Sullivan.

"His limousine picks me up and takes me to his apartment."

Marty grinned, "I think he might be even more unhappy that he's not going to get to spend the afternoon with you, because I'm pretty sure we destroyed the front end of a black Cadillac limousine as I was making our escape."

The corners of Billy's lips lifted slightly, "Oh, he'll be upset, that's his pride and joy. He rides around town feeling like he's a big shot, when he's really just a greedy corrupt pig."

Sally took the handkerchief from Sullivan, "Here, let me take a look at that."

The prostitute winced as she lifted the bloody cloth and dabbed at a ragged laceration torn open between the edge of her eyebrow and the top of her right ear. The bleeding seems to be under control and you might not have much of a scar, if we can get you some treatment."

"Sister, in my business, looks are my second most important asset."

"What's your first," asked Sally with a grin.

"Brains!"

Fifteen minutes later, the injured woman lifted her nostrils to the sweet scent of hickory smoke, as the bus eased along the alley behind the theater. "What's that smell?"

"A friend of ours from out west is smoking some ribs," said Sally. "Think you might want to stay for dinner?"

"Shit yeah, I'd be happy just to stand downwind until they're ready."

"Where are we?" asked the attorney.

Sally waved her hands gracefully back and forth in front of his eyes, "You will forget every detail and have no memory of being here."

"I'm overwhelmed by your mystical powers," replied Sullivan, "and beholden to your kindness."

Marty pulled the window back, as the bus crept through Ned, Katherine, Alison, and a dozen children playing in a thin blanket of snow to stop next to the smoker, "I'm surprised you don't have the Fire Marshall down here giving you summons or something."

Nellis's ruddy face lit up and he rubbed his hands together, "He'll be back at 6:30 to join us."

"Mom said that you came with a reputation."

"Can't help it, I was born this way. What the hell did you do to this poor bus?"

"Well, we got kinda crossways with a squad of commandos and I had to improvise."

"I sure hope the other vehicles look worse and you got a good bodywork guy, she's gonna need some love."

"Hey, we grabbed the last two on our list, that's what counts. You got enough food for a couple more."

"Your old man had my initial request from the butcher tripled after he smelled the smoke. I've got a feeling this could turn into a neighborhood event."

"Looks like you've got an audience," said Marty, opening the door to allow Sally and Sullivan to escort Billy off the bus.

"Yeah, I keep wondering why you deprive these poor malnourished children from learning about real food that comes from the Earth, instead of all that Italian stuff they serve up here…pizza and spaghetti and lasagna, there's no nourishment in that crap!"

"If that didn't smell so good, I'd be asking when you were leaving?"

"See! These kids think food comes out of a microwave! They've never seen raw meat cooked over a wood fire before, that's sacrilege that's what it is!"

"Hey Ned! Would you go inside and open the overhead door? The cops are lookin' for this girl so we need to stash her inside for the night."

Ned saluted and trotted inside, "Sure."

Katherine walked over to Sally, "Can I help?"

"Well, this is Billy Holiday and she had a little tangle with a bully commando."

"Let me see." She leaned close as Sally lifted the bloody cloth to reveal the wound. "Hmmm, might need a stitch or two. Let me see your eyes."

Billy looked up, her eyes dilated but tracking, "You're…you're that lady from All People Matter…Katherine…Kennedy."

"Yes dear, I am. Now, let's get you inside where we can get you cleaned up."

Sullivan followed them through the gaping void into the overflowing warehouse, "This is incredible."

Ned turned to look, "Yeah, they say it's more than fifty-year's worth of props and costumes."

Marty marched a parade of kids towards the door in a hail of snowballs, "Okay, we need to move enough stuff out of the way to fit the bus in here, without making a huge mess. Let's see if we can just slide these racks and tables without dumping everything in the process."

Everyone joined in to move each mountain of props one at a time until they cleared a patch of empty floor for the damaged bus. The children cheered as Marty pulled into the warehouse, until he tapped one of the tables and an avalanche of fifteenth-century armor tumbled across the hood with a mighty clatter that echoed down the alley.

Nellis ran inside, "Was anyone hurt?"

"Only Marty's pride," laughed Ned, as little British-born Anton and his older Irish stepbrother, Patrick, grabbed swords for a duel, while the rest of the children stacked shields and weapons against the Memphis Belle in the corner.

~

Matty led the family doctor into a guest room behind the kitchen, where Billy was convalescing. "Billy, this is Dr. Schumer, who looks after all of my kids. I've asked him to tend to your wounds, if that's alright with you."

The beauty squinted as she lifted her face to the light, exposing purple bruising on her cheek beneath a swollen eye and the gash across her temple. "I've had worse."

"That doesn't excuse what this brute did to you," said the doctor, extending a gentle finger to turn her chin. "I don't think anything's broken but I'm fairly certain that you've got a concussion."

"You can't send me to the hospital, that bastard will find me!"

"I understand and I wouldn't think of endangering you any further. You're in good hands here."

Matty smiled, "We've a houseful of mom's, what more could you ask for?"

"You've been so kind," replied Billy, taking her hand.

"If you don't mind, I'd like to examine you to make sure that I'm not missing anything."

"Have at it, Doc. I haven't been checked out by a real doctor in a long time."

Matty squeezed her hand, "I'll leave you two for the moment. Call me if you need anything."

"Thank you."

After examining every inch of her body, listening to heart and lungs, conducting every test he could manage outside of a clinical setting, and taking blood and urine samples for the lab, he said, "Is there anything else I should know?"

"I haven't had a period in a couple of months and I feel like I'm going to throw up when I wake up in the morning."

Schumer smiled, "M'dear, I suspect that you are perhaps three months pregnant. I'll confirm that when we get the results of the test back."

"I knew that bastard knocked me up!"

"Who?"

She broke down sobbing, "Craig Hobson, mean white honky and corrupt former New York district attorney, who skipped out on federal indictments by becoming an advisor to our slime-ball vice president-elect. He wasn't satisfied getting his rocks off, he had to prove the brutality of his manhood by beating the shit out of his nigger whore."

The doctor comforted her, "I can arrange an abortion, if that's what you want?"

Billy leaned into his shoulder, "I don't know what I want anymore. I'm too scared to make any big decisions right now."

"Please understand, you are my patient and I will do anything I can to help you get back on your feet."

"Thank you," sniffled the black beauty. "Can you get me strong enough to defend myself or take revenge on all these racist johns who've been abusing me?"

"We'll work on that but, for the moment, I suggest you put your faith in Matty and her marvelous family. They'll protect you."

∼

Milly rose from napping in the soft chair and wiped Mac's brow as he awoke with a start. He sat up gazing around the shattered room in confusion, "Where are we? Is this the White House?"

"It's alright, I'm right here and we're safe."

"Where's Doc Billings, I need my meds!"

"We're seeing Doctor Schumer now, you like him," replied Milly, gaging which Mac was driving his illusions.

"I don't know any Schumers." He jumped up and stepped to the window, pulling the torn curtain aside to peer out through a gentle snow into the smoky alley, "Where's my Secret Service detail? I know I won the election, so I'm the president now, when do I give my victory speech?"

The little woman walked over to hug him, "You said you wanted to retire because Turner Graves and his buddies decided that you were going to be their crazy puppet spokesman and nothing more."

"Graves supplied buckets of money and gorgeous women and he never tried to tell me what to do or how to do it."

Milly shook her head, "Don't you see, that Mac Murphy is just a character you made up. He's not real and neither is your presidency. It was all a grand performance and it's over now, the final curtain has fallen and you've taken your bow."

"I got elected, I should serve."

Flustered, she replied, "The inauguration isn't until January, so you have time to rest and begin planning your administration."

There was a knock at the door and Matty appeared with a tray bearing a teapot, cups, saucers, sugar and lemons, and a plate of tiny raspberry tarts. "I thought you two might need some nourishment."

"Who's that?" shouted Murphy. "Did Graves send over another beauty?"

"No, it's just me," said Matty, picking up on the look of frustration in Milly's eyes, "just a sweet grandmother bringing tea and biscuits to tide you over until dinner."

He grabbed the tray and tossed it across the room with a clatter before darting for the door. Matty stuck out a foot and he plunged through the open doorway to sprawl on the carpeting in the hall. A half-dozen children rushed to his aid.

"Here let me help you up," said Little Mac, Sally's teenaged son with the tri-color mohawk, reaching to roll him over.

Murphy screamed, "Who are you? Where are my guards, I'm being attacked!"

The boy recognized the partially elected president and stood up, "You really are screwed up, even if we do share the same first name. I'm glad you decided to bolt the presidency because you'd suck at it."

Matty marched into the hallway, "Now, all of you, observe that he's not well and not really aware of what's going on at the moment, so be kind. Help me get him back to his bed."

The children gathered around to lift him upright, surrounding him to prevent another fall until they settled him onto the bare mattress.

Matty put her hands on his shoulders, "Mr. President, your doctor called and said that he would be coming by shortly to attend to you. Do you think you can be patient for a few more minutes until he gets here?"

Murphy groaned and toppled over on his side.

Matty hugged Milly, "He'll come around, it's just going to take some time."

Her college roommate buried her face in her friend's shoulder, "You have to believe that he's a good man under all the bluster. He's been playing this part every day for more than five years and after taking handfuls of pills and drinking buckets of booze to keep going, he doesn't really know who he is anymore."

Matty patted her gently, absorbing her sobs, "I know you believe he's not really the character that everyone assumes he is and that's good enough for me but...if he tries to hurt you or anyone else, he'll have to answer to the lady of the house!"

Little Tom Baker knocked on the door and led the doctor inside, "I found the doctor down in the kitchen and brought him to you."

Matty hugged her adorable grandson and kissed his forehead, "Thank you, Tom. That was good of you."

"Oh, and Mr. Gray said that the ribs would be ready in an hour," said Alison's youngest blond tornado, grabbing two strawberry tarts that landed on the bureau, as he scurried out the door and along the hallway.

"I just came from your young lady, Billy, and she will recover from the beating. I'm fairly certain that her wound will heal without much of a scar but she was rather surprised to learn the she is with child. Perhaps, three months or so," said Doc Turner, placing his long coat and bowler hat on a battered bureau and approached his delirious patient, "I assume he's a bit disoriented, since he woke up?"

"That's an understatement," said Milly, sadly. "It feels like there's a battle going on inside his mind and he's not sure which delusion is real."

"Neither, at the moment. His tests showed a potent cocktail of powerful drugs from amphetamines to barbiturates, valium to Viagra, and extreme malnourishment. Everything's out of whack and his organs are revolting, it's a wonder he's alive, let alone conscious."

Milly started crying again, "I worried about Doc Billings getting him jacked up before every performance and then bringing him down really fast. Sometimes Mac would pass out cold before the limo left the venue and other times it was like he couldn't let go of an electrical cord."

"That's dangerous and unprofessional." The doctor listened to his heart and his raspy lungs, "He sounds terrible and, if he wasn't who he is, I'd call an ambulance right now."

"Well, he is who he is, so what can you do for him?" inquired Milly.

"Let's start an IV to rehydrate his body and, hopefully, flush some of the toxins out of him. He's exhausted and in need of bedrest and nourishing food for the next few days, if we can keep him under control. Then we'll start making him move a little bit to stimulate all those nerve endings and ramp up his circulation. The downside is that the only way he beats this is if he beats it himself. He has to reclaim who he was before he became a drunken renegade president."

Chapter Six

A guard with a mirrored helmet pointed an automatic rifle from a tower overlooking the gravel path traversing the perimeter of the massively expanded DeSoto Correctional Institute east of Arcadia, Florida, and motioned Jessie and Kate away from the twelve-foot electrified fence.

Kate took his hand and walked south, "We're already marked, we don't need to give them an excuse to shoot us."

"There have to be better ways to go," laughed Jessie.

"You bastard, every time we go on a date, you get us kidnapped and stuck in some god-forsaken hellhole with a really good chance that we're going to end up dead!"

He pulled her close, "I'm surprised they haven't shipped us off to some secret prison somewhere far from civilization."

"Maybe they don't have the transportation system set up for all the people they're kidnapping. There have to be at least two-thousand in here and we're all from this area. What if they're doing this everywhere in the country? That could be millions of people."

"You're right, of course, but I think they've been selective about who they're rounding up to avoid embarrassing Republican candidates during the final days before the election."

"Yeah, but rumor around here has it that something went wrong with the balloting and Murphy abdicated or something."

"Wouldn't it be cool if it was true? What if Spratlin won by default?"

"I know the real Stanton, he'd figure out what's happening and get us out of this mess!"

Jessie paused to scan the fencing and the bleak landscape of scrub, small trees, and marshy ponds, home to lots of critters who would love a man-sized meal. "Meantime, we haven't figured out a way to escape, too many guards, sensors, and electric fences. We'll see whether the boys found any weaknesses during their sojourn around the park."

Kate waved, "Here they come now."

"What'd you find?" asked Eddie.

Jessie hugged the stout biker, "Guards, sensors, fences, and a forbidding environment outside the compound. There's a state highway about a half-mile north of the main entrance but you know they've got that covered. You?"

"About the same. There's a dead spot over near the far corner but there's no place to go. There's a hefty foundation under the fence all the way around the complex and the outer fence surrounding the whole property has sixteen guard towers, so I'm bettin' you couldn't sprint, pole vault, or dig out either."

"What about vehicles coming in and out?" asked Kate.

Benny grinned and shook his head, "They've got a separate secure depot in a satellite lot that's serviced by their fleet of white trucks, driven by armed guards, with a fenced tunnel connecting it to the command center. There's no in or out there."

"We did run into lots of people from the little village under the Pelican Way bridge," said Eddie. "They might have been desperate and defeated in their homeless camp but, even though they've got food and shelter in here, they're ready to mutiny. A callous system robbed them of their jobs, their homes, and their lives, and finally, their freedom."

"Did you notice that there are three other slammers peeking out from behind those trees over there, the little hillock off to the west, and on the other side of the administration buildings out near the road. If they're holding as many prisoners as this joint, we're talking eight-thousand pissed off jailbirds," added Sammy Ball, diminutive former administrator of maps and surveys for the town of Dolphin Bay.

Jessie grinned, "There's an original concept – if you can't break out, take over from the inside."

"That sounds like something Nellis would come up with," laughed Kate.

"First problem is communicating with the other camps," said Benny.

"The second is where's the weak spot in their airtight security?" said Jessie. "If we can find one here, I'm bettin' it will be the same for our neighbors."

Hank Miller and Rex Tatum, original members of the Dolphin Bay workers group that started the protest against the city, strode along the path. Rex hugged his neighbor, Sammy, "Have you heard the news?"

"What news?"

"They're culling prisoners and I noticed a convoy of white trucks backed up to that long white building by the main gate. Word has it that they're going to start shipping us out to a central processing center someplace in Georgia."

"Where'd you hear that?" asked Kate.

"We saw them hauling people away, mostly Hispanics," added Miller. "And one of the women said that they've seen this evacuation play out several times in the past few months."

"I wonder whether everyone goes to the same place or will they separate illegal immigrants from political prisoners?" asked Eddie.

"They probably toss the illegals over the fence at the border but folks like us are another can of worms, if you'll excuse a rather morbid pun?" said Rex with a smile.

"You're right, they intend for us to disappear permanently," said Kate. "If the press had proof of what happened to us and who's behind it, all hell would break loose. Unfortunately, the fascists own a big chunk of the media, so they can slant any story to fit their narrative."

"The only way they win is if they can dispose of the entire opposition," said Jessie. "So, the key to our future is going to have to be so spectacular, so off the wall that the whole world will be forced to accept the truth for what it is."

"We better figure out how to make that happen before they ship our happy asses off to never-never land," said Benny, "or we're toast."

～

The guards made no attempt to segregate women and children from men or to distinguish between the remaining aliens and political prisoners. Each cell block was fouled by the stench of overflowing toilets and herds of unwashed human bodies crammed into forty-eight tiny chambers in each wing designed for two prisoners rather than ten or twelve.

Jessie, Kate, and Sammy took shelter against the chill in the stairwell near the side door to avoid the crowd. Kate squeezed Sammy's arm, "Don't you think it's kind of romantic that Jessie's got us stranded in another hellhole and there's a very real chance that we might not get out of this one?"

Sammy patted her hand, "I always knew there was a good reason to avoid that bastard but he's so…charming, I fall under his spell."

"Me too," laughed Kate. "At least we can get outside here."

The lights were extinguished at precisely nine o'clock, just before Eddie, Rex, Benny, and a gagging Hank Miller lumbered down the stairs.

"What's with him?" asked Sammy.

"The perfumed aroma upstairs," said Eddie, as Miller lunged outside to throw up. A guard in a black uniform and a mirrored helmet appeared, the glare from his headlamp illuminated Hank on hands and knees, vomiting on the gravel.

The Enforcers yelled, "You're not allowed outside after curfew!"

"Have you smelled the inside of that place?" mumbled Miller between coughs.

The guard extended a black prod hissing green static to jab Hank in the ribs. He screamed as his body arched onto the ground. Eddie charged through the doorway when he unloaded another jolt into Miller, only to be dropped by troopers hiding in the shadows.

In the tradition of Andrew Jackson's 'Kitchen Cabinet', newly elected Vice President Creighton Steil and his staff were ensconced in Blair House, across Pennsylvania Avenue from the White House, within twenty-four hours of the declaration of Murphy's election. Officials loyal to The Forge in the Department of State and the General Services Administration evicted the French Ambassador and his entourage, to install Steil as a placeholder for the missing president-elect or the official 'next in line', should Murphy fail to reappear.

Perfunctory Secret Service and FBI searches for the missing president uncovered no clues, witnesses, or ransom demands but his disappearance or abduction unleashed a stampede of faithful senators and representatives to initiate bills to ensure that the vice president-elect was entitled to the office.

Effeminate and pugnacious evangelical Creighton Steil wore a tropical peach jacket with a burgundy ascot and just a flash of red at the pocket. He was surrounded by four heavyset uniforms, each with a mass of ribbons and gold on their chests and stars on their shoulders, as well as his chief-of-staff, political advisor, communications director, and security advisor.

Four-star General Truman Kent intoned, "We support a smooth transition without delay or interruption and we've shared our view with President Gonzalez. If President-elect Murphy fails to claim his office, we will stand behind you."

"We hold the reins in the House and a majority in the Senate, so Gonzalez's investigation isn't going to get off the ground and his efforts to delay the consummation of the election will die before they get started," injected political consultant Tony Spears. "Our people are all over the airwaves and gumming up government efforts to figure out what happened."

"Is there any other way to rise above the investigations?" asked the vice president.

"How about moving before anyone has a chance to consult the Constitution?" asked security advisor and former New York District Attorney, Craig Hobson.

"Sort of claim the office and ask questions later?"

"Is there a better alternative?" asked Steil.

Admiral Hawkins leaned across the table, "In the entire history of our nation, the military has served at the pleasure of the president but, in the last twenty-four hours, we've entered the Twilight Zone, where no one has a clue about what's going to happen next, let alone who's in charge!"

"Gonzalez doesn't control anything, so foreign enemies might be inclined to seize the opportunity to take advantage of our situation, whether that's through a political, military, or terrorist threat," added Simons, a three-star Marine Lieutenant General, overseeing the Middle Eastern theater. "The Joint Chiefs have already put our forces on high alert and all of the intelligence agencies have activated every feeler they can muster."

"It's our sworn duty to protect these United States, so either take control or we will. You have two days to sell the public on the transition or we'll step in to snuff this anarchy before it has chance to become entrenched. Then we can arrange new elections when things settle down."

Steil stood up, "So, am I to understand that I'll have the full backing of the military, if I claim the presidency?"

"Yes, Sir, that's exactly what we're saying," replied the Admiral. "At the moment, you're the only civilian in a position to right a foundering ship but, if you cannot or will not accept this responsibility, we'll be forced to take the unprecedented step of temporarily removing and replacing the elected government of the United States."

"Gentlemen, give us until Monday and I believe we have an agreement. Before I offer champagne, may I request that you set up surveillance on the White House? I want to know everyone who enters or leaves."

"Yes, Sir!" The generals saluted and excused themselves.

Tony Spears dropped a file on the table, "You do realize that there is one small problem with all of this, don't you?"

"What's that" inquired Dan Elliot, Steil's chief-of-staff.

"Murphy."

"What about him?" asked the vice-president.

"Well, for one thing, he might not be inclined to stay in hiding for long. Knowing him, the old drunk might decide to show up and fight to take it back before he goes down in flames, dragging all of us with him."

"What are you saying?"

"I'm saying that there would be a far greater chance of avoiding conspiracy investigations, if we could be sure Murphy was out of the picture permanently."

~

Murphy awoke with a start and rolled onto his back, staring up at Milly, who was wiping his brow with a cool damp cloth. His eyes darted to the darkened windows, "How long have I been asleep?"

"Hours. How do you feel?"

"Like I got run over by a bulldozer." He sniffed, "What's that smell?"

"Oh, Nellis has been smoking ribs all afternoon and I think it's turned into a neighborhood cookout."

"I haven't smelled real hickory smoke since I was a randy student at the University of Georgia in Athens. There was an old black man, Ben Triplehorn, who had a big smoker out behind his barn and he'd sell us all the ribs we could eat for a quarter a piece."

"I'll see if I can get some sent up for you."

"I want to go down there and stick my face in the smoke," replied the almost president, wavering as he tried to sit up.

"First, I don't think you're stable enough to make it down three flights of stairs and, until we figure out what our plan is, I don't think you should be seen in public. That's unless you want the Secret Service grabbing you?"

He looked up at her, his eyes struggling to focus, his mind syrupy and slow, images and thoughts flashing, then fading as quickly as they appeared. "Where are we?"

"We're staying with some of my friends in New York. We're safe here."

"What about…I'm so confused. Where's Doc Billings? I need some meds to get my mind right."

She sat down next to him on the mattress and patted his knee, "You decided that you're done with that, remember? It's time to bury candidate Murphy and reclaim your soul. This is your chance to evict the demons and free the person who's been hiding inside for too many years. I know you can do it."

His face puckered into an impish grin, "You don't happen to have a little splash of Jack, do you?"

"No, you finished off your bottle in the car last night and I'm pretty sure our hosts don't drink."

"What kind of people don't drink? No one wants to be sober in this world."

"Some people are intelligent enough to discount the bile they hear on white-trash radio, it's all lies and you know it."

"That's why my people consume massive quantities of booze!" said Mac, wiping is dry lips. "Hell, real patriots depend on Jack Daniels to stoke the fires before they have their morning coffee."

"Trouble is that most of your audience actually believed the salacious nonsense you spewed over the airwaves night after night. Your target demographic wasn't smart enough or sober enough to separate truth from lies and your election proves they don't care about the difference."

The president-elect chuckled, "Actually, the further it went, the easier it got. I could take a little gem from one of those racist rags and gin up the most outrageous crap to drag out the show on a slow night. Sure as shit, they'd lap it up and be back for more on the next show, because I was feeding their addiction to hate."

"When you start feeling better, you're going to have to make some tough choices."

"I know but I'd feel a whole lot better if I had some of those ribs in my stomach."

"Fine, I'll go down to the kitchen and see if we can get some sent up."

"That would be wonderful," said Murphy, lying back on the mattress.

Milly gathered the little pile of broken tea cups and saucers and opened the door, "You stay put and I'll be right back."

"Can't wait."

She closed the door and walked down the quiet hallway and the stairs to the kitchen, where she found Sally ladling baked beans into two large bowls. "Where are all the kids?"

"They're all hanging around the smoker and who could blame them?"

"The food smells so wonderful, I wonder whether we might get a plate for Mac?"

"Sure," said Sally. "How's he doing?"

"He's confused and exhausted but I think he'll come around."

"How are you holding up?"

Milly sighed, "I'm tired but, while I was sitting there watching him sleep, I realized that helping him escape was the best contribution I could make to his welfare and the future of this country. If the Murphy that everyone saw on television moved into the Oval Office, his backers from The Forge were planning to shove him out of the way in a mad dash to dismantle our democracy, so they can replace it with their own personal kleptocracy."

"The Forge?"

"A very exclusive consortium of super-wealthy families and individuals who control great chunks of the economy and they've been buying elections, from the school board to the presidency, for decades with the goal of owning it all…at the expense of everyone else."

"Sounds like feudalism at its worst."

"If they succeed, it will be. They exploited Mac's outrageous persona to rile up the base, so they could win more down-ballot elections."

"I'm surprised you stayed with him through the whole campaign. His rhetoric was really disgusting."

Milly shook her head, "I know but the loudmouth bigot was just a character that Murphy dreamed up years ago because he was desperate for a job. After all this time and too many drugs and way too much booze, he loses track of which is which."

They turned as Murphy tumbled down the stairs, jumped up with a mischievous wave, staggered through the hall, and pushed through the double doors to slither down the metal staircase to the warehouse. Milly ran out of the kitchen yelling, "No, wait!"

Sally turned off the burner on the stove, grabbed a bowl of beans, and dashed after her in pursuit of the delirious escapee. He was trapped halfway down the staircase overlooking the crammed repository by Nellis, Burt, and a half dozen children at the bottom and two frantic women scampering down the steps behind him.

"Wait up," said Milly as she reached him. "I'm sure there's plenty left for dinner, right Nellis?"

"I can guarantee you the best ribs you've ever had."

Murphy slumped onto a steel tread, "I don't know, I got spoiled in Georgia back in the day."

"I lean towards a sweet sauce myself but some of those East Coast smokers like the tartness of a little more vinegar. What do you prefer?"

Milly sat down beside him as he said, "My first bite of smoked meat was so sweet and tender, with a little bit of heat hiding under a rusty bark that had a little chew to it. I was hooked from the git-go."

Nellis hiked up three steps to look him right in the eye, "I promise you won't be disappointed but I think it would be better if you'd let me fix you a plate of my finest and bring it to you. There's a fire marshal and some local officials out there who might recognize you and that wouldn't be good for you or these kind folks who are putting us up. Can I get you to go along with that?"

"Hell, I'm so hungry I might take a bite out of that blue horse over there," said Murphy pointing to a collection of cantering pastel horses.

Burt laughed, "They pulled a golden chariot that flew across the stage in a children's fantasy called, 'Zambarina' by Joey Hyatt, an obscure playwright from up in Harlem with an enormous imagination. I pay attention when he pitches a script because I know it's going to be totally nuts and completely wonderful."

"I was an actor once..." muttered the president-elect. "Crowds cheered my performances."

"Hell, after learning a little more about you, I'd say some of your performances at the rallies qualify as Emmy worthy. You're not that man, are you?"

Milly wrapped an arm under his and looked into his eyes, "You know he's right."

Murphy buried his face in his hands and Alison's youngest, Tom Baker marched up the steps with Bridgette, a seven-year old Dutch beauty who had been abandoned in the theater by parents who never returned, and brown twins Bailey and Thomas, whose talented and outspoken Muslim parents died in a questionable auto accident on the Jersey Turnpike.

Little Bridgette reached out to touch the backs of his hands, which eased away from sad, confused, and tearful eyes. "I don't think you're the nasty man we saw on television. He just looks like you."

Mac was touched by their concern as his gaze moved from one beautiful young face to the next, pausing on Bailey and Thomas, "You look just alike."

"We're twins," replied the boys in unison.

Tom Baker handed him a napkin to wipe his eyes, "You'll feel better when you've had some dinner."

"I think you're right, son, and I hope that this beautiful young maiden is right too. I was very much like you, when I was a child, and somehow, I became that horrible person you saw on the television, and now I have to figure out whether I can find my way back to who I used to be."

"That's easy," said Thomas, his dark eyes gleaming, "just be the best person you can be, simple as that."

Murphy grinned, "Leave it to the children to strike the heart of the matter. I thank you for your kindness."

"Hey, here comes Mr. Gray, with food," said Bridgette, taking his hand. "C'mon, there's a table and chairs in the Goblin's forest."

"Forest?"

"Yeah, Burt and Marty arranged all the trees and shrubs around the path behind the weapons armory," said Tom.

"They even hid ghosts and goblins in the foliage," added Misty, Sibyl's exuberant preteen red-headed daughter who was wearing a pink tutu and dramatic purple eye-shadow.

Milly followed the procession through the narrow pathways between mountains of props and racks of costumes, past an alcove with guns, knives, swords, and cannons, into a small garden with a long table nestled under overhanging trees shading shrubs of every shape and size that concealed small magical creatures in broad leaves and dark shadows, all lit with streamers of white Christmas lights snaking up trunks and dangling like luminous serpents from branches.

Nellis set a large tray on the table and laid out a platter stacked with ribs, bowls of Sally's beans, Matty's salad, and Alison's sweet biscuits to soak up the drippings. He added two bowls of sauce, pointing, "Sweet and kinda fiery. I like a little of each."

They sat down on a bench facing six smiling faces intent on watching them eat every bite, Milly said, "I can't believe how good this smells."

Mac picked up a meaty rib and held it under his nose, inhaling, "There's something primal about the earthy scent, the rich aroma of smoked meat. Maybe we possess a leftover bit of our distant ancestors who hunted for their meals and roasted the kill over an open fire in a forest somewhere."

Burt turned and walked over to press a button behind a fiberglass rock, which ignited a fake fire in a stack of sticks piled on a shallow prop beach. Milly and Murphy applauded.

The almost president took a bite from his rib, closing eyes to savor the texture of the spicy bark before his teeth mashed through soft moist pork, dripping with a deep molasses sweetness balanced with just a dash of vinegar tartness mellowing a final rush of red pepper at the back of his tongue. "Oh, my, one bite is certainly insufficient to explore so many layers of flavor. My compliments."

The children smiled as he closed his eyes for a second morsel, chewing slowly, overwhelming every taste bud in his mouth. Milly leaned close, "This sure beats hotel chicken, doesn't it?"

"If I never saw another rubbery chicken breast again in my lifetime, I wouldn't be disappointed."

Nellis grinned, "Road food can be a pleasant surprise, once in a while, but I can testify that those rare meals are the exception not the rule."

"I take it you've had experience?" inquired Milly.

"Yeah, I traveled the blues circuit from Chicago through the South to Atlanta for years and years."

"What's your instrument?" asked Murphy.

"Guitar, mouth harp, and singing sad songs to make all the girls cry."

Misty turned around, "I heard you playing on the stage last night and I wanted to dance!"

"Well, thank you young lady. I'll be happy to play for you anytime."

"We could be your chorus," said Nikki, Sally's dainty young songstress, with a little 'Doo-Wah' for effect.

"Your grandpa told me that every one of you could perform just about any part in any play. I think that's fairly astonishing."

"Well, we can't help it," said young Tom. "There's a new show in here every couple of weeks. The King Lear rehearsals start tomorrow."

Murphy pointed a juicy rib dripping with sauce from one child to the next, "I hold fond memories of my last theatrical part when I was in college because I got to play Lear."

"I'll bet you were great," said Burt.

"I wasn't great, I was Lear and the audiences loved him."

Nellis sat down on the bench next to little Bridgette, "What part do you intend to play next?"

Mac munched on a mouthful of pork and lowered the bare rib with a trembling hand, "I honestly don't know that I have another part in me, after living this Murphy guy for so long."

Milly looked at him lovingly, "We have to figure out who you are today before we can begin to chart a course for your tomorrows."

"You struck a chord with millions of people who need and want the same things as the folks who supported the All People Matter movement and it took skill to make them coalesce into a political movement that carried you to victory. The only difference between your people and our people is hate."

Murphy shook his head, "Hate's an easy sell. Don't have to discount it or dress it up in fancy packaging or expensive advertising. The audience wants and needs to believe that someone out there, preferably someone of color, is responsible for their wretched lives being a complete failure. There has to be someone to blame for their misery, their ignorance, and their gullibility. It's easier to rant about some faceless group threatening their little piece of hell than to admit their own deficiencies."

"I heard a replay of part of your show from the other night and the news reports say that your people still don't believe you weren't really their racist nationalist spokesman. I'm not sure who's more disappointed, the Democrats who lost or the folks who supported you?"

The newly elected president chortled, "Maybe that's why nobody seems to be working too hard to figure out where I went. Nobody wants me back!"

Burt laughed, "I think you might be on to something. Didn't they have a tracking device on you?"

Mac brushed the lapel of his jacket, "I tossed it out the window during our escape, I think that was the moment I committed to not being him anymore."

Nellis stared directly into Murphy's jaundiced bloodshot eyes, "Instead of him becoming president, maybe you should."

Milly gasped, "But…?"

The actor laughed, "I don't have any qualifications and lack even a basic knowledge of how government works. I'm a joke not a president."

"I suggest that your grasp of the very essence of what makes people tick can only come from an honest heart. You might lie to yourself about yourself but your audience accepts your outrageous proclamations without hesitation because you've mastered the ultimate acting skill…salesmanship. Whatever you lack in executive skills might be balanced by the depth of character of the decent human being who has a unique ability to make people believe."

～

Young Rusty was waiting in the kitchen when Nellis and Katherine led a parade up the stairs with baskets full of plates, glasses, and cooking utensils for the line of Adel, Anton, Little Mac, and Patrick at the sinks, loading dishwashers and scrubbing pans. The boy reached to take a smaller basket dangling precariously, "Would you have a few minutes to look at something I found on the railroad computer?"

"Sure, let's land these baskets and you can show me what you've found." He kissed Katherine on the cheek and followed the young wizard down the stairs behind the stage to the basement.

Nellis stopped to gawk at the incredible detail in the miniature world of sunshine and puffy white clouds where everything worked exactly on schedule, the buildings shimmered, the street lights changed in sequence, where the trees grew straight and tall, and the sheep in the meadow cantered in play. Rusty leaned out of the control station, "Come on, I've got something up on the monitor."

The boy pointed to a satellite map that showed the rail lines snaking through the endless metropolis from Maine to Florida, "This is the image that we were looking at before."

He zoomed in on individual white trains parked on side tracks throughout the Northeast, then backed out slightly, "Now here's a speeded-up version of what they're doing tonight."

The slender white serpents slithered along the tracks, converging towards central Pennsylvania. The image switched to white trains parked throughout the southeastern states that loaded prisoners and started moving toward a railyard splaying into a dozen branches next to a very large warehouse recently constructed just east of Macon, Georgia. "I've got at least six more groups of trains that appear to be heading for rendezvous in the next day or two."

"They're moving prisoners to these processing centers, where they can sort out the illegal immigrants from the political hostages. The question is where are they going to take them next?"

"I can't tell yet because their route tickets are renewed every twelve hours and I haven't broken that part of the code."

"This is a great start but I need to contact some people in the real world who can help."

"Your friend Bruce left a number for me to call, if you needed to talk. He said it would take a while to get through all the connections. Do you want me to try?"

"Sure, but how long will this take?"

"Well, I have to call a number in Tampa and they'll send me through three more operators before I finally get to Sister Gwen and she'll have to get ahold of Bruce to call us back. This could take a while."

"In case nobody's reminded you lately, you are one incredible kid. Thanks for your help."

Rusty blushed, "I'll come find you when I get Bruce."

"I'll be the guy pacing back and forth waiting for the call to go through!"

~

Milly followed Mac up the metal staircase from the warehouse into the hallway behind the stage. Murphy stopped to stare at a regal woman in a long velvet robe silhouetted in a single amber spot, her deep raspy voice molding 'Lost my Baby' into a solemn dirge, a poignant plea to the empty seats rising up into darkness.

Lost my baby on Monday and Tuesday was twice as bad
Lost my baby on Monday and, Lord, Tuesday's twice as bad
Couldn't get up on Wednesday and Thursday's just too sad

His soul flew off on Friday and the sun didn't rise on Saturday
My heart is broken 'cause my baby's gone away
Best kneel down on Sunday and learn how to pray

Murphy was mesmerized by the grief and sorrow in the soulful tone of her voice and approached slowly, quietly, until he added a low harmony to her chorus.

Lord, have mercy, life's a mystery
Lord, have mercy, I'm wrapped in misery
Bring back my baby, please bring her home to me

She turned to his voice and raised a hand to cover the bruising on her face, "How did you get here?"

He stopped, "I was rescued by someone who actually cares about me."

"After watching some of your rants, I don't see how anyone with a heart or a soul would have anything to do with you. You're a complete bigot."

"The Mac Murphy the public saw was guilty as charged but I'm beginning to believe that the person who lives inside my tortured soul is not that guy."

"After pledging to deport every person of color in the nation, I find that kind of hard to believe," replied Billy. She lifted her hand to reveal her injury, "I suffered this beating at the hands of my former pimp, who is now an enforcer for the Alien Relocation Command which is tasked with removing anyone of color from our society. If I didn't know better, I'd bet this whole concept of racial tyranny was your idea but you're just the salesman, our founding fathers institutionalized it long before you came along."

Murphy's jaw dropped, "I have no earthly idea of what you're talking about."

"You supported removing illegal aliens, all people of color for that matter, from the country and the government formed a secret paramilitary division to execute that delusion. I know dozens of people who went out for a walk or to the grocery or the post office and never came back. The commandoes snatch people off the street or barge into their homes to take someone into custody but there's no record of the arrest and they never appear in any court before a judge, they just disappear."

"But my whole rap on that was plagiarized from cheap pulp-fiction about third-world countries," exclaimed the president-elect. "Those things don't really happen here."

"They do now and your bullshit excuses every ignorant racist's belief that it's perfectly acceptable to destroy the lives of people just because their skin's a different color or they speak a different language or worship their God through different rituals. You gave them permission to hate and they elected you to the most powerful office in the world because you promised to legislate their racism into law!"

Murphy sighed, "That's why I'm here...because I wasn't supposed to win and accepting the mantle would just compound the tragic consequences of what started as a prank. I never had any intention of becoming President of the United States and we both know I'm not qualified."

"Obviously!" shouted Billy. "You're a disgusting maggot who transformed hate and bigotry into an entertainment phenomenon that reinforced the very worst perversions of the dregs of our society. Real people suffered, disappeared, and died because you shot your mouth off! Get the fuck out of my way!"

She stormed past him and disappeared behind the curtains.

~

Thirty minutes later, Rusty found Nellis sitting on a metal office chair on the stage, strumming a guitar and talking with Burt, who was tidying up in expectation of the first Shakespeare rehearsal later in the day. "I got through and Bruce is waiting on the phone."

Nellis stood up, leaned the guitar against the chair and trotted after the boy, down the metal stairs to the wonderland in the basement, picking up the phone from the table in the computer alcove, as his eyes danced across the miniature landscape, "Bruce?"

"Yeah, we can't go on meeting like this. What do you know?"

"Well, lots of weird stuff happening on this end but my young friend, Rusty, has a talent for breaking into computers and he's managed to wrangle his way into the system that runs all the trains in the country. I'm looking at a screen where he's identified some of the Alien Relocation trains and we're watching them move in real time."

"Brad's guys have been scouting them too and watched some of those trains being loaded with prisoners but we don't know where they're going."

"I think we can lead him right to their destinations, where the illegal aliens will be separated from the political detainees. It looks like they've got processing centers near Macon, Georgia, and another one up near..." He looked at the map, as Rusty zoomed in on two trains heading into central Pennsylvania from New York and Maryland, "Maybe Scranton or someplace with a big rail yard west of there."

The boy added, "Looks like they've got one in Ft. Worth and another up around Indianapolis."

"We think the trains were parked until they got past the election but there's nothing stopping them now," said Bruce.

Rusty grinned and pointed to one of the trains headed for Macon, "Watch this."

He punched in a few lines of code and the train stopped.

"Did you do that?" asked Nellis.

"Yup."

"Can you do that with all of them?"

"Sure, but I'd need a lot more computer power."

"Bruce, my young tech wizard just made one of the trains stop dead."

"Really?"

"Yeah. Hey, can you make them go wherever you want?"

"If you give me a couple of techs who know how to work some things out, yeah, I think so. It's all about the switches."

Nellis smiled, "Bruce, I think we're on to something here. Let me buzz you back when I know more. Meanwhile, put your brother on alert. We might have a plan."

"I'm all ears," replied young Spratlin.

"How's your old man holding up?"

"He's heading for D.C. to put some pressure on Congress to begin formal hearings tomorrow or the next day."

"That might be too late to save our friends and change the course of history. He needs to be in Washington now to set up a speech at the Lincoln Memorial night after tomorrow."

"Who's the speaker?"

"Well, he will be for sure but we'll supply another voice to the mix. It'd be great if someone could line up a good band and a couple of famous activists who haven't been picked up yet and aren't afraid to stand up for what they believe in to get the crowd warmed up."

"This is starting to sound like one of those Nellis schemes," replied Bruce.

"Get your brother to line up his guys and your dad use his pull to sell this as a major event. I'll get back to you on the rest of it."

"Roger that."

The line went dead and Nellis watched as Rusty typed in some commands. The white smudges started moving in reverse. "Okay, you don't have to have it all worked out, just enough to be confident that you can make them start and stop where our guys can intercept them."

"I'll identify as many as I can."

"Great. I think I know where you can get all the computer power and expertise you need. Do you have your whole program on your laptop?"

"Yeah, I'm using it as a satellite workstation that's wired into their mainframe, so I can only do so much but, with a computer with heavyweight chips, we could take over their whole network."

"Get your stuff together and we'll go pay a visit to some people who will really appreciate your talent."

He ran through the warehouse and up the stairs, through the hallway to the kitchen, where he found Katherine consoling Billy. "Could I have a minute?"

Billy pursed her lips, "I need to talk with Matty, so I'll leave you two lovebirds to it."

"Thanks," said Nellis, hugging his bride as she walked away. "What was that about?"

"She had a confrontation with Murphy and it sounds like she was not kind."

"I don't blame her. I think I've got a basic concept on how to make this whole thing work but it's going to take a lot of coordination."

"What are you talking about?"

"Rusty has identified some of the Alien Relocation trains and he can make them stop or run backwards or, with the help of those guys over in the underground, he can make them go where we want them to go."

"That's amazing!"

"More than that, I've just talked with Bruce and brother Brad's got his guys lined up to hijack some of them."

"Could they hijack all of them?"

"With the help of the techs over in Oz to guide Rusty and enough manpower on the ground, I don't see why not. I'm guessing they have a skeleton guard on those trains because they only run at night and they don't expect any interference."

"So, what happens after you pull this off?"

"What if we had all of the protestors, plus all the people who are hiding out in the underground and every other hidey-hole across the country…" He paused, "All of the prisoners and refugees, supported by all the All People Matter movement, descend on Washington in a mass protest?"

"What's the goal?"

"To expose the rich guy's conspiracy and shut down the government."

"And who's going to lead this revolt?"

"The guy upstairs."

"Are you out of your mind?"

"Of course, that's why you married me isn't it?" laughed her husband. "But, after talking with Murphy earlier, I'm pretty sure he's a lot more sane that he's letting on. Dry him out and he might be useful."

Chapter Seven
Election +2

Conrad Blaho sat alone in his penthouse suite high above FDR Drive, sipping one final snifter of rare Remy Martin Cognac to tame the ominous apprehension in his gut. His tired eyes wandered across the East River to the lights of Brooklyn flickering on one-by-one, as a cold cloudy morning threatened to erupt from the dark Atlantic.

Allies, surrogates, and members of The Forge crowded the news channels but far too many rushed the idea of a Steil presidency with a complete lack of restraint in light of the inconvenient fact that the newly elected president was missing. Even ardent supporters were hesitant and confused by the sudden rupture of their white-nationalist victory during Murphy's final radio show. With Gonzalez's support of Spratlin's call for investigations and a suspension of placing elected officials in office, navigating the media quagmire to instill confidence in the proposed line of succession would prove challenging.

The light on his phone blinked a millisecond before the ringer on his private line chirped. The 313-area code indicated Detroit. He picked up the receiver, "Hello."

"Conrad, it's Stanley."

"Have you been up all night too?"

"Yes, just considering the possibilities. Do you know anything new?"

"Our contacts at Justice say they've got their best people running down leads but they don't have any idea of where Murphy went, let alone what his intentions are." He paused, "In the process, I got a tour of the Kernel, our surveillance project, the central core of the Nucleus last week."

"Is it fully functional?"

"Oh yes, the quantity of data on nearly every human being on the planet is astonishing and the potential for mining that information to manipulate the population is staggering. It isn't just a big computer system, it's a living breathing creature, with a consciousness of its own, and it's watching everyone, all the time."

"But it can't find Murphy?" asked French sarcastically.

Blaho smiled, "Not a clue."

"What's Tomlinson have to say?"

"He's got all hands on deck but I'm not sure the country's ready for a full-scale blitz to sell Steil as heir apparent. Polls suggest that most of his supporters still cling to the hope that Murphy will surface to become the next president."

"Most of his supporters are illiterate Christian morons who'd vote for a pit viper if it promised an end to abortions and restrictions on gun ownership. Once they cast their votes, they became excess baggage."

"Speaking of baggage, any word on all those displaced traitors?"

"With the election behind us, the wheels are turning and the spigot is open. I'm told that many will be sorted and sent on their way by tomorrow."

Blaho took a last sip of his Cognac, "With most of the opposition out of the picture, it should be easier to frame the junior Representative as a sore loser trying to manipulate the system to fulfill his own inflated ego. He's the presidential wannabe who wasn't elected."

"I think we have to be careful with him, he's placed himself as the paternal moderate trying to calm the nation and he's suddenly developed that television magic that makes him believable," replied French. "The latest polls show that a vast majority has no problem seeing him as qualified and presidential."

"The problem is that we used up all the ammunition we had on him and most of that was bullshit to begin with, so a blatant attack at this point is probably counter-productive."

"How long are we going to keep Steil under wraps?"

"Maybe tomorrow or the next day. We don't want him to come off as the eager young pup trying to grab the golden ring."

"Even with that horrible air of pious concern, everything that comes out of his mouth has to be carefully scripted. One mistake could play right into the headlines and our whole campaign gets screwed."

"I'll put Tomlinson and his people on it, while we let this whole thing play out for a day or two. I keep waiting for the protests to die down but, if anything, they're getting bigger and more vocal."

"They've shut down every city in the county. They're dominating the headlines and the media is running with their message."

"I'm told that our warriors are on standby and I'm inclined to give the protesters one more day to claim the headlines before we send them in to stir things up a bit."

"The media would rather show video of riots and insurrection than chanting crowds moving in slow motion. Their ratings go up with every breaking story," replied French. "There will be a perfect moment to move and our people need to be ready when that moment arrives."

"Patience my old friend, we've come this far together and our long campaign is close to succeeding. If we allow the system to settle, besides the presidency, we'll take the House and the Senate, a half-dozen governorships, and an additional eight state legislatures. Victory is in sight."

A dull gray haze leached across the landscape outside Blaho's window smothering the twinkling lights across the river, "I'm waiting for it to come to fruition but, after all these years, we both know how easily it can be disrupted."

"We'll just have to make sure it goes our way."

"Destiny demands it."

Milly sniffed the fatty scent of frying bacon, as she opened the door to a rush of children stampeding along the hallway and down the stairs to the kitchen for breakfast. Murphy slumped against the door jam, "I always assumed that having children was a decision that doomed formerly liberated people to twenty or thirty years of thankless servitude and I'm fairly sure this confirms my premonition."

"You'd make a lousy parent, you're too wrapped up in yourself." She picked up a deep blue towel and clasped his arm to guide him to the massive boy's bathroom six doors down. "Matty said that you'd find soap in the showers and she left a new razor on the sink. Go get cleaned up and I'll bring a clean shirt before you get out."

"I think we're both going to need some clothes. We didn't really have time to plan our little excursion."

"Actually, I've got a suitcase with my basic necessities and I snuck into your house last month and pilfered shoes, pants, shirts, socks, underwear, and another jacket. Besides, the warehouse downstairs has hundreds of costumes from every period in history. We could dress you up as Henry the Eighth if you like?"

"I'm having trouble enough with my current notoriety." He wavered as he perused the black and white tiled room with sinks down the left wall, urinals and toilet stalls on the right, showers around the corner, and four large baskets filled with rolled up towels in a rainbow of colors. "I think these folks have got this children-rearing thing worked out."

"These are real people who believe in our democracy, each other, and the common good and they're willing to fight for it." Milly squeezed his arm, "Now, go wash the road slime and toxins off your body, so we can go down to breakfast before those kids eat everything in the house. And, by the way, you smell like an old wet dog."

"You don't think we could find a little nip to get the day started, do you?"

The little office manager pinned him against the wall, "You have this one chance to get your shit together and become the man you know you should be…or you can go back to being a disgusting lush and your masters will probably make you the pretend President of the United States, until you're not longer useful. Personally, I think that second choice is a prescription for your personal hell but you have to make that choice right here and right now or I'll have Burt throw you out on the street. Believe me, I'm not kidding."

The president-elect struggled to focus on the anger in Milly's dark eyes but, in that instant, he realized that she was his only salvation, his lifeline out of the depraved facade he cultivated over the past five years. She had always been there at the ready to serve him, to save him from himself, and he never acknowledged his debt to her. An inner tension that sustained the outrageous persona of his radio personality surrendered to her sincerity and the corners of his lips curled as he timidly leaned to kiss her forehead. "I've never been grateful for another human being in my long miserable life but I am very thankful that you are who you are and humbled by the fact that you are foolish enough to care about me."

She released her grip on his shirt, "There are a lot of folks out there who'd like nothing better than to string you up, so do your part and stop making this harder than it has to be."

The slap of the heels of his leather wingtips echoed back and forth from tiles to mirror, floor to ceiling, as Murphy turned into the bathroom and slowly trudged around the corner to the dressing area outside the showers.

Hot water blasted the noxious oils from his skin, the grime from his hair, and softened the knots burrowed into the aching muscles in his neck and shoulders. He lathered up twice and lingered under the splatter, watching the foam slither down his bony legs to circle into the drain before he closed the valves and dried off.

He wrapped a towel around his flabby waist and wandered over to the two taller sinks, standing next to two shorter basins for the younger children, where he found a new razor and a can of shaving cream. A switch on the wall illuminated a lamp above the mirror and he reached for the hot water tap before he looked up, stunned by the ghoulish reflection staring back at him. His skin was pocked and pallid, his eyes gaunt and yellow, his hair thinning and dull, the flesh on his body stretched into bulging swells sagging from a frail skeleton that stooped under the weight. "Yup, you sure look like presidential material to me, bub."

A woman's voice said, "That's not what I see."

He turned to find Billy dressed in yellow sweats standing in the doorway, "Nor I, young lady, nor I."

"Without the spotlights, the giant video screens, and the thundering sound system, you look just like any ol' white honky slob with a big mouth, a giant ego, and a teeny-tiny brain."

"I don't disagree with your attitude, Lord knows I conjured up some truly awful lies to keep the racists tuning in every night."

"Maybe they would have found salvation in truth, if you'd kept your mouth shut."

"I don't know whether you know anything about radio ratings but they are the announcer's meal ticket. They go up, you make money and have security. They go down, you're looking for a new gig.

Five years ago, I started with an audience of about four listeners, when I sat in for a revolting son of a bitch, who was laid up in the hospital and finally died. In the beginning, I had no intention of staying past his convalescence and I thought I was just a down-on-his-luck actor playing a peculiar part in some dystopian Fellini movie that would end when they found a replacement racist."

She interrupted, "You said you had no intention of winning the presidency either but here we are."

"Which exposes the awful truth that I haven't maintained control over any part of my life since I climbed onto this roller coaster."

"What makes you think you can change any of that now? Everyone in the world identifies Mac Murphy with the disgusting bullshit you spouted on your show every night and, even if you were faking it, that's your image, your public persona. You're the face of bigotry and hate and you'll never live that down!"

Before he could say, "But I can try," Milly stepped between them. "It's too early in the day to be debating these issues. How about coffee and breakfast before we start hurling lethal epithets and angry accusations?"

Billy turned on the heel of her white tennis shoe and started for the door, "Fine. I'm going for a run with Alison and we'll finish this when I get back."

Milly shook her head slowly, as she handed him a small pile of clean clothes, "There are millions of people out there who detest everything they think you stand for, just like that young woman. That's a big hurdle to overcome. Are you sure you have the strength and determination to fight for your life as a real human being?"

Mac looked down at her with one cheek shaved and the other covered in suds, the razor in his trembling hand slicing the air, "You said that I have to make a choice and I know I don't have the energy or the stamina to pretend to be that character ever again. I've been rotting from the inside out since I lost my soul to this role and I can't do that anymore."

"Then we'll find your path together."

~

Billy followed a fit and trim Alison down the alley behind the theater, through a thicket of honking cars and cabs, to dart into another dank gauntlet disrupted by brilliant gashes of warm morning sunlight slashing through narrow gaps between towering buildings.

"Is this the scenic route?" laughed the graceful black woman, dodging trash overflowing reeking dumpsters into rancid puddles and the snarl of a scrawny dog defending fetid scraps.

"I usually try to stay out of view, if you know what I mean," replied Alison, adjusting a purple band around her thick black hair. "There are a lot of weird assholes wandering around the city who'd jump either one of us, given half a chance."

Billy brushed the deep bruise on her temple, "I know what you mean."

"I know it's none of my business but why did that jerk pick you to beat on?"

"Because that's Credo, my former pimp before he got busted and drafted into being an enforcer for the Alien Relocation Command. He's a thug who's been deputized to beat up and incarcerate anyone who isn't white and he still thinks he owns a piece of me."

"That explains a lot."

Billy stopped and rested her hands on her knees, panting, "There's more. I'm pregnant by another asshole who beat the shit out of me about three months ago."

Alison rubbed her back, "I'm so very sorry you endured that brutality. There are good people in the world and some of them are even men."

"I know. I'm lucky to have fallen in with your family. They're quite a crew."

"It's...unusual, to say the least, but I wouldn't change anything about any of us." Alison laughed, "Actually, Sally, Marty, and I all took off to chase our dreams when we'd finished school. I ended up being resident groupie for my husband's band for several years on the road but, after we got that youthful quest for adventure and meaning out of our systems, we all came back independently to live with the family."

"I'd say you're lucky to have each other."

"I agree but I should explain that I love my ex-husband with all my heart but he's stuck being a promising eighteen-year-old rock star and his life is an endless string of one-night gigs that are going to lead to the next big opportunity but they don't. That doesn't work when you're trying to raise three precocious kids."

Billy rubbed her belly and glistening tears rolled down her cheeks, "I don't know what to do about this little person growing inside me. The father is a mean arrogant asshole, a political climber who used to be a district attorney but now he's a Security Advisor on Creighton Steil's staff."

She spread her hands to caress the promise in her stomach, "Somehow, I already know I love my child, like we're supposed to be together, like it was meant to be."

"Then, that's how it will be. We'll help you." She took her arm, "C'mon, I'll show you one of my favorite secret gardens."

They trotted to the end of the lane and turned onto the sidewalk along West Houston, hesitating for the traffic light at Sullivan and scampered across six lanes of traffic. Billy ducked around Alison, who asked, "What's wrong?"

"Don't look but there are two black Command Humvees three cars back and I know I'm on their list."

They trotted across the white stripes of the crosswalk and sprinted down the block to escape a blaring siren, flashing red and blue lights, and a metallic voice yelling, "Hey Bitch, stop right there!"

Three enforcers in black uniforms clambered out of the first vehicle and chased the women at a dead run, screaming at bewildered pedestrians to clear their path. Billy tripped on a curb, twisting her ankle and hesitating for an instant.

Alison turned just as one of the commandoes caught up with her and raised his baton to strike. The former groupie interrupted his lethal blow with a solid roundhouse kick to his groin. The baton clattered on the sidewalk as he squealed in agony and tumbled back into his comrades. The brunette yelled "Run!" and twirled to dislodge the gleaming helmet from the shorter thug, revealing terror in the eyes of a pale red-headed teenager. A drop kick to the jaw dissuaded a moaning but determined Credo from reaching to grab her legs, as she dropped the other fierce commando with three quick blows to his sternum.

She grabbed Billy's hand and charged along the pavement, through an open coffee shop into isolated serenity inside a broad open square surrounded by the buildings lining Houston and Bleecker along MacDougal, with gravel pathways snaking between tall trees and open lawns with tables and chairs.

Billy stopped for a moment to marvel at the quiet in the midst of the chaos of a bustling city and the threat of the commandos but Alison shoved her behind a boxwood hedge, as the black Humvees screeched to a stop outside the coffee shop. The glaring glow on the street silhouetted the uniformed figures intimidating the proprietor, who pointed into the garden. "C'mon, we've got to get out of here now!"

The prostitute grabbed her arm, "How'd you do that?"

"A black belt comes in handy when drunks get handsy in roadhouse bars."

They sprinted along a path to the north into an unmarked wooden door, up a long flight of stairs, through a quiet carpeted hallway lined with apartment doors, then down another staircase to crash through a solid metal security exit onto the sidewalk on Bleecker Street. Alison scanned the boulevard and pointed to a tattoo shop across the road, "They'll be coming from both sides, let's hide out there!"

They squirmed through a snarl of tooting cars to duck into the shop, just as the two SUV's barely avoided crashing into each other across the street. A deep voice behind them inquired, "May I help you ladies?"

They turned to greet a gargantuan woman with green hair, brilliantly blue eyes, and swirling tattoos covering every part of her body from the neck down that wasn't draped in a baggy Hawaiian floral tent. Billy stammered, "We just wanted to see a sample of your work."

The woman leaned to peer out the front windows and smiled, "Come with me and I'll show you around."

She walked silently through a small gallery lined with photographs of beautiful tattoos floating on dark walls, softened by a thin cloud of sandalwood incense drifting on mellow rhythms of soft jazz dulling the drone of the city outside. They followed her into a workroom with a giant rainbow scorpion designed into the white tiled-floor between two men inscribing intricate patterns on the flesh of clients lounging in padded dental chairs swaddled in pools of warm light cast by large adjustable work lamps, and finally a hallway of dressing rooms. At the far end, the woman opened a door into a storage locker with an exit into an alley. "I think you'll find what you're looking for out here. Why don't you come back sometime when you're not so rushed for time and I'll show you our best?"

Alison curtsied, "Thank you."

"I don't know why those bastards are after your two ladies but I'm sure you don't deserve whatever nightmares they're handing out today. Too many of my friends and associates have disappeared when those government sanctioned gangsters were barging around the neighborhood. I don't need any better proof than that."

Billy said, "You probably saved our lives."

"Then pass it on to someone else who needs a hand." She pointed to the right, "Go down to Sullivan and there's another alley across the street to the left. There are three more that will get you all the way to LaGuardia. Run through the co-op to make sure you're safe before you head home."

"Thank you," said Billy, turning to follow Alison down the cluttered alley.

~

Kate clutched Jessie's arm, surrounded by Sammy, Eddie, Rex, Benny, Hank Miller and many of the people from the squatter's camp beneath the bridge at Pelican Turn in Dolphin Bay. Their clutch of stragglers bunched together towards the end of a long scraggly column of prisoners being force-marched up to the administration building in a cold gray drizzle by several dozen armed Alien Relocation guards. The parking lot was jammed with white windowless buses parked in close formation.

"Not exactly the revolt we had in mind?" queried Kate, eyeing the guard waving an automatic rifle with a large ammunition clip and deflecting her terror with gallows humor.

Jessie hugged her, "As long as we're together, we'll survive."

"You keep saying that…and then bad shit happens over and over. I'm beginning to think hanging with you might be dangerous."

"At least it's not boring."

"Boring, no. Deadly, maybe."

As they approached the security gate, Jessie noticed detainees being separated into two lines, women and children into a chain link tunnel on the left and men through the other passage. "This doesn't look good, they're splitting up the men and the women."

Kate stretched to see over taller people ahead, "I need to stay with you."

Jessie pulled her closer, as they approached the guards directing inmates into one line or another. A stout sentry waved a baton at Kate and his metallic voice droned, "Women to the left, men to the right."

Kate clung to Jessie's arm, "I'm going with him."

Two other guards stepped forward, presenting batons with squiggly wisps of silver static dancing on the tips, but the first guard raised a hand, palm out. "This is just to complete the paperwork and a cursory medical evaluation. You'll be reunited for the remainder of your journey after your assessment."

Jessie stepped in front of her, "I'd prefer you allow her to accompany me."

"I don't give a damn what you'd prefer!" replied the sentry with a wave of his hand, directing the two guards to apply fifty-thousand volts of electricity to his torso.

Kate screamed as Jessie dropped to his knees and Sammy, Benny, Eddie, Rex, and even Hank Miller jumped to his defense, tackling the guards in a donnybrook of flying fists and swinging clubs until the director fired a single shot into the air from a pistol. The prisoners released the guards and stepped back.

"Insubordination or any attempt at mutiny will result in immediate execution. I have every reason to believe that you are intelligent people who would not sacrifice your own lives or those of your comrades over something as insignificant as this." He pointed to the left with his club, "Madame, please follow these ladies without further violence or I will have your defenders shot!"

Kate made no attempt to hide the fear in her eyes as she leaned to kiss Jessie and moved into the procession of women. "Meet me on the other side."

Jessie reached for her but the two guards swung their batons across his chest and shoved him into the other column. "I'll find you."

After a few steps, Kate lost sight of him as the women shuffled along the gravel path in single file until they entered a large concrete block room through heavy metal doors that creaked as they swayed on their hinges. A troupe of uniformed sentries inspected the identification cards each prisoner wore on a lanyard around their necks and directed each to a line according to the colored classification letter.

Kate stepped before a black uniform with a club in his hand, which he shoved between her breasts to flick her identification tag with the prominent red "P" and his metallic voice said, "Political offender? I'd like to teach you to mind your place, if you know what I mean?"

He stepped closer and whipped the club to strike her behind her knees. She dropped to the ground, her face inches from his crotch and looked up at her reflection in the mirrored visor of his helmet, terrified at the prospect of being at the mercy of these cruel vengeful thugs, who had the power to send her to the farthest reaches of a black hole in the government's new detention program, buried so deep her desperate cries would be lost and forgotten before the ink dried on her conviction notice. The realization stymied her anger but reinforced her determination to survive long enough to change the future.

An old black woman, standing in line, reached down to help Kate to her feet but the bully produced a slender blade to rip open her blouse and bra, exposing her breasts. The tiny woman stepped in front of her, "What's the matter with you people? Didn't your momma teach you how to behave? You should be ashamed of yourself, this is America!"

The thug pointed to a line on the far right, "Go!"

The old woman flashed her badge and latched on to Kate's arm as they moved into the din of chaos under the dull green glow of fluorescent lights, with guards shoving prisoners from one station to the next for identification, mug shots, fingerprints, a blood sample, a cursory check for outstanding warrants or any criminal records, and an interview with a court clerk, who took basic information.

The man looked at her badge, tapped his keyboard, and grunted.

Kate crossed her arms to hold the remnants of her blouse across her chest. "What did you find?"

"A list of charges and sworn testimony to back them up."

"What exactly am I being charged with?" inquired Kate.

"Publishing propaganda against the state, inciting a riot, resisting arrest, assault and battery, the list goes on and on."

"I must qualify as superwoman because I'm a reporter who's been covering a national political movement and a presidential campaign all day every day for the past year."

"I don't know anything about that, I'm just a clerk who fills out forms and files the paperwork for the prisoners who are brought through this facility."

"That's what the Germans said about the victims of the holocaust after the war and no one believed them either."

"I'm sorry but I'm forced to follow procedure and send you on to a holding cell, until you are called up for a preliminary hearing. We're kinda backed up, so it might be a while before anyone comes for you."

"I have a question, do you take pride in what you do? I'm thinking you don't believe half the shit they're accusing people of but you're writing them up and stamping the forms with your official seal. Fuck, how much are they paying you?"

"I don't get paid anything."

"Then why?"

"Because they have my whole family and, if I ever want to see my parents, or my wife, or my two kids again, I'll do as I'm told."

Kate sighed, "You know the revolution's coming. There will be an end to this."

There was a tear in the man's eye, "Much as I love our current president, even the Secret Service can't keep him in office. They're gonna replace him with a hateful monster, who will destroy everything this country stood for and he and his people won't quit until it's all just a sad memory."

The reporter caught herself, "I just have to believe that some brave soul with a good heart and a vibrant spirit is going to change all of this and I believe it's going to happen soon."

"Not soon enough to save you or me," said the clerk, stamping each sheet in her file with a red stamp that read, 'Hold for Trial'. "I just hope we live long enough to see that happen."

A tall uniformed guard pushed her along a dank corridor, fouled by the stench of cells crammed with prisoners, to a desk where a severe looking woman, with close cropped silver hair, a permanent scowl, and a dull gray uniform that was two sizes too small for her stout frame, took her file and leafed through the pages. "Looks like you're a real threat to society, so you'll be staying with us for the next few hours, until a judge has time to review your case. I think you'll enjoy our holiday suite and you'll have forty-six roommates to keep you company."

"I was told that I would be reunited with my people."

The woman chortled as she threw a hard right that caught Kate's cheek and knocked her to floor, "We can't waste time with prisoner's personal desires, it's cheaper for the system if more of you die in transit. Take her to Cell 17!"

The guard unlocked a thick soundproof slab and the chatter of dozens of women fell to silence as she stepped inside, feeling the cold steel of the door close against her back. An aging Hispanic woman approached, reached up with a gentle finger to turn the girl's chin to inspect the bruise on her cheek and the tear in her lip, "Honey, what have they done to you and what happened to your clothes?"

"One of the guards liked my breasts and the militant dyke out in the hall decided to teach me a lesson about power in the penal system."

"Those bastards!" hissed the woman, clacking a wad a gum.

Two younger girls stood up from a cot that was chained to the wall, "Here sit down and let's see if we can scavenge some clothes for you," said the redhead, turning to the other women. "Do any of you have an extra shirt or coat for this poor woman, the mental midgets out there tore up her blouse."

A tattered orange hoodie passed from hand to hand. A tall bleached blond held it out, "Here try this, those guys probably never saw a real pair of tits in their sad demonic lives other than their momma's or some girlie magazine."

Kate put on the sweatshirt and zipped it up, "I'm not going to die at their hands and I'm sure as hell going to fight for my freedom."

"Good luck with that, girlfriend," said a punk rocker with flaming orange hair and a leather jacket. "No one ever gets out of here, except to move on to one of the death camps on the ghost trains."

A voice from the back of the cell added, "I heard they're using old military bases out in the boonies and throwing up thousands of ready-made barracks to house tens of thousands of prisoners."

"Yeah," said another, "there's no release for good behavior. Once they've got you, there's no escape. You're guilty until proven innocent and, in their eyes, everyone is an enemy of the state."

She leaned back against the cold damp wall, "I believe that all of this is going to change very soon but the only way that a revolt can succeed is if we, all of us, are ready to defend everything that used to make this country great, before Murphy's dark victory crushed our hopes and dreams."

"You're chasing a pipe dream, girl."

"That's the kind of positive thinkin' that could've stopped all this before it got started," added a middle-aged woman.

"Well that, and getting all those lazy assholes off their couches to vote when it counted," said a tall brunette. "All of this could have been avoided, if another two or three percent of the voters bothered to show up on election day."

"Yeah, maybe next time they'll get their shit together, although I doubt that any of those losers ever had it together in the first place."

"If there is a next time."

An older woman sat down on the edge of the cot, "I think we can presume that with this sham, if there is any doubt about the outcome of the next election, it will be cancelled."

"No presidential election has ever been cancelled in history, even during the Civil War and the World Wars," said a tiny Puerto Rican girl. "We studied that in American history. That's what makes American democracy the envy of the entire world, the government bows to the will of the people, not the other way around."

An Asian woman added a touch of sarcasm, "It used to, before the ignorant and illiterate elected a total fraud."

"It wouldn't surprise me to find that the folks who run their dodgy club, what is it? The Farce, no, The Forge, always intended to put Steil in office, even though he couldn't win an election for dog catcher in his hometown," said another.

"But a blowhard like Murphy, who spouted fiery fascist fantasies and an endless barrage of outrageous charges against his opponents, was a perfect candidate to block for their stealthy anointed champion," said the thin black woman who helped Kate escape the brutal guard. She had blue-gray hair, sad drooping puppy-dog eyes, and a dignity she wore as a cloak of honor. "Didn't take long to clear him out of the way and pretty much everyone in his inner circle. Steil's people will take over and he'll be insulated from the endless hearings and investigations by grateful Republicans, willing to bow and scrape to save their own skins."

Kate asked, "What's your name?"

"Keisa."

"That's a beautiful name and thank you for helping me earlier but you're absolutely right. Even if they take down The Forge, there are still people behind the scenes paying the bills and pulling the strings. That's never going to change until 'we the people' rise up and demand it like the peasants in the French Revolution."

"You might watch what you say in here," said the red-head, pointing to a black dome in the ceiling. "They've got cameras and I'm guessing microphones too."

Kate sat up and looked up at the black plastic ball, "The one thing I will say to you and everyone else is that I think we all love this country very much and we want to restore everything that made it the envy of the entire world…before the fascists who support Murphy and Steil and their buddies started tearing our society apart twenty years ago." She waved her hand around the room, "I'm sure that we're just a tiny fraction of the people that you've kidnapped but, no matter how many corrupt Enforcers you put on the street, there will always be more of us who will stand up and fight for freedom and democracy."

The lock in the steel door clanked and six armed and armored guards entered, followed by the steely woman jailer, who bellowed, "Gather your things, you're being moved."

"Where are you taking us?" asked Keisa, the old black woman.

She held up a sheaf of papers, "Our monitors have determined that all of you have been corrupted and, as certified enemies of the state, you will never be candidates for rehabilitation. My orders don't include your final destination but you are to be transferred to the Dispersion Center in Georgia for passage west."

"Why have we been chosen?" asked the little Hispanic woman, clacking her gum.

"The monitor notes suggest that you've been programmed to act as a cell in revolt against the government, so you'll be interrogated individually before being convicted and assigned your final destination."

The women closed around Kate, "How is that possible, when no one in here has ever seen any of the rest of us before today?"

"I don't make these decisions but it's my duty to enforce the orders of my superiors precisely and without question or hesitation."

"If you had a brain, you'd realize how absurd this is," said the lanky brunette.

An Enforcer smashed the butt of his rifle across her face and snapped back to attention. Blood spurted from her nose and a gash above her eye, as she collapsed into the arms of several women around her.

"What the hell is the matter with you people," shrieked the Keisa. "have you no honor or decency?"

The warden pointed to three guards on either side, who lit up electric prods that crackled with hissing fingers of static, "Unless you want these gentlemen to prompt you along, close your mouths, get in line, and do as your told!"

The women marched out of the cell in single file until the matron stopped Kate with her baton, "Say your goodbyes, you'll be lucky to make it to dinner, let alone your destination."

"I'm not afraid of you."

"You don't seem to understand that we don't care whether you were rich or famous, if you push it, I get to decide whether your death's quick and clean or slow and painful."

Keisa pushed the baton away and steered Kate down the hallway.

After finger-printing and a cursory strip-down medical exam where the gruff male doctor spent considerable time inspecting Kate's breasts, under the watchful gaze of two leering guards with sizzling batons, they were confined to a sweltering chain-link box with other dangerous women wearing the red 'P' on their tags.

Keisa led Kate to a corner away from the gate where they found a young black woman wearing a heavy cloth coat over a tattered hospital gown and clutching an infant to her breast.

"How old is your baby?" asked the old woman.

"She's not even twenty-four hours old yet, they dragged me out of the maternity ward!"

"What's your name and why did they arrest you?" asked Kate, her hand gently caressing the baby's back.

"I'm Bridget and this little miracle is Tasha." Her eyes brightened as she hugged the tiny bundle. "I made the national news protesting the arrest of my boyfriend when I was nine-months pregnant!"

"They're going to try to take that baby from you," said Keisa calmly. "Stay close to us."

"They'll have to kill me first," stammered the frightened girl.

Kate shook her head, "From what I've seen since our arrest, that's not out of the question."

A murmur spread through the crowd as keys jingled and the gate swung open. Bridget tucked wee Tasha under her coat, as the women trooped past six uniformed troopers in single file to climb onto a white windowless bus that reeked of sweat and urine. Kate noticed men being loaded onto buses from a gate to the east and she could only hope that Jessie and the rest of the prisoners from Dolphin Bay would end up at the same destination.

A convoy of buses eased on to Highway 70 for the short ride to a rail spur in a dense forest just west of the Peace River, where a sleek white train with more than twenty windowless carriages idled in expectation of leaping north, given the slightest nudge of the throttle.

Kate and Keisa, along with several other women clustered around the new mother and the baby as they climbed down into blazing sunlight and marched the few feet to the steps into the train through a short gauntlet of menacing guards in mirrored helmets tapping sparking truncheons against their leather boots. One of the troopers thrust his baton in front of Bridget, intending to inspect the bundle under her coat but frail Keisa stumbled into him and pushed the girl up the steps.

He raised his club but the old black woman looked up at her reflection in his shield, "Oh, I'm so sorry, I'm just a clumsy old woman and I hope you'll forgive me."

The metallic voice crackled, "Get on the train, you're holding up the line."

"Yes, Master, I'm going as fast as these old legs will carry me."

Kate took her arm to help her up the first stair and Keisa winked at her with a tiny grin. The younger woman whispered, "I think you're too brave for your own good!"

"Take notes, your time will come," laughed the spry old spinster.

"I survived most of the attacks on the All People Matter rallies."

Keisa stopped and turned, "You're that reporter who wrote those wonderfully honest articles. I thought I recognized you."

"Just don't spread it around, I like being alive."

Bench seats lined each side of the car, each separated from the next by a plexiglass shield, and every prisoner was wrapped in a mechanical sash that cinched as soon as they sat on the seat. A lone guard stood at the front, pointing to assign the laggards to open spaces, "Take your seats, you'll be belted in by an automatic restraint. You'll refrain from talking to your neighbors and there will be no potty-breaks until we reach our destination."

"How long will that be," whined a tall blond woman with short cropped hair. "Women need to use the restroom more often than gents do."

The mirrored helmet hissed, "You'll know when the train stops."

~

Billy settled onto a tall stool, hidden in the darkness at the back of the stage between staggered flats painted with an interior room of King Lear's castle on one side and a dark forest on the other, and rubbed her belly. She refused to let the doctor predict the sex of her baby, because she wanted to give it a name of its own, not something out of a book or a family tree, and she was absolutely sure that she would know the instant she looked into those eyes. A tiny grin curled the edges of her lips, she had an inkling that it was a boy because it never stopped fluttering around in her womb.

Rugged and weathered Greenwich Village actor, Kevin Haines, summoning the essence of Lear in a black turtleneck, old jeans, a bright red beret, with a voice that reverberated around the theater in rhythm with a drummer tapping out a syncopated beat,

"To thee and thine hereditary ever
Remain this ample third of our fair kingdom,
No less in space, validity, and pleasure,
Than that conferr'd on Goneril. Now, our joy,
Although the last, no least, to whose young love
The vines of France and milk of Burgundy
Strive to be interess'd' what can you say to draw
A third more opulent than your sisters? Speak."

Henny Rhine, a petite brunette with a pale complexion and brilliant blue eyes, playing Cordelia, replied a melodic, *"Nothing, my lord."*

Lear, incredulous, *"Nothing!"*

Cordelia, *"Nothing."*

Lear, *"Nothing will come of nothing, speak again."*

Cordelia, *"Unhappy that I am, I cannot heave*
My heart into my mouth. I love your majesty
According to my bond, nor more nor less."

Haines started to reply with, *"How, how, Cordelia…"* but haughty director Mason James stormed across the stage to interrupt. "You're not projecting the sexual tension! The old man's soliciting love and passion beyond the affection of a daughter for her father and he's desperately disappointed that she's not forthcoming. This is palace political gamesmanship overshadowed by tantalizing and scandalous family secrets and Cordelia's need to defend her independence against her father's predatory bullying."

Burt walked up behind Billy and whispered, "How are you feeling?"

She sighed, "It's busy today, probably too much excitement being chased for blocks by the Black Shirts."

"I'm glad you were with Alison."

"She was amazing! I'm never going to cross that girl ever!"

The old man patted her shoulder, "She is her own woman."

"You should be proud of everyone in your family."

"I am and I'm also fairly certain that you'll make a great mom."

Billy pointed through the gap between the flats to the shadows on the far side of the stage, where Mac Murphy was watching the rehearsal, arms crossed, a curled finger at his lips. "Is he supposed to be wandering around where anyone could recognize him?"

"Actually, Sally took him down to makeup and added a few touches that make him look like he resembles Murphy but not quite," replied Grandpapa. "Besides, I'm pretty sure he hasn't had a drink since Marty poured out the last few drops of his Kentucky whiskey from a bottle he found on the floorboards of Milly's car. He hasn't been spouting campaign nonsense or made any attempt to run, so I loosened the leash a little. Milly needed some rest, so one of us is watching all the time."

"Not that I approve of anything about the guy, but once you get past the bluster, he's far more aware of his place in all of this than I gave him credit for."

"I'm guessing it might be the first time in years that he's been sober. Doc Turner told me he found liver damage and a cocktail of pharmaceuticals in his system and warned that he'll probably go through withdrawals and hallucinations, as it all starts washing out of his system. He got away from Milly after things settled down last night and I found him sniffing around the smoker in the alley, completely lost and delirious and wondering when his Secret Service detail was going to pick him up."

"We had a pretty good argument earlier but I realized that it's gotta be a weird trip, falling from being king of the world to hiding out in an old theater because it would be more convenient for your political allies if you turned up dead."

"I doubt that Shakespeare could have said it better," laughed Burt, as the director marched off the stage.

Billy whispered, "I never got to read much Shakespeare. What's going on."

"Shakespeare's a long discussion because he was probably the first author to refine the way a story is told, down to its most essential elements, and most of his plays were based on loosely fictionalized real-life personalities and events that were making history in the late 1500's."

"So, what's Lear want from his daughters?"

"He's facing his own mortality and he's decided to divide up his kingdom among his three girls but the one who convinces him that she loves him the most, will get the biggest slice of the pie."

"That sounds like incest or something."

"You're right, sex is the underlying motivation in these discussions, especially with Cordelia, because she has yet to marry, in spite of 'the vines of France and milk of Burgundy', two rich and noble suitors trying to win her fancy. She refuses to acknowledge that she could feel any love other than what she's always felt for her father and her king."

"And he's not satisfied with her honesty?"

"Of course not, this is the opening scene of the first act. It can't end here!" laughed Burt, watching Murphy react to the actors. "I did some research on our house guest and one curiosity was that he was a lead actor in the drama department at the University of Georgia, while he was earning his M.F.A."

Billy squeezed Burt's arm, "That explains his ability to rile up a crowd."

The old man wrapped an arm around her shoulders, "I hate to interrupt your education but Doc Turner took Murphy's vitals a little while ago and wants to check your blood pressure."

She patted her tummy and stood up, "Whatever's best for this little critter."

~

The rehearsal continued through the afternoon with different groups of actors working through various scenes against bits of musical accompaniment. Murphy remained steadfast in the shadows and during a break, Kevin Haines wandered over to inquire, "I'm sorry to bother you but I couldn't help noticing that you've been standing here completely glued into what we've been doing. You seem very familiar, are you an actor?"

Not quite confident in Sally's disguise, the president avoided Haines inquiring eyes, "No, I haven't acted since I was in college, a long time ago, but one of the last parts I got to play was Lear and I must admit, I enjoyed playing the crazed and terrified king."

"Do you remember any lines?"

Murphy blushed and coughed to clear his throat, before his practiced baritone cried,

"Howl, howl, howl, howl! O, you are men of stones
Had I your tongues and eyes, I'd use them so
That heaven's vault should crack. She's gone for ever!
I know when one is dead, and when one lives,
She's dead as earth. Lend me a looking-glass,
If her breath will mist or stain the stone,
Why, then she lives."

Mason James walked across the stage, applauding, "That was brilliant!"

Mac grinned, "It's been a very long time."

"You've still got it, old man. I wonder whether I might ask you to do that bit again, out here at the front of the stage, where all my actors can see how it should be done."

"I wouldn't want to interrupt your rehearsal."

"I think you'd give us motivation," said Haines. "We need your energy."

"Alright, shall I start there?"

"Yes, and I'll be Kent, Kevin can be Edgar, and we'll grab Harold to be Albany," said James. "Just start us off and we'll follow along."

Murphy walked to the front of the stage, flashing on enormous crowds chanting through his raucous rallies, pumping the edgy rage burbling just under the surface, ready to erupt into mayhem, empowered or restrained by his tone and cadence. The adulation was addictive but maintaining that mania required pushing the narrative farther and farther into the paranoid propaganda of the racists and nationalists, twisting rumors and suspicions into front page news every time he made a public comment. The exhilaration was an opiate for his ego but the alcohol and prescriptions could not mend his mental and physical exhaustion.

Haines walked up behind him, *"Howl, Howl..."*

The president raised his arms, as if holding his dead daughter and joined in. His mind cleared and his voice rose from a desperate whisper to soar through the auditorium, with the anguish and horror of a broken king.

The lines came easily and the other actors fell into character, as they worked through the final scene and he was well into his final speech before Lear dies, when the doors at the back of the theater burst open and six Special Unit Enforcers marched down the aisles with weapons at the ready.

Murphy remained in character, finished his lines, and tumbled over, dead on the stage, but Mason marched to the front and demanded, "How dare you interrupt my rehearsal. What could you possibly want?"

"We're looking for a woman named Billy Holiday," said the metallic voice from behind the mirrored faceplate of the helmet of the Second Lieutenant, with the single silver bar on the shoulders of his tight black leather uniform.

"I have no idea who you're inquiring about, everyone here is involved with this play and none of them is named 'Billy'."

"We have reason to believe that she was in this theater this morning," snapped the Black Shirt.

"How do you know that?" asked Mason.

"That's classified information."

"What's she look like?"

"She's tall, black, and she used to be gorgeous."

"How would you know that, Sire?" asked Harold Hamm, projecting Albany's bearing and demeanor.

"It's in her file."

Haines jumped in, "Well, there won't be any black actors in this company until we do Othello in the park next spring and I'd invite you to the premier but I'm fairly certain you have no concept of theater, let alone Shakespeare, so perhaps you could clear out so we can get back to work. Our first performance is Thursday, so we're kind of under the gun, if you'll excuse the pun."

"I hope you're a dramatic actor because you suck as a comedian," replied that leader's mechanical voice, as the posse turned to march up the aisle and out through the swinging doors into the lobby.

Haines walked over and stood over Murphy's limp body, "You can get up now, they're gone."

The president sat up and then stood, reaching to shake his hand, "Thank you for letting me sit in, I certainly enjoyed it."

The actor held his hand a moment too long, "It was an honor to work with you, sir."

The president-elect bowed slightly and wandered off through the shadows and up the stairs to the apartment, where he found Burt seated in his favorite chair reading the Times. "We just got raided by a squad from the Special Unit."

"What'd they want?"

"Billy."

"From what she told me, there's only one bastard who would track her here and he was sentenced to jail for the next five years before he signed on with Black Shirts."

Murphy shook his head, "I hate to admit that I didn't know the force really existed until yesterday."

"From what I hear, you sure preached about the need for it on your show for years."

"Guilty as charged, just one of too many reasons I have to ditch that character before he succeeds in consuming my soul." Perspiration dripped from his forehead, his eyes twitched, and a spot of drool dribbled from the corner of his mouth. "Tell me, how's Billy?"

"Your whole campaign was built on white-supremacist nationalistic nonsense, I'm surprised you even acknowledge a pregnant black girl from the wrong side of the tracks," replied Burt, rustling the newspaper. "Incidentally, there isn't one story about our missing president in the front section of today's paper. They buried two paragraphs about the stalled investigation on the back page of the City Section next to an obit about a disgraced former councilman."

"That's it?"

"Yup. I think you qualify as out of sight, out of mind."

"I'm humbled by my former position on the front page plunging to relative obscurity in a matter of hours." Murphy stared at the floor, for a moment, shaking his head, then looked up, "So, how's Billy?"

"Why do you care?"

"Damn it, because she was direct and honest when we argued this morning." He paused, "I was a debate champion at Georgia, an actor, a radio host, and a fake politician and I don't lose arguments, so I found her complete lack of restraint in expressing her thoughts and feelings audacious and annoying at first, then challenging, and finally intriguing, because they weren't developed by some conservative think tank or lifted from the pages of some ridiculous tabloid.

No, she spoke from her heart and the brutality of her reality, which made me realize that our acceptance of racism as a social norm is the original sin of our society. The white race gains nothing by oppressing minorities and depriving them of hope and opportunity. Every high school or college graduate has the potential to change our world, every dropout costs us money."

Burt stared for a long moment, "Which Mac Murphy am I speaking with?"

Murphy straightened up, "The one that's trying to understand how I became the asshole that all those lunatics love…and whether there's some way I can rectify at least a smidgeon of the damage that I've done before an assassin shoots me or I'm hauled off to jail."

"That could be a long struggle."

"Maybe my realization about Billy is the first step."

"I guess we'll see," replied Burt.

Chapter Eight

Marty Sutton, Burt and Matty's eldest, a combat vet and facilities manager for the theater - could fix just about anything. His abilities as a rigger, climber, and trapeze artist who grew up clambering around the inaccessible reaches of this old building, qualified him as an advance scout when he joined the Marines. He still suffered flashbacks from his service in Iraq, doing deep reconnaissance across the border into Syria and Iran from 2002 through 2006 when the superiors started shipping in the amateurs. He was forced out after barely avoiding a dishonorable discharge for slugging a Second Lieutenant who had a college degree and no instinct for survival or the slightest commitment to protecting his men.

Marty directed Ned's ebony and chrome pimp-van with the silver bow tie glittering in the lights of city traffic around the toe of Manhattan and down a ramp to a steel gate at the entrance to a pair of barricaded tunnels. "Flash your lights twice, then turn them off."

Ned clicked the lever and doused the headlights.

A wandering flashlight appeared in the darkness and a hooded figure unlocked and waited while the heavy gate rolled out of the way so the truck could enter, then closed and secured the grate.

Rusty raised his head to peek through the windshield, "Where are we going?"

Marty turned, "This is where we stash all the people we've been rescuing."

"How come I've never been here?"

"Because you had no need to know," replied his father. "Now you do."

Ned followed the sweeping light of their guide into the tunnel on the right and parked at the bottom of a stairway.

Nellis grabbed Rusty's heavy knapsack from the back of the truck but the boy took it from him, "Lemme carry it, so I know it's safe."

The troubadour raised his hands, "It's your gear, I'm just a roadie until we get inside."

The hooded phantom led them up the darkened staircase, the flashlight sweeping back and forth across each step, until they reached a landing and pushed through swinging doors into a dimly lit hallway. Their footsteps echoed around the unfinished arched corridor with blank alcoves for advertising along the walls, as they followed the hobbit to a bright crosswalk and the faint sound of people moving and talking in the distance.

The guide flipped back her cowl to reveal a pretty face with a mane of wavy strawberry blond hair and started to say, "I'm…"

But Nellis wrapped her in a bear hug, "You're Amy Martin from Atlanta! How did you escape?"

She hugged him back, "I was out running errands when the Enforcers raided our offices and took Althea. One of the secretaries warned me and some friends hooked me up with the modern version of the Civil War's underground railroad. Two days later, I was here. How about you?"

"Some young friends rescued us on horseback and, like you, we were whisked across the country in the dead of night," replied Nellis. "I'm sorry about Althea and all the other people who got picked up. That's why we're here, we're working on a plan to get them back."

She turned to Tate, "I've seen that face before."

"Tate Sloan…and, yes, I'm supposed to be dead. This is our savior, Ned Perkins, and this young man holds the key to unlocking the secrets of the prison trains that are transporting our friends to oblivion."

"I'm pleased to meet each of you. I was instructed to take you to Oz, so, if you'll follow me?" She turned into the cross-tunnel and stopped before a sky-blue elevator and pressed the glowing button. The doors slid open and they all piled in, rising two stories to a balcony overlooking crowds moving about the platforms and tunnels below.

Rusty walked up to the bannister and peered down, "Who are all these people?"

His father wrapped an arm around his shoulders, "These are the people who were rescued before the Black Shirts could nab them."

"There must be thousands…"

"Somewhere around forty-five hundred, I'm told," said Amy. She pointed to a pair of frosted glass doors on a balcony on the other side of the atrium. "That's Oz."

"Why do you call it Oz?"

"Because that's where we keep our wizards and they're anxious to meet you."

Rusty looked up at his father and then Nellis, who said, "You can do this son, I know it and you know it. So, don't doubt yourself, just do your best."

The boy nodded, took a deep breath, and followed Amy around the gallery to the frosted glass slabs that shrouded the wizards' lair where programmers toiled on a level he could only envy. His father reached for the handle to pull the door open, "This is what you've been working towards since the first time you sat down in front of a monitor. These folks might know things that you haven't mastered yet but you've managed to hack into a vital transportation system and that knowledge might save thousands of innocent people from disappearing forever. Don't hesitate, share your talents and know how very proud I am of you."

Rusty leaned against his father for a moment before stepping across the threshold into a warm, hushed technological womb with multiple monitors glowing on two-dozen workstations arranged in clusters like the leaves of a four-leaf clover amid towering black granite columns. Red power lights on endless rows of servers marched into infinite darkness behind a wall of glass at the back of the huge room.

A petite woman in a black pants suit, with gleaming blue eyes, a soft pale complexion, and a mane of gray waves gathered into a loose bun, scurried across the black floor to greet the new arrivals. She reached a hand to Rusty, "I'm Madeline and I'm so very pleased to meet you. I understand you have a special talent."

The boy blushed, "I just figured some stuff out and I hope it's helpful."

"Oh, I think we're in desperate need of your expertise to find a way to rescue our missing friends. I see that you've brought your computer, you can set up at this station right next to mine but I'd like to scan your system for security before we log you into our circuits, if that's alright?"

"Sure, I ran an antivirus program earlier but I'm sure yours is more thorough."

Marty hugged his son, "You don't need us hanging around and we've got other things to attend to but Nellis is going to coordinate your information with our troops. Buzz me when you want to be picked up…and don't forget to eat, you get cranky when your blood sugar drops."

"Okay," replied Rusty, following Madeline to a broad desk with four displays. He pulled his laptop from the case and the screen glowed electric blue as he opened it.

His hostess inserted a drive and keyed in a password. "Nice machine, bet she screams."

"Twelve-core processor, tons of memory."

She pointed to a red band moving across the screen, "This shouldn't take long."

Two young programmers got up from their desks and walked over, just as the machine beeped.

"You're clean," said the taller of the two, who might have just started college. "I'm Evan and this is Carl. We heard you were coming over to help out."

Rusty shook their hands, "I hope so. I hacked into the rail system to hijack their software to run my HO trains and figured out that their software sucks. It looks like one of our grandfathers wrote the code on an ancient Commodore 64 computer and there is no security. Any fool could take over the whole system if they had half-a-clue, so I rewrote it."

"You did what?"

"I made it work better but they don't know it…yet."

"Show us," said Madeline.

Rusty opened his program and zoomed in on the trains converging on the Macon railyard. He toggled a couple of switches and the identity badges appeared over each train. He pointed, "See the white trains lining up over here near this giant warehouse, they're the prisoner trains and they're really easy to spot."

170

"I'll say," said Evan. "The only way they'd stand out more was if they used phosphorescent paint! They literally glow in the dark."

"You've been watching this, what's happening?"

"I think these trains are bringing in prisoners from collection sites in the surrounding states. After watching them last night and today, I'm guessing this processing center sends the illegal immigrants south to the border in Texas and the other people on these trains over here on the other side of the building. They haven't been moving that much until today, so I don't know where that final destination is, other than out west someplace."

Nellis inquired, "Do you have a secure phone line?"

"Yeah but you have to be careful about picking up a trace from the other end," said Carl.

"I believe the good Lord himself is going to be guarding this call."

Madeline produced a phone, tapped in a twelve-digit code and handed the receiver to Nellis, who dialed into the Pope's switchboard. "Hello, Sister. This is Nellis Gray and Sister Gwen in Cameron told me that you might be willing to help me make a secure call."

There was a pause while he listened, "918-596-9378."

"Hi, Maybelle, it's Nellis. Could I speak to Bruce?"

"Yes, it's good to hear your voice too. Yes, we're safe for the moment. Thank you."

A minute passed, "Bruce? Nellis, listen we're set up here and we're looking at Macon. Is Brad in position?"

He paused, listening.

"Cool, looks like we've got one of these white snakes loading up to head north."

~

The prisoners were unattended in the darkened cabin, cinched into plastic seats and unable to move or stretch, as the sleek white train lumbered north along aging tracks through central Florida. Kate could see Bridget nursing tiny Tasha under her coat in the seat next to Keisa across the aisle towards the rear of the car. They yelled at each other around the frosted plexiglass partitions separating each detainee for the first hour or two until one-by-one, all of the women withdrew into silent contemplation of the horrors ahead.

After the humiliation and degradation suffered during their interrogation, demeaning medical examinations, and 're-classification' in the cruel gauntlet of the first processing center at the camp outside Arcadia, they shared the realization that their former freedoms had been erased, absorbed into a brutal bureaucracy, a sinister system within a trusted American institution dedicated to removing the threat of those who dared stand up for democracy. That terror proved a pungent elixir that deterred any hope of mutiny and fed a sobering despondency that shrouded fading dreams of normal life.

Each time they slowed to pass through populated areas, Kate had to stifle any hope of satiating her urgent need for a bathroom. From the odors wafting through the fourteenth-carriage, there was little doubt that every other woman was enduring the same torture.

After nine grueling hours, the phantom train slowed to a full stop. Sliding doors hissed open with a welcome blast of fresh air and the guard with the static lisp stepped inside, "We have arrived at our destination. You'll be released from your restraints to proceed through the exits fore and aft in single file. Follow directions and do not speak or you will suffer the consequences."

He turned to press a release and the moment the latches clicked, a heavyset woman in the front seat jumped up and pinned the startled trooper against the wall with her full weight, lifting her long, soiled dress to urinate on his black boots. She pressed her nose against his mirrored face-shield, "What kind of disgusting animals are you?"

Before he could raise his club, several other women surrounded her and shuffled off the train onto a long, crowded platform where endless lines of prisoners entered a row of open doors. Kate stood on tip-toe to scan the people filing off the train but could not spot any familiar faces.

She held hands with Keisa and Bridget as they entered an enormous room filled with the murmurs of fear and anxiety buzzing through thousands of female detainees. She guessed that the men were suffering a similar experience in the north half of the huge facility.

A battalion of uniformed guards funneled the captives through a gauntlet of administrators identifying and classifying each prisoner. The two older women crowded in front of Bridget as successive clerks glanced at the red 'P' as they scanned the tags that each of them wore, stamped their papers, and motioned them into the next queue through another set of stations that segregated them into holding pens awaiting transportation to their ultimate destinations.

Latin and Hispanic captives were crowded through a broad doorway into another room, while the political prisoners were grouped according to their potential threat. Activist housewives and young protestors were separated from those who organized and promoted rallies and marches or led national movements. Kate wondered if she would be reunited with Jesse and the rest of her comrades. The hope made her shudder because she had to assume that those with the highest profiles were destined for execution or banishment to die slowly in the worst of the concentration camps. Their incarceration in the derelict jail in Naples before the first rally in Dolphin Bay the previous year was terrifying, this misadventure would probably prove fatal.

After nearly twelve hours packed into their chain-link coop without food or water and taking turns using a floor drain as a toilet, a dozen guards with fizzing batons wrangled them down a long corridor and out onto a platform where another long white windowless train, impatiently awaiting its human cargo, hissed like a serpent preparing to strike out into the night.

~

The train crept out of a sleeping Macon well after midnight and began to pick up speed as it passed Arkright heading north into dense pine forest paralleling the Ocmulgee River. The tracks curved right then left into a long dark channel carved through the timbers but the signal lights flashed red and the train came to an abrupt stop.

Chief Engineer Eddy Deacan picked up a microphone, "Delta thirty-seven to ComCentral, come in."

Static rattled the speaker. "Delta thirty-seven to ComCentral, come in please."

Again nothing.

Scotty Ditkins, his second in command, said, "We can't sit here all night. Other trains will be coming up behind us as soon as they're loaded."

"Well, we both know we sit until we're told to move. That's the rule, so we'll just have to enjoy the full moon peeking through the trees while we wait."

Curved windows around the nose the engine provided a panorama of the thick forest of tall slender pines fading into nightfall. A flickering light appeared rounding the curve far down the tracks, a tiny orange blob screaming out of twilight. A few moments more and the apparition sped closer, close enough to distinguish massive flames flaring up into the darkness, a glowing cloud illuminating the trunks of individual trees guarding each side of the tracks like stoic sentries as it roared towards the stalled train.

"If we don't back up, that thing is going to ram us and this plastic turd will go up in flames!" shouted Ditkins. "I hate hauling people to these camps and I sure as hell am not willing to die tryin'!"

"I agree," said Deacan, heaving the lever into reverse to begin propelling fifty cars back down the tracks but the lights in the cabin flickered and the fly-by-wire system failed to respond. Beads of sweat appeared on the engineer's forehead, as he looked up at the approaching inferno and grabbed the microphone. "Abandon the train immediately! Guards, release the prisoners and everyone run for your lives! This is not a drill! I repeat, this is not a drill! Get out now!"

The ultra-secure hatches slid open along either side of the silver serpent, releasing hundreds of frantic prisoners who leapt into the night followed by untrained troopers, who charged away from the tracks and into the trees, anticipating an enormous crash but the billowing firestorm screeched to a halt, barely singeing the sleek snout.

Through panicked screams and shouts, bagpipes wheezed against a steady drumbeat as a dozen pipers, in kilts and sashes, led a small army of Scottish warriors flaunting family tartans, brandishing shields and golden Celtic broad swords and belting a war cry that would curdle the blood of any veteran. They marched past the dumbfounded engineers to the open door of the first car, which was reserved for high-security prisoners, and Brad scrambled inside while the Gaelic invaders moved down the endless chain of cars.

The guards fled, when the engineer posted the warning, leaving more than fifty frantic women chained to their seats. Kate yelled, "Brad!"

He rushed to her, "I can't believe we found you! Are you alright?"

"No, get me out of this chair! Push the button on the panel up there!"

Brad leapt to the front of the car and released the restraints.

The women cheered and Kate jumped up to hug him, then leaned back to inspect his kilt, "We can never thank you enough but I should have guessed you Spratlins were of Scottish heritage."

"It's a long story that started with my brother and his buddies leading a brigade dressed up as clowns to rescue the kids when they were kidnapped. We figured we could hijack the train without a shot, if the amateur troopers were totally freaked out by our attack, so we loaded up a flat car with straw bales and set them ablaze, the rest was just showmanship."

Kate grinned, "Come to think of it, I don't think I saw any of the guards carrying a gun. They all had batons that work like cattle prods."

"Good for them because we have snipers in the trees surrounding the train and I'm fairly sure they picked up the troopers as they fled because I haven't heard a shot.

Another clansman in a red and black tartan kilt pushed through the women, "We just released the next two cars full of men. The rest of the train is abandoned."

"Start rounding up the freed prisoners and get them back on board."

The Scottish warrior saluted with a broad smile, "Aye, Sir!"

Jessie appeared in the doorway and Kate rushed into his arms, "I was so worried."

He hugged her and offered his hand to Brad, "We're all glad to see you and your guys, even if you are dressed in your little plaid skirts."

"At least we showed some style."

"Stopping the train is all well and good but what do you plan to do with all these prisoners now?"

"Actually, with some help from a young friend of Nellis's, we're going to use the train to evacuate everyone who wants to go," replied Brad. "We even have a qualified engineer in our squad who can drive her if the engineers don't want to cooperate."

"Yeah, but where are you sending the train?" asked Kate.

"I'm told there's a plan but I haven't been told what it is yet. Security and all that."

"If this is one of Nellis's crazy schemes, I might want to know a bit more before I sign on," said Kate.

Jessie laughed, "Ah, c'mon, you're never turned down an opportunity to face a horrifying death in all the nightmares I've put you through. You can't bail out now!"

She looked up at Brad's bearskin hat, "Every time this guy tries to take me on a date, we end up in some God-forsaken hell hole with little or no hope of escape or survival."

The artist hugged her, "But we're still together."

She punched him in the arm, "No thanks to you, buster!"

"I assume these operations are going on with other ghost trains?"

"We've got squads speeding to intercept every white train in the country. We should have most or all of them before sunrise."

"Who's the brains behind the technical part of this scheme?" asked Jessie.

"I'm told he's a fourteen-year old computer genius."

"Where did Nellis find him?"

"I have no earthly idea."

Tabitha sat alone in her salon, sipping a snifter of ancient Port and staring at Jessie's raging ocean storm framed above her mantle when the phone on the end-table rang. She picked up the receiver, "Hello."

"Tabitha, it's Mavis. I've got some news."

"It's always lovely to hear that pep in your voice, which makes me suspect that you have some positive little tidbit to foist me past my frustration and depression," replied the aging editor.

"What do you have to be frustrated about? You've inspired literally millions of our protestors to peacefully jam up just about every city in the country, demanding a recount and an investigation. They wouldn't be out there without your leadership and coordination."

"That's true dear but Bobby Warmington deserves most of the credit for coordinating everything. I'm getting on in years and I find that I am most impatient about those things that could slip away if I don't pursue them to fruition before I die."

"Well, you're not dying tonight because we have a date to hear Spratlin speak at the Lincoln Memorial tomorrow night and we need the biggest crowd that's ever assembled in the Capital."

"And what's he going to say?"

"I haven't been told but with Nellis and Katherine behind it, I'm not going ask questions."

"Nor should you dear. Did they give you anything else?"

"Bruce quoted Nellis as saying, 'We're going to put things right.'"

"Knowing Mr. Gray as we do, we should probably be terrified…but hopeful."

"You make sure the troops are heading for D.C. and I'll call Bobbie. I'll have a plane waiting at the airport at noon, you both need to be there."

~

Ernest Cummings, Creighton Steil's very personal secretary handed him a sheaf of documents with a kiss to his cheek. He turned to answer a knock at the door of the Dillon Drawing Room in Blaire House, across from the White House, where presidents lodge their most important guests.

The vice-president elect was seated in a comfortable armchair, sipping thick black coffee spiked with just a few drops of Cognac to spice the evening. He was entranced by the illusion of birds fluttering through the branches painted on the antique aqua Chinese wallpaper in the dancing firelight warming the cold gray chill of Washington leaching through the heavy curtains drawn across tall broad windows.

Craig Hobson, Steil's Security Affairs Advisor, marched into the room with the arrogant stride of a corrupt legal predator puffed up with his potential status.

Steil looked up, "To what do we owe this honor at this hour?"

"Sir, Representative Spratlin has reserved the Lincoln Memorial and lined up the press for a major speech tomorrow night."

"Do we have any idea of what he intends to say?" asked Cummings.

"No, even our spies within his campaign have no idea."

"Perhaps he's finally ready to concede the election," suggested Steil.

"That might be wishful thinking."

"Has the Secret Service made any progress on finding Murphy?" asked Cummings.

"As far as I know, no. They really don't seem to have a clue," replied Hobson. "To be quite honest, I'm not sure that anyone wants him back."

"You've never been 'quite honest' in all the years I've known you but no news is good news," mused the vice-president elect. "We need to have our people there to handle the media."

"I can promise that security will be tight because the Service guys are still protecting Spratlin but we'll have plenty of our people in the crowd to control the situation."

"I want to know everything you know before you know it. Do we have an understanding here?"

"Yes, Sir!"

"Thank you for informing us," said Cummings. "You can contact me at any hour of the day or night."

"You can count on it," said the security advisor. "I'll see myself out."

"Thanks for coming by," said Steil, watching the door close behind Hobson as he left. "This could be trouble!"

"Don't worry, I'll put out some feelers, so we'll know what to expect."

"The fact that he's using old Abe as a backdrop makes me suspect that he's planning to make some grand announcement. It's pure theater."

"I'll go make some calls and inform our sponsors, while you approve the corrections Ted Johnson made to tomorrow's speech," said the secretary, caressing his shoulder as he turned to leave. "You should get some rest, so you're fresh in the morning."

The vice-president elect lifted his spiked coffee cup in a toast, "Nothing the makeup people can't fix."

Chapter Nine
Election +3

Marty leaned over Rusty's slumping shoulder, "Have you had anything to eat since all this started?"

"Yeah, someone brought some donuts by earlier," replied the boy without glancing away, his tired eyes tracing every detail on the four screens lined up across his work station.

"That doesn't help your hypoglycemia."

"Yeah, I guess."

"Well, they're bringing sandwiches and stuff up from the cafeteria in a few minutes, so let's make sure you get some nourishment in you," said his father. "I've been watching the intercepts on the big screens and it looks like you brought every train to a halt at exactly the right spot."

"The rescue squads have intercepted fourteen so far, from Alabama to Chicago and all across the eastern half of the country, and they'll get a few more before morning. They're attacking trains farther west but we don't have time to turn them around."

"Can you get the rest through to DC by tonight?"

"Yeah, I've got the other guys programming the system to clear out the tracks so the ghost trains have smooth sailing to arrive in plenty of time to transport the passengers to the rally. There are a bunch of other trains loaded with protestors from other cities that will unload at various stations around the Washington."

"Aren't the Railroad authorities going to try to stop dozens of renegade trains?"

"Well, all the other trains are going to run on time or a little ahead of schedule and our trains are going to slip into the open tracks, hopefully without interfering with anyone else. Oh, and they aren't supposed to move during daylight hours, so we're altering their identity badges and destinations so it looks like they're idling on sidings, when they're really moving. The computers won't flag them as missing until they all start converging on the capital."

One of the techs rolled a small food trolley up to Rusty's station. Marty handed his son a turkey sandwich, a drink, and a banana, "Here's some food. Eat."

The boy devoured half the sandwich without taking his eyes off the screen or missing a keystroke.

"Can't they just shut you down?"

Rusty looked up at his father with bloodshot eyes, "We've taken over the system. They just don't know it yet."

"You're amazing!" said Marty with a kiss to his forehead. "Did you know that your peers have nicknamed you 'The Wizard'?"

The boy blushed, "No, they haven't."

"Yes, they have and they're using it as their callsign."

He looked around at the other techs, all staring into screens as prancing fingers scurried across keyboards, working furiously to move and position the captive trains without raising suspicion at the Federal Railroad Administration.

"What about trains to transport the folks downstairs?"

"Should start arriving at eleven twenty-four."

"They're clearing the dormitories out of the tunnels now and Nellis's bringing Katherine over to give them a pep talk before we head out."

"What about Murphy? Is he going too?"

"I honestly don't know."

The boy turned to look up at his father, "Why would anyone with any brains vote for that guy?"

Marty shook his head, "First, from what I've heard, it was all a show and he was playing the part of the racist pied-piper leading the ignorant and the gullible to support his nonsense. People will always unite when they have something in common to hate."

"Does he really believe any of the stuff he talked about?"

"I don't think he really does but he's so strung out from being on drugs and alcohol for years that he's having a hard time figuring out which personality he really is."

"That's nuts," said the boy, turning back to his keyboard. "At least machines don't turn evil on their own."

~

Nellis climbed the stairs from a harried kitchen nourishing waves of noisy children heading off to school. He stopped midway down the broad hallway to knock on Murphy's door. Milly Clark peeked through the crack, "Nellis, come in."

He stepped inside to find Murphy pacing the room back and forth, back and forth. "What do you want?"

"I'd like to talk to both of you about something important."

"What's that?" snapped the president-elect.

"Now, Mac, be polite."

He stopped moving to stare down at her, "Every molecule in my body is primed for violent mutiny and my brain is screaming for a fix but you people don't seem to understand."

"We understand," said Milly softly, "and so do you. Which Mac are you going to be?"

"I can't give you a fix but I might be able to offer you something better," said Nellis, leaning against a battered chest of drawers with a sly grin.

"What's that?"

"How about revenge?"

His eyes widened and his jaw dropped open.

"Do you want to end this, once and for all?"

Murphy paused, trying to absorb the question. Spastic flashes of static charges recoiled through his brain, a wash of sheet lightning splattering brainwaves into crashing surf exploding in a tidal storm, "Yes, yes, I do."

"Fine. We're having a little shindig at the Lincoln Memorial tonight. Stanton's going to give a speech. I think you should too."

Mac reached a hand to steady himself. "You want me...to speak?"

"Yup. I think it would be good for you to set things straight with your people and explain the conspiracy to the rest of the country too. It'll be broadcast on every station."

Milly wrapped an arm around his waist, "What do you think?"

"I think they'll have snipers in the crowd to take me out! But...damn it, I'd rather go out in a spectacle of blood and guts than hiding out for the rest of my life…pretending I'm not the character I pretended to be."

"That's the spirit. Do you want some help with your speech? Katherine's a pro and we won't be leaving for a couple of hours."

"I already know what I need to say…hell, I've known for years," replied Murphy. "But there is one thing that I will need, if I'm going to be marched out for execution."

"What's that?"

"I want Milly and Billy at my side the whole time…and all these damned kids too!"

Milly squeezed his arm, "Do you want me to ask Billy?"

"How 'bout if you ask her if I could have a moment of her time?"

"I can do that," said the little woman offering a small supportive smile as she turned to leave.

Struggling to grasp the veracity of this scheme in his molting reality, the president-elect stared at Nellis, "Think you can get us there and then out again without someone trying to shoot holes in my sorry ass?"

"I'll be disappointed if there aren't at least a hundred-thousand people in the crowd and most of them are going to be pissed off at you…but I'm sure you and Stanton can win them over. If you do it right, maybe there's hope for the nation…if you fuck up, there'll be a riot and we'll all get shipped off to concentration camps…if we survive."

"Yeah but the feds, the guys who are supposed to protect me, are going to be armed and they probably work for The Forge, so there's no assurance that they won't try to take me out!" He flopped down on the bed, "I need a drink!"

"No, you need to decide whether you want to be that asshole on the radio or you want to help mend the wounds you caused. I know the real Murphy who keeps peeking out from behind your phony bravado can make a difference but it's your call."

Before Mac could answer, Milly opened the door to allow Billy to enter. "You wanted to see me?"

Nellis winked at Murphy and followed Milly into the hallway.

Mac hesitated, "Actually, I have a confession and a request. Would you like to have a seat? Coffee?"

"I'm not sure I'm staying that long. What do you want?"

Mac cleared his throat and stared into her beautiful dark eyes for a long moment, "I guess I should start by apologizing to you and all the immigrants and people of color across this nation for my crass campaign that played to the ignorance and bigotry of a sad, forgotten, and unappreciated class of our citizens. Ginning up their hate and channeling their energy paid big bucks and I have to admit that I played them for all they were worth."

"That's still despicable."

"I agree," replied Murphy, gazing out the window. "The point is that I'm just beginning to realize that the character that I played is not the person I am." He turned back to her, "I'm being given an opportunity to begin to make things right for the country and take the first steps on my journey towards earning some tiny shred of redemption."

"How's that and what's it got to do with me?" asked the lanky black beauty, crossing her slender arms across her chest, her jaw tight, her eyes hard and focused.

He shook his head slowly, "Stanton Spratlin and I are going to make a joint appearance tonight at the Lincoln Memorial to talk directly to the American people about what happened and how each of us would like to fix the mess I created. I need two people to help me fulfill that obligation."

"Who?"

"My best friend, Milly…and you."

"Why me? I think you're a piece of shit. A hundred years ago, you would have been one of those monsters riding around on horseback, dressed up in an old sheet, torching and raping and lynching colored folk like me for being black. The only difference is that now those same bastards are walking around in fancy suits calling themselves 'Conservative' Republicans, which is code for arrogant racist asshole."

"I accept your honesty and your bravery for standing up for your beliefs. That's why I need your support. I want the two of you standing beside me when I speak tonight and, if someone doesn't try to assassinate me, I promise not to embarrass or disappoint either one of you. That's the best I can offer at the moment but I hope you'll consent to my request. This conversation is about as open and honest as I've been with anyone in decades and proving myself to you has become very important to me."

"Why's that?"

"Because I respect your honesty and your grit. You don't have any doubt about where you stand in your world or what offends your sense of right and wrong, which is more than I can say for myself."

She walked over to stand beside him, contemplating the bitter gray dawn creeping across the city. "Why should I say yes?"

He turned to stare at her profile, "Because you have the courage to defend your principles and in a previous lifetime, those are the values I used to believe in, so that's what I want to talk about tonight. Between now and then, I want you to teach me your truth."

~

Ethan Tomlinson sat at his desk watching a syrupy fog oozing over Dune Point, glistening in dawn's first light outside the broad curved window of his office in the expansive contemporary architecture of interconnecting forms strewn like children's blocks behind tall undulating walls snaking around the perimeter of the ImageSculptor complex in Malibu.

After a long night of strategic brainstorming for a campaign to sell Steil as the legitimate president the nation needs, he sipped a 1985 Taylor Vintage Port from a deep snifter to greet the dawn while contemplating those first tentative meetings decades ago at Stanley French's majestic retreat in the forest overlooking Jackson Lake. French, Conrad Blaho, and the Reverend Joshua Godwin laid out the rough outlines of an audacious campaign to dismantle the federal government, eradicate laws and regulations that limit industrial productivity and the unencumbered accumulation of vast wealth, and return the world economy to the natural balance of a two-class system.

He could hear Conrad Blaho's voice defining the goal with firm conviction, "We need to forge an alliance of kindred spirits, those brave souls willing to raise an iron fist to crush the sniveling liberals and erase everything they've installed since Roosevelt instituted the New Deal."

The vision evolved into 'The Forge', a clandestine community of like-minded patriots dedicated to establishing a thoroughly modern fascist state. The list of prominent ultra-conservative contributors was extensive and they proved more than enthusiastic in their substantial targeted contributions but the key to their campaign's ultimate success was provided by Reverend Godwin's delivery of legions of ignorant, illiterate blue-collar white evangelical bigots who lined up to vote for the supremacist candidates promoted from the pulpit.

They started stacking school boards in Oklahoma, then city councils across the Midwest, gradually infiltrating and overwhelming state legislatures, and occupying governor's mansions, before posting a slate of obedient candidates for the House and the Senate in every state in the nation.

In the process, thousands of small newspapers and hundreds of rural radio and television stations were gobbled up by new ownership that transformed the medium and the message to fire up an exploding audience with a barrage of blatantly false propaganda and bizarre conspiracy theories. Foundations were formed to contribute buildings and endowments to every prominent law school in the nation to garner the influence to place ultra-conservative deans with the authority to realign the curriculum to produce armies of radically programmed attorneys to serve the requirements of corporate titans as future justices.

The struggle spanned nine administrations and now, the stars were aligning to place their well-groomed candidate in the Oval Office.

He was startled by the chirp of his personal phone. "Hello."

"Tomlinson? Blaho."

"What's up?"

"I'm getting warnings that Spratlin's reserved the Lincoln Memorial for a speech this evening. No one seems to have a clue what this is all about. Do you?"

"I hadn't heard anything but I'll make some calls and see what I can find out."

"This is trouble we don't need. Steil's giving his speech outside Blair House later this morning and I want that to dominate the national news tonight."

"Yeah, I made some improvements in his script. Even with that sincere schtick he does, it was a tad too syrupy. He needs to appear calm and focused on taking the reins of government in his strong steady hands during this time of turmoil, reassuring the public that he is the only person who can lead the nation down the path to renewal. I'm sure he can pull it off but anything less than total commitment will just hand the protestors more ammunition and make him look like the fool he really is."

"Once he takes office, he'll do as he's told."

"I have hours of truly disgusting tape if he gets out of line."

"Is there anyone in public life who you don't have files on?"

"Nope."

"Lemme know when you have some solid intel on what's happening in Washington tonight. I want our media people all over that event."

"Will Terry's got Steil's event covered and he'll have a promo out before news-time. I'll make sure he's got crews and lots of agitators at Spratlin's show at the Memorial. If things get crazy, some well-edited film could tip the scales of public opinion to install Steil to protect the voters from anarchy."

"All the networks are covering the marches in every city across the county and selling them as peaceful protestors exercising their first amendment rights but our merchants and corporate execs are fed up with the chaos and loss of business and they expect our people to step in to protect them."

"Our media is trying to slant it the other way."

"Hell, send our militia guys in there to cause some damage, so we can blame it on the hippies!"

"Actually, we've got incidents planned in thirteen cities for later tonight. Tomorrow's headlines will be dominated by photos of violence and mayhem. Our local officials will demand federal troops to protect lives and property."

"That's more like it!" shouted Blaho. "We need to take charge of this opportunity and drive that final nail into the coffin of democracy before we lose control."

"Fine, I'll get back to you when I have real details."

"Make that sooner rather than later."

"Roger that," replied Tomlinson, reaching for his desk phone to speed dial Will Terry.

The number rang three times before the videographer picked up, "How's life in sunny California?"

"Damp, why?"

"It's cold as a witch's tit in D.C."

"You got Steil's speech covered?"

"Yeah, no problem. I've got two crews on it."

"Great, did you get Stanislawski and his guys lined out for tonight?"

"Boston, New York, Philly, D.C., Detroit, Chicago…we got all the biggest protests and I promise there'll be fireworks going off everywhere."

"We need to make it big and loud enough to convince the populous that Steil's the only guy who can save then nation."

"Gotcha."

"Have you heard that Spratlin's giving a speech at the Lincoln Memorial at eight tonight?"

"Yeah, there are rumors going around."

"Make sure you've got your crews there and plenty of Stanislawski's guys in the crowd. No matter what he has to say, we want this to look like a riot, an insurrection to steal the Oval Office."

"We know all the D.C. protestors will be there anyway, so I'll just shift the entire operation to the mall. Shouldn't be any problem to insert a hundred of our guys in the crowd to stir things up."

"Loud and proud, brother. Make sure you let Hobson know because this could be the Hail Mary that wins the game."

Terry laughed, "Hell, we're the best team on the field!"

~

Marjorie Spratlin was sitting before of the mirror on her dressing table adjusting pearl earrings when Stanton knocked at the door. "Come in, come in."

"The car's waiting to take us to the airport."

"I'll just be a minute. Mr. Charles took my things down a few minutes ago."

"Are the girls ready?"

"Yes, dear." She stood to face him, "Are you alright, you seem anxious?"

"To tell you the truth, I only have a sketchy idea of what Nellis is cooking up but I know my speech could change the course of our democracy. Murphy and I were both appealing to an enormous class of undereducated, underpaid, or unemployed working poor. All the impoverished folks on the right and the left share the anger and frustration that the oligarchs have foisted upon this country but they're blaming each other for the stalemate in government, the loss of jobs, stagnant wages, the list goes on…but when you take a broader view it becomes clear that they're all suffering the same nightmares and the only issue separating the two sides is bigotry and racism."

"That is the original sin of this nation," replied his wife, "and, try as they might, no one in the past two-hundred and fifty years has solved the problem or quelled the anguish with a single speech. You go out there and tell your truth, just as you have throughout your campaign. You're a uniter and I'm very proud of the person you've become."

His eyes met hers, "We've been through our own personal challenges but I think we've finally become the people, the family we were meant to be, all of us."

"I don't think we've reached redemption yet but we're closer than we've been since we were newlyweds." She wrapped her arms around his neck and touched her cheek to his, "We should be going, Mr. Charles will be impatient."

He kissed her forehead, "I'm glad I found that girl I fell I love with all those years ago. I thought I'd lost you."

She turned to pick up her coat and purse from the bed and looked up at him, "I just needed to know that I was still important to you."

He took her hand, "I'm delighted to have you beside me."

Sissy and Sammy, dressed in matching coats and dark blue berets, waited with the family's nanny, Sibble Savage, in the hallway. "I can't believe you're going to give a speech in front of the Lincoln Memorial. The crowd at the convention was gigantic and I know some of your rallies were huge but this is going to be way bigger," said Samantha.

"I'm going to be intimidated by his eyes staring down on us," added Sissy.

"President Lincoln's?" inquired her mother.

"Yes, it's like he started trying to put this country back together and daddy's doing the same thing."

"I hope he approves," said Stanton with a hug. "C'mon, we have cars and planes waiting to take us to Washington."

Sibble took his arm, "I believe in you, just as I did when you were a precious wee boy. You will make a difference."

"I'm so pleased you're coming with us." Stanton hugged her, "We're all your children."

Mr. Charles was holding the door of the shiny Fleetwood Cadillac and tipped his hat, as they trooped out the side door. "My you young ladies look stunning today!"

The girls curtsied and giggled as they climbed into the car, just as Mama Louise and Maybelle Brown with her children trooped down the kitchen steps.

He helped the mistress of the house into the back seat and turned to Stanton, "Looks like we're going to be full-to-overflowing on this ride to the airport. Is Mr. Bruce coming?"

"Oh, he's coordinating communications and he's going to catch up with us at the Capitol. Mrs. Sloan is sending a plane to pick him up at three o'clock. You're welcome to join us if you like?"

"I don't want to intrude."

"You are as much a part of this family and this struggle as any of us. I'd be honored if you would stand with us."

Mr. Charles smiled, "Thank you, I'll be there."

~

Bruce Spratlin looked up as Sister Gwen knocked gently and swept into her tiny office, nestled in the peak of the roof of the orphanage, carrying a tray with a small pitcher of hot tea and a tiny bowl of sugar, two thin wedges of lemon, and some warm biscuits. "I thought you might be hungry and thirsty and I know how cold this room can be this time of year. The heat from the house never seems to get up here."

"Oh, lovely. I sure appreciate it," replied young Spratlin. "So, you chose the coldest room in the house as your own?"

"Should I ask my sisters or some of the children to suffer the cold while I'm snug and warm? I think not."

"You are the face of empathy and compassion," replied Bruce, sipping the steaming tea.

"How's everything going?"

"Latest word is that Brad's troops intercepted and commandeered at least twenty prisoner trains overnight and they're waiting for clear tracks into DC."

"What about Mr. Gray?"

"I just got off the phone with him. They're loading up several thousand fugitives from the Alien Relocation Command and leaving New York in the next hour or so. He said he's got a guest speaker coming along but he wouldn't tell me who. Oh, and the All People Matter folks are transporting thousands of protestors from around the country to be there by tonight."

"Are you going to be able to attend?"

Spratlin grinned, "Yeah, they're sending a plane for me this afternoon."

"Just shows how important you are," said Sister Gwen, turning to the door. "I'll just leave you to your calls."

"Sister," said Bruce, "you should be there too."

"I couldn't," blushed the nun.

"Yes, you could and you should. I'm sure there will be plenty of room on the plane and we'll be back tomorrow, if we don't get arrested first."

"I'd gladly get arrested with you in this fight."

"Then be ready when Mr. Charles comes by to pick me up at two o'clock."

"Fine. I'll make the arrangements."

The rotary telephone on her desk jangled and Bruce picked up the handset, "Hello."

~

Brad, Jessie, and Kate sat behind Chief Engineer Eddy Deacan and his second in command, Scotty Ditkins, in the cockpit of the prisoner train, as it slowed to a stop on a siding in dense forest just north Roxbury, Virginia.

Deacan turned to his new directors, still clad in their kilts and colors, "Digital message from The Wizard says we're to wait here until further notice."

"Can you open the doors in the other cars?" asked Jessie.

"Yeah, there's the master switch," replied Ditkins, pointing to the control panel.

"Our people could use some fresh air," said Kate.

"Lemme use your intercom," said Brad, taking the microphone. "Attention everyone, we're stopped here for a while, until we get the command to roll into D.C. for the rally tonight. We're opening the doors so you can move around but stay close because when they say 'Go', we're moving out."

A cheer went up as the latches released and the doors hissed open. The fugitives edged into the breach, squinting at flurries of tiny snowflakes falling from a cold overcast sky and collecting in crowns on graceful pines, forming sculptures on the barren twigs and branches of slumbering deciduous trees.

Benny helped Sammy down onto the roadbed before they strolled along the length of the train, greeting other escapees gleefully, to climb up into the cockpit.

"We've got a trainload of happy campers," said Sammy.

"We passed the guards' substantial stash of rations around, so everyone got a little something to eat," added Benny. "Now their only complaint is that we're not moving,"

"Soon enough," replied Jessie. "What'd you do with the guards?"

"Stashed 'em in the last car with some unfriendly company to keep them in line," said Sammy.

"If truth be known, they're all a bunch of ignorant thugs who traded a free pass out of jail for a commitment to be cruel and heartless to anyone who isn't white," said Ditkins.

The Chief Engineer shook his head, "After what we've witnessed, I'm all for sending them back to jail where they truly belong, disbanding the Alien Relocation Command and indicting the ringleaders for crimes against humanity. That's after freeing all these prisoners who had no business being arrested in the first place."

The second officer said, "I still don't understand why our folks in the Command Center don't know where we are?"

"I wish I could give you a technical answer but I'm no expert. The only information I got was that some patriotic genius hijacked their software and can start and stop these trains where we need them. Maybe we'll find out more when we get to Washington," said Brad.

Kate asked, "Why do you drive these trains, if you don't believe in what they're doing?"

Deacan hesitated, "Because…they've got my brother and they've threatened my kids."

"I'm sorry," said the journalist. "When there's time, I'd like to hear your story because, when this is over, I'm going to write the whole truth about all of this from our naïve beginnings to bringing the conspirators to justice."

"There's a book I want to read," said Deacan.

"There's a book every American ought to read," added his mate.

Milly, an unwavering sentinel weathering a thinning rush of children scampering to the kitchen for a fast breakfast, watched Billy back out of Murphy's room and close the door gently. "What do you think?"

Startled, the tall black beauty looked down at her, "First, I want to know why you decided to help him disappear?"

The dowdy receptionist sputtered, "Because…I fell in love with the person I saw hiding under all the bullshit the first time I met him and I believe he's worth saving."

"Not because you wanted to spare the nation a nightmare?"

"Everyone who has a brain knows that Mac doesn't have the qualifications or the capacity to run anything, let alone the country. He's an actor who was consumed by the horrible character he created out of desperation…I know that's not who he is."

Billy leaned against the door jam, "He claims he's going to give a speech at the Lincoln Memorial tonight and he wants me to be with him."

"I know," said Milly, wiping a tear from her cheek. "Did he tell you why?"

"He said that he wants me to coach him on my truth."

"And what truth is that?"

"I grew up in the ghetto and I struggled to survive from the day I was born. I learned to play the system and I used some of the money that I made to help some of my sisters escape the business to start a real life in a different reality. My Mama used to call me tough and tender and always too honest for my own good."

"I think she was right. Are you going to help?"

Billy's eyes glowed, "The only way we're going to change the world is by taking some chances and making some noise. This isn't what I had in mind but, hell, I've never seen the Lincoln Memorial at night. Besides, for a brief part of our conversation, I saw that person you were talking about and he seemed almost sane."

Carpenters erected panel walls, with steps, doors, and windows, that could be rolled into various configurations, crafting different scenes, while the lighting crew braved tiny catwalks and towering ladders to place dozens of lamps with scrims and colored gels to evoke different moods during each scene. Stagehands carted furniture and props and organized them in the alcoves on either side behind the velvet curtains, while the musicians tuned up.

Theater mascot, Josie, a small Shetland-collie, marched around the stage, inspecting the efforts of the crew and collecting pets from old friends and new acquaintances. She settled down on the edge of stage, with her head on Billy's lap. The young woman closed her eyes, feeling the warm silkiness of Josie's ear, and embraced the tiny infant in her belly, swaying slowly as she sang along with a horn player in the pit, who was wailing through a slow passionate rendition of 'St. James Infirmary'.

> *It was down in old Joe's barroom, on the corner of the square*
> *They were serving drinks as usual, and the usual crowd was there*
> *On my left stood Jean McKennedy, and her eyes were bloodshot red*
> *And she turned her face to the people, these were the very words she said*
> *I was down to St. James infirmary, I saw my baby there*
> *He was stretched out on a long white table,*
> *So sweet, cool and so fair*
> *Let him go, let him go, God bless him*
> *Wherever he may be*
> *He may search this whole wide world over*
> *Never find a sweeter woman than me*

Burt walked to the front, applauding, "That was beautiful."

The trumpeter looked up with a cockeyed grin, "What's your name girl and why haven't I heard that voice before?"

Billy ducked her chin to pet the old dog and hide her bruises, "My name's Billy."

"Well, I'm pleased to meet you, Billy, and I definitely want to jam with you, as soon as we get finished with this rehearsal. Are you up for that?"

"Sure. I'll meet you right back here, when the music stops."

"Promise?"

"I won't promise until you tell me your name."

"Oh, I'm John, John Duvall. I'll catch you later."

She turned to Burt, "I see what you mean about this place being a living breathing creature. With all these amazing people transforming it into a palace, it feels like the whole building is vibrating with its own energy. I want to learn how to contribute something to all of this."

The old man turned around to take in the mad scramble of bodies preparing the stage for the dress rehearsal, "It's a mad-dash ballet and I'm always amazed that these folks don't run over each other but they're all pro's, the best at what they do. Look around, there are probably fifteen or twenty different areas of responsibility, from set design and construction to backgrounds, lighting to sound and music, costume design and wardrobe, makeup, it goes on and on for months before the production hits the stage. Watch what they're doing and find the task that's closest to your heart. Heck, just follow Josie around, she's friends with everyone in the theater and all of them could use a hand."

Billy touched the gash on her face. It was beginning to heal and the swelling had subsided but the deep purple bruise would linger as a harsh reminder. "I can't believe you just said that."

"What?"

"A week ago, I was literally a slave. I'd given up my body, my pride, and my soul but all of you helped save me and my baby from that hell, and now you're saying I can be anything I want to be…just pick a craft or a skill and learn how to do it…just like that?"

"Well, yeah, that's how it works in our world," replied Burt. "Every one of our kids can sing and dance and build a set and paint a background, run wiring and take over the lighting or sound consoles, or do pretty much everything. They just seem to pick it up as they grow, so why should you be any different? You're just a kid who's getting a late start."

Billy tucked her chin with an embarrassed grin, "My front job was as a makeup artist in a photographer's studio."

"Well, there you go," said Burt. "All I'm saying is, you can choose where you want to begin but the learning never stops, it just leads you from one step to another. You already know how to sing and, I don't mean to be insensitive but considering your prior profession, you're probably a fine actress to boot. With a little training, you could probably step right into a role on stage."

"No, I couldn't."

"Why not? Do you honestly think that actresses are born with their talents? Of course not, they all had to work hard to learn their craft but anyone can do that, it's just work."

Billy took his arm, as the work lights dimmed and an engineer eased the background lights from cool blue to warm amber, fading spots on and off chalk marks on the stage, where the actors would stand to give their lines. "I never had an opportunity to think about getting to choose who or what I wanted to be. Those dreams were just some fantasy lingering from when I was a little girl."

Burt patted her hand, "Look at all these people scrambling around this stage. They don't see it as work, they live for the chance to contribute to a production, to show what they've learned, to try out their latest ideas and techniques, and to learn something new, so they'll be better prepared the next time. None of these people do what they do for the money. Heck, this show is booked for eight shows over two weeks and then it's gone, because we've got a pair of concerts back-to-back the following weekend with a couple of groups from England. Even with a full house, no one's going to make a killing on this, most won't make enough to cover their expenses, but it's exposure and the promise that this might lead them to something bigger that keeps them going."

She squeezed his arm, "I want to be a part of this."

"You already are!"

Billy had briefly scanned the CliffsNotes of a few of Shakespeare's works for a high school literature class but never had an opportunity to see a play. There had been one john who took her to a weird off-Broadway avant-garde production, where the audience seemed to be tripping through a garish spinning light show, oblivious to the fact that the cast was naked and shouting incomprehensible nonsense, but the guy only wanted to jump her bones in the middle of the crowd. She left him in pain and walked the forty-seven blocks to her apartment in spike heels through a thunderstorm.

She smiled up at the old man, "Thanks for making me feel like it's okay to dream again."

"Don't ever stop dreaming. That's what this wonderful magical Playhouse is all about!"

~

Adel and her younger sister, Misty, were hiding on the catwalk above the stage, spying on Burt and director Mason James, who were discussing the sequence of scenery changes.

Kevin Haines approached from behind the curtains, "Are we set to open tomorrow night?"

"It's postponed until next week," replied James.

"Why?"

"Because there's going to be a show in Washington tonight and everyone who cares about this country needs to be there."

Burt turned, "One of our house guests has arranged a giant rally and our mysterious actor is going to speak."

The actor asked, "Is he who we think he is?"

Before the theater owner could respond, the swinging doors at the back of the auditorium burst open and Sybil, Marty's wife and manager of The Playhouse, charged down the aisle and up the stairs at the side of the stage into Burt's arms, "I couldn't stop them!"

"That's alright, I'll handle this," replied her father-in-law with a hug, as a dozen troopers stormed down the burgundy carpeting.

The leader stopped in front of the stage, "We have a warrant to search the premises for illegal aliens and persons wanted for treasonous acts."

Burt looked down at the gleaming helmet, "We don't have anyone who falls into those categories and, as you can see, we're busy."

The metallic voice screamed, "Shall we arrest you for impeding our investigation?"

"You're wasting your time," shouted the actor with a street-wise Cockney accent, moving to stand beside Burt, "and it's time for you to leave."

"Are you the same asshole who interrupted my rehearsal yesterday?" asked Mason James, assuming his haughty-gay-bitch persona. "You are, aren't you? Well, no one meeting your descriptions has joined my company, so can we get back to work?"

Black clad guards with sizzling batons mounted the steps on either side of the stage as the leader said, "We're going to search the entire building and anyone who tries to interfere will be taken into custody."

Adel whispered to Misty, "We have to warn Grandmama and hide the guests."

One of the guards raised a gun, as the two girls scampered across the catwalk and disappeared into darkness.

Misty darted into the kitchen to find Matty at the stove, "There's a squad of troopers in the theater and they want to search the building. Adel just went upstairs to warn everyone up there."

Her grandmother pressed a button on the intercom and said, "I need you girls." She turned to the stove and started rattling pots and pans, making an awful racket, just as her daughters, Sally and Alison emerged through the dining room to intercept four guards in black uniforms storming into the kitchen.

Sally confronted the first guard, "Where do you think you're going?"

The thug shoved her out of the way but Alison stuck out a foot and dropped him to the floor with a savage chop below the back of his helmet. The second sentry raised his crackling truncheon to maul Alison but Matty swung a cast iron skillet and shattered his gleaming face shield. Jagged shards of rainbow plastic exploded in his face, blood gushed from flesh and eyes, as he dropped to his knees with an agonizing wail, while Sally and her sister charged the last two before they could warn the rest of their squad.

Adel scanned the mayhem in the kitchen and rushed along the bedroom hallway, to Milly and Billy, who were talking in quiet murmurs. "The scary guys are back and they're trying to search the building."

Billy sighed, "It's Credo, my old pimp turned government enforcer, and he's looking for his revenge on me."

Adel said, "Get the president and follow me. I know a secret place they won't find."

Milly opened the door to the bedroom, "Grab your coat and follow me, we're under attack!"

"Are you sure it's not the Secret Service?" mumbled Mac, stumbling after the women scampering to keep up with the slender girl. She pulled open a small hatch in the wall at the end of the hall, "This is the laundry chute. Burt built it when all the new children started moving in but all of us ride down it like a slide and it dumps out in the basement. There's a secret room down there where we can hide until they can sneak you out of the building."

Milly looked at Mac, "How are you feeling?"

"Hopeful and scared," muttered the president-elect, struggling into his jacket and turning to stare back down the hallway in bewilderment.

"C'mon, we have to go," whispered Adel. "There's a racket downstairs, so more troopers are in the kitchen."

Billy pulled Mac close to the wall, "I'll go first and catch you at the bottom."

The lanky woman climbed into the tiny closet and disappeared into darkness. After a long moment, she whispered, "That's fun! C'mon, you can do it."

Mac scrunched himself into the cubbyhole, looked up at Milly with anxious eyes and scooted off to the left, with a very quiet, "Ahhhhh."

Billy caught him as he flopped onto a load of dirty clothes and grinned, "The doc who kept me jacked up for the past year provided a lot of chemical rushes but nothing like that!"

Adel stuck her head into the shaft, "Are you okay?"

"He's fine, send Milly down."

Milly hopped into the bin and slid down the ramp, followed by Adel, who stood up and rushed to peek out the door. "Okay, they aren't coming this way. We're going out this door to the right and down the old staircase. It's kind of rickety, so watch your step."

They tiptoed along the hallway and down an old steel stairway that creaked and swayed a little as they descended to a landing two flights down. Adel held up her hand and listened but there were no footsteps following. "Okay, we've got to go through this dark creepy room where they used to store coal to fire the boilers in the old days. Milly put your hands on my shoulders, Mr. President you follow her and Billy can bring up the rear. Just stay in line and follow me."

A faint glimmer at the far end of the long dusty chamber illuminated a narrow path between rows of large boxes and piles of wood and rusty steel. Adel turned with a finger to her lips as they exited the dungeon into a dim hallway past concrete steps leading up to a pair of utility doors that opened into the alley behind The Playhouse.

A metallic voice said, "Check those steel doors."

Someone pulled one of the doors up just enough to splash a blinding flash of daylight through the crack, then jiggled the latch before stomping on it with a heavy boot but the heavy slabs were bolted closed from the inside. "Naw, it doesn't look like anyone's used these in years."

Chapter Ten

Cameraman Jackson Bell pointed to an angry sky and growled to his sound man, Jamie Allen, "Why do these arrogant bastards always show up twenty minutes late, while we're stuck out here in crappy weather?"

A cold north wind drove low clouds across the city, dumping rashes of frigid drizzle on the crowd of reporters gathered in front of Blair House, awaiting Creighton Steil's announcement. After another twenty minutes, the vice-president-elect emerged from the residence wearing a tailored black trench-coat with a patriotic red and white striped scarf accentuating his chiseled features, and stepped up to the cluster of microphones.

"Ladies and gentlemen, my fellow Americans, it has been three days since a record number of citizens fulfilled their civic duty and voted to elect my running-mate, Mac Murphy, to the Presidency of these United States. I'm afraid it is my obligation to report that, in spite of a relentless, diligent, continuing search by every branch of government security, no trace of our future president has turned up since his disappearance.

Our nation has never faced a mysterious dilemma like this before but constitutional experts have declared that if President-elect Murphy is not found or is not willing to accept the office he won in the election, then the vice-president elect should be sworn in at the inauguration in January.

I look forward to his imminent safe return but I want to assure the nation that I am prepared to stand in for him. My staff is working with his transition team to assemble an exceptional group of extremely talented and devoted experts to form the next administration. The country is facing challenges on every front - from the economy that the current president has driven into recession; to a complete lack of a coordinated or cohesive foreign policy; to the ongoing invasion of filthy illegal immigrants streaming across our borders to sully the integrity and the foundations of our society, steal American jobs, and cash in on benefits that should rightfully go to needy Americans. Not to mention, a crumbling infrastructure and unrestrained violence in the inner cities, failing health and medical services and an educational system in complete collapse and ranked thirty-second in the world."

The ruggedly handsome vice-president-elect paused to allow the cameras to zoom-in as his tanned face sagged into a well-practiced 'sincere' guise, "I promise that our administration will unite the feuding factions from left and right to cure the ills of the nation with common-sense solutions to all of these problems and many more, starting on day one. We campaigned on the promise of returning America to our roots, to the goals and aspirations of the Founding Fathers, and restoring pride in our power and our might after too many years of misguided impotent policies that have destroyed our standing in the world.

I'm sure Mac Murphy would agree that it's time to join together to rebuild our military and re-establish our dominance of friend and foe alike. We are The United States of America and our guiding principles, grounded in the word of God, used to be the envy of the civilized world and I'll see to it that they are again.

I look forward to keeping you informed of any developments as our transition team announces the nominees who will take office in January. God bless America and protect our troops around the world. Thank you."

Reporters surged to ask questions, as he morphed into his gallant paternal guise and stared into the cameras, "What can you tell us about Murphy's disappearance?"

"Surely, the Secret Service can't lose a future president!"

"Was he kidnapped?"

"The American people demand the truth!"

"I wish I had an answer to your questions but the truth is – no one seems to know what really happened that night or where he is today. If and when I receive any information, I will share it with all of you." He turned away from the microphones with a wave and climbed the few steps to enter a warm and inviting Blair House.

His very personal secretary, Ernest Cummings took his arm and leaned close, "Perfect! You were strong, sincere, and succinct and you dodged the questions with the simple truth. I think 'presidential' is the perfect descriptor for your performance!"

Security advisor, Craig Hobson, waiting just inside the door, greeted the two men with, "Well played, the public is confused and anxious and you came across as calm and steady. The press is scrambling for any new piece of the story, so the talking heads can stop repeating the same scraps of misinformation and unfounded rumors over and over."

"That might be wishful thinking," replied Steil. "The press doesn't want a Republican in the White House, especially me!"

"The voters needed reassurance and you provided it," added his secretary.

"Might I have a few minutes of your time in private?" asked Hobson quietly.

"Certainly," said the vice-president-elect, marching down a corridor to his temporary office. He dropped his coat on a chair, walked over to a credenza and poured himself a stout Scotch. "What have you got for me?"

"Spratlin's speech tonight is being put together on the fly by multiple Democratic and independent organizations taking on different pieces of the event and everything's being coordinated through his office. No one in the know seems to have a clue about why it has to happen today, let alone what he intends to talk about."

"So, basically, you don't know any more than you did last night!" snapped Cummings. "You're the senior Security Advisor to the future President of the United States, you're supposed to know everything!"

"I've been informed that the powers-that-be will provide video crews to record every facet of the event, dozens of our spokespeople to address and distract the media, and a small army of infiltrators to ensure carefully edited tape of a full-fledged riot for the morning news."

"We need to know what this is all about…now, so quit screwing around and do your job!" Cummings turned to his boss and smiled, "I'll have Ted and Nancy start drafting your statement."

"Spratlin's gambit might make you look like the white knight ready to save the kingdom from certain ruin," said Hobson.

"We all better hope you're right." Steil took a sip of his whiskey, "I'm ready to play my part."

~

Ned glanced at Nellis and Katherine in his rearview mirror, as he guided his pimped-out ebony step-van with the glittering chrome bow-tie across the grill through morning traffic down Seventh Avenue to swing around Battery Place and drop into the closed construction site, "You okay back there? We're almost at the station."

"I can't believe you got us out of the theater just as it was getting raided by the troopers. Capturing us would have been a coup for the Republicans but I don't want to imagine what they'd do with Murphy. I sure hope he's safe."

"Nellis, you've been my best friend for a lot of years and I trust in your…unconventional ways, but if you get this wrong, it's going to put a whole bunch of folks in a big hurt."

"Ah, we've survived lots of crazy stuff over the years. This is just bigger and badder."

"What if the Secret Service or the FBI or, hell, those damned militias figure it out? They could have a battalion of storm troopers sitting on the steps in Ol' Abe's monument just waiting for us to drive up so they can inflict heavy casualties before they escort us off to some concentration camp in the boonies!"

"Those are contingencies we can't control and we've got other folks dealing with all that. Our best protection is to make sure that a bazillion people show up and Spratlin and Murphy are on those steps with a live microphone at eight o'clock."

"Yeah, what could go wrong with that?" replied the driver, stopping at the top of the ramp to flash his lights before the huge gates at the entrance to the tunnel swung open.

Katherine leaned close to Nellis and squeezed his hand, "I sure hope you're right."

"Have I ever let you down?"

"Well, there was a time when you got in front of the cameras in Denver."

"Ah, that's just little stuff. No one remembers that crap."

"Those clips are played over and over on the news channels and the internet every day. You're a cult hero and a villain!" said his new wife.

Ned interrupted, "Maybe they'll know something inside about what happened at The Playhouse. Tate's supposed to come back with me to help make sure Murphy's on the train when it's ready to leave in a couple of hours."

He eased the truck down the ramp into darkness, as the gate closed behind them and Amy appeared in the headlights next to the staircase. Katherine said, "I always feel calm when she's around, because she's not going to get ruffled and knows how to deal with everything."

"She is a cool head," added Nellis, hauling the sliding door open to a frigid blast of winter.

Ned hopped out and hugged Amy, "How's everything going here?"

"I'm amazed at how fast four-thousand people can get motivated and organized just for the chance to see the sky again."

"Well, that is a fairly good reason, even if it's threatening to storm, but taking back our country might add a little incentive to the cause," said Nellis.

"I have no doubt that every person will be ready when the trains arrive and the sanctuary will be spotless," said Amy, turning to Katherine. "I know that Dr. Cohen is looking forward to your talk to keep everyone focused on what we're trying to accomplish."

"No pressure there," laughed Nellis, hugging Katherine. "I know you can handle this, unless you want me to take the mike?"

"Small chance, buster. Let's get moving, we've only got a couple of hours before they'll start loading up."

They trudged up the stairs, along the broad unfinished hallway to the balcony overlooking bustling crowds carefully folding up the tiny shops on the platforms and carting away the tables, chairs, and workstations lining the track-beds. Nellis leaned on the railing, marveling, "That's just incredible, they're like a well-organized army of ants clearing away the clutter."

Amy gazed around and sighed, "I know it's weird but I'm almost sad to see this community rise up out of the darkness. Every person down here contributed their best for the common good and you don't find that in normal society, everyone's too wound up in their own stuff to notice what's really happening around them."

"I understand how you feel," said Katherine, "but I don't agree. There are hundreds of thousands of people protesting in every city in the county and I can only hope that millions of them are heading for DC to bear witness to the emancipation of our tattered democracy."

"These people figured out how to live together in peace and harmony, with a common cause that was the common good," said Amy.

"We've got to find a way to bring the country back to one for all and all for one," added Nellis with a grin. "How about we make you Minister of Proper Attitudes?"

Amy blushed.

"Sounds like a good title for one of your country songs," said Ned.

"I sure hope Lucy's still snug in her case under the bed," said Nellis, following the ladies to the elevators.

"Chief Billings has the farm covered. The only people getting in or out of there are the girls."

"I'm going to owe them big when this is over."

"Oh, from the reaction I got from them, I think they'll just be glad to have their cranky neighbor home," said Ned.

"All we've got to do is make it through the next twenty-four hours or so, without getting killed or busted, and we'll be fine."

Katherine kissed his cheek as the doors closed and the lift started to descend, "That doesn't give me a whole lot of confidence."

"You just gotta believe darlin', you just gotta believe."

∼

Captain Martin emerged from the cockpit, as Representative Spratlin stepped into the aircraft, "I'm pleased we get to serve you again, Sir. It's an honor."

Stanton offered his hand, "This might be the most important and the most consequential leg of the journey yet. Tonight could be our last chance to save the nation from self-destruction. If we can't remember how to stand together, we might as well draw new borders and split the country into warring states. It can't go on like this and I plan to explain that to the nation."

"I think a majority of our citizens agree with you, I know I do."

"Then get us to Washington as fast as you can, so I can get to work."

He glanced at the gaggle of children accompanied by Mama Louise and Maybelle Brown, "I see you've brought an entourage, let's get everyone buckled up because we're heading out!"

Spratlin smiled, "They're my conscience."

Marjorie settled in beside him in the forward cabin, "I know we agreed to allow the children to come along but I'm still a bit anxious about their safety."

"I know exactly how you feel but we couldn't very well deny them the chance to participate in the making of history and, besides, we both know there'd have been a rebellion if we'd decided against it."

His wife nodded, "Have you had any updates on what's happening?"

"I handed the reins over to my office manager, Gloria Lang, and told her take charge and not to communicate with me until I was in the office. We don't want to give anything away to the opposition but, from what I've heard through other sources, they're going crazy trying to find someone in our command center to spill the beans on what's going to happen."

"I'm betting your people know how to deflect the infiltrators."

He patted her hand, as the jet raced down the runway and lifted into a brilliant blue sky to cheers from the children. "I'm blessed to have their support and expertise. Considering how fast everything has to be moving to get a massive rally organized in a little over a day, I wouldn't want anyone else running the show."

~

Adel settled Mac, Milly, and Billy in a small alcove with an old dusty desk and a tattered couch, "They won't find you here, so stay quiet while I go find out what's going on and how Grandmama plans to get you out of the theater. I'll be back as fast as I can, promise."

Murphy leaned on the desk, "Well, it sure isn't the Oval Office but I guess it'll have to do for the moment."

Billy smiled, "This is reality. That wasn't."

"Point made," said Milly, brushing a smudge of dirt from the shoulder of Mac's jacket. "Are you okay?"

"Fleeing armed government agents certainly puts a lot of things into perspective and I can see a tiny glimpse of the horrors that people of color have suffered for centuries. I'm sure that same injustice must apply to every wave of new immigrants who brave the journey to our shores, only to face bigotry and oppression, hatred and violence. It should have ended after the civil war but white people were never going to allow minorities to determine the future of their 'white' nation and that holds true to this day.

I have to admit that I regret reinforcing that racist fantasy since I first started this gig and, if we can survive the journey to Washington, I'll do what I can to make the American people accept our national sin for what it is."

Billy smiled, "You're going to become my best student."

Within minutes Adel reappeared with her Aunt Sally, who was carrying a small white suitcase, which she laid on the desk. "I'm so glad the girls got you out of danger."

"What about everyone else," asked Milly.

"Well, several of the troopers met with untimely accidents like falling down stairs and tumbling off the roof. They needed medical assistance, so their buddies took them to the hospital and left two reinforcements outside the lobby and another three or four trolling the perimeter but I'm pretty sure they're afraid to step inside the theater because no one seems to know what happened. They might think they've got the building secured but I'm absolutely sure that my sister-in-law will prove a worthy distraction."

"What's in the suitcase," asked Billy.

Sally hooked a thumb at Mac, "This guy's way too recognizable, so we're going to give him a new look."

"How are you going to get us out of here?"

Adel grinned, "Oh, you're gonna love this."

Sally sat Mac on the desk and draped a towel around his neck before applying thin layers of latex over his cheekbones and along his jaw, changing the contours and shape of his face. She smoothed out the wrinkles and puffy bags around his mouth, covered his thinning hair with a tousled salt-and-pepper wig, stippled his cheeks with pock-marks and hollowed out his cheekbones with several day's stubble. She plumped thin gray brows into bristling bushes and muted his glistening blue eyes to brown with contact lenses. Sally sat back to inspect her work and handed him a small mirror.

Billy looked over her shoulder, "You're good, he doesn't look anything like Mac Murphy."

His mouth dropped open as he stared at the tramp in the glass, "I've been through a lot of makeup and wardrobe over the years but this is astonishing. I look the way I've been feeling for the past five years. What am I supposed to be?"

"A trashman," replied Adel with a laugh, "and you look the part."

Sally handed him a grimy pair of overalls, a rumpled leather hat with fur earmuffs, and a filthy pair of boots, "In about ten minutes, an oversized trash truck is going lumber through the alley and you're going to hop into the cab as it goes by. At the same time, you ladies are going to become seamstresses at Betsy Aberson's seamstress shop next door and we'll sneak you out in a delivery truck in plenty of time to catch up with the president-elect."

Mac handed his jacket to Milly and pulled the overalls over his clothes. He yanked the thick zipper up to his chin and pulled the mangy hat down to his eyebrows, "What do you think?"

Billy wrinkled her nose, "If I didn't know better, I'd swear you were just some stinky low-life working a lousy gig."

"You need to bend forward a little bit, as if you've got a sore back from lifting heavy trash cans all day. You're an actor, become this part," added Milly.

Murphy straightened up for a moment before his shoulders sagged, the curve of his spine compressed his flabby torso into a slouch, and his knees bowed slightly, which made him appear several inches shorter with the flaccid bearing of a weary toad who has suffered the ages."

"There you go," laughed Adel. "I'd definitely cross the street to avoid you!"

~

Adel's mother, Sybil, once a ravishing starlet who was abused by Hollywood producers and directors, passed around like a mirror covered with lines of cocaine. She found sanctuary in Marty, who was taking Production Management courses at UCLA, started a family, and assumed the duties of the business office of The Playhouse...but she still knew how to vamp.

Matty turned from the stove as Marilyn Monroe, dressed in a low-cut clingy white dress under a tailored black coat that enhanced her curves, strolled through the kitchen, clipping a large rhinestone dazzle to her earlobe beneath a platinum blond wig. "I'm always awed by your ability to transform yourself into her character. I'd swear that you're her reincarnation."

Sybil cocked in her hips, stuck out her chest, puckered her lips, batted her false eyelashes, and lifted a long cigarette holder to her mouth expecting a light. "I do so enjoy making arrogant men feel weak and inadequate."

Her mother-in-law laughed and glanced at the clock, "You'd better get going, the truck's going to turn into the alley in about five minutes. We'll bring everyone else over to the underground in a little while."

She whispered, "Wish me luck!" above the clickety-clack of her stiletto heels skittering down the stairs and across the warehouse to emerge through the metal door as a brilliant spark amid overflowing dumpsters offering up a foul bouquet to a cold damp morning.

Two troopers were patrolling each end of the lane and she could hear the squawk of their radios, as four mirrored helmets turned to watch her sashay towards the street. The two black uniforms ahead raised their sparking truncheons and moved to block her path, while their comrades abandoned their station and hustled to close on the phantom, mesmerized by the sway of her hips.

Sybil stopped between the guards, let the coat drape from her shoulders to expose her cleavage, fluffed her hair in the reflection in the helmet, and held up her cigarette holder, "Either of you macho-men happen to have a light?"

The face shield scanned her shape and a gloved fist produced the blue flame from a lighter. She inhaled and blew a long slow puff that curled around his rainbow visor. The metallic voice inquired, "Where do you think you're going?"

Sybil fluttered her eyes, as the other two approached from behind, "I was going to look for some…action." She reached out to rub his bicep, "Maybe I don't have to go too far to find what I'm looking for, if you're half that man I think you are?"

"I'm man enough for you, girlfriend."

She turned to his partner, "Or are you the alpha who knows what a woman needs?"

A squeaky high-pitched voice stuttered, "I've got…everything you could possibly want."

Sybil stepped between them and hooked their arms, just as an enormous trash truck trundled into the alley, the engine roaring and squeaky brakes hissing as two men jumped off the back to start rolling trash bins onto battered steel arms that screeched as they dumped their rancid contents into the belly of the putrid beast.

Her troopers shuffled to the side of the lane to protect her from splashing puddles, as the truck moved and stopped, with a thunderous growl and a deafening shriek. The guard on her right raised his baton to flag down the driver but she grabbed his arm and leaned close enough to yell, "I'm afraid I'll have to take a raincheck unless you have someplace we could go that's…more conducive to intimate conversation."

"Our personnel-carrier is just around the corner. Would that do?"

She flashed her Marilyn smile and wiggled her hips, "Let's go take a look."

Her son, little Mac, waited until they turned the corner and propelled Murphy out of the warehouse and boosted him into the passenger seat, while Adel scurried ahead of Milly and Billy to dart into the back door of Aberson's Alterations. Murphy shrank low in the seat as the burly driver checked his mirrors to be sure the guards had not reappeared and tooted the horn twice. The workers jumped on the back of the truck as it groaned and lumbered its way around scurrying critters and stray dumpsters into traffic on the street.

~

Nellis peeled off to visit Rusty and the Wizards in Oz, while Dr. Cohen escorted Katherine down to the mezzanine to enter the west entrance above a brewing hive of activity. The swirling human eddies slowed and stopped as the restless residents turned to cheer and applaud.

The director handed her a microphone and she turned to take in the crowd spilling out of the tunnels to crowd into the track bays, fill the opposite platform, and hang over the balconies. She shook her head with a smile, "This is truly amazing. Thank you! Thank you!"

The applause continued until she raised her hands, "Thank you! I haven't been on the run as long as most of you have but this is our chance to end the nightmare and begin our journey back to salvation. Are you with me?"

The chamber exploded with cheers and laughter and more than a few, consumed in the mayhem, stared around in disbelief.

"In a few minutes, several trains will arrive to take us to the biggest, rowdiest rally the nation's capital has ever seen. Democratic Presidential candidate Stanton Spratlin will be speaking to the nation from the steps of the Lincoln Memorial in Washington, D.C. I'm told that trains and buses filled with patriots just like you are heading there from all over the country to support our demands and your freedom!"

Someone below her yelled, "Why's this any different than all the protests we've seen on TV and who's going to protect us from the ARC thugs?"

Katherine looked down at the elderly Hispanic refugee and offered a warm smile, "I'll answer your questions in reverse. Our sheer numbers are going to protect you and you're going to protect each other because you know and I know that the fascists are going to send their goons to disrupt the rally with violence and chaos. That's a given but we'll outnumber them a thousand to one."

"What else?" asked the man.

"My good friend, Representative Spratlin, isn't going to be the only speaker. I believe, if we can protect the dignitaries and allow them to speak to the American people who will be watching from all over the nation, tonight's event will be the first step in restoring our country to real democracy and civility. We the people need to show up and make ourselves heard."

"Why now? What's changed?"

"How long have all of you been cooped up down here, hiding from the Gestapo? What's it take to motivate you to fight back, to reclaim your lives, your families, your place in society? The country's in flux, no one knows what's happening since Murphy disappeared and I'm fairly sure that no one with half a brain is going to be satisfied with Creighton Steil claiming the Oval Office. This is the moment to rise up, this is our chance to change the future! Are you with me?"

"Yes!"

The whole building shuddered and masses of people climbed out of the opposite track bed as the first train eased into the station.

~

The frosted glass doors into the lair of Oz opened as Nellis approached. Supervisor Madeline was waiting and reached to shake his hand, as he asked, "How are things going here?"

"Your young genius has earned the respect of every programmer in the suite and, as a result of his talent, we're controlling almost all of the white trains across the country."

"I didn't doubt him for a second. You should see the set-up he's got in his basement."

"I'm sure it runs like clockwork. Come with me and he can show you what's happening."

Nellis followed her across the broad foyer and beneath the black granite arches into the rarified hush of the clustered terminals. Marty was leaning over Rusty's shoulder watching the monitors and turned to greet Nellis, who reached out to pat the boy on the back. "I hear you're causing trouble again."

The boy turned with a tired grin, "We've got lots of trains running on our schedule and I'm pretty sure the operators in the Administration have no idea of what's happening or how to take back control."

"Can they do anything about it?" asked Nellis.

The young programmer pointed to three giant screens displaying the movements of all trains running east of the Mississippi. Normal traffic was flowing around a hundred streams and creeks pouring into a mighty river surging towards the Atlantic. "Unless they're brave enough to shut the whole system down to reboot, probably not. We disabled their identification system, so they really don't know which trains are which. They can see their normal traffic moving on schedule but they can't tell who all these other trains are or how they're being controlled."

"I'm impressed," said Nellis marveling at the spectacle. He looked down at the boy's droopy eyes, "When's the last time you slept?"

Rusty yawned, "Ummm...I don't know what day it is but it's been a while."

Marty rubbed his shoulders, "I tried to get him to take a little rest but he's determined to get all the trains to D.C. in time for the rally."

"I know I'll never get another chance to do anything like this again."

"Why?"

"Because, if we succeed in delivering all these trains nose-to-tail in D.C. on time, I don't want anyone to ever know who did it. It should become myth or legend."

"And if you don't?"

"I gotta hope that you and Ned can find a way to hide me, 'cause there's going to be a whole bunch of pissed-off grownups looking to lay the blame on someone."

"I think you're going to be a hero to a lot of people," said Nellis with a grin. "I'm always impressed when anyone combines clever and devious to make good things happen."

~

Amy scurried down the utility stairs to the cold dark service entrance and tripped the switch to open the gates. The chrome bowtie across the grill of Ned's ebony van shimmered in the dull gray gloom of winter but the bane was broken by the excited chatter of children in a variety of exotic costumes hanging out the windows of the gayly painted and still damaged Village Bus that pulled up beside her.

She flipped the lever to close the barriers as Ned and Tate and a posse of adults herded the rowdy mob of children towards the stairs. Ned grinned at the young firebrand from Atlanta, "I'd like you to meet Burt and Matty Sutton, their daughters, and a herd of grandkids, adopted kids, and a few more for good measure."

"You must live in a house with a huge kitchen and lots of bedrooms."

Alison's youngest, wee Tom Baker who was dressed as a tiny green leprechaun, piped up, "We do and someone stuck a theater on the front!"

"That must be why you're all dressed as different characters!" She laughed and let her eyes scan the crowd of performers approaching behind him but her jaw dropped open, "That man looks sort of like…"

"Someone who sort of resembles a missing president-elect?" inquired Matty, quietly. "How about we assume it's just a vague resemblance for the time being. We don't want to start a riot amongst all the refugees who've been hiding out down here for so long, before we have a chance to explain what's happening."

"Trust me," said Ned, "Nellis has a plan and if we can pull this off, there's going to be some spectacular fireworks in DC this evening."

"But…?"

Alison, still dressed as Marilyn Monroe, took her arm and batted her extravagant eyelashes to enhance the actress's famous look of naïve innocence, "Honest Honey, we'll explain everything as soon as we figure it out ourselves."

Tate took her other arm, as the crowd marched up the steps, "You've been around Nellis enough to understand that he doesn't approach things the way normal people might."

Ned leaned over, "More a matter of hanging on for dear life…he'll get us through but I promise he'll scare the crap out of you before it's over."

Amy shook her head, "I've seen him in action and the only words I could come up with were unpredictable and brilliant in a scary sort of way."

"Well, no one else has managed to put any kind of organized plan together to defend the movement or our democracy for that matter. This is the moment in history when things can change in a flash. Just gotta hope we get all the pieces in the right order," said Matty. "Sort of improvising on how to sort out the future of the country. This should be entertaining at the very least, don't you think?"

"I'm not privy to senior planning but I have to wonder how we're going to get to Washington without getting tangled up with the authorities?" replied Amy, pulling open the doors at the top of the stairs.

"You mean without getting executed," laughed Burt. "We're being protected and directed by the young genius who's working with your tech team."

"Yes, young Rusty. He's very special."

"There are worse things that can happen in life," added the man who resembled the president-elect.

Amy turned, "I'm not sure what to make of you."

"Young lady, do you understand what redemption is?" asked the man, his intense brown eyes focused on hers.

She stared for a moment, "For most people, it's about repairing their guilt and regrets with the people they've hurt."

"Very good," said Murphy, the corners of his lips curling into a knowing smile. "This is my one and only chance to set things straight with the American people and, if I'm going to consider myself a member of the human race, then I have to reach for that brass ring and atone for my sins."

Billy was holding his arm, "This morning, I would have handed this asshole over to the ARC troopers without a second thought but now, I'm starting to believe that he's beginning to grasp his own truth and, if I'm right, his speech could save the nation."

"Which you is real?"

Murphy's shoulders sagged slightly, his jaw relaxed, and his eyes softened, "I've been playing...no living the role of a disgusting loudmouth bigot for the past five years and I allowed that character to consume my spirit, to commandeer the very core of my being. That person did and said horrible things for all the wrong reasons and convinced thousands of our citizens that their hatred and lunacy was perfectly acceptable. It is not."

He turned to Milly, who was grasping his other arm, "My good friend Milly rescued me from my self-inflicted nightmare and probably saved the nation from certain damnation in the process. If I am to reclaim my soul, I have no choice but to see this through and I hope you'll help me get to Washington, so I can talk to the American people tonight."

Amy looked up, her eyes probing his, "What are you going to say?"

Murphy smiled, "This character never worked from a script, the monologue just starts and I improvise from there, so how about I start with the truth, the real truth, and we'll see where that takes me?"

"I'll be listening."

"How about you come stand with me and Representative Spratlin on the steps of the Lincoln Memorial tonight and, if you don't approve of what I have to say, I'll hand you the microphone and you can tell your own truth? I've watched your performances at the rallies. You have an irresistible presence because you treat your audience like they're your best friends and people react to that."

"They also seem to latch on to hate and lies and conspiracies."

"True, I've proven how easy it is to coax people along from being semi-intelligent to believing any hokum I could throw out there. The magic elixir was hate. Not just any hate but focused mutual hate for anyone of a different heritage or religion or skin color or language. Mankind has merged into tribes to annihilate those 'other' people for the communal good since the beginning of history. I think it's time we put a stop to it."

Katherine's voice echoed down the long hallway, as the group approached the balcony over the rail station. "… I'm fairly sure that no one with half a brain is going to be satisfied with Creighton Steil stealing the Oval Office. This is the moment to rise up, this is our chance to change the future! Are you with me?"

An enormous cheer, "Yes!"

Ned and Tate led Murphy and his ladies down a corridor to a suite of offices, while the children ran ahead to lean over the railing to peer down on an enormous crowd packed along the platforms on either side of the cavern. Hundreds of people climbed out of the track bed on the far side as the first train eased into the station.

Dr. Cohen's voice rebounded off the white tiled walls, "Ladies and gentlemen, we've spent these many months together in exile and we've become each other's keepers. I'm proud that we've triumphed over the ARC Gestapo and the isolation and terror that we have endured and, in the process, transformed our personal torment into a smoothly functioning society of righteous caring brothers and sisters."

Applause!

"I know that each and every one of you is anxious for fresh air, sunshine, and freedom but this is just the first train, so please be patient. To simplify this process, we will board by our section numbers, starting with group 'One'. Make room for the first passengers and move away from the train until your section is called. Our second train will be arriving on the west track momentarily and we will begin loading group 'Two'.

Please remember that we must maintain our security protocols until our mission is completed. You can wait a few more hours to reach out to your loved ones while you protect each other just a little bit longer."

A thinning swarm cleared the other track as a sleek silver engine towed an endless line of carriages into the station. Squads of retired police and military volunteer security emerged to board anxious passengers who lined up in orderly queues

More than an hour later, Ned and Burt clambered aboard the engine of the last shiny train as it slid down the tracks to load the final few cars. Matty emerged from a corridor, her salt and pepper hair gathered into a loose bun, hunched shoulders covered with a black peasant's shawl that trailed around her tiny frame, and stage makeup smoothing the age lines around her eyes and mouth, expressive and exquisite islands in a parchment complexion.

With the vibrant soul of an aging shaman, the effervescent matriarch led her flock to venture on a journey of salvation, with wisdom, compassion, and a wicked cackle. Her pale blue eyes glistened in the dull light, as twin pink rabbits, Misty and wee Melody, scurried across the platform pursued by Adel, as a stylish fox in a black leotard with pointy ears and a thick bushy tail. Matty's eldest son, Marty, who was completely out of character, marched out with the short quick steps of a British diplomat in a dark tailored suit, slender black tie, and a bowler hat, carrying a briefcase out in front of his body, as if it might contain something dangerous or, perhaps, reeked of foul malodorous perfumes to be delivered to someone someplace yet to be determined. He was followed by a tribe of American Indians, a cowboy strumming a guitar, a court jester bounding after a wizard in a purple cloak, a bride pushing a stylish carriage wide enough for twins, a peck of giggly children in stiff blue and white school uniforms, and several other curious characters, including a tall man dressed in an eighteenth-century mourning coat with a slender black woman on his left arm and a rather dowdy maiden on his right, both wearing broad skirts under long furs.

Katherine, as a stylish celebrity with a bright red scarf covering her auburn tresses and large dark glasses hiding her eyes, and Nellis in buckskins with a coonskin hat with a furry tail, and a very French Tate in an oversized black beret and a tiny black moustache escorted Marilyn and two peroxide blonds in spiky heels across the landing to scamper onboard as the coachman yelled, "All Aboard" moments before the doors slid closed with a soothing "Shusssh."

The last carriage was sealed off from the rest of the train but excited chatterer and ebullient energy rattled the car. Katherine waded through the jovial crush of merry characters to the front and picked up a microphone from a small communications bay as the train began to roll. She pressed the button and a crackly voice erupted from the small speaker mounted in the panel, "This is your engineer Patrick Smith, to whom am I speaking?"

"This is Katherine Kennedy."

"Welcome aboard. According to whoever has commandeered Central, our trip should take about three hours."

"Great! I was wondering whether I could use this system to talk to the passengers?"

"Yes, just press the 'Intercom' button and you'll be live."

"Thank you." She winked at Nellis, "You look like Daniel Boone! All you need is a musket," and pressed the button.

Tabitha Hall's houseman and protector, Hannibal Davis pulled the Cadillac up next to the Lear on the tarmac at Dolphin Bay International. Mavis Sloan appeared in the doorway of the jet and waved, as he opened the rear door to help his boss, Bobby Warmington, and her son Johnny step out of the car.

The owner and editor of the Dolphin Times turned, "Go park this beast someplace and hurry back, I'm sure that Mavis wants to get going."

"You expect me to join you?"

"Of course, this is about the future of our nation…as in all of us…and you know I feel more secure when you're close by."

Davis tipped his hat, "I am honored and humbled."

Young Johnny trotted up the stairs to hug Mavis, "Thanks for letting me come along."

She roughed his ginger hair, "I heard that Jessie and Kate are safe."

"Yeah, my mom told me. I can't wait to see him."

"Well, did you know that my dead husband has turned up alive? I get to see him for the first time since Hurricane Dot tore through town last year."

"Then we both got our wishes, didn't we," smiled the boy, his blue eyes twinkling with the boundless hope of youth.

She kissed his forehead as Bobby and Tabitha started to climb the stairs, "I think we did and, if this all works out, a lot of other people are going to get their wishes too."

He peeked inside, "Wow."

"Is this your first ride on a Lear?"

"Yeah. Does it go really fast?"

"Well, we'll be in Washington in less than two hours. Is that fast enough?"

"Yeah, I can't wait."

"Well, go inside and say 'Hi' to the pilots and have a seat in the back."

He turned into the cockpit, where two pilots were going through their checklists. The woman in the left seat turned, "Who are you?"

"I'm Johnny Warmington."

"Well, welcome aboard, Johnny. I'm Captain Martin and this is my copilot, Jones."

"This is cool. How did you learn to fly?"

Jones smiled, "We were both in the Air Force. He flew fighters, I flew transports and when we got out, we got lucky enough to get hired to fly planes like this."

"Boy, I'd like to learn to fly when I grow up."

"Hang on to that dream, son. One day, opportunity will present itself and you be smart enough to say, 'Yes'."

Hannibal Davis returned to help the women crowd on board and Bobbie retrieved her son, "C'mon, let the pilots finish their preparations, so we can get going."

Jones got up from his seat to close and seal the hatch, then turned into the cabin. "We'll be rolling out in just a minute and we should be in the air in no time. I'll be back to get drinks for you when we level off."

Mavis smiled her cover girl smile, "Thank you."

"Thank you for picking us up," said Tabitha. "Have you heard any news?"

"Just that at least some of the prisoner trains were intercepted and hijacked by Brad Spratlin and his buddies. I've been assured that

Jessie and Kate are safe and that planes and trains and buses with thousands of protesters are being cleared through to D.C."

Bobbie hugged Johnny, "This guy's been terrified since they were snatched."

"Well, it looks like things are being turned around," replied Mavis, buckling her belt as the engines revved and the jet taxied out to the main runway. "I got a call from Representative Spratlin's office manager, Gloria Lang, verifying that everything is on schedule. They'll have a car waiting for us at Reagan International. The entertainment starts at six and we're to appear on the steps with Stanton and his family shortly before eight."

Tabitha shook her head slowly, "We've been through this preparation in so many cities across the country, so I have to admire the hundreds of people rushing around taking care of all the details of putting this rally together in basically a day. That's organization."

"Yeah, we sent a whole caravan north last night and I've been getting calls from coordinators across the eastern half of the country, moving thousands of people by any means of transportation available. If this works, it's going to be the biggest protest in the city in decades."

"I was honored to hear Reverend King's speech to the biggest crowd I ever saw in my life," said Davis. "There was an energy, a power that swept through all those people and we were filled with hope and determination that somehow, some way we could set things right."

"America could have accomplished that feat right then but the Republicans wouldn't tolerate sharing their power with 'niggers and Jews' and they still won't," said Tabitha. "Segregation and the enslavement of your people is our national failing. It's time we changed that and made amends with everyone who suffered through it."

"The vengeful crowds who voted Murphy into office will never give up their right to hate but someday it will be harder for the racists to get away with abusing minorities when there are more of us than there are of them."

"Amen to that," said Bobbie.

"I think we have to be careful to forgive their hate and provide a path to redemption, so we don't end up replacing their sins with our own," added Mavis.

"I believe history provides many examples of righteous revolutionaries becoming total failures as administrators. Mao killed off half the population of China through sheer ineptitude after his Communists took over. He had to release the clerks and managers, who'd been consigned to 're-education' camps, to turn things around," said Tabitha. "The goal must be to restore our democracy."

"Power to all the people," grinned young Johnny.

"And all people matter," added Mavis.

Mr. Charles eyed Bruce Spratlin's bright pink parka and lime-green beret as he stopped the limousine outside the kitchen door of the St. Francis Orphanage, "I won't have to worry about losing you in the crowd tonight."

The gay artist looked down at his clothes, "I'll make an easy target."

"Do you think there'll be violence?"

"I'd be surprised if there wasn't some kind of confrontation or an attempt on my father's life."

"So, you're planning to be a human distraction?" asked Mr. Charles.

"I don't know what's going to happen but, after all that's gone down in the past year, I'll do whatever I can to make sure he lives through this."

"Don't worry, I'll be there because all of you are my children," said the driver, getting out of the car as Sister Gwen appeared at the gate dressed in her stiff habit under a long black coat. He glanced up at dozens of small faces peering down from the windows and tipped his cap, as he walked around the car to open the rear door. "Good afternoon, Sister. I'm glad you could join us."

"I'm honored to be included and I even asked the Lord to make it just a little bit warmer in Washington than it is here today."

"Amen to that, Sister," replied Mr. Charles, as a dusting of snow wafted down the alleyway.

Bruce climbed out of the front passenger seat to join her in the back, "I'm so glad you decided to come along. You've helped all of us and you should be there to see how all of this is going to play out."

"I prayed on it and decided that the very core of my belief system is based on caring for the least among us…and that includes my small contribution in assisting all of you who have worked so hard to lift a huge segment of our society out of poverty and despair. That is the Lord's work," replied the nun.

Bruce laughed, "I don't think I've ever been in such exalted company!"

She took his hand, as the car slipped into traffic, "In the Lord's eyes, you're perfect just the way you are because he intended you to be the person you are."

He blushed, "To tell you the truth, I think I'm finally beginning to accept that."

Her face lit up with an angelic smile, "Heroes come in all sorts of shapes and sizes."

Mr. Charles' deep voice reverberated from the driver's seat, "I agree. This whole family redeemed themselves during the past year or so and I give most of the credit to your little sisters."

"I can't argue with that," replied Bruce. "We were a classic example of the dysfunctional family, self-destructing in every way we could."

"Well, I'm proud of all of you," laughed the graying houseman and surrogate father, as the car rolled out on the runway to park next to the sleek silver dart. "And now you're going to help save the country."

Chapter Eleven

Young Rusty leaned back in the padded office chair and laced his fingers behind his aching neck to watch hundreds of trains slithering across the four screens, long slender worms slipping into traffic without disrupting scheduled service, at least until the final phase of the operation.

Supervisor Madeline walked up behind his chair and rubbed his shoulders, "Looks like it's all working."

"Yeah, we've got it all programmed to fill every station and crossing in the metropolitan area. They'll be really stacked up but Evan says they'll all fit."

"Any trouble with the high-command in the Rail Administration?"

"They can't see the ghost trains but they know something's up." He pointed, "They tried to roll a slow freight into a gap in front of one of our trains over here in Pennsylvania but Carl changed a couple of switches and moved it onto a siding."

"Gee, think they might wonder about that?"

"The only way they can interfere, besides putting army guys with bazookas on the tracks, is to shut down the whole system and they can't do that during rush hour. And besides, their trains are all running on schedule for the moment."

"What about when the big crush happens?"

"Well, some of their passengers might get stranded a little farther from their destinations than usual but they'll have so much company, they can all share their complaints," replied the boy.

"Has anybody thought about how you're going to untangle this mess, when it's over?"

Rusty looked up at her, his tired eyes glimmering in gray circles of exhaustion, "Hey, I only got hired to get the trains to DC. Nobody mentioned getting them turned around, somebody else is going to have to figure that out later."

Madeline grinned, "Could they just run your program in reverse?"

He stared at the screens and pursed his lips, "You know, it's possible but I don't have the energy to figure it out right now."

"What time do you think all the trains will arrive?"

"We're aiming for five o'clock, so there's time for people to get to the Memorial before the speeches."

"Was your family on the train that left earlier?"

"Yes, but I'm flying out around five-thirty and my dad said the plane can hold twelve passengers, so the team can come along, if you want?"

"Are you kidding, of course we would. I'll arrange transportation to the airport."

~

Dressed as tourists in cowboy hats and faded jeans, Lincoln Todd and Roger Stanislawski strolled around the Washington monument surveying the mall. Todd stopped to lean back, inspecting the huge tower, "That'd be a convenient roost but the getting up and down might be a hassle."

"Ya' think?" replied his comrade, heading across the grass. "Do you see the irony of you working on this project in this space?"

"You know he was my great-great-great grandfather, don't you?"

"You're full of shit."

"Well, there's that but you don't have a memorial dedicated in your name, do you?"

"Let's go over and see what the view's like from the War Memorial before I punch you on general principles."

Security had closed off access to the reflecting pools and the walkways beyond the waterfalls but the pair could see armies of workers scurrying up and down the broad stairs setting up a podium and speakers, towers for lights and video cameras, and miles of barriers to contain the crowd.

"You know they're going to have this covered and I doubt you're going to get a clean shot from the trees, so the only choice is to get in close," said Todd, turning to stare up at the Atlantic tower. "I'll bet there's a nice perch up there."

"I'm not sure anyone could scale that, with all the security."

"We both know shooters who'd go up that thing like a monkey in about two seconds," laughed Todd.

"Let's keep it in mind."

"How many guys are we going to have in the crowd?"

"Probably a hundred. They're trashing the protests this afternoon and they'll be all primed for action tonight."

"I'm told that our people are going to have four or five video crews with reporters on site. We could stash weapons in their gear to get past security."

"That'll work. They park the vans and celebrity limos behind the trees on either side of the Memorial. Easy access guarded by the feds," laughed Todd.

"Our people already have security passes, so they should be able to walk right through the checkpoints. You get the weapons together and I'll line up some veteran shooters and put you in contact with the equipment manager for the propaganda machine."

"Cool, call me when you have it worked out."

"Can do."

～

Chief Engineer Eddy Deacan turned to a beep on the communications screen and reached to sound the whistle, "Get your folks on board, we're cleared through to D.C."

Jessie, Brad, and Sammy jumped down to the track-bed in a flurry of puffy snowflakes as a shrill shriek shredded the serenity of the whispering pines and hundreds of bodies emerged from the forest. Brad yelled, "Get everyone on board, we're moving out!"

Small herds of liberated prisoners flocked to the open doorways and helped each other climb aboard. Brad marched to the last car and peered inside, where more than a dozen ARC guards were strapped into plastic seats lining one side of the car. Rainbow shards from the shattered shields of their imposing helmets glimmered on the gravel around the tracks and the tyrannical sentinels appeared frightened and submissive. "Any problems with these guys?"

"Naw, they're just sad little sheep in wolf's clothing," laughed Milton Shepherd, former tactical commander of a Seal team, picking up one of the guard's batons and igniting the sizzling static. He pointed it at the largest prisoner who turned away, whimpering. "Take their torture tools away and they plead for mercy."

"Not that they offered any to all these folks they were transporting to hell," replied Brad. "Make sure they stay under guard, when we get to D.C., so they can be arrested."

A brawny trooper sneered, "They're going to arrest all of you as soon as this beast pulls into Union Station."

Brad pointed, "Brother, by the time we get there, your guys will be running for cover. We're going to make sure that you're brought to justice, not in some secret kangaroo court but before a real military tribunal. You all claim to be working for a secret security branch of the government, don't you?"

Terrified eyes stared but no one responded.

"After tonight, ARC will be disbanded and everyone involved in this mockery will be in custody. Keep them under control, we're heading out."

He trotted back to the engine and climbed into the cockpit, "Looks like everyone's on board."

"Say a little prayer that there isn't a squad of armed goons out there waiting to hijack us," said Kate.

"We won't let that happen," said Spratlin as he took a seat and straightened his kilt. "We've got an experienced squad who've seen more than their share of combat, even if we are dressed in traditional uniforms."

"Broad swords and shields?" asked Benny, with a smile. "And skirts!"

"And enough combat weapons to take Bagdad, if we need to."

The train picked up speed as it rolled north and Ditkins said, "From the route they've laid out, we'll be running through forests and marsh country, away from most of the rail traffic. According to the schedule, we should arrive a little after four o'clock."

Deacan settled back into his seat and eased the throttle forward, "Next stop Liberty."

An hour later, the sleek white train slowed to pass through Brooke, Virginia, just north of the Crow's Nest Preserve, and picked up speed heading northeast through a series of curves to cross the bridge at Aquia Creek but Deacan pulled back on the throttle.

"What's up?" asked Brad, pulling binoculars from the sporran or leather pouch on his belt.

The engineer pointed to a tanker truck parked across the tracks beside the marina, "Roadblock."

"Stop the train here. We've got special ops to deal with this inconvenience." He picked up the microphone and pressed the button, "Morgan, Henke, we have an obstruction. Bring your gear."

The nose of the sleek serpent emerged from the forest where the track straightened out more than two-hundred yards from the bridge. Ditkins pressed the button to open the sliding door and two soldiers in camo fatigues stepped into the cockpit.

"Folks, these are two of my best guys, Morgan and Henke," as he handed the field glasses to the hulking black officer, "Take a look."

"A couple of dozen of those fake troopers and it looks like someone loaned them some weapons." He offered the glasses to Henke.

"Why would anyone use a tanker truck against a train? Unless that thing's full of milk, they've got a big problem."

"We could just push it out of the way," said Deacan.

"Nah, it'd be too easy for them to blast us," said Henke. "Let's just blow it off the tracks and them too."

"Uh-oh," said Morgan.

"They're setting up artillery," laughed Henke, jumping through the door as two soldiers in kilts set up a large gun on the tracks.

"That looks heavy duty," said Jessie, leaning out the door.

Brad looked up, as the shooter in front of the tanker truck fired a blast that shredded the trees on the north side of the tracks, "It's just an old 806 but I guarantee these boys know how to use her. You might want to cover your ears."

Before Jessie could cup his ears, Henke fired off a spray of fifty caliber tracers that sent the ARC troopers scrambling for cover, toppling their heavy weapon. "Shall we aim for the tanker?"

"Think you can take it out without damaging the tracks?" asked Brad with a grin.

"Ah, Sarg, you know my talents better than that. Do you want me just to take out the tank and leave the cab sitting there?"

"Sure, the less damage we leave behind the better. You're the man!"

Morgan straightened the belt of shells, "How many you going to waste on this sucker?"

"Ah, I bet I can take it off the tracks with a dozen."

"Why waste so many?"

The gunner laughed, "Alright, Scots in skirts are always frugal, aren't they? How about nine?"

"Go for it!"

The former marine hunched over the weapon and eased off three rounds that blew out the tires, aimed again, and spread five rounds across the belly of the tanker, which erupted in orange flames spewing from a jagged tear in the mangled torso of the trailer as it arced over backwards with a mortal roar, splintered a line of trees, and tumbled into the frigid waters next to the marina with a steaming splash. The rear window of the cab was shattered and the paint blistered by the heat, but the tractor was otherwise undamaged.

Henke grinned, "Eight!" He and Morgan collected the 806 as six more retired soldiers appeared with automatic weapons and scattered the remaining ARC troopers into the brush along the shoreline.

"You're still the best!" Brad turned and yelled, "Head 'em up, move 'em out!"

Everyone scrambled on board and he told the engineers, "Leave the doors open, so my guys can protect the train until we're clear of the bridge."

Deacan pushed the throttle forward and the white snake rolled east, "I sure hope you didn't damage the tracks or we're in a heap of trouble."

"Have faith, brother, my guys are pro's," laughed Brad. "Don't slow down or they'll try to shoot up the prison cars."

He grabbed the microphone, "Everyone hit the deck, we're running through a gauntlet, so let's be safe!"

Morgan leaned against the jam of the open door, grinning as he peered down the bank along the tracks, where several snipers were hiding behind large trees. He fired a short burst and they all dove for the dirt. "Pussies!"

Another gunner a few cars back laid in some cover fire to pin them down as the train picked up speed to cross the bridge, heading north.

~

Ethan Tomlinson's phone chirped as his shoe touched tarmac, exiting the jet with a nod to the driver holding the door of the limousine outside Signature Flight Support at Reagan International. He settled into the rear seat and touched the screen on his phone, "Hello, Stanley. What can I do for you?"

"I want to know what the hell is going on with Spratlin's circus tonight. My people tell me the streets are already clogged with protestors coming into the city from every direction!"

"To tell you the truth, I've only just landed but I talked with Will Terry a little while ago and he's setting up video crews to capture every angle on this event. He told me that the crowds have been building since this morning but Spratlin's people haven't had time to work up much marketing, so this is all word-of-mouth and social media."

"Why do I get the feeling we've already lost control?"

"No one, and I mean no one, has offered the slightest clue about what it is Spratlin wants to say and who's going to be there as back up? I did pick up a rumor that Jazz Taggart and his Band of Merry Men are playing warmup."

"Aren't they…"

"Yeah, the band that Nellis Gray fronted for at every All People Matter rally."

"Coincidence?"

"I think not," replied Tomlinson. "I'll get back to you after I have a chance to check in with our people."

"Our supporters in The Forge are climbing down Conrad's back and he's about to have a stroke, so check in with him as soon as you have some news."

"Stanley, we've always been straight up with each other, so I'm not going to blow smoke up his ass to quiet your money guys until I know what the fuck is going on. We've accomplished a lot in fifty years but there's a long way to go, even if Steil takes the Oval Office. After all we've been through, this is just another obstacle to be overcome and we will succeed."

"I know you're right but don't blame the troops for being anxious to push this thing across the finish line."

"They're sophisticated tycoons, so they ought to know the old adage that my mom used to say, 'Don't count your chickens…'. In this case, it's don't let your greed and lust for power destroy the whole campaign."

"Amen to that. Let me know what you know when you know it!"

The line went dead and he turned to stare out the window as the limo turned north on the George Washington Memorial Parkway. He noticed fleeting glimpses of a sleek white windowless train without any identifying marks running between several passenger trains rolling nose to caboose into the city on the tracks beyond the trees.

Chief Engineer Patrick Smith pushed the throttle to propel the long train south from Baltimore into dense forest in the Patuxent Refuge. He turned to Burt, riding shotgun in the cab, "I don't know who's running the scheduling on all this but it's been smooth so far and they've kept us out of metropolitan jams. We ought to be in the station in forty-five minutes or so, if they keep everyone clear."

"Actually, the brain behind that operation is someone very dear, who I have absolute respect for. He knows what he's doing."

The train cleared the bridge over the Patuxent River, approaching the campus of Bowie State University, but Harrington grabbed the throttle to brake, pointing through the windshield. "Trouble."

A flaming pile of telephone poles were strewn across the tracks in front of an old school bus. Yellow bursts flared from the open windows followed by sputtering explosions of rock and dust along the rail bed.

Brad's former commander, Muncie McCoy, snapped, "Stop and back up fifty yards or so. Open the doors!" He grabbed the microphone, "All hands on deck, we found the resistance!"

Two-dozen battle-hardened professionals leapt from the retreating train, taking up positions in the trees on either side of the tracks. Two scouts scurried south to scan the barriers. Muncie's radio squawked, "Looks like a bunch of militia guys in fake camo totin' AR's."

"Anything besides the bus behind that pile of logs?"

"Naw, but they've got nests in the brush on both sides of the tracks."

"Think we could blow right through the blockade?"

"Yeah, it's rinky-dink. Hell, they ain't no boy scouts, their fire's going out!"

"Okay, you guys take out the snipers and the bus. We'll push through the barricade and pick you up on the other side."

The remaining liberators took up positions in the open doorways and McCoy ran to the engine, "Ned, hike back and make sure everyone's under cover in the last car. We're going to run the gauntlet."

He raced along the tracks and climbed into the final passenger car, as the train inched forward following a pair of explosions farther down the line. Businessman Marty was standing in the doorway before a table surrounded by Marilyn Monroe next to a mustachioed Tate, Nellis in his coonskin cap, and Katherine the radiant movie star. A cast of Indians, cowboys, a wizard and a jester entertained a gaggle of uniformed children seated in the back of the carriage. The president-elect, in a black mourning coat with ample makeup to erase twenty years of hard living from his haggard face, looked anxious.

Matty asked, "What's happening?"

"A squad of militia guys are trying to hijack the train but our guardian angels are dealing with the situation. They asked me to get everyone down on the floor in case the bad guys start shooting."

Murphy looked up, "Who ordered them to stop this train?"

"I'm sure it's the same folks who terrorized the All People Matter rallies. They've got volunteers everywhere."

"I guess my question should be more direct. Did they choose this train because I'm on it?"

Nellis replied, "I'm fairly certain there's no way anyone could know, because we didn't know which train we'd be on, so it could be coincidence."

"I don't believe in coincidences!" snapped Murphy.

"Now, Mac," soothed Milly, clutching his arm.

Ned stepped in with gentle authority, "Mr. President, our security forces are taking care of the situation. The engineers are going to push through the barricade and proceed to Washington. They've asked all of you to take cover until we've moved past the danger. Your cooperation would be appreciated."

Billy leaned close to whisper in Murphy's ear, "This is just the first threat you're going to face today. We could die here or on the steps in front of Lincoln's statue but we're going to see this through no matter the obstacles, so do as the man says and get down on the floor."

Murphy stood up and walked to the back of the car, "Children, we've been asked to lie down on the floor until we get past the danger, can I play with you?"

Tiny Indians and uniformed students cheered and everyone took cover.

Burt and Smith turned as McCoy leapt into the cockpit and pointed through the windshield, "Our guys are going to take out their snipers and move the bus."

"Then what?" asked Burt.

"We're going to push the barricade out of the way and proceed with your journey."

Engineer Smith pointed through the windshield, "Might not have to."

An ancient decrepit diesel locomotive rumbled up behind the yellow bus, which bowed from the center ejecting gunmen out of doors and windows, the tires grabbing the ties beneath the rails, and rolled over twice before landing on top of the smoldering pile of logs in the ditch.

"What is that?" asked Burt. "I haven't seen one of those in decades."

Smith grinned, "That's a SD7. I thought they went out of service back in the seventies or eighties."

"Well, I'm damned sure glad to have their help."

Burt smiled, "I think the brains behind this operation sent the cavalry to help us out."

~

A parade of black Suburban's pulled up, as Chief Engineer Patrick Smith nestled the train into the only open track in the crowded railyard just north of Union Station, sandwiched between a tangle of trains that blocked the view from either side in the dull evening light.

Murphy peeled the latex mask from his face, rubbed the makeup off with a handkerchief, and removed the brown contacts from his eyes, "I need to be myself when I meet Spratlin."

Billy reached to flip up the collar of his long black coat and pulled the brim of his broad-brimmed hat low over his eyes. "You keep your head down and we'll get you to the podium on time."

"I appreciate you ladies for making this journey possible."

Milly patted his hand, "We'll get you there, the rest is up to you."

Nellis pointed out the window, "The cars are waiting, if you're ready."

The president-elect took a deep breath and exhaled very slowly, "Let's begin!"

Billy took his arm and looked up at him, "Your supporters wouldn't stand for this."

"I was just thinking about the frenetic racist fever I used to spin up in the crowds of ignorant bigots, who needed someone spewing rubbish to justify their hate. And you're absolutely right, I would be stoned or worse."

"No tellin' what they'd do to a pregnant nigger ex-whore like me."

"I would protect you with my life."

The statuesque beauty stopped to stare, searching for the soul behind the determined focus in the eyes beaming in the shadow of his fedora. "I can't believe you just said that."

"You've become quite precious to me. I owe you and Milly a great debt for helping me begin the journey to find out who I'm supposed to be."

She pulled him close, "Convince us and you'll convince the nation."

"Let's go," said Matty.

A small herd of enchanting characters climbed down the few steps into the frigid cold of the gravel yard, before the two women helped Murphy to the ground, where Stanton Spratlin waited with an astonished squad of Secret Service agents.

Nellis grinned, "Brought you a special guest, thought you might need some backup."

"I had no idea…"

"It'd probably be good if no one else had any idea either, so do me a favor and ask your guys with the earplugs to keep this off the airwaves until we need him on stage."

He turned to Tom Walker, Head of Security, "See that this remains our little secret. I don't want a word of this gentleman's reappearance to get out until I say so. Is that understood?"

"Yes, Sir."

Spratlin shook his head and extended his hand, "I'm not really sure how to react to this whole situation but I believe we have much to discuss and little time to get acquainted. So, why don't you ride with me and we can talk on the way." He turned to Nellis and Katherine, "And why don't you two join us?"

Nellis took Katherine's arm, "I was afraid you'd never ask."

"I wish I could say that it's great to see you but we both know that I'm just another character in your latest Fellini film that could change the course of history or doom our democracy. Do you have any idea how this is all going to work out?"

"Not a clue," laughed Nellis, "but you of all people know that I always deliver a stunning finale."

"Yeah, that's what I'm afraid of," replied the almost president.

Before the limo started moving, Nellis asked, "How are your girls?"

"They're safe and warm at the hotel and all the kids are anxious to see you. Brad commandeered the train carrying Kate and Jessie and their crew and, as you know, Bruce has been handling secure communications from home. He's flying in with Mr. Charles and Sister Gwen."

Katherine wrapped her hand around Nellis's arm, "And he's anxious to see all of them too, even if he won't admit it."

Spratlin stared at Murphy for a moment, "I have to assume that there's a very long story behind your disappearance and sudden reappearance with Nellis and Katherine of all people. So, considering our limited time, let's cut to the chase. Why are you here now?"

Murphy grinned, "Well, now that I understand that you have a 'relationship' with Nellis, I guess we should both blame him."

Stanton laughed, "Fair enough! We do have some rather jaded history."

Mac winked at Katherine, "The honest truth is that I've been an actor, a performer all my life and what started as a short-term stand-in gig for an ailing radio bigot, evolved over the past five years into a prank run for the presidency. The personality that the white-nationalists revered was a drug addled and alcohol fueled contrivance who consumed and destroyed the person I once was."

"What changed your mind?"

Mac looked from Milly to Billy, "These fine people had more faith in me that I had in myself but the moment of reckoning happened as I was preparing for my last radio show on the night of the election, when one of my campaign staffers informed me that I should enjoy the revelry of our impending victory because I was about to become just another employee of the folks who financed my campaign. In that instant I sobered up and realized that my candidacy and the prospect of winning the White House would enable a tiny group of greedy bastards, who call themselves The Forge, to literally buy absolute control of our government. I was to be the mouthpiece, the distraction from the deconstruction of the government and the demolition of the middle class.

Milly convinced me that the only solution was for me to flee before they had a chance to control my movements. So, we ran and my new friends gave me the chance to take a serious look at my sins and then they offered me this path to begin my redemption. I've screwed up a lot of things in my life, I couldn't let this opportunity pass me by."

"So, what do you want to say?" asked his opponent.

Murphy's stone-cold eyes focused in on Stanton's, "The truth. Simple as that."

"Can you be more specific?"

"Let's be straight with each other, okay? I never had any intention of being president of anything. I got into this charade to embezzle a fortune and have some fun mocking my fans and the Republican Party. I owe it to my redneck supporters and the citizens of this country to tell the truth about what happened, what I did, and to convince them that it was all a lie. I never believed any of the crap I spouted on the radio or in my speeches at the rallies. It was pure improvisational performance driven by lots of drugs, buckets of Jack Daniels, and the reaction of the crowds. They know none of it was true, even if they're desperately afraid of anyone who isn't fat, white, and stupid coming to take their lives and their privileges away."

Nellis looked at Spratlin, "Having been a performer all my life, might I suggest you go out and say what you have to say and save the surprise for the finale?"

Stanton nodded and hesitated before he turned back to Murphy, "Why should I trust you?"

Mac roared, "I sure could use a shot of Jack about now! But you have no choice. You can go out on the steps under the gaze of old Abe and say whatever you want and, short of starting an insurrection, everyone's going to agree with you and go home. Nothing will change.

If you let me follow you up, we bring everyone in the nation together against the rich bastards and the party machinery, while we create a peaceful revolution that might actually make things better."

Katherine asked, "So, who's going to be president?"

"Not that bastard, Creighton Steil," replied Murphy, pointing at Spratlin. "He's the only guy in the race who's actually qualified to run anything."

"But I wasn't elected," said the Democratic candidate.

"You got the most votes, didn't you?" said the president-elect with a grin. "Besides, you said this was another one of Nellis's Fellini movies, so we're making it up as we go along. If we have to have another election, so be it, but I'll make damned sure that the folks that voted for me don't ever vote for a Republican again."

~

Roger Stanislawski edged the truck through a dense throng of bodies clogging the streets and sidewalks and offered his official network pass to the guard at the barrier on Henry Bacon Drive at Constitution.

The cop scanned it and asked, "You with The Patriot Network?"

"Yeah, man, our motto ought to be we ain't jivin' you!"

"What's in the van?"

"Just lighting gear." He checked his watch, "Actually, we're running late. The boss wanted this all set up for a live clip on the six o'clock news. We're gonna have to hustle to get it together on time."

The officer handed the card back to Stanislawski, "Just make sure you park over in the parking lot by the gift shop after you unload. Security will be closing things up in about twenty minutes."

"We'll be outta the way in plenty of time," said Lincoln Todd, with a wave from the passenger seat.

The van rolled around the plaza in front of the memorial and parked next to another Patriot truck. The two men hopped out to greet Harvey Green, who managed the broadcast equipment on location. "Sorry we're late, traffic and security," said Todd.

"Yeah, they've got this place locked down." He turned to point to thousands of protesters jammed against a chain link barrier constructed around the edge of the drive and another at the bottom of the broad stairs beneath the imposing statue, with armed security eyeing every possible threat, "Ain't no one gonna get close."

"Is it just Spratlin?"

A female singer with a large guitar tapped on the microphone at the top of the stairs, "Is this live? Can y'all hear me?"

Green cupped his hands to yell, "Don't know, they don't tell me shit. We've suffered through a couple of lame folk-rock bands and a few speeches by local liberals. I'm pretty sure no one's gonna tell us until it happens."

"Hey, did our helpers show up?" asked Todd.

He pointed, "Those vagabonds have been hanging around for the last thirty minutes, asking when you were going to arrive."

"I'll deal with them," said Stanislawski. "They're just wanna-be's looking for a chance to try out for a gig."

"Just get this gear set up so Sonya can spout her bullshit for the six o'clock and get this truck out of here as soon as you get the gear on the ground. The cops have been hassling me since I got here."

"Yes, Sir."

"Y'all Lewis and Clark?" asked Stanislawski, motioning to the four amateur roadies, who looked like displaced mountain men with heavy beards and camo clothes fit for the wilderness. "I can't fucking believe two of you are working together with names like that."

"Hey, blame his daddy," said Hector Clark. "I had nothing to do with it."

He pointed to the tallest of the four, a bear-chested man with long brown curls falling across the torn shoulders of a tattered leather jacket, "And I suppose you two are Sacagawea and her Indian brother?"

"Fuck you," said the smaller balding man with red fringe and dark deadly eyes.

"You sure you're up for the task at hand?"

The men shuffled and grinned. Lewis said, "It's a pleasure doing business with you, brother. We're gonna save the country from a nightmare."

"Question is whether you can shoot straight?"

"We're all Special Ops. We know the drill."

"Ever used an old Delta?"

"Yeah, I shot a few rounds with one a couple of years ago. Old school but nice balance."

Todd opened the rear door of the van and pulled out small satchels.

"What'd ya do, cut off the barrels?" asked Clark.

"No, we made a few improvements. The stock and barrel both lock in with a half twist. There's a half-dozen clips with twelve rounds in each case."

"Hell, I'll only need one," boasted Lewis.

"Here's the deal," said Stanislawski leaning close, handing each an ear piece, "we don't know what's happening here or who's appearing when. Our troopers will be raising hell all evening but they'll start a ruckus in front of the podium as he's finishing his speech. Save your shot until the crowd gets rowdy, the chaos will provide the perfect television diversion, but you get to remain invisible until I give you the word when I get a handle on what's really going down tonight."

An anxious Johnny Warmington sat on the edge of his seat, peering out the window at enormous crowds gathering along the mall in front of the monument, as the van passed through security and pulled around to the back.

"Will we get to see the statue?"

"Of course, dear," replied Tabitha. "It's just inside the memorial. But before we go, tell me, do you know why this place is so special?"

"Because Lincoln stopped slavery."

"How'd he do that?"

"His armies from the North fought the rebels from the South, who broke away from the rest of the states because they didn't want to give up their slaves."

"That's very succinct young man," replied the editor. "So, here are some facts that you should notice, while we're here. The architect, Henry Bacon, emulated the classic style of the Parthenon in Athens and was very careful to include special numbers of elements, like the thirty-six columns representing the thirty-six states in the union at the time of his death, the eighty-seven steps from the reflecting pool to the statue come from his Gettysburg address, which included the phrase 'Four score and seven years'."

"So, a score was twenty?"

"Yes, you're exactly right." She continued, "The marble for the building came from Colorado but the marble used in the statue came from Georgia and it sits on a pedestal from Tennessee."

"North and South, East and West?"

The matron smiled, "I won't bore you with much more but notice the two paintings on the ceiling dedicated to Emancipation and Reunion and do pay attention to the murals in the alcoves on either side of the statue. One is a stone etching of his address at Gettysburg and the other his second inaugural speech, which he gave a few months before he was assassinated. If you take a moment to read it, you'll see how much he wanted to reunite the nation."

"I'll look for it." The boy jumped out of the car and clapped his hands over his ears against deafening music and the roar of the crowd, as he scanned the crush of bodies lining both sides of the reflecting pools for as far as he could see. Four police officers guided them across the lawn and through a cluster of trees to a small door that revealed an elevator, "Is Jessie up there?"

Tabitha shouted over pounding music, "I don't know dear, but we'll find out as soon as we get there."

The editor turned to Mavis, while the boy hopped into the car as soon as the doors parted, "Are you prepared to see Tate?"

The beauty pursed her lips, "I guess we're about to find out."

Bobby Warmington took her arm, "Try not to make him bleed. After all, what would Abe think of a cover-girl beating the crap out of her former husband on this historic occasion?"

"He'd probably approve," laughed Tabitha, as they followed Johnny.

The boy stepped into a large alcove next to the imposing statue in the central chamber of the temple, where a growing flock of familiar faces gathered in the vestibule. He spied Jessie and Kate talking to Brad Spratlin amidst the throng from Cameron - Sissy, Sam, with Marjorie, Mama Louise, Maybelle Brown and her children - Daniel, Hubie, Muriel, and Martin – Mr. Charles with Bruce, in a garish pink parka and electric-green beret, next to sister Gwen in her black and white habit. He glanced at the enormous marble president as he sprinted across the smooth stone floor through Matty and Burt's herd of children to leap into Jessie's arms.

"I'm so glad to see you," said the artist with a squeeze. "I swear you've grown since we got kidnapped."

"I'm so glad you're alive! I thought…"

"I know and I'm sorry those horrible men scared you."

Kate leaned in to give him a kiss on the cheek, "They scared us too!"

"How's Gracie?" asked Jessie.

"She recovered from the poison on that dart but she's been really blue since you've been gone. She goes down to the dock and just stares across the bay, as if the Kate Too's about to come motoring in and when I take her to your house, she just lies on the drive looking up the lane."

"Ah, I've missed her almost as much as I've missed you and I can't wait to see her when we get home. I sure appreciate you looking after her. Have you been fishing?"

"Naw, it's not the same without you."

"Fine, first thing we're doing when we get back is going fishing down in the little bay. Your boat or mine?"

"MissU 2, of course!"

Mavis appreciated the security and comfort her friends provided but nothing they could say or do could calm the pounding of her heart or pacify the butterflies flitting around her stomach as her eyes searched the crowd. She was startled by a gentle touch on her shoulder and turned to fall into her husband's arms.

He held her for a long moment before she pulled away, "I'm so very glad you're alive but I want to throttle you for letting me go through the grief of your death…and now, the embarrassment of your resurrection!"

He turned his head to expose his cheek and winced, "Okay, I'm ready."

Tears trickled down her cheeks as she clenched her fists and pounded his chest, "You son of a bitch!"

He wrapped his arms around her and pulled her close, "I'll explain the story and take my punishment when there's time, but right now we've got a rally and a cause to attend to."

"That's a lame excuse to avoid taking responsibility for this incredibly awkward situation," said Mavis, clutching his lapels. "Who's in charge of this show?"

He pointed, "Spratlin's Chief of Staff, Gloria Lang. I think that's her talking to Security over behind the statue but we just got here and I haven't met her yet."

"What about our security team and Brad's guys?"

"I don't know about your team but I'm told that Secret Service, FBI, and every police officer in the District is here in force, so it's their game. From what I've heard, Brad and his comrades hijacked and escorted a number of prisoner trains into town. Actually, he got lucky and took down the train carrying Jessie and Kate and all the folks from Dolphin Bay."

Brad walked over to add, "We've got thousands of freed prisoners nearby and they'll fill the plaza in front of the monument before my dad starts his speech."

"That should be dramatic," said Mavis, looking up at her reborn husband. "We'll talk later, if we survive this event."

Tate took Brad's arm to escort him to Matty, who was still dressed as a peasant woman, Burt in his striped railroad engineer's cap, Marty in a stiff black business suit, accompanied by Marilyn Monroe and two other platinum blonds shepherding a scurrying fox with two pink bunnies, several small American Indians, and a classroom of children in formal uniforms. "I want you to meet the folks who sheltered all of us and thousands more in New York."

Brad grinned, "Do all people in New York dress this way?"

"Only the cool ones," replied Amy, stepping out of the throng to hug Brad, who gathered her in his arms.

"I was worried that you'd been captured."

"No, I got lucky enough to be out of the office, when they came to arrest the rest of our staff. I haven't found Althea yet and I'm worried about her."

"If she was traveling on one of the trains on the East Coast, I'm pretty sure my guys got her back." He looked into her eyes, "If we survive tonight, I'd very much like to spend some time with you."

"I'd like that," said Amy, reaching on tiptoe to kiss him.

~

The last glow of daylight dimmed behind dark clouds promising a cold mist, if not a frigid downpour before the evening passed. The column of black cars approached the Lincoln Memorial and Murphy turned to watch thousands of jovial protesters marching west along Constitution Avenue and down the side streets to swell the crowds jamming the mall and the surrounding parks all the way to the Capitol.

He turned to Billy, "Those are the real faces of America – every size, shape, and color."

"Our diversity makes this country great and every one of us needs to be recognized as equal and legitimate, vital and unique."

"There are more than seventy-million who think otherwise," said Spratlin. "I'm not going to convince more than a few of those people to join the cause, that's up to you."

Mac nodded slowly as Milly patted his knee, "This is the performance of your lifetime but this time it's not an act, it's the real thing and I know you can do this."

"I'm glad you believe in me, both of you." He glanced at the roiling crowd jammed against the barriers across the drive in front of the memorial, flashing on the anger and hate that throttled his rallies into furious frenzies of unrestrained violence. The tenor of these protestors was a display of joyous determination to conquer and rebuild the system that demolished their lives. The entire working class suffered the same brutal frustrations and nightmares but these people intended to end the corruption and oppression and rebuild the middle class for everyone, while his audience would consume the crumbs of our democracy, anointed by their ignorant dedication to fraudulent candidates representing the interests of the shadowy titans who dominate corporate America.

As the van parked behind the Gift Shop and an identical vehicle pulled up next to it, Spratlin extended a hand, "If we do this right, perhaps we can save our democracy."

"I'm honored to have the chance to say what I should have said a long time ago."

"That's good enough for me," said Stanton, who knocked twice on the window. The door cracked open to reveal a narrow tunnel between the doors of the two cars. "Mrs. Gray, would you be kind enough to accompany me?"

"Of course!" replied Katherine with a kiss to Nellis' cheek and a little pout. "Try to stay out of trouble until we get through this."

Her husband chuckled, "Fat chance!"

Security Chief Tom Walker stuck his head in the door, "We have two agents in the front seat, dozens surrounding the area, and another car following for the two-hundred yard journey to the entrance. We'll be in constant contact with these gentlemen and you can reach us through them. I'm told that Mr. Gray is expected to play some music in a few minutes, so we'll take you over when they give us the word."

The door closed with a gentle thud that silenced the music vying with the human thunder reverberating along the length of The Mall.

Murphy stared out the tinted window as the other car pulled away, "Will it be just us?"

"No, the rest of the family is already inside the building, along with everyone from Cameron and Dolphin Bay, thousands of prisoners rescued from the ARC roundup, as well as tens of thousands of supporters and members of the All People Matter movement," said Milly.

"We'll stand with you," added Billy, "because we've all come to bear witness to history."

"I doubt the freed prisoners will be a receptive audience."

"You didn't order the institution of a government program to disappear thousands of enemies of the fascist state but you did justify the concept and millions of your fans bought into it."

"I was so successful at rallying the worst of our society, I can only hope that I might redeem myself with the rest of our citizens by offering the truth."

Nellis nudged him with a grin, "You won't accomplish that in one speech or ten, but you can't begin the performance until you recite the first line. This is your premiere, give the critics something to write about!"

"Well put," replied Murphy.

Katherine ducked as she scooted between Suburban's and climbed into the seat next to her former boss and lover, "We can't go on meeting like this."

He took her hand, "We've both come a long way in a little over a year."

"I'm very proud of who you've become. You're the man I always knew you should be."

He kissed her fingers, "You managed to motivate millions of people to stand up for their rights and the future of our democracy and I would never have been able to mount a real campaign without your support, so in spite of how things have changed for us, we're still a team."

"Question is whether we can pull off Nellis' latest scheme," replied the beauty.

"We have to give your new husband credit for seeing things from a slightly different perspective than the rest of us and, as a result, freeing thousands of political prisoners, putting on the biggest show in D.C. since the great marches of the sixties, and providing a platform to expose the tycoons trying to devour our democracy and control the world, in what, the last forty-eight hours?"

"He does think in mysterious ways."

"I'm happy for you if you're happy?"

"I'll be happy when this is over and we can go back to the quiet of the farm to live in peace," said Katherine with a sigh. "I thought I could hide from the insanity when I moved in with him. I felt safe and secure but the whole world turned upside down before I could get settled, so I'd really like to find out what's it's like without all the violence and drama."

"I'll do everything I can to see that you're protected when this is over."

She grinned, "Nellis won't put up with security people hanging around. He's got a loaded shotgun, a pack of noisy dogs, and a locked gate to keep the world out!"

"I am familiar with his security arrangements and his wonderful dogs, but we both know you married a good man."

She looked into his eyes, eyes that could not mask his affection and caring, if not passion. "He keeps saving me from myself."

"Something he's better at than I ever was," replied Stanton, with a gentle squeeze to her hand. "Do you know what you're going to say?"

Katherine gazed at the raucous but peaceful crowd pressed against the fencing in front of the Memorial and smiled, "Like you, I've given the same speech hundreds of times but tonight is different. Those people have the motivation of desperation, now they need permission to coalesce around a solid plan to fight for an end to this madness. You and Murphy are going to provide that spark but I can prime the audience."

"I have to admit that I'm concerned about Murphy following through. He could march out there and go into his old routine and this whole effort would be for naught. What do you think?"

"He was drunk and stoned, a physical and mental wreck when he arrived at our refuge and, to be quite honest, I was repulsed by the man and everything he represented...but then something happened over just a couple of days, the family doctor got him dried out and sobered up, Milly and Billy got him focused on his own redemption, and the idea that each and every person has value and a place in our society, not just the white racists." She paused and glanced back at the crowd as the van slowed and stopped, "We were staying in a home with fifteen children from diverse backgrounds and I'm not sure that they didn't reveal the truth to Murphy. He's bounced back and forth between sanity and madness a few times but after the ride down here on the train, I have my fingers crossed that he's sincere in his intentions."

"I trust your judgement. I have no doubt Tabitha will have something profound to say to get things started."

"From the energy in that crowd, I'd say the warmup speeches and great music are keeping them engaged."

Chapter Twelve

Lincoln Todd stood atop a camera platform, scanning the roiling mass of humanity stretching for as far as he could see in every direction. Famous activist singers and celebrities took turns rallying the crowd to wrest control from the autocrats and resurrect democracy – equality and inclusion, minority rights, expanding health care for every citizen, and confronting climate change. The common theme reinforced the necessity of joining together to bring down the incoming fascist administration, before it could destroy everything that made America the envy of all nations. None of the performers had any idea of what Spratlin's message would be but they repeated the campaign themes and built a torrent of energy and enthusiasm to engage the audience.

His sixth sense prickled when Jazz Taggart and his Band of Merry Men took the stage to warm up the audience with a medley of Sixties anti-war anthems. His earpiece buzzed and he touched the plastic bud, "Greetings from the top of the world."

"How's the view?" asked Stanislawski.

"It's as cold as a witch's tit up here and, from the looks of those clouds, I wouldn't be surprised by a blizzard blowing in to make things cheery but I'll bet all the folks stacked tight all the way to the Capitol building are toasty warm. Hell, you can see the moisture from their breath condensing into a cloud above their heads! Where are you?"

"I'm helping out on the camera stand near the north corner of the steps."

"Everyone in place?"

"Yeah, we've got an outfielder on top of the Arch up at the World War II Memorial, another on the platform right below you tending to the switching gear, and two more close by. I sent the rest of our guys out in eight-man squads to burrow in where the cameras are most likely to catch the ruckus when things get rowdy."

"I'm seeing layers of security everywhere. Looks like Secret Service and FBI around the memorial, city police on the front lines,

National Guard on the perimeter and undercover agents wandering through the crowd."

"Yeah, I'm seeing them too," replied his partner. "Just from the way they're setting up, I'm pretty sure they don't know much more about what's going down than we do."

"Are we clear to let it all hang out?"

"Yeah, I talked to the boss a little while ago and he's good to go."

"Stir up a little chaos on demand?"

"Just hang loose until we get a handle on what's happening. We want to pick our moment, as soon as I get a final sanction."

"Can do. Did you notice who's playing?"

"Yeah, I did and I'm half-expecting Nellis Gray to show up to sing a few tunes."

"Don't put it past him, even if the ARC troopers disappeared him and his bitch mother of the All People Matter movement."

"I'll be damned!" muttered Stanislawski, scanning the supporters near the statue. "Somehow, he got reincarnated."

Nellis emerged from behind a column picking a solo on a Stratocaster as he strode down the steps and marched up to a microphone. "How's everyone doing tonight?"

Cheers and applause buzzed through the crowd as they recognized his identity.

"Here's a little song I wrote that seems appropriate tonight. It's called 'Choices' and I'm thinking that's why we're all here together, because we've already made our choices!"

Stanislawski's earbud buzzed, "Can I shoot him now?"

"No! Damnit!"

Nellis began to sing and the audience pushed forward, squashing thousands of bodies against the barriers and a determined column of officers in riot gear.

Dedication
To our cause
Hides the fear
In the applause

Once it starts
There'll be no pause
We march into morning
Despite the cost

Stand together
Brave and strong
A legion for justice
We'll right these wrongs

Man the barricades
Stout and strong
To defeat the tyrant's
Mindless throngs

"You might have heard some rumors about lots of folks like me disappearing off the streets all across the country and I'm here to tell you that everything you heard or suspected was true. There's a secret militia force called the Alien Relocation Command within the government who've been capturing and shipping thousands of immigrants and patriots to concentration camps out west." He pointed to motionless herds of people in the shadows on either side of the monument. "I know because all those people were captive on the ghost trains headed for oblivion until an archangel swooped down and turned those human cattle cars around, so they could be with us tonight to testify to the truth!"

A cry of 'Freedom' echoed across the reflecting pools.

"So, I'll ask you to welcome them home! Can we get a little applause here?" Nellis held his arms wide as thousands of former captives marched into the lights and filled the steps up to the memorial. He turned to look up at Lincoln's statue in the warm glow, "I think ol' Abe is smiling tonight!"

The crowd cheered and applauded, sensing the promise of their gathering.

"I'll tell you what, we've got some old friends here tonight, who have a few words to share with you before we let Representative Spratlin have his way with us, and I'm pretty sure we have a few surprises for you too. I know it's cold out here, that north wind is vicious, so huddle up and hang tough because you're about to change the world!"

Sissy and Sam hugged Katherine, as they peeked out from behind a column to watch the performance, "We're so glad you're safe!"

"We probably wouldn't be here without your bravery and ingenuity at the farm that morning. It's been a long scary trip but I know Nellis has missed you every day and his ultimate goal is to sit on his porch and play a game of chess on the antique game table with you."

"I might even go easy on him," laughed Sissy.

The enormous crowd swayed back and forth and sang along through an extended version of Woodie Guthrie's 'This Land Is Your Land' and roared a final "This land is made for you and me…" Nellis pointed to Jazz, who was sporting a toothy grin, "I'm very pleased to be reunited with my old friends, Jazz Taggart and his Band of Merry Men!"

Jazz leaned into a microphone, "And you know we're pleased to have you back amongst the living!" He walked over and hugged Nellis and shouted in his ear, "I sure am glad to see your ugly mug!"

"That makes a whole bunch of us!" laughed Nellis, as he turned to the mic. "Ladies and gentlemen, we're having a bit too much fun up here, so I think it's time to hand this over to the matriarch of the All People Matter movement, a woman who has motivated, inspired, and guided us through the many traumas of the past year. There would be no unity and certainly no direction without the leadership of Tabitha Hall!"

The matron appeared on the arm of Hannibal Davis in a spotlight in front of the amber glow surrounding Lincoln, her white hair a beacon in the chill, her smile warming the hearts of thousands braving the frigid darkness. Mavis and Bobby Warmington followed with Sammy and Benny and a mob of children to escort them down a narrow gap that cleaved the enormous sea of former prisoners. When they reached the podium, the youngsters scampered up the staircase to disappear behind the columns.

Tabitha waved and held her hands high to acknowledge the adulation with numerous "Thanks you's" and "God bless you's" before finally standing patiently, silent and unmoving until the roar subsided. She turned to stare up at the statue for a long moment before beginning. "Our most famous president was dedicating the battleground at Gettysburg when he said, 'Four score and seven years ago our fathers brought forth upon this continent, a new nation, conceived in Liberty, and dedicated to the proposition that all men are created equal.

Now we are engaged in a great civil war, testing whether that nation, or any nation so conceived and so dedicated, can long endure. We are met on a great battle-field of that war. We have come to dedicate a portion of that field, as a final resting place for those who here gave their lives that the nation might live. It is altogether fitting and proper that we should do this.

But, in a larger sense, we cannot dedicate—we cannot consecrate—we cannot hallow—this ground. The brave men, living and dead, who struggled here, have consecrated it, far above our poor power to add or detract. The world will little note, nor long remember what we say here, but it can never forget what they did here. It is for us the living, rather, to be dedicated here to the unfinished work which they who fought here have thus far so nobly advanced. It is rather for us to be here dedicated to the great task remaining before us—that from these honored dead we take increased devotion to that cause for which they gave the last full measure of devotion…"

The crowd was silent.

"…that we here highly resolve that these dead shall not have died in vain—that this nation, under God, shall have a new birth of freedom—and that government of the people, by the people, for the people, shall not perish from the earth." She paused for a moment to take in the breadth and depth of humanity braving brutal temperatures on this most consequential night. "I don't believe that our former president could possibly have known how meaningful his words would be to all of us more than one hundred and fifty years after his speech but I can think of no quotation that fits our circumstances more perfectly.

I feel as if the violence of the past year was driven by the same evil forces that prompted our Civil War. The voices of freedom have been attacked repeatedly by white nationalist militias, hundreds of peaceful protesters have died and thousands were injured. Even more were accosted on the streets of our nation and kidnapped by a secret government army dedicated to cleansing our nation of immigrants, people of color, and many of the leaders of our resistance.

If you doubt my words, please let these thousands of freed prisoners explain how sweet their freedom is tonight!"

The former hostages chanted, "Freedom! Freedom!"

"You might have heard Mac Murphy's final broadcast where he said that his entire campaign was a cheap, sleazy carnival sideshow to keep his audience angry and riled up enough to vote for the kind of shady people you wouldn't allow in your living rooms. He's right about one thing, the tyrants who own the Republican Party, who've been stealing elections for decades, need to be brought to justice and our recent elections need to be christened null and void!"

Raucous cheers!

She looked directly into the camera on the scaffolding in front of her, where Stanislawski peered back, "I know there are thousands of patriotic people who were hoodwinked into casting votes they might now regret and I want to say to each and every one of you, we…all of us…are facing the same nightmares, the same oppression, and the same dismal future if we do not band together to demand free and fair…let me repeat that…FREE and FAIR elections for every contested office from your school boards to the White House and no one should be sworn into office until that happens!

Mr. Murphy refused the job and his vice-presidential candidate, Creighton Steil, is a complete and total fraud, an incompetent shill in servitude to the same oligarchs who financed the violence against our volunteers. Representative Spratlin, though certainly qualified and worthy, has no desire to accept the office as a compromise or second choice. The next president of our country needs to be elected by a majority of the American people in a contest free of campaigns based on bigotry and lies, campaigns without dark money contributions or PAC sponsored advertising.

We live in a world of communications, so let's give each candidate for every office the same allotted time on television and the internet to run their ads or make speeches to present their platforms to the American people. And these opportunities will be available for a limited time, say a month or two, instead of years of political showmanship!

Our citizens demand the election of government officials on every level who will do the work of governing our nation with honesty, integrity, and a commitment to serving us, We the People, for a change! There are plenty of bureaucrats who have benefitted from the tycoons' purchase of their elections, in spite of having no qualifications for office or intention of making a sincere effort to solve problems instead of creating them! We demand change and now is not soon enough!"

A glacial gust drove flurries of feathery snowflakes flickering through the spotlights above the bellowing crowd.

"I don't want to keep you from hearing from our next speaker but, before I introduce her, I want to thank each and every one of you for braving these conditions to save our democracy from certain ruin. I salute you for your courage and your commitment!"

Applause.

"And now, it is my sincere pleasure to introduce a woman who represents the very soul of our cause, a woman who was only freed from sanctuary from certain doom this morning, my dear friend, Katherine Kennedy!"

~

The roar of thousands of protesters chanting, "Welcome Home! Welcome Home!", echoed around the chamber like thunder rumbling ahead of a storm, as Katherine, Jessie and Kate marched down the steps. In the chaos, the friends and family huddled in the niche beside the statue failed to notice Milly and Billy escorting Murphy out of the elevator until Spratlin walked over to shake his hand.

Mavis gasped, "I can't believe it…"

Tate pulled her close to whisper, "We've been drying him out since he vanished and we all believe that he's going to contribute to the cause tonight as the final speaker."

"That bastard's going to speak?"

"Just like us, the public figure is not who he really is."

The Sutton children swarmed around their houseguest, as Stanton asked, "Are you ready?"

Mac's lips curled into a gentle smile, "I've never been more ready since opening night when I played Lear in my final production in college."

Adel took his arm, "The children want to escort you down to the podium."

He hesitated, patting her hand, "My dear, I would be honored but I also worry about your safety. There are a lot of people out there who really don't like me very much."

The precocious teenage actress grinned, "Then we'll protect you! Besides, there's thousands of prisoners surrounding the podium who might not take kindly to someone trying to threaten this rally."

Murphy glanced at Burt and Matty, who nodded their approval.

"Who's going to escort Representative Spratlin?"

Sissy and Samantha walked over, "He brought his own delegation, so we'll take him down and the rest of you can bring Mr. Murphy."

Katherine's words ricocheted around the marble walls, "When Lincoln talked about 'We the People' he was talking about all of you. Because of his dedication to life, liberty, and the pursuit of happiness for all our citizens, we are a nation of diversity and we have a responsibility to stand up for the rights and freedoms that he and so many others fought and died for!

We lost hundreds during the attacks on our rallies and we have no idea of how many political prisoners died during their internment at the hands of the ARC enforcers. It's time to put an end to this and you have the power to demand a new beginning. Are you with me?"

Cheers and applause.

Mr. Charles followed Bruce as he walked over to his father, "I think she's about to introduce you."

Spratlin admired his son's colorful clothing, "Are you determined to be a distraction or an easy target?"

"Both."

"I am so very proud to have you by my side tonight." Stanton hugged his son and kissed his cheek, "Where's Brad?"

Brad and Amy ushered Marjorie Spratlin to her husband, "We'll face this together as a family."

Samantha grabbed Johnny Warmington with Sissy, Sibble, Mr. Charles, Mama Louise, Maybelle Brown and her children – Daniel, Hubie, Muriel, and Martin to usher the family, with Tate and Eddie escorting Sister Gwen.

Jessie and Kate applauded, as the entourage at the top of a narrow undulating human corridor started down stairs with the rowdy approval of the fugitives, and he leaned to whisper in her ear, "Someday this story needs to be a book and you're the only person who could write it."

She kissed his cheek, "I'm fairly certain it wouldn't all fit in one book, it would have to be a series."

"Does that mean I can keep you locked up in our little house by the bay for an extended stay?"

"After all you've put me through, I don't think you could get rid of me anymore than you could live without Gracie."

"True that, I can't wait to see her."

Katherine yelled, "Let me introduce my dear friend, the Honorable Representative Stanton Spratlin!"

The enormous audience cheered and chanted, oblivious to the stiff north wind driving icy slush across the mall, as Katherine turned to applaud Stanton. Following Brad and Nellis, with Marjorie on his left arm, he clutched the sleeve of Bruce's vibrant pink parka with his right. Leading the entourage through gleeful greetings from hundreds of freed prisoners and waving to the thousands of desperate souls who sensed history in the making.

Stanislawski tracked the congressman's delegation descending the stairway but was distracted by a small group of people moving around in the shadows behind the columns to the right of Lincoln's statue. His earbud buzzed, "What?"

"Time to start agitating?" asked Todd.

"Let's see how this unfolds before we send in the clowns. Sit tight."

"You're no fun at all, you know that, right?"

"Fuck you. Your time will come."

Spratlin reached the podium, waving to the crowd, as the ringleader clicked off, but something was off in the sequencing of the talent. It was too early in the program for Spratlin to deliver a grand finale and he suspected that, while the congressman was the feature, he might not be the last to take the stage.

The Representative kissed his wife on the cheek, hugged his sons, and caressed each of the younger children, before turning to the lectern. "Ladies and gentlemen, our freed compatriots, and all of our citizens watching across the country, I'm proud of every one of you out here tonight for braving these brutal conditions to stand up for democracy before it's too late!"

The crowd cheered, "Spratlin! Spratlin!"

"Tabitha Hall quoted from Lincoln's Gettysburg Address, which is etched on the wall inside the memorial and I hate to imitate her lead, but I noticed the other inscription inside. It's Lincoln's Second Inaugural speech, in which he said, 'On the occasion corresponding to this four years ago, all thoughts were anxiously directed to an impending civil-war. All dreaded it – all sought to avert it. While the inaugural address was being delivered from this place, devoted altogether to saving the Union without war, insurgent agents were in the city seeking to destroy it without war – seeking to dissolve the Union, and divide effect, by negotiation. Both parties deprecated war but one of them would make war rather than let the nation survive and the other would accept war rather than let it perish. And the war came.'

Today, we're fighting the same battle against a contemporary version of the same enemy – those select few who would destroy our democracy to satisfy their greed for money and power. The Southern Gentry seceded and shattered the union in order to maintain ownership of their African-American slaves.

It was a matter of dollars and cents, owning a slave was far cheaper than paying a free man and if he didn't work hard enough or fast enough, the owner could beat him, kill him or sell him to another slave owner. That same mentality is the driving force behind the crimes and insurrection of the cartel of tycoons who view anyone beneath the top one percent, as mere servants. Keeping all of you in debt and desperation is far cheaper than paying a living wage or providing real benefits or job security to America's working class, for that matter."

The vast audience howled.

"Evidence is piling up to support a demand for an investigation into the corruption of our electoral system and the complete suspension of the installation of any elected officials into office until it is finished! The Republicans don't want to govern, to find mutually agreeable solutions to solve the dire problems our country is facing. They want to whine and complain, lie and confuse, obfuscate and disguise the real purpose for their very existence…to dismantle the government and demolish our democracy – one law, one right, one benefit, and one marble column at a time until the very foundation of our nation is buried and forgotten.

This must stop right now and we, all of us, must close down our country until We the People can have confidence that our votes count, that the candidates are real live intelligent human beings willing to work for all the citizens not just the wealthiest few, and the flow of dark money that has bankrolled this criminal activity is shut off permanently.

I propose that every legitimate candidate for every office from your local school board or local council, to the governors and legislators in every state, and every member of Congress or the President of the United States be given a reasonable amount of money from the treasury to fund their campaigns. Outside contributions of any kind would be prohibited by law. I would also propose that every active campaign be no more than three months in length. Today, the campaigning for the next contest starts before the votes are counted from the last election and I don't know about you, but I'm sick and tired of being bombarded with endless 'look at me' ads and promotional gimmicks that drag on for months and years.

Our elected officials need to take their oaths and go to work and after two or three terms in office, they must be forced to resign so new people can move the country forward and all retired elected officials must be barred from becoming lobbyists or using their influence for profit. The days of old men abusing their power for decades have to end!"

Representative Spratlin's truths reverberated around the marble chamber as Bridgette, Burt and Matty Sutton's tiny adopted golden Dutch girl, clutched Adel's hand, and scanned a churning sea of people stretching into the night beyond a blazing bank of lights above a crush of television cameras and photographers vying for position along the press barricades, anticipating the first shot of a possible mystery speaker. Soulful green eyes looked up at her big sister, as she crooked a finger and whispered, "Are you scared?"

Adel knelt and took both of the little girl's hands with a gentle smile, "We stand up for what's right and true, that's what our family has always been about. Tonight, we're here to support Mr. Spratlin and President Murphy, while they try to explain to the people what's happened to our country and what we can do to fix it." She leaned close, "And, to tell you the truth, I hope all those people out there are smart enough to understand what they're talking about."

Bridgette grinned, looking up at the swarm of brothers and sisters, aunts and uncles, gathered behind a massive column, "I'm not scared, as long as I'm with all of you."

"We're family and, no matter what happens, we look after each other."

Spratlin's words echoed across the tidal pools, "We all know that the only way to force the Republicans to meet our demands for truly free and fair elections is to shut this country down from border to border, from sea to shining sea. We the People are on strike in defense of our democracy! Are you willing to stand up for our rights?"

The audience erupted in a deafening roar.

"I had a hunch we'd probably agree on that!"

Katherine led the children in clapping along with the crowd chanting, "Spratlin! Spratlin!"

"Thank you! Thank you! But I'm not the star here tonight, it's all of you who believe in the American dream, who are willing to fight to make things right. We don't need violence, we need mass…we need every citizen with a functioning brain, a compassionate heart, and a courageous soul to join us to bring our national nightmare to an end. I believe that, together, we can make our country into the shining sanctuary we all know it should be!"

Through cheers and clapping a deep warm chant of 'Amen…Amen…Amen' rose above the din and the congressman bowed to his audience. "Pray to your God to give us the strength and wisdom to see this through." He raised his hands for calm, "There's one more thing that all of you need to understand, so I'd like to introduce someone who offers a unique perspective on all of this and I want you to welcome him graciously."

The spotlights dimmed as a horde of silhouetted supporters streamed out of the alcove to spill down the stairs through the meandering passage between thousands of freed captives who applauded missing leaders, famous faces, a troop of costumed personalities, and a crush of children escorting Burt and Matty, Billy and Milly flanking Murphy incognito. He strode down the broad treads without acknowledging the curious crowd, his face was obscured by his hat and the collar of his trench coat.

Mac stopped on the step above the slender podium to thank Spratlin and shake the hand and greet every member of his family and staff, kissed Marjorie Spratlin's fingers, and patted little Bailey and Thomas on the head, before turning to gaze back between the imposing white columns framing the giant statue, humbled by history and his own guilt. The president-elect removed his hat and held it to his chest, bowing slightly as he whispered, "Forgive my insatiable craving for power and glory, my ignorance and impotence to alter the course of my campaign, and my indefensible sins against everything that this country must stand for, if life on this planet is to continue to be worth living."

Thousands of curious and rejuvenated escapees, along with a broad coalition of anti-fascist activists, peered up with hope and anticipation, raising deafening cheers and applause, thundering around the magnificent monument in surging volume and blaring intensity. He handed the fedora and coat to Burt and stared out through twilight over a churning sea of humanity, suddenly still and silent until a single spot flashed through the darkness to illuminate the mysterious figure.

A stunned gasp rolled through the audience, as his giant image appeared on video screens and they realized who was about to speak. Boo's and jeers flared above a roiling tide of confused murmurs that morphed into rage. Stanislawski's agitators initiated violent tussles with stunned protestors in locations covered by Patriot Network cameras, while speechless reporters mumbled, "It's…Murphy?"

Jeers raged above a raucous roar, "Bastard."

"I thought he was dead."

"He needs to be tried for treason!"

"Let's lynch the motherfucker!"

The president-elect turned to stare into Lincoln's knowing eyes for a long moment, his stomach churning, his body trembling, his mind screaming for a shot of bourbon and a cup full of Dr. Billing's magic pills to ramp up his courage and spike his libido to endure the battle raging between the inebriated demon, famous for hateful performances to ecstatically ignorant audiences, and his damaged soul striving for redemption from the smoldering ashes of a wasted life.

Every muscle in his aching body quaked and the blood rushed from his head, as a dazzling cascade of photographers' flashes blasted the monument with waves of cold blue radiance flickering through pelting flurries of puffy white snowflakes. He waited until the persistent fury of the protestors slowly settled into a modest growl of seething confusion. "Ladies and gentlemen, my name is Mac Murphy. Some of you made the mistake of voting to elect me to the office of President of the United States and, unfortunately, I won."

He paused, his eyes blurring in and out of focus, his mouth dry, his lips quivering in the cold, while the endless mass of humanity stretching into the darkness booed and jeered.

"I stand before you humbled and disgraced by my own deeds and actions. I could plead ignorance and innocence, I could sight my former rather disgusting addictions, of which there were many, I could blame the people who manipulated my entire campaign with lies and subterfuge, or the tiny cabal of incredibly wealthy donors who bought the election with money they stole from their workers and the taxpayers.

I will choose none of these options, because the only truth is that I was willing to sell my soul to the devil in exchange for ultimate power and self-glorification. When my darkest wishes were granted, I realized that accepting my responsibilities meant handing the keys of governance to those who would destroy everything the United States of America has stood for since revolutionary whispers about freedom and justice ignited the inception of our grand experiment in democracy, nearly two-hundred and fifty years ago."

The snarling crowd quieted.

"I must also admit that I was blind to the strategy and ultimate goal of the real powerbrokers, who had no intention of allowing me to discharge my naïve ambitions or legal obligations, by eliminating me and installing their unelected champion, my vice-president-elect, in the Oval Office to ensure quick and unrelenting delivery on their programs to dismantle every branch of the Federal Government, rescind all laws and regulations that inhibit the profitability of their big banks and industries, scrap taxation and social benefits, and turn the corpse of our former glory over to international corporations to administer by a dictatorial committee.

You've all heard me spout some outlandish and ridiculous drivel to rile up my audiences but every word that I utter this evening is the absolute truth as I know it. So, while you have every right and reason to doubt my candor and my intentions, listen carefully. The future of our nation is at stake and it's going to require responsible, intelligent, and dedicated citizens like you to take it back!"

A smattering of applause drowned out rowdy chants from tiny pockets of fights and scuffles in the bewildered crowd.

"I've recently learned that a coven of these international corporations have installed massive computer surveillance systems, that monitor every movement or communication by every citizen in the nation, and it won't be long before they have a complete dossier on every human being in the industrialized world. They already have access to everything from your background to your financial accounts, your family and friends, your political persuasions, and your most private secrets. As many of you can attest, the Security Units know exactly where we are at any moment, because we're all being monitored by corporate command."

More than half the crowd erupted in angry taunts, hundreds rushing the barriers, as two-dozen armored vehicles rolled around the drive to park bumper-to-bumper unloading squads of riot police clad for battle, with many more moving in to block access to the roads surrounding the park. Six Secret Service agents started up the steps, attempting to push through the dense mob of unmoving and uncooperative prisoners recently liberated from Federal custody. Murphy held up his hand, "Gentlemen, I would prefer you secure the perimeter. I've brought my own security for this event."

The emancipated closed ranks and the Sutton and Spratlin children moved to surround the president-elect. The agents backed down the stairs, their hands gripping weapons inside their coats.

"To those of you who have suffered the indignity and terror of political assassination and incarceration, I must apologize, and I mean that sincerely. Until recently, I really had no idea or interest in the depths of depravity that justified shock troops being deployed by a secret agency within the government to round up and disappear tens of thousands of loyal citizens, like all the patriots on these steps, for the crime of expressing their rightful beliefs. I know that seems preposterous but it's true, which brings me to the point of my appearance.

I want to speak, for a moment, to those who rallied behind my campaign and voted me into office, because I know that you'll claim that I've been brainwashed by the liberal elite, that I've abandoned the cause of defending a great swath of our society in your time of need. Hell, my constituents will hate me as much as the liberals in this crowd but that's what we need to talk about."

Howling jeers and raucous cheers erupted across The Mall.

"You devout Christians bowed to a disgusting phony idol who gave you permission to hate…and you willfully accepted the invitation because it was easier than facing your own delusions and ignorance! Republicans have masked their racist mantra of white-supremacy for decades but I gave it voice, I brought the truth of their hypocrisy and lies out into the open and you embraced it all. Christ would be ashamed of every one of you hypocritical liars! I'm absolutely sure that Peter will bar the pearly gates to every fake Christian who attempts to enter because there is no room for hate in the hereafter and there sure as hell shouldn't be any in this world either!

Your belief system is a fraud and, if you ever believed in the word of the Lord, now is the time to admit your sins and stand up for what every religion should stand for…freedom and equality for everyone everywhere!"

An enthusiastic cheer rolled through the crowd.

"To those frustrated voters, who are working their asses off and struggling just to make ends meet, I must say that I am truly sorry that you're having a hard time during this phase of extraordinary inequity between the greedy bastards at the top and the rest of our society. The people who sponsored my campaign don't care about your problems, let alone your hopes and dreams. They're doing everything possible to make matters worse by keeping you uneducated, in debt, and without hope…and they won't stop until they own everyone.

Their goal is a two-class society, those who have and those who serve, and they'll blame your misery on any convenient scapegoat like immigrants or people of color or the Democrats or even renegade Republicans who aren't marching in lockstep with their agenda. Those groups are just convenient foils that ignorant supremacists can all hate together but they're not responsible for your misery. The fascist pundits scream and yell about the threat of 'those people' coming to destroy White America but you know and I know that all of you are 'those people' and you're not trying to take anything from anybody. You're just trying to defend your rightful place in our society! If you truly believe in all that America stands for, there is no 'Them', there is only 'Us'.

The loss of your jobs, rights, benefits, and security are the result of a coordinated campaign by the very richest Americans who have commandeered the Republican Party to expand their already vast fortunes to own and control everything, including you.

They won't reopen the coal mines in West Virginia, they won't bring manufacturing jobs back to the rust belt, and they have no intention of fixing health care…they'll just eliminate funding and destroy it, leaving it to all of you to figure out how to pay for your own medical expenses.

Far too many rich folks don't believe they should have to share their wealth to support immigrants and 'freeloaders' who are too lazy or stupid to fend for themselves, let alone create their own fortunes. They view those at the bottom, those toiling to break out of poverty to begin their journey to earn the American dream, as the undeserving, the unworthy, the dispensable…but they're wrong. All of you are the people who will build the next empires, create new technologies, employ thousands, and support our way of life."

The crowd cheered as he glanced back at a look of assurance in Milly's eyes, a smile of approval playing on Billy's lips, and a nod of approval from young Amy.

"When their monitoring system is fully functional, their statistical experts will decide where you live, how you can serve them, whether your children will be chosen to go to school and what they'll be allowed to become as adults. Job security and a thriving middle class will become fanciful memories and the economy will be planned and controlled to produce maximum profits for a very small group of these wealthy families and everyone else will accept the lives assigned to them by a machine…or they will starve."

A curious silence muted the massive audience, broken only by scattered knots of noisy agitators attacking those around them without collaboration.

"They've been erasing the middle-class little-by-little for more than fifty years, as their international corporations shuttered factories and shipped jobs overseas or installed robots, who don't need scheduled breaks, vacations, or benefits. All of this didn't happen by chance or circumstance, they've been planning this for decades, starting with the John Birch Society in the 1950's and gerrymandering voting districts to isolate and dilute opposition strongholds, so their chosen candidates could begin destroying our society from within at the state and local level. They invented the radical racist Freedom Faction fanatics to clog up Congress and soften up the resistance a decade ago, before they swooped in to get me elected, so they could finish the job!

They even set up test projects in most of the red states in the middle of the country to try out their cockamamie theories of trickle-down economics and preservation of racial purity. Kansas was chosen to eliminate taxes with the promise that the economy would bloom from the spare change that would dribble down from the massive tax cuts for the super-wealthy but infrastructure and every public service stopped functioning and the state's budget is billions of dollars in the hole. Oklahoma got to eliminate funding for public education, so the radical evangelical morons could rewrite the curriculum to deny science, history and common sense and make it conform to their bizarre and hateful religious propaganda. Indiana got to persecute the LGBT segment of our population, Wisconsin destroyed their unions, and parts of Texas did away with zoning and building codes that protect everyone, so contractors could make more money faster without any oversight or legal jeopardy. Every state had committees dedicated to restricting the minority vote by claiming voter fraud, when the only fraud being wrought was by those who yelled the loudest."

A modest cheer rose from tens of thousands of anxious and hopeful faces staring up out of the darkness.

"The real story behind the campaign for my election reads like some weird dystopian novel, a script conceived by an inebriated demented author with no talent and a sick imagination…but none of this is fiction, although it will certainly be the stuff of history and legend by the time you complete this crusade.

Most of the appointees and nominees approved by the Republican Congress for positions within the current administration were selected for their commitment to deconstructing our institutions, removing the checks and balances that guarantee our rights and freedoms, eliminating all regulations that affect corporate profits, and destroying anyone who stands against them. I was the fraud who made their nonsense sound reasonable…but, if we let them continue, history will be turned back to the dark ages!"

Raucous 'Boo's' rose from the human sea, while tiny clusters raised signs of 'Hang Gonzalez', 'White Power' and 'Deport Filthy Immigrants' tacked to baseball bats spiked with ten-penny nails, deadly weapons to pummel unarmed protestors as television cameras pivoted to capture the turmoil for instant international consumption. Confederate battle flags fluttered on long poles at the core of roiling melees of flying fists and splattering blood. Thundering munitions and dozens of caustic smoke bombs exploded on either side of the reflecting pool, scattering demonstrators in frantic waves, eddies spinning closer and closer to the cameras, which captured the ferocity of the carnage inflicted on anyone in the path of the rampaging rioters.

Stroboscopic images pulsed across the giant screens along each side of the pond of bloodied and unconscious bodies being carried along in the human current; a woman clutching a baby was struck from behind by a huge man wielding a massive club, lofting the child out of the frame as she disappeared, trampled under the flailing feet of the stampede; a bludgeoned elderly couple desperately reaching for each other as they were dragged in opposite directions; hysterical children screaming, the injured wailing, hundreds pushing and shoving to escape the slaughter, and throbbing through the uproar, the attackers chanting, "Save White America!"

Murphy pointed to a savage human vortex swirling across the plaza, "I believe those are the same thugs who were sent to turn my rallies into vicious riots and wreaked mayhem and death on the All People Matter gatherings. Why don't you real patriots escort them out?"

The combat flags and hateful signs were gradually consumed by swells of thrashing bodies surrounding the goons and lurching toward heavily armed National Guard troops at the edges of the crowd.

Mac waited silently, while surging human breakers slowly settled into restless ripples. "Ladies and gentlemen, I finally sobered up and was fortunate enough to have some good friends force me to confront a few of my personal demons." He paused, as raucous rioters were routed and the ruckus receded, "In the process, I've discovered my absolute respect for people who get up and go to work every morning, who love and care for their children, who take responsibility for their neighbors and offer kindness and compassion and generosity to complete strangers, and have hope and dreams and cherish what this country truly stands for." He turned to wave his hand towards the young guardians surrounding him, "I'm humbled to have recognized these truths through the grace of these children who are with us tonight and I say to you, to all of you and the citizens of this great country, I was wrong! I was wrong and I apologize to the nation for my lies and my failures."

The crowd gaped in stunned silence.

"Until the Supreme Court or the United States Senate decides that I am not eligible or worthy to become President of these United States or the corporate conspiracy sends their assassins to take me out, I will use this opportunity to repair the damage that I've caused."

Stanislawski's earbud beeped, "Now?"

"Don't have clearance yet!"

"What the hell are they waiting for? Take him down before he exposes everyone!"

Murphy's words blared through the microphone, muffling Stanislawski's response.

"The members of The Forge twisted our democracy to dismantle the government and it is my hope that they will all be rounded up and brought to justice. I will gladly testify before Congress or a special counsel to expose the villains directed by The Forge to do their bidding.

The shadowy autocrats, who've been buying local and state elections for decades, are the very same people who manipulated the media, so they could buy Congress and the Presidency. Who do you think owns the vast majority of our nation's newspapers and broadcast networks that skew national polls and public opinion?" He paused, overwhelmed by the sensation that Abraham Lincoln's eyes were burning into the back of his skull, reminding him that this crowd was far more obligated and genuinely impassioned than any of the right-wing crazies who showed up at his speeches during the campaign. "I ask all of you to help take back our country and restore its glory, before the brilliant beacon that has guided this great nation for centuries is extinguished and we're all dragged into servitude!"

Little spasms of applause spread through the murmuring mob and morphed into a bellowing howl that melded into the rhythm of a chant, "Take it back! take it back! Take it all back!"

Murphy glanced over to Milly and Billy, then leaned into the microphone, "We need to have everyone onboard this march into the future, shall we see whether President Gonzalez is accepting visitors this evening?"

Todd screamed over the roar, "What are we waiting for?"

Stanislawski checked the blank screen on his phone, hesitating for a moment before barking, "Go! Go!"

"One or both?"

"Take them all out!"

A seething mass of revolutionary fervor oozed around the barriers to surround a thicket of riot police, FBI, and Secret Service agents trapped at the bottom of the staircase by a peaceful but determined crush of humanity.

Special Agent Mike Thomas' eyes locked onto the president-elect, who stepped away from the slender podium to shake Spratlin's hand, as a tall black woman with a smaller lady, a soldier in a Scottish kilt, and a man in a hot-pink jacket stepped up to stand close beside them, oblivious to the danger in the enormous quagmire of angry protestors surging along the promenade, their frenzy reverberating all the way to the Capitol in pandemonium and revolt. The agents and riot police pushed and shoved people to clear a path but the dense throng swarmed to shield their resurrected hero from the authorities.

The deafening din spawned by thousands of clamoring partisans was interrupted by the crack of a shot and the ping of a bullet ricocheting off the base of a marble pillar behind Murphy in a puff of white dust. The renegade president did not flinch, suddenly grasping the depth of Tyrone Turner's gallantry in his dogged stance before the approaching airplane or his spiritual conviction in the moment of his assassination at the debate in Madison. Instinctively, he stepped in front of Milly and Billy to point in the direction of the shooter lying prone on the planking of a camera tower to his left. He saw a brief flash of blue reflecting in the glass of a scope as the assassin found his mark.

Unfazed and undaunted, he waved his hands to shepherd the children away from danger. Adel, Little Mac, Johnny, Sissy, and Sam pulled Sibble and their younger siblings away from the podium.

Wee Bridget looked up at her big sister, "Should I be scared now?"

Little Mac and Johnny Warmington crawled over to shield them, as Adel wrapped her arms around the girl and whispered, "Yes, I'm scared too but whoever is out there shooting isn't aiming at us."

Voices shrieked through Thomas's earpiece, "Someone get to the president-elect before that bastard gets off another shot!"

Another agent replied, "Who's to say it's not one of ours?"

"Look at him, he didn't even duck! Is he drunk?"

"Who are those women and the idiot in the pink coat?"

Thomas growled, "Everyone shut up and do your jobs. Protect him!"

Federal agents fought through a flood of frantic marchers, hell-bent on defending a man they would gladly have lynched an hour before, as a second shot knocked Murphy backwards, blood spurting from his shoulder.

The calm relief of freedom shared by thousands of partisans on the stairs devolved into churning chaos, former prisoners crouching or diving for cover until Murphy rose up, holding his bloody shoulder and staggered to the microphone with young Amy at his side. "A real president once said that the only thing we have to fear is fear itself and, to tell you the truth, I'm not afraid of that bastard with the rifle up on that tower. He can shoot me again but I'm not moving. He and the traitors who sent him have already lost because all of you know the truth!"

Murphy saw a tiny spit of yellow flame off in the darkness high above the far end of the pool, his eyes tracing the reflection of an orange ember skipping across gentle black waves. Time slowed and he was suddenly aware of minute details in the surging mayhem, the individual expressions on the faces moving in every direction amid screams of panic piercing the rumbling roar of the raucous mob, the terror in the eyes of dozens of children huddling on the pavement, two men scampering down the scaffolding of the nearest camera turret and security units pushing through scrambling bodies to apprehend them.

His lips parted to utter, "I'm sorry" as he turned to glance at Milly and Billy and pushed Amy down on the pavement. Benny Young, the headstrong young landscaper who started the original movement in Dolphin Bay, tackled him as the bullet shredded snowflakes fluttering through a cloud of ice crystals condensing in the frigid air above the frightened crowd. Mac watched Sammy grab Bailey and Thomas, sister Gwen protecting Maybelle Brown's youngest, Muriel and Martin, while Eddie, Brad, and Tate dove to cover women trying to protect terrified youngsters but his eyes focused on Bruce Spratlin's fuchsia sleeves wrapping around his father to wrestle him to the pavement as the slug seared into his temple, the side of the boy's head exploding across his father's bewildered face in a shower of red droplets shimmering through the lights to splatter over the children gazing up at them in fear and awe.

Murphy cried, "No! They want me, not that boy!" as he crumbled to the steps under Benny's weight while another spray of wayward shots skittered across the plaza, spouting puffs of pulverized granite and splintering the lectern in their quest for victims crouching in the icy glow of spotlights blazing through the darkness.

Suddenly aware of a staccato patter of gunshots in the distance rising above the screams in the crowd and groans of the wounded, he struggled free of Benny's grip and crawled towards a wailing Spratlin covered in the blood of his son's shattered head, while Brad shielded his hysterical mother as they scrambled to Stanton. Mac reached to touch the broken father's bloody hand and said, "We have to end this. It can't go on."

Realizing that the shooting had stopped, Nellis, Tate, Burt, Sammy and the rest of the men rose from sheltering the children. Sibble tottered after Sissy and Samantha, who ran to their parents. Katherine turned to a cry from Kate, who was clutching young Johnny in a pool of blood seeping from beneath a motionless Jessie, shaking his body, screaming, "Oh my God! Wake up! Wake up! I just got you back, you can't leave me now!"

Nellis grabbed his coat and rolled him over, reaching to his jugular. He looked up at Kate and Johnny, "He's got a pulse but it's weak. Let's figure out where he's wounded."

The boy unzipped Jessie's jacket to find blood dribbling from a small wound in his stomach. Nellis lifted his shoulder to spot a larger exit wound. He pulled off his scarf and stuffed the wad into the hole, pointing to Johnny's soft hat, "Use your hat to cover the wound on his stomach and press as hard as you can."

He scanned the people tending the wounded and spied Brad cradling his parents and sisters, "Brad! You got a radio on you? We need ambulances now!"

The former commando pulled the radio from his belt and pressed the button, watching four crews muscling stretchers through a swirling crush of frightened protesters. "You guys on this? We need…" He paused to count, "At least a couple of dozen ambulances up here, Stat! I see four medics coming up the steps but we've got wounded and dead all over the place."

Benny helped Murphy stand to look out across acres of bedlam and turmoil, the audience stampeding to escape the slaughter, the press scaling the barriers to capture images of the victims and the butchery. He spied the microphone on the pavement and stumbled through splintered wood and twisted metal framing to pick it up, his right hand covered in Bruce's blood, his left pressing a handkerchief into the oozing hole in his shoulder. "Ladies and gentlemen, my fellow citizens…"

His words echoed down The Mall and the terrified crowd slowed. "We have lots of wounded patriots up here, so let's get some medical help right now!"

Amid the din of sirens blaring, red and blue flashing lights approaching from all directions, and two helicopters with sweeping searchlights appearing overhead, he noticed the red lights on the cameras swivel in his direction and wiped blood and grime from his face with the sleeve of his jacket. "Ladies and gentlemen, we and the entire nation have just witnessed and survived yet another attempt by the powermongers to remove the only two people who can stop their march to dominance…" He turned to Spratlin, "And they missed both of us!"

Brad lifted his brother's body from Stanton's grasp and a weeping Marjorie helped her husband to his feet,. His face, hands, and clothes glistening with Bruce's blood. Bewildered, he gazed at too many limp bodies surrounded by volunteers trying desperately to help until the ambulance crews could cart the wounded through the mayhem to proper care. A small mob of children surrounded him and Sissy and Samantha took his hands to lead him to Murphy, who lowered the microphone to wrap his good arm around Spratlin, leaning to whisper, "I am so very sorry about your son."

Stanton, staggered by the violence and devasted by Bruce's heroic death while trying to shield him, hugged his former opponent back and took the microphone, hesitating as he stared out at thousands of frightened faces peering out of the darkness, trapped in that juncture of fight or flight, bravery or survival, "Ladies and gentlemen, as you can see, we will not be defeated, we will not give up or give in, and we…all of us…will march together to reclaim our nation from the clutches of fascism! We won't rest until everyone involved in this massacre and the desecration of our elections and our democracy is brought to justice."

He looked up into the camera lens, "To those who spawned this senseless violence, your vast fortunes will not protect you from our truth!"

Mac leaned in, clutching his shoulder, "And the authorities might start with my complicit vice-president elect. I believe he's staying in Blair House and I'm absolutely positive that, once he's taken into custody, he'll sing like a frail little sparrow."

A weeping Johnny clutched his mother, while Katherine hugged Kate as she trotted after an ambulance crew carrying his mortally wounded Jessie through a solemn motionless crowd to an ambulance. Nellis took her arm to join Tate and Mavis, Tabitha and Hannibal Davis, Benny, Sammy, Sibble, Sister Gwen, Amy, Mr. Charles with Marjorie and Maybelle Brown, shepherding all the children to surround Brad, who was still standing at attention holding his brother's body behind his father with tears streaming down his cheeks.

"And I'm calling on Congress to convene a special session tomorrow morning to begin an investigation into the thugs, who smuggled trained marksmen with high-powered rifles past multiple levels of security surrounding this event to assassinate the presidential candidates from both parties, as well as the tyrants who control the real money behind this well-orchestrated coup attempt."

Stanton tightened his grip on a weak and unsteady Murphy, and added, "There's been enough madness and bloodshed, it's time for true American patriots to stand up to defend our democracy from the real enemies of the state, those who have worked so hard and spent so much money to buy and own our country, to corrupt the very meaning of patriotism and honor, and destroy the dignity and dreams of millions of our working-class citizens. We are one nation, one people and there is no future for any of us unless we, all of us, come together to build a new and better nation."

Murphy took the microphone and stared into the camera, "Everyone has been referring to The Forge as some mythical mysterious group of faceless gilded demons hiding in their ivory towers. I think most ordinary people think it's some sort of country club for rich guys, not the heart and soul of a sprawling international conspiracy by the traitors they really are. Can you imagine the arrogance and audacity of these people who conceived and executed a plan to overthrow and dismantle every level of our government to preserve and enlarge their wealth and power beyond anyone's wildest dreams?"

He paused, snowflakes fluttered through the spotlights and the crowd was still. "You've seen these people interviewed on the news, their faces on magazine covers with stories touting their contributions to society or a hospital or university. That's glossy public relations and a big tax right-off but none of their very public generosity is real. None of that money comes out of their pockets.

You've all heard of Turner Graves? Big shot oil man, who's actually a little runt of a guy, paid millions of dollars to support my campaign and every penny of it was illegal. He manned my campaign staff with the very best people he could find and every one of them was working for him not me. He even hired a doctor to follow me around and make sure that my many addictions were satisfied and expanded. He supplied beautiful women, booze, drugs, hotel suites and all the things that wealthy people expect, just to make sure that I'd be too preoccupied with my own gluttony to notice how he and his people were using my hateful blather to pave the road to victory for the autocrats.

I'm told that Stanley French, CEO of Dynamic Devices, and his pal, Conrad Blaho who runs Lebanon Steel, had a little powwow with their buddies more than fifty years ago to plot out the road map from being wealthy assholes to owning and controlling the economy and dismantling the government. They don't like federal regulations interfering with their companies polluting the environment or having to pay even a tiny bit of their profits in taxes to support the needs of the peasants. They've been buying elections from your school board to the White House ever since and…oh by the way…eliminating the middle class and all rights and benefits provided by our laws and constitution.

They bought up American manufacturing and shipped those jobs to Asia or Mexico and blamed it on trying to maintain a competitive edge in the international market. Their only competition was foreign companies that they bought up along the way to make their lies seem reasonable. Demolishing the middle class was the real purpose behind their manipulations.

Their lackies in all your state legislatures have been passing laws to make it more difficult for anyone who isn't a pearly white Republican fascist to vote! And, if you do go to the polls, they're giving themselves the power to decide which elections in your state are legitimate...if any Democrat wins, they'll contest your votes and install a Republican instead!"

A great roar rose from the thousands of protestors huddled around the reflecting pond, as he pressed his palm into the oozing hole in his shoulder to dull the pain and slow the bleeding. He could feel the warmth trickling down his arm to pool in the fold in his shirt at the elbow and blood was dripping from the hem of his coat into a puddle on the granite pavement. His eyes faded in and out of focus and his knees were weak but he was in his groove, guiding his flock to embracing his vision, his truth, and perhaps the inauguration of his own redemption.

"Don't you see? The nightmares that have plagued our nation and our government for the past fifty or sixty years were all part of their plan to make Americans doubt the validity and honesty of our elections and our system of democracy. We're on the verge, ready to tip over the very edge into darkness by handing our country over to a pack of wolves, unless we put a stop to it right now!"

He pointed into the crowd and to the cameras, "You! All of you have the power to save our nation by shutting down every city in every state and demanding that the conspirators be brought to justice! Hell, they should forfeit their ill-begotten fortunes, we can use the money to hoist our neediest citizens out of poverty.

Nothing moves until we have new elections for every office in the nation and you can help make sure they're legit by boycotting all the media outlets and networks who have been spewing lies and propaganda in support of these gangsters. If they're not real journalists confined by facts and truth, they shouldn't be allowed to broadcast or publish their fabrications...I don't know about you but I think those pompous morons who vomit these lies every night on radio, television, and the internet are primary actors in the conspiracy. I should know because I was one of them! Haul them off to jail too!"

The audience cheered.

"Ladies and gentlemen, fellow citizens, the time has come to declare the Republican Party a domestic terrorist organization. If we don't thwart their assault on our liberties, there will never be another free and open election in this country ever again. It is, quite simply, a choice between democracy and autocracy, between our rights and freedoms or eternal servitude to wealthy despots, between the vision we all share of what this country should be or hate and bigotry, lies and deceit in the gloom of fascist tyranny.

This is our last chance to reclaim our democracy and I can promise you there's no cavalry ready to charge over the hill to save the day. We're the only folks who can make this happen and that means that every one of you out there across the country needs to be out in the streets, protesting with peaceful determination until these traitors are removed from positions of power and the institutions of government are returned to the citizens. Some of you are natural born leaders and we need real patriots to step up to run for office because there are going to be a whole bunch of vacancies!"

He waved to the cheering audience and turned to Milly and Billy, pointing to a shattered Stanton, covered in blood and leaning on Brad, who was still standing ramrod straight holding his brother's mutilated body, the family surrounded by a herd of children. "And here's the guy who should be elected president because we all know that he's got the guts to stand up and fight for all that's right and true! Elect him and everyone can go back to sleeping soundly at night!"

Chapter Thirteen

Katherine found Nellis sitting on the floor of the porch in front of a blazing fire in the wood stove radiating warmth against a frigid north wind whipping through the farm. Gracie was stretched out on his lap for an extended belly rub, while Mamasan, Brandy, Chacha, Cody, and two litters of mewing cats nestled close, vying for attention and affection. A dozen chickens, a knot of goats, a tussle of raccoons, a family of fox, bounding bunnies, chattering squirrels, a passel of possum, and flocks of fluttering birds rustled around just outside the screens.

"That's the first real smile I've seen on your face since you came up with your scheme to overthrow the government," said his wife, settling in on the chaise to gather a blanket against the cold and an armful of feline adoration.

"I wish I could say it's self-satisfaction but really, it's just being here at home with you and the critters."

"I've wanted to be here, alone with you, since the day I first moved in but the real world kept intruding. To tell you the truth, I'm terrified that something's going to tear us away again."

He looked up with a sarcastic grin, "I'd still have peace and quiet, a locked gate, and no uninvited guests if you'd minded your own business instead of barging into mine!"

Her lips drooped into a miserable pout before she tossed a pillow at him and all the dogs jumped, "You were just a sad lonely curmudgeon before I rescued you."

Nellis lifted Gracie off his lap to sit on the edge of the chaise, "Sure 'nough, it was nice and quiet and the biggest hassle I had was keeping my grow a secret and preventing the dogs from chasing after teenagers out on the lane. I never had Federal Marshals wandering around the property or traitors sending their goons to burn down my barn or clandestine militia guys trying to send me off to some godforsaken hellhole."

"You were lonely and bored with yourself, even if you did put on a good show of irascible independence. If it wasn't for your true and undying love for me, you wouldn't have had the opportunity to save thousands of innocent prisoners or put on the biggest protest in history or topple the government for that matter. I think you should be thanking me," laughed Katherine, leaning to kiss him. "This is home and I love being here with you."

"I'm awfully glad you took pity on me, dragged me out of my shell, and tried so hard to get me killed."

She punched him in the arm. "Okay fine! I'm moving out in the morning!"

He reached to tickle her, "Not a chance, I'll lock you in a closet."

"How about the bedroom?"

"You've got a date, sister, but first I want to know what Kate had to say about Jessie?"

"He's had three surgeries and lost a lot of blood but the docs think he's going to make it."

"Is he conscious?"

Katherine laughed, "Yeah, after being astonished and thankful that Kate had survived, his first words were about how soon he could get out of there to go fishing with young Johnny."

"Sounds about right. I sure was glad to see Sissy and Samantha."

"Sissy's itching for a game of chess and I don't think she'll go easy on you."

"Yeah, we're playing tomorrow after she gets finished with school and I'm already regretting coming home."

Katherine shivered, "You know, considering you have a live-in chaperone, you could bring the game inside while it's cold."

"And give her an advantage, not a chance."

"You act so tough and that little girl has got you wrapped around her little finger."

"What did Stanton have to say during your hourlong phone call?" grumbled Nellis. "I should be jealous!"

"You keep forgetting that you are the 'other' man in my life…well, maybe not anymore, now that you're my husband but you know the drill."

"So, what'd he say?"

She sat back, stroking an armful of kittens. "He's still very fragile and Marjorie's being his strength in spite of her own grief but he said that their ancient nanny, Sibble is completely shattered. They're planning a funeral for Bruce in Washington next week and a burial here and we're invited to both."

"Can do."

"Where to begin?" Katherine smoothed the mother cat's shiny fur as she snuggled close to allow the youngsters to nurse, "He and Murphy got together with President Gonzalez yesterday and they're hoping to convince Congress to hold a new round of elections in about three months. Until then, everyone who's in office will stay in office, unless they're implicated in the scheme."

"Gonzalez has agreed to stay?"

"Yes, and several committees in the House and the Senate will begin investigations in coordination with the FBI, DOJ, and the Secret Service within the next few days. Creighton Steil was taken into custody and many of the people involved with the violence at the rally have been arrested. Inside word suggests they're cooperating and this whole thing has spawned a deluge of resignations in every department."

"This is going to be huge. Once the first guy starts talking, they'll go down like dominos." replied Nellis, as the dogs nestled around his legs. "Maybe it's the new beginning that we've needed for centuries."

"If We the People don't take advantage of this moment, we'll never get it back."

"There's a huge group of voters who are going to have to learn the difference between propaganda and real facts and make a choice between democracy for everyone or fascism benefitting the few, if this is going to work. Is Stanton going to run again?"

"I think he has no choice. He's earned the stature and the people seem to believe in him because he's honest and up front, the only sane voice in a chorus of contemptible propaganda!"

"What about Murphy?"

"So far, no one seems to be talking about indicting him but Stanton is keeping him close, as an advisor in a show of unity to pull his supporters on board."

Nellis laughed, "All it took was some real barbecue to get that guy turned around."

"You were the one who saw through his schtick and realized that he wasn't who everyone thought he was."

"There was a moment, that night when I served him those ribs, where…it's wasn't so much what he said but the look in his eyes, the tone of his voice that exposed the real Murphy just for an instant and I knew right then how we could use him to win this thing and we did."

"He doesn't really have any qualifications for office," said Katherine.

"He has the ability to make people believe what he tells them, even if it is total bullshit, and that's a valuable gift in these times."

"I think Stanton should ask him to run as his vice-president."

"That's a sure win but he'll need a strong leash to keep Mac in line."

"See, we've settled all the problems of the world and created a roadmap for the future of our democracy."

"Not bad, considering everything, except you know and I know the oligarchs are already moving on to plan 'B'. The Republicans are going to raise a stink and try every trick in the book to portray all of this as a Democratic coup. Hell, I wouldn't be surprised to see their militia morons causing violence and mayhem to spice up our protests, so this ain't over and we're not done," sighed Nellis. "We'll have to jump back in tomorrow."

"I know but can't we pretend the world outside the gate doesn't exist for just one night?"

"Maybe we could trust the millions of patriots in the streets to hold things together until tomorrow," said Nellis wrapping his arms around her. "Can we go to bed now?"

She kissed him tenderly, "Just promise you won't start another insurrection before morning."

"Just with you, darlin', just with you."

The Characters

Nellis Gray

Stanton James Spratlin – father – distinguished, aristocratic, proper – CEO of Stanton Oil Products - Temporary Congressional Representative who became Tyrone Turner's VP candidate until Turner was assassinated and he became the presidential candidate.

Marjorie Murray Spratlin – mother – recovering from being a bedridden alcoholic hypochondriac and reclaiming her place as matriarch of the family.

"Sissy" Shirley Ann Spratlin – 3rd grade, blond curls, pug nose with freckles, big green eyes - spritely, giggly, inquisitive, determined, and frightened. Chess aficionado.

"Sam" – Samantha Spratlin – 8th grade – slender, pale skin with dark eyes and auburn hair,

Bruce Spratlin – brother – gay artist / musician and activist, lives in a renovated loft in the barn, where he paints erotic art, and drives a baby-blue VW bug.

Brad Spratlin – oldest brother wounded in the war, post-traumatic stress, angry, violent, alcohol, drugs, flashbacks – hulking, burr cut, shrapnel scar on his right cheek, a dragon tattoo to chase away his demons on his right shoulder. Reclaimed his life to become security chief for his father.

Mama Louise – cook – the good-humored backbone of the staff and the family, lives in renovated servants' quarters over the garages. Originally from southern Georgia.

Sibble Savage – nanny / housemaid – slender, aging waif, who looked after this generation and Stanton and his sister before them…more parent than their real parents and knows all the family secrets, which guarantees her place in Spratlin House until she joins her husband, who died in the Korean War.

Maybelle Brown – deceased Representative Curtis Hall's former black mistress and mother to his four bastard children – Daniel, Hubie, Muriel, and Martin taken in by the Spratlin family.

Mr. Charles – houseman / chauffer – distinguished overseer - everything on the property must meet his approval, things are done as they have always been done and the honor and social graces of the family are to be protected.

Nellis Gray – cranky, craggy, lives with Katherine in an old farmhouse in a garden wonderland with five dogs and six cats, chickens, a few goats, plus raccoons, fox, bunnies, squirrels, possum, and flocks of birds.

Gracie – Nellis's Shepherd/Doberman mix

'Lucy' – Nellis' 1959 Goldtop Les Paul six-string electric guitar.

Nanny - his wife, who died of cancer and haunts the house

Katherine Kennedy – Stanton's former secretary, mistress – long, lean, thick auburn hair, dark piercing eyes, high cheek bones, strong jaw, wide smile – intelligent, organized. spokeswoman for the All People Matter movement and living with Nellis.

Ned Perkins - a beanpole with long straggly rusty blond hair and a full beard, accountant and transport driver for Nellis' marijuana crop, who has another identity and vocation keeping Tate Sloan out of sight.

Hank Garrett – runs the soup kitchen in Cameron

Constance Calhoon – homeless shelter in Cameron

Sister Gwen – the St. Francis Orphanage in Cameron

SunnyBreeze

Jessie Cotton – former junior quarterback for the Wisconsin team that lost to Oklahoma, successful landscape painter in Dolphin Bay, leader of the All People Matter movement

Gracie – Jessie's Shepherd

Kate Crocket – Jessie's old college girlfriend and former lifestyle reporter for 'American Style' magazine in Atlanta, until she became the published voice of the All People Matter movement. Tall, willowy, horsy, thick blond hair, piercing amber eyes, pretty without being glamorous

Johnny Warmington, 9-year-old, who lives nearby with his single mother and younger sisters, loves to go fishing with best friend Jessie, and has an innate connection with animals and nature in the bay. Blue eyes, ginger hair

Bobbie Warmington – Johnny's mom – Secretary for the All People Matter movement

Derek Rangle – Tropical Paradise art gallery owner - a shock of white hair, dancing blue eyes behind thick horn-rimmed glasses, and the grin of an aging wizard

Sammy Ball – tiny clerk in the Dolphin Bay Planning Commission's archives, bushy gray eyebrows, green eyes, leader of All People Matter movement

Benny Young – landscape maintenance for the city, original face of the movement

Alva Thompson – Benny's sister

Eddie Glover – motorcycle shop – movement security

Hank Miller – original leader of the Dolphin Bay protest

Rex Tatum – Sammy Ball's neighbor and original leader of the Dolphin Bay protest

Tate Sloan – from Senders Creek, Oklahoma, as quarterback, he led the OU football team to a National Championship by defeating Jessie Cotton's Wisconsin team in the Rose Bowl. started TMS Oil Technologies, financed by his father-in-law, became notoriously rich and developed SunnyBreeze with his wife Mavis before disappearing during Hurricane Dot.

Mavis Simonson Sloan – Former OU cheerleader and sorority girl, who believed that there are only two classes of people, those special few who have and deserve enormous wealth and those who serve them, until she was confronted with the inevitable collapse of the American society and became the money behind the All People Matter movement.

SunnyBreeze – idyllic community on the south end of Breezy Key, created to bilk and brainwash wealthy tourists by Tate and Mavis Sloan, providing 'elite' vacation housing and every amenity in a safe, exclusive environment, until Hurricane Dot devoured it completely.

Tabitha Hall – aging heiress who owns the newspaper, The Dolphin Times. Tall, slender, mane of white hair, green eyes and pale parchment complexion.

Hannibal Davis – Tabitha Hall's houseman

The New School at Dolphin Bay – Mavis' exclusive school in SunnyBreeze

Mac Murphy

Mayor Tyrone Turner – black former Mayor of Atlanta - six-six former Rhodes Scholar, with a doctorate in economics from Yale, and all-star linebacker for the Atlanta Falcons and Democratic Presidential Candidate

President Phillipe Gonzalez – current democratic president

Alien Relocation Command – Black Shirts – Special Unit Enforcers – para-military force directed and protected within Homeland Security. Tasked with enforcing the conspirator's directives, rounding up enemies of the state, immigrants whether legal or not, liberal democrats and protesters, and anyone of color. They are free to use as much violence as necessary to control the situation without judicial oversight.

Martin McClintock Murphy – rogue radical right-wing radio show host, who becomes a candidate for president on a lark - beady dark blue eyes, pudgy face, thin lips

Jack Hannah – WBFK – engineer / station manager – Cincinnati

Milly Clark – secretary / receptionist - fields calls during Murphy's broadcast.

Casper Wein - political organizer extraordinaire – convention coordinator

Shepherd Stone - political operative from Boston – Murphy's campaign manager

Dr. Theodore Billings – greedy physician hired to keep Murphy upright

Haden Crawley – video director for the campaign

Penny Baker - voluptuous makeup girl

Austin Crouch – Nashville producer and promoter for campaign rallies – big stars, big shows

Turner Graves – Oil / mining – first mega-contributor to Murphy's campaign

The Forge

Conrad Blaho – COO Lebanon Steel – founder of The Forge conspiracy

Stanley French – CEO Dynamic Devices – founder of The Forge conspiracy

Sons – John and Michael French

Reverend Godwin – tele-evangelical preacher and founder of The Forge conspiracy

Ethan Tomlinson – ultraconservative PR consultant, behind the scenes campaign director for the conspiracy

Will Terry – produces all the syndicated right-wing radio and TV shows, advertising and public announcement

Bill Mendelson – broadcasting

Nucleus / Kernel – worldwide web of massive computers, controlled by advanced artificial intelligence, monitoring every citizen in the industrialized world and programmed to manage everything from the global economy to organizing the population to serve the foundation of the new order.

Harry Wilson / Primary Tech – cutting-edge chip production and the entire Nucleus program

Harry Summers – international real estate developer who founded The Golden Key Golf Resort – proposed the scheme to turn rednecks and racists into true believers

Augie Phillips – agricultural production and chemicals

Casey Buck – owner of the largest privately-owned oil company

Sam Snider – resorts and cruise ships

Jack Simpson – international heavy construction

Jefferson Hicks – North Carolina Representative, con artist and pedophile

Creighton Steil – Murphy's running mate – handsome charming, sleazy, homophobic, gay, evangelical VP – former governor of Indiana – The Forge's chosen candidate

Ernest Cummings – Steil's personal secretary and lover

General Truman Kent – Four-star Head of the Joint Chiefs

Admiral Hawkins – Joint Chiefs

Simons –three-star Marine Lieutenant General

Dan Elliot – Chief of staff for the VP

Tony Spears – the political consultant for the VP

Craig Hobson – former NYC district attorney - became Advisor to the Vice President on Security Affairs

The Playhouse

Matty Sutton – Grandmama, matriarch and director of the theater – fussy, obstinate, and always right – small, gritty, feisty – domineering and demanding but bound to each member of the family with real love, even if she doesn't show it very often. pale blue eyes, small mouth and thin lips, a beautiful complexion wrinkled and sagging, long salt and pepper hair rolled into a loose bun at the back of her head.

Burt Sutton – husband, technical wizard, writer – small, stout, bald, little glasses, tinkerer, knows every system in the building and the tricks to keeping everything running. Matty Sutton

Nell Carey – Matty's mother who suffers from dementia and appears to be totally uncommunicative with everyone except Adel

Marty Sutton – eldest child, combat vet and facilities manager - which meant that he could fix anything. Rigger, climber, and trapeze artist – grew up clambering around the inaccessible reaches of this old building – which qualified him as an advance scout, while he was in the marines - flashbacks of Iraq, doing deep reconnaissance across the border in Syria and Iran from 2002 until 2006 and they started shipping in the amateurs.

Sybil Sutton – beautiful starlet who was abused by Hollywood producers and directors, passed around like a mirror covered with lines of cocaine, before escaping to marry Marty, who was taking Production Management courses at UCLA, and taking over the business office. Nell – Matty's mother

Dakota – Marty's eldest daughter- Dakota – vivacious, headstrong, talented, and anxiously awaiting a reply from Peter Oppenheimer's new drama school.

Adel – mid-teen daughter, dancer, acrobat, and precocious actress – inherited the best of her parents – anxious to begin her journey – but mature enough to understand the value and power of the family. Long, lanky, walks like a ballerina, dirty blond hair, seductive brown eyes

Rusty – juvenile son – awkward, withdrawn, shy - just coming of age and unsure of his place – brilliant tactician – wants to study physics – wavy blond hair, green eyes, goofy smile – limbs too long for his body, hands and feet too big – not athletic. possesses math and IT intellect and the ability to visualize in three dimensions

Misty – preteen daughter – bright, smiling, cheery to everyone, charmer – red-head, freckles, blue eyes – likes girly things, pink, wearing her hair in different styles, loves dressing up in costumes and pretending to be a character for a few hours

Sally Sutton Stewart – middle daughter – went off to college to study Literature but ended up living in a commune for a year, where she met her husband. Black hair, dark eyes, fair skin, curvy shape, the perfect look for dark smoky dramatic parts – always looks as if she's the subject of a 1930's Hollywood promotional photo.

Little Mac – teenage son – tri-color Mohawk, dangly peace symbol earring – stony, creative, guitar, lyrics, has a little band and several girlfriends

Nikki – teen daughter, songstress – tiny, dainty, pale, ginger, blue eyes

Alison Sutton Baker (Ally) – youngest daughter and firebrand, divorced from musician husband. Jet black hair, piercing amber eyes, fit and athletic, nannies all the kids. In a blond wig, she does a perfect imitation of Marilyn Monroe, black belt.

Tom Baker – son, youngest of the children – little tornado, constantly into everything but so cute no one can discipline him. Longs for his father but is always disappointed when he shows up

Bibi Baker – preteen daughter – tough tomboy - resents sharing her mother with all the other children and getting hand-me-down clothes. Wants to run away to be with her father – not afraid of much. Dirty blond hair, ponytail or pigtails, bubblegum, overalls, red Converse high tops, basketball

Adopted kids

Bailey and Thomas – black 8-year-old twins, taken in after their Muslim parents, Tom and Juanita Roberts – talented tenor and soprano with the Metropolitan Opera and outspoken critics of the racist president, were killed in a questionable hit-n-run automobile accident on the Jersey Turnpike.

Melody – tiny 6-year-old Japanese girl, handed to Alison at one of Earl's Jamband concerts at Central Park by an elderly Japanese woman, dressed in a black floral kimono, her thick white hair tied with a simple ribbon, who bowed very formally and keeled over dead on the spot

Patrick – 12-year-old Irish red-head, rescued from an overflowing Catholic orphanage, parents killed in a bombing in Ireland

Bridgette – 7-year-old Dutch girl, abandoned in the theater by her parents, green eyes, cinnamon colored hair, freckles

Anton – 10-year-old British born son of a tragically flawed leading lady, Avanti Prime, AKA Geraldine Forester from Cleveland Heights, who had a weakness for Champagne, cocaine, and leading men and disappeared, after a run in a remake of 'Who's Afraid of Virginia Wolfe, without her child.

Dr. Cohen – Manages the underground sanctuary for thousands rescued from the ARC commandos

Tatum Freese – television anchor

Madeline Post – co-anchor

Dixville Notch, New Hampshire

Mindy Hoffman – voter

Bobby Thompson – mayor running balloting

Warren and Fred – selectmen

Sally Yoder – town clerk

Chief Shannon – police

Betty Barnes - citizen

Barry Hinkle – citizen

Paula Paulson – reporter for International News

Other Characters

Don Seamans – Spratlin's press secretary

Captain Martin – pilot on Spratlin campaign plane

Amy Martin – Atlanta – founder - Worker's Union of the Unemployed

Althea Dodson – abducted Worker's Union founder

Billy Holiday – beautiful black prostitute

Credo – Billy's pimp and ARC enforcer

John Duvall – trumpeter

Dr. Nathan Schumer – pediatrician for the Sutton family

Stanley Sullivan – attorney rescued by Marty and Sally

Bridget – prisoner with baby Tasha

Kevin Haines – Shakespeare actor

Henny Rhine – actress

Mason James – director

Eddy Deacan – Chief train engineer – prisoner train from Macon

Scotty Ditkins – second engineer

Milton Shepherd – former Seal

Morgan & Henke – former special forces

Patrick Smith – Chief engineer on train from New York

Tom Walker – Spratlin's head of security

Roger Stanislawski – terrorist organizer

Lincoln Todd – terrorist organizer

Harvey Green – Patriot Network location equipment manager

Lewis and Clark – former Special Ops assassins

Mike Thomas – Secret Service special agent

Novels by Rick Stiller

Fiction

Dealer

The Redemption Series

Nellis Gray – Volume I
SunnyBreeze – Volume II
Elect Mac Murphy - Volume III
The Forge – Volume IV

Young Adult

The Morgan's Knot Serial Fantasy

Morgan's Knot
Island of the Children
Ice Island
Islands of Concrete and Steel
Islands of the Mind
Islands in the Sky
Islands of Dark Miracles
Islands of Wisdom

Visit: www.rickstiller.com for more of his books,
photographs, and music and www.morgansknot.com for
the latest on the Morgan's Knot series.